The Photo That Launched 160,000 Words

The Father...

...that's what the natives called the maneater that preyed on them during WWII. The massive reptile was finally killed by these soldiers who counted more than 30 bullets in its thick hide.

"On one of my trips to the island, I discovered this amazing photo. Known to the people as 'The Father of the Crododiles,' the greatest reptile on Earth began to swim through my imagination. The result is this epic historical fiction and predator story."

- Timothy James Dean

I0608885

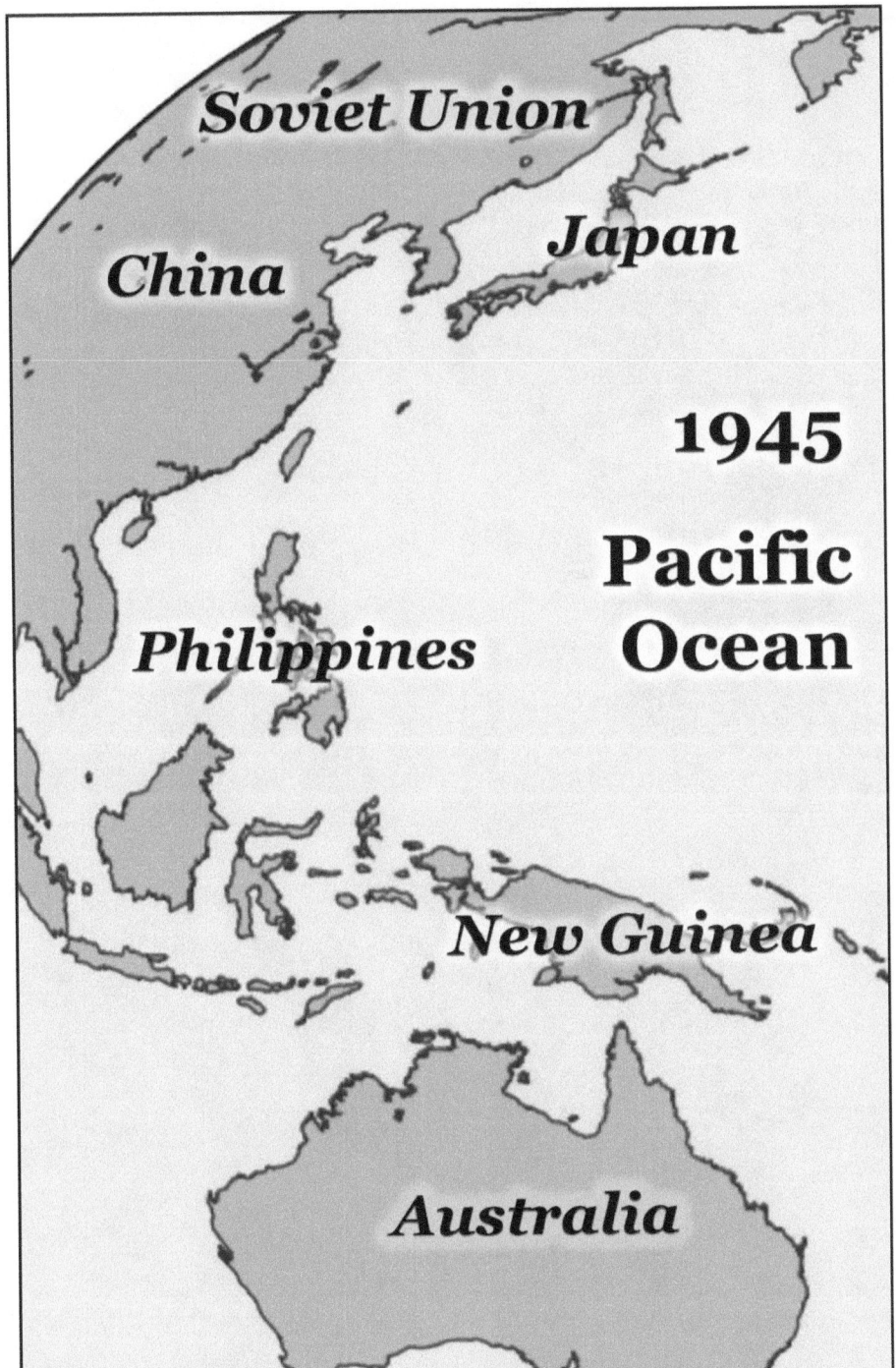

DEDICATION

To Deborah

For being there at every step

For my parents

Jim and Glady Dean

Who took me to the island

and let me roam free

And to the native people

of the island of New Guinea:

may you remember your culture,

live long and prosper

TEETH

Prologue

July 1945

Valley of the Cannibals

The young soldier is surrounded by thousands of attacking tribal warriors. His cheeks are dark with stubble from the trek through the jungle and his eyes look older than his age.

Now his future is measured in heartbeats. He glares at the dark-skinned cannibal chief who wears his GI helmet. He fires his rifle at a warrior, ducks a swinging axe, and scrambles the man's brains with his pistol.

Beside him, a companion shoots an attacker, and another swings a sword, nearly slicing an adversary in two.

He grips his smoking rifle in one hand, pistol in the other. Gunsmoke stings his nostrils.

There comes a roar so deep, it rattles the bones. Warriors freeze in mid-strike and turn to face a new, but far more ancient, enemy.

The crowd parts as the giant reptile bowls through – a nightmare from the mists of time.

A crone rises before the river deity and shrieks its name. It crushes her beneath its massive weight.

The beast's head bobs strangely as it runs and the soldier's eyes go to the cause. One foreleg is a bloody stump and he knows, he is the one who hurt it.

There is one slim chance.

"Run!"

The earth shakes as the attacker thunders up. The soldier wheels away. He strikes the wall of warriors with the butt of his rifle, but time has run out.

The monster spreads huge jaws, billowing a stench from the pit.

It shows its terrible teeth and bites.

44 Years Earlier

November 1901

The enormous South Pacific island looks like it belongs to the age of dinosaurs. On a map, New Guinea resembles a Tyrannosaurus rex. Its backbone is the formidable Owen Stanley mountain range. The second-largest island in the world is so remote and rugged, it is famous as "the last unknown." It sprawls across the tropical South Pacific Ocean, but hundreds of miles inland, the soaring peaks are crowned with snow.

The Big River starts in those mountains as a trickle that soon becomes a stream. It gurgles down rock faces and leaps into canyons. Now it chuckles over boulders, growing in power until it forms boiling rapids that roar from one drop to another.

At the lowlands, it becomes a mighty river. It disappears into the rain forest and emerges again in great brown coils across the grasslands.

Within its swollen body, it carries predators of such savagery, they rival the river itself.

The torrent splits in fingers at the delta, and then is swallowed whole by a far greater body of water, the South Pacific Ocean.

The widest channel is fifty yards across. Its banks are choked with jungle, but here and there are curious patches of bare clay.

A neon-blue butterfly flits along the foliage. A fish leaps at it and splashes back. The flier flutters down and finds a perch where it flares its wings in the sun.

A cave seems to yawn in thin air. An elastic shape flicks out, the butterfly's wings fold sideways, and it jerks into darkness. A bullfrog detaches from the background. It waddles a few steps, a blue fringe quivering around its lips. One gulp and it's gone.

The butterfly's former perch begins to shake. Cracks web across the surface. An end falls off, trailing mucus. A sharp snout bursts from the gel. Yellow eyes with vertical pupils fly open. The frog tucks its head into its chins and watches as the newcomer struggles to birth itself.

With only its tail stuck, the hatchling attempts to walk away, claws raking the mud, but the shell will not let go. The infant regroups while the frog dozes in the heat.

The newcomer goes into a frenzy of lashing and the shards fly off. The bullfrog observes a scaly creature with an olive back, ivory throat, and jaws lined with interlocking teeth. This is not food. It loses interest and turns away.

The hatchling stands on unsure legs. It stumbles, but remains upright and takes several steps, learning to use its limbs as it goes.

This is a small creature, only several inches long, but already it is exceptionally large for its kind, one in many generations. Although its species can stand, walk and swim from the instant they hatch, this one is a prodigy. It bulges with muscle and is full of aggression.

Now, fast as a lizard, it runs at the frog. The amphibian dips its head while the other lifts its snout. They sniff.

At once, the baby leaps up, rising on its tail. It bites across the frog's head, sealing its nostrils. Needles pierce green flesh and agony explodes.

Now the frog leaps, but its rider hangs on. Again, it bucks and the two somersault. The frog cannot breathe and its panic soars. It gathers its great hind legs and makes its most prodigious leap yet. The combatants cartwheel across the sky and the amphibian slams down on its attacker. The hatchling crashes upside down, a knob on its head striking a sharp stone. It is slashed deeply across an eye and knows its first pain.

Still, it will not let loose.

The bullfrog staggers a step towards the river, dragging its terrible appendage. Its throat spasms as it stares at the water – so near, but forever out of reach. Jade eyes bulge and the world goes dim.

It topples onto its side, dragging its nemesis with it.

The hatchling lies beside its first kill and keeps its teeth in the flesh. The spotted legs scissor out and go still.

Only now does the baby release its grip. It nuzzles down the flank to a hind leg, and bites again. Blood gurgles down its throat – its first ecstasy. It jerks its head from side to side, tearing skin and tendons.

The leg pops off and the hatchling takes an end in its mouth. It chomps and swallows, chomps and swallows. When only the webbed foot is hanging from its jaws, the infant rests.

The earth shakes as heavy feet approach. A basso rumble comes from the sky. The tiny one flinches.

A head a thousand times its size descends. A fence of stained teeth settles beside it on the mud. Instinct kicks in and the hatchling grows calm.

With twin pupils, it stares up at the enormous eye of its mother. The cut has not damaged the baby's vision, although it drips blood.

For a time, the two are lost in reptilian love.

Eventually, the hatchling chokes down its first meal, its belly distended. In the aftermath, it turns to the river to bellow triumph. It spreads its jaws, but only a squeak emerges.

Then its dam joins in – a guttural rumble that makes storks defecate and mount the air. For this is the call of Crocodylus porosus, the Saltwater crocodile, the largest and most fearsome reptile that still walks Planet Earth.

Upon hearing this, the bones of all animals, including humans, turn to water, for this predator feeds on them. It tracks its victims with the cunning of the ambush hunter.

At last, all animals must come to the river. And then, the hidden crocodile strikes. It splashes up and seizes its victim in its merciless teeth. The prey is pulled underwater, the reptile goes into its death roll, and drags it to its doom.

But at this moment, the female belies that reputation. She is the epitome of fond motherhood. Behind her stands her nest, a mound of clawed-up mud and leaves. In it are scores of stained eggs, some whole, others shattered. This morning, hearing the chorus of chirps and taps from within, she nuzzled away the covering.

Across her mudslide, a dozen miniature reptiles take their first steps.

Curiously, every one is male, but this, too, is the way of the species. The precise temperature at which they incubated determined their sex. If there had been a difference of a few degrees, all would be female.

Of the hatchlings, only the biggest bull has killed and eaten. He lies by his mother, gorged and sleepy.

Lured by the scent of blood, a sibling comes for the frog. It finds the sloppy belly and bites. At once its brother's head comes up. It is consumed by new sensations – rivalry and rage. Again, it rises on its legs, surer this time, and charges the interloper.

It slams the smaller brother over and seizes him in long jaws. The two twist away across the mud. The mother raises her head and grunts.

In her world, all is as it should be.

The throaty vibration echoes through the jungle. A wild boar forages there, and the sound makes its hackles rise. It snorts and charges off, tossing tusks.

An arrow flashes through the light. The pig topples squealing with the projectile standing in its side. The arrow is as long as a spear, featherless, with a bamboo tube on the killing end, sharpened to a razor point. The boar roots at its affliction while its lifeblood gurgles through the tube.

A brown man steps from the foliage. He, too, has heard the call of the great pukpuk, but knows he is at a safe distance. He is brawny and young and carries a black longbow and a clutch of pig arrows. White beads are woven in his kinky hair, and in the hole punched through his nasal septum are two crocodile teeth, bound together, points out.

He is naked except for the cucumber-sized gourd that encases his genitals, tied around his waist with bark string.

A stone knife presses against his side. The hunter crouches and cuts the pig from ear to ear.

The boar thrashes and the man puts a hand on its flank and speaks quiet words until death comes. He stands, pulls out his arrow, grasps the trotters, and slings the carcass around his neck.

An arrow slams through the man and emerges from his back. The hunter's features contort as he gawks at the long hardwood head, carved in backward-swept barbs. His own blood flows with the boar's and he falls to earth.

Five more dark-skinned warriors emerge from the jungle. They look so different from their victim, they might almost be another species. Their facial features are broader, and their bodies shine coal black. Patterns in red, white, and yellow mark their faces and torsos. Through their pierced noses are bound pig tusks, turned up, signifying war. Floating over them are headdresses of white egret feathers, delicate and beautiful.

Two of the newcomers wear grisly trophies. Freshly cut human heads dangle from their necks. These faces resemble the pig hunter. The shot man sees his kin.

These warriors also carry longbows, but all their arrows have the barbed tips made for killing men. Some bear stone-headed axes and cudgels. They, too, are naked except for their penis gourds – but these are long, and curl in strange shapes.

The most powerful of the headhunters steps to the victim. This is the Mambu-Ato, the most feared war chief on the entire river. He crouches and taunts the pig-hunter. He reaches to the place where his arrow pierces the ribs, dips a finger in blood, brings it to his lips and sucks. He flashes a smile of shining black teeth, now stained red.

7

He takes the stone blade from his victim's fingers, cuts a slice of the hunter's forearm, and puts it in his mouth, chewing loudly, relishing the horror on the dying man's face. The pig-hunter's eyes glaze over.

One warrior goes to the fallen boar and grins at the curved tusks. He slings the pig around his own shoulders.

The chief takes the hunter in an embrace and begins to slice the neck. His men steady the body while their leader de-capitates it. This will be a prize memento back at the spirit house. They chatter lightheartedly as they work, as men do af-ter a successful hunt.

The she-crocodile rests beside the river, jaws wide to the sun.

Blood crusts over the hatchling's eye. He watches the end-less swirl of the Big River toward the sea.

TEETH

Book 1

Operation Teeth

"Yea, and if some god shall wreck me
in the wine-dark deep,
even so I will endure...
For already have I suffered full much,
and much have I toiled in perils of waves and war.
Let this be added to the tale of those."

– Homer, The Odyssey

"They died hard, those savage men
– like wounded wolves at bay.
They were filthy, and they were lousy,
and they stunk.
And I loved them."

– General Douglas MacArthur

"You may not be interested in war,
but war is interested in you."

– Leon Trotsky

1

July 1945

Port Moresby on the Southern Coast of New Guinea

Dingo Hawsey was talking with his men on the shortwave radio. They had found something extraordinary. The patrol officers had been on a sortie a couple of hundred miles out, looking for enemy encampments. This time, they hadn't found signs of the "Yellow Peril," but they had come across something so unusual, it piqued the major's curiosity.

"Keep on coming," Dingo said into the mike. "I'll meet you along the road." He was a deeply tanned man with a shock of dark hair, in robust physical condition. He jumped behind the wheel of the jeep the American army had kindly provided for his use. He drove out of town along the coastal road, sliding around the corners made slick by the rain.

At forty-six, Major Dingo Hawsey felt more at home in New Guinea than anywhere else. He'd been a planter before the war. As soon as he'd heard that Japan had invaded the Philippines, he'd joined the Australian Army. Others hadn't seen it right off, but Dingo had known from that instant, the belligerent Japanese had their eyes on the ultimate prize, the sparsely populated continent of Australia.

They must be stopped, and New Guinea, located between the Japanese islands and Australia, was the strategic place to do it. This was world war, after all, and it was clear to Dingo that the Japanese were taking full advantage of the German action in Europe to carve off as much of Asia and the South Pacific as they could manage.

Their momentum had been halted on the massive island of New Guinea by the Australians in a series of bloody battles. Port Moresby on the southern coast, one jump from Australia, had been bombed. You could still see the evidence in burned down buildings and the hulks of ships in the harbor.

Dingo had led his men many times against the Japs along the Kokoda Track. Even now in '45, there remained great hordes of enemy soldiers across New Guinea. These days, it had fallen on Dingo, under the direction of the Americans, to mop up the Japanese.

The major had not liked it when Australia put the Yanks in charge of the Australian military, but he'd come to understand. Their top man, General MacArthur, had arrived, and the Australian politicians understood that American might, money and manpower, were their only hope to stop the Japanese Empire.

This time out, the patrol had come across a native runner carrying something unusual. This fellow had apparently made the treacherous trek hundreds of miles from his home.

Dingo drove along the rough road. When he saw the army truck lumbering his way, he pulled to the side and lit a smoke. "G'day," he greeted his three officers as they clambered down.

"Now let's see what you've got." The item in question turned out to be an envelope, folded and filthy. The messenger had carried it from the wild interior.

"The bloke said he's from Kissim," the driver explained. Dingo gave a whistle. That area was so dangerous, not even armed patrols ventured there.

"That is just up river from the Valley of the Cannibals!" Dingo exclaimed. "Struth, mate! No white man's ever gone in there and been seen again." He turned the envelope in his hands.

A letter from that wild place was unheard of. On the outside, the major made out English words, cursive in faded ink, through the stains.

"You were right to call this in," he said. "I know the man this is addressed to. I'll see ya later. We'll hoist a pint and you'll fill me in on the rest. Now I need to shake a leg."

Dingo wheeled the jeep and sped back the way he had come.

2

Three years earlier

July 1942

A Village near Buna, North Coast of New Guinea

Thunder rumbled across the sea and Dez's skin prickled with unease. The young missionary, so far from home in this strange land, peered towards the ocean but saw only a wall of impenetrable fog.

Molly's worrying must be rubbing off, he thought. The mist drifted inland, turning palm trees into towering ghosts. Dez glanced up at the tendrils around the white cross fixed to the peak of the mission's main building, then down at the dark-skinned men gathered below. They spoke in their native tongue – a language he still struggled to grasp after a year here – but he barely registered their words.

The thirty-year-old Australian scanned the inland huts, their grass roofs darkened by rain. People moved among them, women tending the gardens beyond.

The settlement resembled countless others scattered across the massive South Pacific island of New Guinea, but with one significant difference: three foreign buildings dominated the high ground near the shore. Unlike the traditional huts, these structures stood rectangular and imposing with corrugated metal roofs and cement panel walls inset with real glass windows and timber doors – a slice of Australia planted on this remote coast.

Dez, dressed as usual in shorts and a light shirt, was a cheerful, practical man. This morning, he oversaw the village carvers. He was paying them to make benches for the school by smoothing the planks they had split from logs. They used the iron adzes he'd brought from Aus in place of their traditional stone-headed ones.

The men were nearly naked. Most had a leaf hanging front and back to protect their modesty. A few had *laplaps* – lengths of cloth – knotted around their waists. Their armbands dangled with pigs' tails and prized shells.

Many wore necklaces, items strung on bark twine. These were mostly dog teeth, with some of crocodile, shark and pig as well.

Everything looked as it should, but Dez could not shake his sense of foreboding. He and his wife, Molly, their young son and baby girl, had arrived on the island a year ago. They'd been commissioned by their church in Australia to come to this place as missionaries. They were to build a church and school. The first necessity had been to learn the local language. It was unique and unwritten, spoken by only about a thousand people in the immediate vicinity. Without the ability to communicate, the couple could get nothing done, so learning the language had been a priority. They had picked up pidgin English, the simplified trade language, and some of the men of the village knew it as well, so that helped.

Dez glanced at Molly some twenty yards off, surrounded by local women, two-year-old Sally on her hip. Nearby, their five-year-old, Stevie, played with the local boys. He was easy to pick out because of his hair, bleached nearly white by the sun. The boys used small bamboo longbows to shoot stick arrows at a coconut husk.

Molly was dressed in a cotton shift, while her friends wore grass skirts, their breasts bare. Many, like Molly, had infants on their hips or playing around their feet. At his wife's side was Kiki, the native teenager they paid in trade goods to help around the house.

Again, Dez saw nothing abnormal, and brought his attention back to the work. But as he did so, from near and far, the gang of skinny village mongrels began to bark. They turned in the direction of the beach and sniffed the breeze. Then, still howling, they ran for the ocean.

The people were always at risk of tribal war with neighbors and they counted on the dogs for warning. The men near Dez, and others across the village, shouted to one another.

Weapons were at hand and they snatched up axes, clubs, bows and arrows, and sped after the dogs.

Dez crossed to Molly. He was anxious, but did not want to frighten her. He forced a grin and gave her a peck on the cheek, then kissed little Sally's head. She looked up at Daddy, smiled and cooed.

"Not to worry, love," he said to Molly. "Probably just a ship going by."

He trotted after the men and caught up with them on the beach beyond the coconut palms. They talked as they watched the dogs bark into the fog. This went on for several minutes, and Dez told himself that it was a false alarm. Then he heard the throb of an engine.

Of course! Just what he'd told Molly. But no – and his flesh rose in goose bumps – the sound was very close. The rumble was joined by another, and another, until there was a roar from the unseen sea.

14

Then, paces away, a black shape, all sharp edges, thrust out of the swirling vapor. It grated onto the beach, shedding water. The dogs went hysterical and the watchers fell back, grabbing the arms of their fellows.

A ramp clanged down and something incredible soared out of the fog. It thumped onto the sand and Dez's senses told him what his mind could not believe. It was a stunning white horse, dancing sideways, tossing its mane. He knew the apparition was real when he heard jingling as it mouthed the bit.

Outlandish as the animal was, Dez's gaze riveted on the rider – a heavyset middle-aged man in uniform, yellow-brown face under the cap. What stole Dez's breath away was the fierceness in the slanted eyes.

The man's gaze met his own across the distance and knowledge shot through Dez.

It's the Japs! The invasion the radio had warned about, against which he and Molly prayed every day, was upon them.

Enemy soldiers swarmed around the rider, armed with rifles tipped with bayonets. One carried a machine gun.

The dogs circled behind the horse, snarling at its legs. It fired back a hoof and cracked a canine skull. Then the stallion stood on its hind legs and pawed the air. It neighed and Dez's blood went cold. The rider expertly kept his seat. He drew a sword and held it high.

There was a burst of automatic gunfire and the dog pack bowled back on the sand in a spray of blood. Dez's thoughts flew to Molly and his children, and he turned to run. Beside him, the men stood stupefied, some with their mouths open.

The Japanese soldier with his Nambu machine gun saw the white man among the blacks. He felt his general's eyes on him as he fired.

Dez saw the muzzle flash and his thoughts flew to Molly, Stevie and Sally. A prayer began to form, but it was too late. The deadly hail tore through him and Dez collapsed onto the wet sand, eyes rolled back in his head.

General Taro Yazawa made a mental note of the first casualties in his invasion of New Guinea.

His soldiers sprinted by the corpses and disappeared through the palms. From beyond came gunfire and screams.

The general heard more landing barges scrape ashore behind him. He touched his heels to his mount and cantered up the beach. Today, a thousand of his fighters, many of them seasoned veterans of the China campaigns, would land here. It heralded the full invasion by the Imperial Army. Hundreds of thousands more soldiers were on their way.

Yazawa charged between the trees, sword at the ready.

Molly heard the shots and saw the Japs come. Her mind screamed that Dez was murdered and her sanity reeled. She snapped back to reality when bullets thudded into the women around her. There were shrieks as they fell to earth.

Time slowed. She saw two more women shot and the girl, Kiki, went face-down. The first soldiers trotted by, shooting into the village.

Stevie!

Molly's gaze flew to her son. His friends had scattered, but her boy stood transfixed. A soldier charged toward him. His dad had taught him to stand his ground, and now his small hands pulled back his bowstring and the sharp stick flew true, striking the man's cheekbone.

The Jap's fingers went to his face and came away red. His face twisted and he sprang at the boy, lunging with his bayonet. He stabbed Stevie through the chest, wrenched the blade free, and the boy crumpled to the earth.

Molly felt the steel through her own heart. At last, she could move.

Still carrying Sally, she dashed the few steps to their house. The shotgun stood in a corner by the door. It belonged to Dez, but she was a country girl and she could shoot. Sally was a burden, but she managed to break open the double barrels and check they were loaded.

She burst back out into the massacre.

Her eyes flew to Stevie's little body and her soul groaned. One last time, she glanced toward the beach where Dez had disappeared.

I'm coming, darling, she thought.

Among those at her feet was Kiki. Molly didn't know if the girl was hurt, but the rise of her chest said that she lived. Molly bent and shook her. The girl glanced up, terrified, and Molly gathered she was unharmed. Gently, she placed her precious baby beside her.

"Run!" she hissed in the language. "Take Sally! Run to the jungle!"

A hundred enemy soldiers were in the village. They walked now, sure of their victory, taking time to aim at those fleeing in the distance.

Molly looked for the man who had stabbed her son. She saw the line of blood on his face. Molly threw up the shotgun and pulled the first trigger of the side-by-side. The 12-gauge pellets blew most of the Jap's head off.

She had seconds left, she knew, and she swung for another target.

The Japanese stood in squads, pointing to runners. They took turns bringing them down. A soldier raised a light machine gun and tracked a woman racing through the gardens. The line of slugs caught up with her and riddled her body.

Molly used the second barrel to blow a hole through his chest. She could not know it, but she had just avenged her husband.

General Yazawa sat easy on the stallion he had named "Ginga" at its birth, meaning "silver river." He had raised it on his ranch in the mountains of Hokkaido, Hidaka. He was of Samurai heritage, and both he and his mount were bred for war.

From his vantage near the *gaijin* buildings, the general watched the slaughter unfold. His men had been ordered to take no prisoners. The invasion of New Guinea was key to the Empire's grand plan of conquest. Victory required an implacable spirit. Most of the savages were dead, and more were exterminated as he watched. From the photos brought back by the reconnaissance aircraft, he had expected to find members of the white race here. It was a *Krishitian* mission, after all. He had seen the Australian male die on the beach. But the female was a surprise because she was armed.

He saw her kill two of his soldiers in quick succession. His *katana* was still in his hand and his heels applied pressure.

Ginga bunched its legs and sprang forward. The woman heard the hooves and saw the stallion loom. Her mouth opened in a scream that never came. The general leaned down as if to embrace her.

The blade passed through and her head parted from her neck. The warhorse pulled up in a shower of mud, and the general wheeled to watch. The body, spurting blood, tottered and toppled.

The general dipped his head – respect. For a moment he savored the piercing, transitory nature of this life. Then he turned the horse to better watch his men, while he pulled a pad of cotton from a pocket to clean the *katana*.

Kiki was still on her belly, one hand on Sally who had begun to cry, when the white woman's head rolled up beside her, blue eyes open. She grabbed the child, leapt up, and sprinted for the village.

General Yazawa saw the movement out of the corner of his eye. He could easily have run her down, but he did not. Killing an armed *gaijin* was one thing, but chasing a mere girl was beneath him. He rasped a command and his soldiers obeyed.

A volley rang out, but the native dashed on. Now she was between the huts. Seconds later, she appeared on the far side and entered the gardens. Sally was jarred and frightened and began to scream. Bullets struck all around, but the girl dodged from side to side and continued.

Kiki was somewhere beyond terror. The vegetation ripped around her, followed by the clapping sounds. She sped toward the fruit trees. A soldier fired and she went on a knee, almost dropping Sally.

There was a sting on Kiki's leg. She stared at the cut that spilled blood down her calf. She felt faint, but a foreign shout, close by, brought her to her senses. Gunsmoke mingled with the fear from her armpits.

Kiki jumped up hugging Sally to her chest and ran on. She was through the papaya trees and into the jungle near the swamp. She had walked these trails all her life and knew not to fall into the water that lapped both sides of her path. That was where the big *pukpuk* waited, and even the trail could be deadly.

The devil-voices followed. She heard the thump of running boots. There was nowhere to go but forward, but that was a dead end.

Kiki pulled up. Before her was black water and she could see the crocodiles basking on the mudflats, more in the murky liquid. She had two bad options – the guns or the swamp.

A bullet whined by her ear and the girl made her choice. She slid down the bank into the water. Her feet sank into mud and when she ran, it was slow motion. She held the howling child in outstretched arms, keeping her from the filthy slough.

The killers were just behind, the *pukpuk* in the water with her. She saw them come from all sides, ripples behind the terrible heads. Fear lent her strength and she leapt on.

Men yelled. Another slap, and the water jumped at Kiki's side. And then, an eternity later, she was at the far bank. She scrambled up and rolled behind a tree. A bullet splintered the wood by her ear. The little girl had screamed herself into hysteria: she made no noise, mouth frozen wide.

Kiki heard the splashes as a soldier leapt into the swamp, followed by others.

There came a mortal scream. She dared a peek back in time to see a foreigner slam over in a wash. The *pukpuk* took him in a roll and foul water churned. Two more soldiers were just behind, and they tried to turn back, but water made them slow and the reptiles were not. There were shrieks and more shots.

Kiki scrambled up, sheltered by the tree, and ran for her life. She moved Sally from one hip to the other as she sprinted on bare feet until the pain in her side was too great, and then she walked. For several hours, she alternated between running and walking, until she was further from home than she had ever been.

She was in thick jungle, on land she knew did not belong to her people. But she could not go back. The place of her birth had changed forever. Yet even here, she found there were trails. The girl went from one to the next. That night, she made a nest of leaves for Sally and left her for a few minutes while she searched for a particular plant. She chewed up a leaf poultice, the way her grandmothers had shown her, and plastered it over her wound, tying it with vines.

Little Sally was beyond exhaustion. Kiki took her up and she sobbed quietly in the native girl's arms. There was nothing for them to eat. She gave Sally a breast and that quieted her, even though Kiki had no milk. They slept where they lay.

In the morning, she woke to find herself surrounded by native warriors she did not know. Fortunately, they were allies of her tribe. She told them her story, and the men took her to their village, the women fed her and the baby, then led her to an army outpost.

An Australian army doctor stitched up her bullet wound. He also checked Sally and found she was exhausted and dirty, but unharmed.

Working through a translator, the military men extracted Kiki's story. They were most interested in what the teenager had to say.

They knew there was no way the youngsters could go back where they had come from. There was no home left and everyone they loved was dead. An officer wrote a report. It would be carried by aircraft to the brass in Port Moresby. Also on that flight – a teenage native and a little white girl.

Kiki and Sally would have to take their chances in the capital.

3

"WORLD WAR II IN THE SOUTH PACIFIC" - BY COLONEL HENRY CHAMBERS III

The Importance of Teeth

Dear Reader, in order to comprehend New Guinea, you must grasp its grand scale. After Greenland, this is the largest island in the world – three hundred thousand square miles sprawled across the South Pacific. It exceeds our vast State of Texas and is more than twice the size of the British Isles.

This land hosts millions of exotic animals and insects, but you do not find the great hunters of Africa – no lions, tigers, or hyenas.

What you do encounter, often at great personal peril, are Saltwater crocodiles. The freshwater variety is here in abundance as well, and while they frequently attack and eat humans, their great cousins are far more deadly. They are called "saltwater" because they can survive the briny ocean, but they thrive in freshwater as well.

Scientists say the "salties" have been on the planet for two hundred million years. Their kin not only shared the primitive world with dinosaurs, they ate them. Their jaws deliver bone-crushing force, equal to Tyrannosaurus Rex.

Most dinosaurs disappeared en masse sixty-five million years ago, but not the crocodilians. They survived the traumatic event that wiped out their dino-kin, perhaps because they could swim. While the old world died, they went forth and multiplied. They voyaged across entire oceans. On the grand island of New Guinea, they found an ideal home. From their first invasion, they were the apex predator. They feasted on the succulent animals. And when at last the two-legged creatures arrived on these shores, they were also welcome to drop by for a bite.

New Guinea has some six million human inhabitants, though this is an estimate. The island remains mostly unexplored and extremely dangerous. The Stone Age people are divided into a thousand tribes speaking a thousand different languages, none of which are written. This makes New Guinea a linguist's paradise and an administrator's nightmare.

It was the 16th-century Spaniard, Ortiz de Retez, who named the island. Perhaps he was reminded of the negroid inhabitants of Guinea in Africa, and he dubbed this island "Nueva Guinea."

In the early 19th century, a vertical line drawn on a map in Europe divided New Guinea in two. Half a world away, the sea-going Netherlands claimed the western portion as Dutch New Guinea.

The eastern half was split again, horizontally. The British colony of Queensland in Australia claimed "Papua," the southern section. ("Papua" is another ancient name, signifying "frizzy hair").

The northern portion was annexed by Germany under the grand title of "Kaiser Wilhelmsland." To meet the demand in Europe for oil, they sought "copra," the dried meat of coconuts. They also bartered for exotic items. Many a fraulein had her ensemble set off with a Bird of Paradise plume from a headhunter's hand.

The challenge for the Germans – beyond keeping their heads in this war-torn place – was how to pay the natives. What coin could they use for people who saw no value in silver and gold?

As elsewhere in the new world, colorful beads went a long way, as did steel knives and axes, but what could they use for currency?

They saw that natives paid one another with teeth. Many types were used, including pig tusks (which are, Dear Reader, teeth), but far more common were the denticles of dogs. Wealthy villagers wore dog-tooth necklaces that turned them into walking banks.

The Germans hit on a splendid idea: mint this coin! Back in Europe, their factories began to spit out porcelain teeth. Bearing this by the caseload, traders of the "Neu Guinea Kompanie" sailed again for the fearsome "Insel der Kannibalen" (Island of Cannibals).

The natives were stunned by what they were offered — translucent teeth, each one perfect. The pale men must possess the master race of dogs!

For a time, the false teeth did increase their bite of New Guinea trade, but they also spread a peculiarly Western malaise; inflation. The factories churned out far more canine currency than Nature could ever produce.

When the Fatherland fell in World War One (a mere twenty-five years ago as I write this), German New Guinea was erased from the maps. The Dutch managed to hold onto the western half, but the eastern side of the island came under Australian administration, now known as the Territories of Papua and New Guinea.

Significantly, even then, it was Japan that laid claim to the other German-controlled islands of the South Pacific.

The world should have been paying closer attention.

4

July 1945

Port Moresby

It was going to be another blistering day in Port Moresby, the capital of the Territory of Papua, and the largest urban center on the island. "Capital," though, was a rather grandiose term for what was, in truth, a rough town on the edge of a brutal frontier. The reason for its existence was its excellent harbor, across the gulf from the northward-pointing beak of Australia.

The equatorial sun twinkled on the waves and glared from the metal roofs of the buildings clustered along the shore. It reflected blindingly off a thousand puddles that pocked the roads, the legacy of the downpour of the previous afternoon.

The rays burnished the dusky skin of hundreds of natives who strolled the streets among the military vehicles and vintage cars from the prewar period.

A jeep splashed along, honking at the pedestrians. The Australian at the wheel shouted at them to clear the way! Grudgingly, they obliged.

The white man is always in a rush!

The fenders brushed by. The driver had business with the Commander of US forces in the New Guinea Territories.

The natives' dark skin and kinky hair attested to their distant African heritage. How their ancestors got here from that far-off continent was lost in the mists of time, but it must have been by water. These people were thickly muscled, outfitted in tribal regalia and the brilliant trade store cloth they favored. Most women were bare-chested.

The warriors carried their homemade weapons – bamboo longbows, arrows, axes of stone and steel, and wooden clubs.

But not guns. Even though World War II had brought millions of firearms to New Guinea, the natives did not possess them — at least not overtly, and never in town, for these were strictly forbidden by the authorities.

This day, the men carried their traditional weapons, not because they spoiled for a fight, but because they never left home without them. In fact, they were in a festive mood. It was Saturday, and that meant market day.

The jeep braked at an office compound. Buildings of white weatherboard were separated by plots of trimmed grass and crushed coral walkways. Beneath the Stars and Stripes, a sign announced American Army Headquarters.

Major D. Hawsey climbed out, grabbed his worn crocodile-skin briefcase, and headed for the entrance. The "D" stood for "Dwayne," a name the major had loathed since he'd had to defend it with his fists in school. As far as even his closest mates knew, the "D" stood for "Dingo."

He glanced at the Stuart tank among the canna lilies. The cannon was impressive, but the broken track told another story. Tanks had been of little use in the New Guinea mud. *Metal coffins*, Dingo thought.

Sentries flanked the front doors. They recognized the Australian officer and he passed without challenge. Dingo felt sorry for them — overly dressed, in his opinion, in steel helmets, long-sleeve shirts and trousers. By contrast, Dingo wore shorts and a light shirt. On his head was the famous "digger" hat, a wide-brimmed affair with one side hooked to the crown. His only nod to etiquette was the pair of white dress socks pulled just below the knees, and leather shoes. Back on his plantation, like the natives, he often went barefoot.

Dingo entered the building, greeted the soldier at the desk, and strode down a hallway.

Inside the complex, in the most spacious office, the sixty-year-old commander of the US garrison, Colonel Henry Chambers, stood at the window, gazing across the harbor. He was distracted from the view by a beetle that careened his way. Wing-cases spread, it struck the glass, bounced down, and landed in a web.

A huge black spider with yellow markings hung there. Henry often watched these predators. They wove a lacy "x" at the center of their webs, and waited there in ambush.

The instant the beetle tangled, the spider ran at it. Henry watched, faintly appalled, as the predator loomed and the bug redoubled its efforts to escape. But the spider pounced and sank in its fangs. The beetle's wings drooped. The end of the predator's abdomen touched it and a strand of web glistened. With its many legs, it spun the paralyzed insect until it was wrapped like a mummy.

This country! Something is always hunting something else! Henry shuddered and returned to his desk. There came a knock at the door and the colonel called to enter. Dingo came in and saw the older man, gray hair clipped close, peering over reading glasses.

A ceiling fan churned the humidity. The colonel came towards the major with a smile and a crisp good morning. Sofas faced one another across a coffee table, and Henry waved Dingo to one while he took the other.

"Henry, something unusual came into my possession this morning," Dingo began as he opened his briefcase. "It's been carried by hand a very long way..." He looked up.

"And it's addressed to you."

"To me?" the colonel asked, surprised. He watched what the Australian drew into the light and his nose came up like a Carolina bloodhound.

The office door banged open. A young native woman backed into the room, carrying a tray with a pitcher and two glasses. She was barefoot and bare-chested. She turned to the men, her full breasts with their chocolate tips proudly on display. Her only clothing was a red and yellow grass skirt hung low on her hips. The colonel looked up and sighed.

Now, what was her name? Ah yes.

"Hala, how many times have you been told?" he said. "You must wear your shirt at work! Go and put it on."

Dingo glanced her way. In the territories, bare breasts were as common as coconuts. The sight of one more set – even ones as well formed as these admittedly were – was barely cause for a raised eyebrow. Still, the colonel was right to insist on decorum.

Hala had recently arrived from the Trobriand Islands. She spoke only a little mission-English, but understood what the boss-man said. Her experience of life, however, told her differently.

Why have good tits, she thought in her tribal tongue, *if you do not show them off?* Men appreciated a girl displaying the evidence that she would make a good mate, worthy of a high bride price. Her response was to offer the boss-man a fetching smile as she poured the passionfruit juice, bending so her breasts bumped together. The eyes of the men, she saw slyly, had a mind of their own. Hala departed, hips swinging.

What Dingo had taken from his briefcase was an envelope so crumpled and soiled that the handwriting on it was hard to make out.

"As I was saying Henry, it's addressed to you – or at least, to your rank. The major read the longhand on the envelope: "To the Commander of the American Forces in New Guinea."

28

He offered the item and Chambers turned it over in his hands. The paper was greasy and soiled, almost worn through at the creases. An unpleasant odor wafted.

Smoke, sweat – Lord knows what else!

The colonel picked up the ornate Japanese dagger on the table, slid it under the flap, and cut.

5

Three Hours Earlier

Port Moresby Military Hospital

This time, Johnny had believed his wound might not heal. He had smelled death often since he'd started fighting in these jungles at the age of seventeen, and he knew this sickly-sweet stench all too well.

Gradually though, during the endless dog days in hospital, he had come to realize he might just pull through. But he still had that deep ache in his chest. Once again last night, it had ruined his sleep. He lay on his canvas cot, sweat trickling down his forehead and sides.

It was early morning and he heard the feathered orchestra tuning up over the tent. Far off, a rooster crowed. His fingers traced the livid welt on his upper chest.

This is an important day, he reminded himself. He had a meeting with the man who controlled his immediate future, and Johnny had his own fervent plan.

I did not fight all these years to miss the invasion of Japan!

It was already mid-July here in 1945, and Johnny figured the US Army would be on the move from the Philippines to the enemy empire any day. Maybe it was already underway!

He felt a stab of anxiety. He hadn't spent all his time in the hellish jungle, just to miss the main event! The only thing that had kept him going during the desperate times was the deep desire to be part of the US invasion of the Japanese islands.

Johnny had sworn by all the things he held dear to be there when Japan fell. His hatred ran deep and it fed him like fuel. Still, it was not something he talked about, not to anyone. It was too personal, too important.

The huge challenge was that he had to get back across the South Pacific Ocean to the Philippines. But here he was, stuck in Port Moresby. He would never forgive himself if, after everything he'd endured, he missed the Big One.

The light intensified through the canvas walls. Johnny made out the forms of the five men on the other cots. They, too, were recovering soldiers, but all Aussies. He was the lone "Yank."

Johnny sat up and felt the pain stab through him. He stifled a groan and ran his fingers through his sweat-damp hair.

Fight to live, he whispered to himself. *Live to fight!*

The words had echoed through his mind during his endless days of suffering – the lost time when even the docs didn't think he was going to make it.

Live to fight, fight to live!

He'd clung to his chant as if his life depended on it, and maybe it had.

During his years fighting for General MacArthur, Johnny had been shot three times and bayoneted once. He'd taken a bullet through the thigh, one in the forearm, and there had been the stabbing. He had a scar that zigzagged down his rib cage – what the Aussies called "a beaut." That knife hadn't killed him, but this last bullet had almost finished the job. It had gone through his upper chest and out his back.

That was four months ago.

Last night, Johnny had stretched out on his army cot under the mosquito netting, wearing boxer shorts in the tropical oven. But every time he shifted, his wound woke him up. He must have slept at last because when next he came to, someone was whimpering. A voice snapped "shadup" from another bed, and Johnny realized he was the source of the whining and felt ashamed.

It's just the nightmares, he consoled himself. Dead men frequently invaded his nights – the ones who had fought beside him, and those he had killed. In life they were mortal enemies, but in death they came together.

Maybe it was the malaria. Like many on the island, he had it. The fever lived in his blood and there was no cure – Doc Mac told him that. Once in a while it came knocking so hard, his teeth rattled. He fretted that another bout was coming on, and that was the last thing he needed today.

A fragment of the night terror came back to him. The dream was a recurring one about the buddy who'd arrived with him in New Guinea. That was one of the first deaths Johnny had experienced. But now Walt was one of the worst of the night riders.

Again, they were in the stinking swamp with the Japs and the crocodiles. The men killed each other and the crocs ate the dead.

Again, Walt took the bayonet through the chest.

The Jap charges and stabs him. Walt grabs the rifle, and they do the terrible dance.

31

In the dream as in life, Johnny had slashed the enemy with his own bayonet. Walt and the Jap fell together in the mud.

But now in Johnny's dreams, they lived on. Endlessly, they writhed and bled and sliced their hands on the steel.

"Why?" Walt asked, staring with his mild blue eyes through cracked lenses.

"Why? *Why?*"

It always happened that way even though it wasn't right. Walt had already lost his glasses by then.

Johnny sighed, pushed aside the mosquito netting and sat up. He reached under the cot, found his rifle, and brought it up. The battered wooden stock was a comfort in his hands. On the very day Walt died, Johnny had plucked the 1903 Spring-field .30-06 from the hands of a dead GI. He'd left his issued M1 rifle behind. The bolt action rifle spoke to the game hunter in him and it was the ideal gun for the sniper he'd become.

Johnny ordered himself to stand. In order to convince the brass to send him back to the war, he had to flog himself into shape. For the last two weeks – the fortnight, they said here – Johnny had worked on his scheme. It started with short walks that left him gagging in agony. But he persevered and the walks grew longer. For the last few days, he'd even managed to run.

More of a shuffle like some broken down geezer. I really do not know if I can do this!

Instantly, Johnny heard the voice in his head. He'd learned early in the war to turn over most of his thinking to the Hard Case. It was the only way to cope with the things he'd seen and done.

No excuses! Today, you'll run! Let's hear those feet hit the deck!

That last part was his father, the Navy officer.

32

Johnny pulled his thin-strapped undershirt over the dog tags around his neck and worked his legs into the army trousers.

Dead men's clothes. They'd provided them at the hospital, washed but worn. He picked up the canvas sneakers and knocked them out on the floor in case a spider, centipede or snake had moved in overnight. He tugged them on, stuffed his Zippo, a box of Camels and a pack of chewing gum in a pocket. He went out through the screen door, catching it so it wouldn't bang.

He emerged just as the sun sailed over the trees. The tropical birds burst into their full paean to the new day. He glanced around at the Quonset huts, tents, and larger buildings that composed the Port Moresby Military Hospital. There were only a few others up this early – medics and native orderlies changing shifts. His own tent was out on the fringe.

Johnny might be only twenty years old, but today he felt weak and worn. As he forced himself to walk the dirt track towards the harbor, he wished he felt anywhere near as fit as he had as a teenager. Back in San Diego, he'd been a star on the football team, a wide receiver who scored a lot of touchdowns. His track-and-field events were sprints and the long jump. He could run like the wind, and when he jumped, he seemed to fly.

Later, in Hawaii, he'd transferred all his enthusiasm to water sports. He'd been sixteen when he arrived in the US Territory, and right away, he'd been drawn to the surfers – the beach-boys with their long wooden boards.

Duke Kahanamoku, the Sheriff of Waikiki and a frequent Olympic medal winner for the USA, had been one of them. Johnny saw him regularly. He'd even gotten a few lessons from Duke.

Back then, Honolulu was growing fast. More and more mainlanders vacationed on the Hawaiian Islands, especially after Pan Am launched its Clipper service with the big flying boats out of San Fran.

The teenager observed that the surfers attracted the prettiest girls and that sounded good to him. During his year on Oahu, he'd convinced his parents to buy him a board. Sure, it was used, but it was hand carved solid wood, as long as a canoe.

He practiced at Waikiki and around Diamond Head. At last he'd become proficient enough to join the men who rode the water mountains that crashed against the island's north shore.

Johnny was breathing better and he picked up the pace. He glimpsed a nurse in the distance and wondered if it was Gwyndolyn. The pretty woman bothered him! Talking with her, he was almost lulled into thinking there was a kinder, softer world out there. But he knew better. The Hard Case told him why.

A man whose job is killing other men has no business with thoughts like that. Forget about Gwyn. You've got your mission!

His legs wobbled but Johnny forced himself on. His thoughts buzzed around General MacArthur and the upcoming invasion of Japan. He turned when his path joined the wide road around the harbor. His heart thumped unevenly – but still he ran.

Fight to live! Live to fight!

6

That morning in July of 1945, Johnny did not know that his plans were already in ruins. Like each one of us, he traveled the one-way street of time. In the crucial direction, the one from which both glory and destruction come, he was as blind as a newborn.

This is true even for a genius who can glimpse the laws that govern the universe. Take Albert Einstein. Back in 1905, he published his famous equation: energy equals mass, multiplied by the speed of light, squared ($E=mc^2$).

But brilliant as he was, Einstein was no more capable of seeing the future than Johnny. Albert could not know that his profound theory would lead to the creation of horrific weapons of mass destruction. He did not glimpse, all those decades earlier, the rise of the Nazis and the conquest of Germany from within. He could not foresee Adolf Hitler's hatred of Albert's own Jewish race or his diabolical "Final Solution."

There was no way he could foresee that the Fuhrer's physicists would seize on Einstein's breakthrough as their greatest hope for world dominion. Nor did he have any clue that it would be a different great nation that would win the desperate race to create the atom bomb.

This very Saturday morning in 1945 that found Johnny on the Port Moresby shore was Friday night in New Jersey. There, Albert stood in his favorite moose head pajamas, brushing his teeth before bed.

Even now, mere days before the practical application of his discovery would alter the reality of the world forever, the famed physicist did not, could not, even glimpse it.

"If only I had known," Albert would sigh after the fact, "I should have become a watchmaker."

7

The colonel wanted to get to the letter, but he remembered his duties as host. He passed a glass of juice to Dingo and took a sip of his own.

"Ta," the major said. He hung his hat on a knee and drank, while the fan lifted the damp tendrils on his forehead. He drained his glass, wiped his lips with the back of his hand, and waved at the envelope he'd given to Henry.

"A patrol brought it in this morning. They'd been out looking for Japs. They ran across a native runner out there – or vice versa, I suppose. My blokes reckon that *bush kanaka* must've spent a month crossing the mountains. *'Onepella moon'* – you know how they talk. The bugger was starved. They had to feed him before he could speak.

"Turns out he'd walked all the way from the Catholic mission at the headwaters of the Raub River. Kissim! Know where that is, Henry? Far side of the bleedin' mountains. The Raub River flows the other way from us, exits on the north coast.

"Much shorter for our man to go down that 'Big River,' as the locals call it, but not a good idea. Very bad one in fact. Get to that in a moment.

"This blighter managed to cross the central range – no small feat itself. I tell you, Henry, few white men could have made it, not even me." Dingo grinned, his ivory-colored teeth evidence of a lifetime of tobacco and strong coffee.

"Somehow this runner managed to avoid his own blood-thirsty countrymen along the way!"

The colonel was well aware that Dingo had lived in New Guinea for decades. It came up frequently in his conversation.

Dingo had grown coconuts at the coast and coffee in the higher country. Of course, that was before the Japs invaded and the Territory went to war. "The wife and sprouts," he shipped back to Aus, to her parents' farm. He'd closed down his plantations for the duration and turned the Moresby house into bachelor quarters.

"We haven't had any contact with Kissim since before the war. Between the crocodiles and the cannibals, Henry, the Raub River is the last place you want to be. The priests used to get their supplies by air – the only way in and out. But all that ended with the war. Truth is, with the Japs on their way, we forgot about the poor buggers. Might as well have dropped off the face of the Earth."

"I want to hear more about that," the colonel said, "but let's get to the letter."

"Ah yes," Dingo said. "Must admit – got my ears perked."

The colonel extracted a sheet of yellow foolscap from the envelope. Moisture had blurred the writing that covered both sides of the page. Henry scanned the first lines, turned it over and glanced at the signature, then began to read from the beginning. He looked up when the Australian cleared his throat.

"Yes Dingo, of course. The writer signs himself 'Father Christopher Bastion' and gives the address as 'The Mission of Our Lady of Perpetual Help, Kissim Village, Raub River.' He says he's an American priest. 'My dear Commander and my fellow American, I am in need of your mercy and urgent assistance.'" The colonel read ahead and paraphrased.

"Bastion and three others established the mission in 1937. In all, there were four priests – two Australians, an Italian, and himself. When war broke out, he and his fellows were 'guided by God' – his words – 'not to return to the outside world.'

"This was because of the Italian, Father Constanti." The colonel read the next passage word-for-word:

"'We knew that in the greater world, Italy was our enemy. This was not so in our mission under the loving guidance of Our Lady. We were two Australians, Fathers Sid Bunn and Bob Delaney, myself – an American, and our Italian brother, Bruno Constanti. Our nations might be at war, but in our Eden, we were allies.

"'Here we laid the foundation for agape, far from the reach of international politics. What example would we set for our new brothers and sisters in Christ, we asked ourselves, if we could not live in His love for one another?'"

"An idealist," the major observed. The colonel nodded and scanned on.

"'No aircraft have arrived since the hostilities began,' Bastion writes, 'but we had everything we needed, provided by our Heavenly Father.' They were even left alone 'by the savages our people fear above all others – the notorious headhunters of the Valley of the Cannibals.' He says, 'Thanks be to God, the Mambu warriors have not ventured through the wild country that separates us.'" The colonel read a passage to himself.

"Ah," he said, "now we're getting to the heart of it."

Dingo leaned forward.

"'Everything changed at the beginning of May of this year,'" the colonel read.

"'Then the Japanese invaded Kissim. A squad of nine arrived, bringing native guides at gunpoint. Eventually, we learned they had come through the mountain passes from the Sepik River.

The day they marched in, they surprised our Australian brothers who were, 'by bad luck or God's will' – Bastion's words," the colonel said – "'working with the faithful in the gardens.

"'The Japanese forced them to kneel – and while Brother Constanti and I watched from the forest, unable to do anything but forfeit our own lives – Sid and Bob were martyred in the most horrific way, by sword. Our people panicked and tried to run, as did the guides, and all were shot down.

"'The war had found us at last, and with a vengeance.'"

"Sodding bastards!" Dingo exploded, rocking forward so his hat fell to the floor. He snatched it up and dropped it on the sofa.

"Indeed," the colonel said. "Father Bastion goes on: 'The Japanese have slaughtered thirty-seven of our people. They have guns, and we have nothing but our faith, and the primitive weapons that are these people's only defense. Still, our faithful men managed to kill two of the enemy. The reprisals have been terrible. They burned down the village, including our home and simple church. They have killed all the pigs and robbed the gardens.

"'We count seven Japanese now. As for ourselves, we can barely keep body and soul together. We exist like animals, eating roots and wild fruit, creeping to a new place every night in order to avoid certain death.

"'My Dear Commander,'" Henry read on, "'we have long surrendered our fate to God. But now we throw ourselves on your mercy as well. I would not ask only for myself and Father Constanti, the two of us who remain, but for the lives of our innocent flock. I beg you, if it is within your power, rescue us.'" Colonel Chambers turned the page over.

"'There is an airstrip behind the mission,' he writes, a natural field where they first landed. He says we can put down there.

"The priest concludes: 'We will continue to hide in the jungle, and we pray that our brave acolyte, Simay, who volunteered to carry this letter across the perilous mountains, will somehow come to you. We pray for your protection, Sir, and your men. We will watch without ceasing for you to come. God willing, you will find us before the enemy does.' And he signs himself, 'Yours in Christ, and Your Fellow American, Father Christopher Bastion.'"

"Called in the heavy guns there," Dingo said with a twitch of his lips. "God and country! When was the epistle penned?" The colonel flipped the page again.

"'Sunday, May 27,'" he read, "'in the Year of Our Lord, Nineteen Hundred and Forty-Five.'"

"Two months ago, give or take," the Australian observed. "No doubt the good Fathers have not heard that the mad dog Hitler found his own 'final solution'..."

"...or that Germany surrendered," the colonel put in. "Peace in Europe! The Italians of course were beaten by then, and Il Duce and his mistress killed by the mob, their bodies dragged through the streets. Father Constanti is no longer an enemy alien. Little do they know."

"Fair dinkum," Dingo agreed. "Little do they know."

"There's something else," Chambers said: "a Post Script." He put his finger on the place and puzzled through words almost obscured by the stains.

"Something strange here," he said, peering at the Australian over his glasses. "He warns me to beware of a 'monstrous beast.'"

"Our people call it 'the Father,'" the colonel read. "We have a difficult time preventing them from worshiping it, particularly after it devoured five of the faithful.'"

40

"My word!" Dingo exclaimed. "The Father! Of course, I've heard of it, but I thought it was a native myth.

"But if it is real, I believe I know what the bugger is!"

8

As Johnny ran along the harbor, he had to make his way through a growing crowd of natives. There were people of all ages walking to town and he realized it was market day. That would give some an opportunity to earn, and the others, an even greater one to spend. Many carried the special shillings minted in Australia for people without pockets. The coins had holes punched through their center, and they wore their wealth on thongs.

Johnny heard a babble of languages as he dodged the huddles greeting their *wantoks* (*"one-talks"* – those cousins and friends from their home village who spoke their unique tribal language). He noticed highlanders with their wide faces, coastal people with narrower ones, and the offshore Melanesians, some of whom reminded Johnny of the Hawaiians.

The market was an opportunity to visit friends and kin, and admire members of the opposite sex. Clutches of young warriors stood together, ogling the girls and making comments. Some females averted their gaze and passed by. Others smiled boldly back. Saturday was an exuberant mixture of commerce, reunions and romance, all rolled into one.

Johnny heard the growl of a jeep, traveling fast. He saw natives jump out of the way. Just then, two boys came running from the crowd, chasing one another across the road. Johnny grabbed them by their shoulders, ignoring the twinge in his own.

"Slow down!" he told them as the vehicle barreled by.

"Yes Masta," one smiled. "Thank you, Masta," the other one said.

"Don't call me that," Johnny said. The word was common but the soldier didn't like it. "It's Johnny. Just Johnny. You want some gum?" He pulled the chiclets out of his pocket and handed them over.

"Tank you Mas...tank you Joe-nee, tank you true!"

"Go on," Johnny smiled, "and watch out!"

The road was so congested he had to walk again. Over the bobbing heads he saw the marketplace among the warehouses. Once a coffee shed had stood there, but it had been bombed by the Japanese and had burned to the ground. The native market sprang up on the ring of scorched earth.

Today at first light, hundreds of vendors had come in from the villages. The women did the gardening and they came carrying nearly their own weight in *bilums*, woven string bags. These bulged with sweet potatoes called *kaukau,* and a variety of vegetables. Many had a baby tucked among the *bilums*. Others had infants on their hips, close to the breast, and round-bellied youngsters at their heels. Other folk carried yellow and green papayas, bundles of sugar cane on their heads, tamarillos called "tree tomatoes," and baskets of purple passion fruit.

On impulse, Johnny went into the market. There were only a few Caucasians in the crush – Australian housewives, shopping for their groceries. Johnny passed between rudimentary stalls made of four posts in the earth with a grass roof, or simply a mat spread on the dirt.

Many sellers offered pyramids of the green and reddish nuts called *buai* – the betel nut of the Areca palm. The stimulant was popular all over the island. People chewed betel and slaked its acidic burn with quicklime. *Buai* stained their lips and gums red, and eventually, turned their teeth black.

42

A chaw stimulated abundant saliva, which caused much spitting, and every road and public place was splattered scarlet. This disgusted the whites, but the people adored their addiction.

Johnny watched fishermen hawk strings of fish and eels.

Other sellers offered chickens, the quick and the dead, and eggs in nests of moss. Some brought the denizens of the jungle; marsupial cuscus (a cuddly possum), wallabies and tree kangaroos with their long tails.

Then there were the feathered set, white cockatoos, green, red and blue parrots, and the flightless cassowaries that looked like the dinosaur age with their horny crests.

Most prized of all, their iridescent plumes desired for head-dresses and body decoration, were the Birds of Paradise. The jay-sized birds looked like they'd fallen into vats of neon paint.

The cacophony was deafening, but above it all rose the scream of the pigs. All their lives, these had been coddled like children. They shared the family home, and some had suckled at a woman's breast with her own babies. But at last their true status in village life was revealed. They had been run down, trussed up, and cheerfully dragged to market. In fact, they were all *kaikai* – food. The hogs did not accept their reversal of fortune quietly. Their outrage was earsplitting.

A million flies and mosquitoes joined the crowd. The people slapped at them and, alternately trading insults and wheedling for mercy, they bargained. Johnny cut through a marketplace ripe with body odor and the stench of animals.

He approached a group from the Catholic mission. A number of teenage native girls were outfitted in plaid skirts, white blouses, socks and shoes. Overseeing them were some nuns and a white-haired priest, all sweltering in dark woolens.

43

Arranged in a line before them were woven baskets piled with fruit from their compound – guavas, mangoes and melons.

Two of the older girls spotted the approach of the tall American. He might be thin, but he was a looker! His black hair hung to his neck, and they took in the muscled arms and chest beneath the undershirt. They nudged one another and turned on dazzling smiles.

"Hey handsome!" one sang out, "You like me?" She turned her significant caboose and wiggled.

"You like mangoes?" another one called, putting her hands under her breasts. There was a collective gasp from the nuns. One stepped to the girls and began to slap.

"Naughty! Verra naughty!" Johnny heard an accent thick as porridge. The teenagers were unperturbed. They warded off the blows, beaming all the while. Johnny grinned and stepped by while the old priest glared at him, jowls aquiver.

"Padre," Johnny said, touching a finger to his head. The gaggle giggled and the scandalized nuns clucked over them.

Johnny took to the road once more. As he got further away, the crowd thinned and he could run again. His muscles were warm, and at last, he felt a welcome surge of energy.

He broke into a sprint, jumping puddles.

9

July 1942

Buna, North Coast of New Guinea

Bullet-riddled corpses were awash in the waves as another barge ground onto the sand. Takano Katsu leapt ashore, boots splashing through red foam. His landing craft was one more in a long line now. Muscular and well trained, Katsu had still been violently seasick during the voyage. Like many, he had "fed the fish." He was glad to be on solid land again.

Katsu was *Rikugun Taii* – a Captain in the Imperial Army with a hundred and fifty infantrymen under his command. Due to scheduling, he had not been among the first to arrive on the New Guinea shore this day, but the officer at the landing place told him that, as promised, General Yazawa had been the first off the boats.

Katsu led his men up the beach, passing squads of soldiers slinging corpses into the waves.

The body of a white man went in. In the fighting to come, he expected to see many dead *gaijin*, and this did not disturb him. Nor did the blacks. They were savages who must make way for the civilized people. But when a child was thrown in, followed by a headless white female, he felt distaste.

In his opinion, killing women and children was not fit work for warriors.

But war is war, he reminded himself. In this age of technology, aircraft and artillery blew up civilians by the tens of thousands. What were a few more unfortunate deaths in the magnificent sweep of the Japanese Empire across Asia and the South Pacific?

Captain Takano knew that victory was everything, and defeat, unacceptable. His father, a high-ranking officer and martial arts expert, had taught him from youth that pity was an emotion for women.

Katsu himself had a wife and two children at home. His family was of prime importance to him, but he had sacrificed himself to his nation's cause. He had sworn his life and service to the sacred Emperor and the royal family.

45

The corpses were merely enemy foreigners – distractions from the higher purpose – and he thrust them from his mind.

The captain led his men into the village. Already, the army flag floated from the tallest building – the rising sun with its crimson rays. He did notice that it had been tied to the cross.

Katsu saw the white stallion being tended by the grooms and knew his commander was nearby. He called an order and the men tightened ranks. Then the general himself appeared in the doorway of the smallest *gaijin* building.

From its scabbard, Captain Takano drew his *katana* and held it aloft. It was a family heirloom, centuries old, and it was a great honor for Katsu to carry it into battle.

He shouted and the men saluted.

The general watched his warriors in their new uniforms, bearing the latest firearms. He felt fierce pride, but did not let it reach his face. He gave the men a nod and re-entered the house. It smelled of the *gaijin*, but he was a soldier, and it would do.

His cook brought a flask of *sake*, warm from the stove, with the earthenware cup the commander preferred. On the table was his oversize book of parchment paper. A bottle of ink and set of calligraphy brushes were at his elbow. Yazawa drained the rice wine, savoring the warmth of home. He turned the pages to the last entry he had made at regional headquarters in Rabaul. This was on the island the enemy had the effrontery to call "New Britain," but what the general had observed was a military city of a hundred thousand Imperial soldiers. They had riddled the mountain with tunnels that turned the place into an impregnable fortress.

Taro Yazawa selected a brush and began to paint the strokes that would recount his glorious conquest of New Guinea.

10

July 1945

Port Moresby

Gwyndolyn Brooks picked her way towards the hospital, trying not to muddy her shoes. She was chatting with Ruthie, her fellow nurse and apartment mate. Even though it was early, it was already ferocious with the kind of heat only the tropics could brew up. Towards the harbor the sky was blue, but purple-bottomed cumuli were stacking against the inland hills.

It will pour again this afternoon, Gwyn thought, loosening the collar of the uniform she'd ironed last night. This morning, she showered in cool water and slipped it on. Just before going out the front door, she bobby-pinned the winged cap to her chestnut curls.

"This heat's enough to curl your toenails," Ruthie complained for the umpteenth time. Strands of her red hair already stuck to her peaches-and-cream complexion.

"Like whining is going to do anything about it," Gwyn smiled.

She was twenty-three, a graduate of the Vancouver School of Nursing. A small-town girl from the interior of British Columbia, her life, like millions of others, had been transformed by the Second World War in twenty-odd years.

Because of it, her experience as an RN had been overseas. When the Motherland called for help from her former far-flung colonies, Gwyn had thought it through, then volunteered.

Gwyn met Ruthie Flynn, an Irish nurse, at the hospital in London. After several months there, both had volunteered to take part in the Allied effort in the South Pacific.

At the military hospital in Port Moresby, their patients remained soldiers, but now they were Australian and American instead of British.

At first the two friends had bunked with other nurses on the hospital grounds. They'd enjoyed the common room where they listened to the news and music on the radio. But before long, as they had done in London, they went in search of private digs. Near the hospital, they located a flat – the floor of a house owned by an elderly New Zealand couple. It had two small bedrooms, a kitchenette with its own kerosene refrigerator, and a bathroom with a shower bucket.

Most of their time belonged to the hospital, but in her spare time, Gwyn had befriended many of the Australian women. These were long-time residents, married to men with plantation-related businesses or government jobs. They set up home and raised their families.

Of course, that was before the Japanese war machine stormed onto the island. In 1942, the Imperial Navy steamed for the capital, while their aircraft bombed Port Moresby.

The Japanese even dared to attack Darwin on the north coast of Australia! Thankfully, the American Navy thwarted their seaborne invasion in the Battle of the Coral Sea. Not to be stopped so easily, the enemy swarmed overland. When it appeared Port Moresby might fall, most women and children fled for "Aus."

But here in 1945, in Port Moresby at least, the threat was over. The womenfolk were making their way back. Once more, they took command of their homes and became the hub around which the men revolved. The women were earthy and practical, Gwyn found, most with a plainly spoken exterior that masked a pillowy heart.

She also struck up friendships with the natives. Contrary to some advice she received – not to get too familiar – she visited their humble homes. Gwyn found them to be respectful, generous with what little they had, and possessors of a lively sense of humor. She enjoyed the laughter.

It was while visiting these sections of town that she first encountered the homeless children. Bands roamed the streets, looking for handouts, sleeping where they could. The balmy climate helped, but Gwyn was troubled that these youngsters had no home, no one to love them. She made inquiries and found they were victims of the war. Some were called "half castes," the mixed-race legacy of soldiers. One way or another, they were all orphans.

Gwyn's heart went out to them and her project was born. In it, she found a powerful ally in the Director of the hospital, Doctor Gillis MacClure. The elderly medical man known to everyone as "Doc Mac," went to bat for her with authorities. Gwyn had been granted temporary possession of a rambling house, run down as it was and in need of repair. The Aussie owners had perished in a wartime mishap, and heirs had not yet shown up. For the meantime, the home was hers.

Gwyn dubbed it "the Good Shepherd Orphanage," and raised funds and volunteer work parties from the local churches. Carpenters replaced the rot, and the place got a coat of white paint, courtesy of the American Army. Gwyn hired a native staff to cook and clean.

Soon she had sixteen boys and girls, ages two through nineteen, living in the house. She set up school in the living room. She cajoled Ruthie and Australian friends to help teach. True, it was little more than the alphabet, simple words, and the addition and multiplication tables, but it was a start.

The Good Shepherd consumed all of Gwyn's spare time. Ever more frequently, her nights were spent sleeping there.

She and Ruthie began to talk about what had become increasingly clear. One day soon, Gwyn would move into the orphanage for good.

But on this Saturday morning as she and Ruthie walked to work, Gwyn was unable to focus on the children. Nor was she following the story Ruthie spun about last night's dance. She was preoccupied by a male friend. She would see him today and Gwyn was both perturbed and more interested than she cared to admit.

11

Johnny was puffing like a steam engine. The drill of pain in his chest had become a general torment down his side. He was jarred in all the places the war had hurt him.

An ambulance truck, canvas sides painted with red crosses, came from the direction of the airport, siren howling. Johnny approached a section of the road lined with stores. Across the way, a man was taking the padlock off Burns, Philp & Company, a general store. His body begged for a breather. His fresh scar throbbed and the old one in his thigh tugged like an anchor. He came to a stop and, panting, gazed across the Moresby harbor. There was a freighter at the docks, men unloading with a crane and net. Further out were two US Navy vessels. One was a destroyer at anchor, sailors over the side on ropes, painting over the rust. The other was a PT boat, just getting underway. Something about that made his chest twist.

Suddenly Johnny had to stare at the gravel road, trying not to think of his father. His dad had been an officer on a Navy warship. He winced under the barrage of images that came at him, and in spite of his efforts to steer his thoughts another way, he found himself in that other lifetime. *His face, his voice.*

To distract himself, Johnny looked at the gunboat. *What a power launch!* He recited what his dad had taught him: *PT – Patrol Torpedo. Seventy-seven feet of deadly force. Barrel in, loose the torpedoes and make your getaway.* Dad had admired the "plywood fleet," although the vessels he'd served on were much larger.

Johnny watched the PT cut around the hulk of a Japanese-sunk freighter. It headed for the port's mouth and she opened up. The roar of the engines echoed across the water. He sat on a boulder, pulled out the Camels and lit one. When he looked again, the gunboat was a dot going over the curve of the world. He did not want to think about his father, so he turned his mind to another PT he'd run across.

It had been a couple of years ago in the outer islands. There'd been a combined military action against an entrenched Japanese stronghold. Enemy snipers had the men pinned down and their commander radioed HQ for help. By then, Johnny was part of General MacArthur's elite core of shooters. He'd been up the New Guinea coast, seeing some action. Johnny was given thirty minutes to throw his gear together, and then he was aboard a PBY Catalina, heading over the ocean. The armed flying boat took him across the channel between the islands they called "the Slot," deep water where the enemy ran their supply ships.

He'd seen the big island of New Britain, and then a lot more dotting the Solomon Sea. The aircraft splashed down near one and taxied ashore.

It was late afternoon. Johnny was just in time for chow and a drink with the men he'd be fighting alongside the following day. As a spectacular sunset set fire to the sky, the men moved to the "cantina." It was really no more than a table, a cooler, and some chairs scattered on the sand, but it had a million-dollar view, and a cold brew from home went down easy.

They'd just settled in when the howl of big engines drowned out the conversation. A PT boat was racing at them. It got close and still came on, barreling for the beach.

Just when it looked like the skipper was going to park on the sand, he spun the launch hard around, threw it in reverse, and came to a textbook stop just offshore.

A dozen sailors swarmed over the gunwales. They swam the few yards, and dripping wet, came up the beach. Their leader was a skinny lieutenant with a mop of hair.

As he reached the Army men, the looey fished a wad of wet greenbacks from a pocket and in what Johnny took for a Boston accent, he said he'd buy "every man-jack a be-ah."

Sometimes Army and Navy didn't mix but the offer of a free round went a long way. The newcomers mingled with the others, sitting wherever there was a chair, or on the sand. The skipper ended up beside Johnny. Still standing, he said in a loud voice his name was Jack, and he launched into a joke about a Texan, a Mexican, a big-chested blonde and a Longhorn bull. Now, Johnny came from a church-going family. Early on, his father warned him that swearing was an indication of a poor education and even poorer imagination. He said men who used foul language were bores who substituted words for fists. Language like the looey's might have been tolerated by his Navy cohorts, but his father made it clear, he would not hear it in his home.

Johnny's mom took it a step further. She promised her boy that if she heard a "potty mouth" from him, she'd clean it with soap. Johnny made the mistake only twice of using the words around her that he heard every day at school, even from his football coach. He remembered each occasion with clarity, because both times he'd found himself suddenly going sideways, his usually benign mother dragging him by the ear. At the sink, he'd been ordered to stick out his tongue. She'd lathered her hands and smeared on the suds.

Even in the Army, surrounded by men who turned the air blue with their language, Johnny didn't like to cuss. If he did, he tasted Lifebuoy.

The story the skipper spun would have been beyond the pale in Johnny's home. But he'd been in the army for years now: he'd heard it all, and then some. But he hadn't heard this joke. The looey delivered the punchline with gusto. The men roared, Johnny included.

Jack sat down, turned to Johnny with an easy smile, and they started talking. First topic was the gunboat, and Jack seemed impressed by how much his new acquaintance knew. Johnny explained he was a Navy brat, and they moved on to various warships. Johnny named a few his forebearers had sailed on. He found himself describing the Pennsylvania-class Super Dreadnought that had been his father's last ship. Jack whistled and asked for his name.

"Johnny Willman." Jack asked if Lieutenant Commander Jeremy Willman was a relation.

"My father," Johnny said, regretting the tack the conversation had taken. That made retired Rear Admiral Horace Willman his grandfather? Johnny nodded. Jack paused and said he knew what had happened to Johnny's old man and he was sorry about it. Johnny didn't reply and found himself needing to stare out to sea.

Jack squinted at him and changed the subject. The skip said he'd found an anti-tank cannon sitting idle. He planned to "commandeer it," he grinned. He pointed at the boat's bow, now a dark line on the waves. He would mount the big gun there. Then he'd really blow holes in the "Tokyo Express." That's what they called the flotilla of enemy ships that delivered troops and supplies through these islands. In order to avoid being sunk by Allied fighters, the Japanese now ran their convoys at night. And that's where PT boats like Jack's came in.

"We're like those huge crocs you see out here," the man said. "We lay in wait. And then we're fast and we've got big teeth." He showed his own. The talk turned to racing sailboats. Jack had done his fair share. He talked about how to tack against the wind. You did that using the keel, Jack said. "Without a good keel," the skip said, "you might as well be driftwood."

Johnny brought up surfing and his teenage enthusiasm showed. He described the massive waves he'd ridden at Waimea Bay and Sunset on Oahu's north shore.

"From the photos, they're like boats without a keel. How do you turn them?" Jack asked.

"You don't," Johnny said. "You go straight out and come straight back."

"Driftwood!" Jack laughed. "You need a keel!"

Somehow, though, every topic came back to girls. Jack told Johnny about a drive he'd made around Europe in a sports car, and some flings he'd had. Johnny realized that the looey had "known" a lot more women than he had, in what his father would have called "the biblical sense."

At 22-hundred, Jack said he had to get back aboard his PT-109. At midnight, he and the boys would head into the slot to hunt Japs. Johnny said he had his own hunt in the morning, and explained he was a sniper. He kept his eyes on his new acquaintance, watching for a sign of revulsion, but Jack only nodded. Some men didn't like snipers: they thought there was something cowardly about shooting a man at a distance. At least, Johnny found, they thought that way until an enemy marksmen got them pinned down. Then they were only too happy for the help.

Jack said it was time to go. The skip called his sailors. Grumbling good-naturedly, they got up.

Johnny walked down with them to the water. The sailors waded in and swam out. Jack stepped into the waves and turned back.

"Let's get together after the war," he said. "Have a few be-ahs."

"I didn't get your last name," Johnny said.

"It's Kennedy," the voice came from the darkness. "Jack Kennedy." There came the flash of white teeth and the looey swam away.

Back on the Moresby harbor, Johnny thought about that.

Sure, we'll get together after the war! More likely, neither of us will make it home.

The PT boat he'd been watching was gone. Johnny flipped the cigarette butt in a puddle and stood.

My meeting is at 9-hundred hours. Get a move on!

He took a few strides and broke into a jog, retracing his route along the harbor.

12

"WORLD WAR II IN THE SOUTH PACIFIC"
- BY COLONEL HENRY CHAMBERS III

I Shall Return!

Dear Reader, when Japan attacked Pearl Harbor and multiple targets in Asia and the South Pacific in December of 1941, the leader of the American Army in the Philippines was General Douglas MacArthur.

This was the man who had once been Field Marshall of the islands, hired by the Philippine Government. Always the egotist, he designed his own splendid gold-braided uniform.

Eventually, in order to assume command of American forces in the Philippines, the warrior had to return to the humdrum khaki and mere title of General of the US Army.

By the late 19th Century, our nation had won the Spanish-American war. The loser was forced to sell us its colonies, including the 7,000 Philippine islands. Just off our own shores, we also took Cuba.

Douglas MacArthur had believed for years that war between the United States and Japan was inevitable. Yet, when push came to shove – when the Japanese invaded the Philippines in force – the general could not mount an effective defense.

In short order, they brutally routed MacArthur's Army.

With surrender imminent, President Roosevelt ordered his famous general to abandon his men and see to his personal safety. And so it came to pass that MacArthur boarded a PT gunboat under cover of night, accompanied only by his family and a few close officers, and slipped away.

Of the 100,000 soldiers he left to the non-existent mercy of the enemy, it is estimated that between 10,000 to 20,000 Americans and Filipinos perished on the infamous Bataan "Death March." From the harsh Japanese view, a soldier who surrendered was worth less than a dog. They often killed their prisoners for sport and sheer machismo.

It was a disgraceful defeat for General MacArthur. He slunk into Australia with his tail between his legs. But then, the Australians laid on a hero's welcome.

They had good reason. They knew Japan lusted for their sparsely inhabited southern continent and they had little hope of defense. Australia had already sent its best fighting men to help the motherland battle the Nazi hordes. Now they needed their soldiers, but Churchill had his own urgent need and would not let the Aussies go home.

So it was a desperate Australia that welcomed MacArthur. America had bottomless pockets and millions of patriots who rushed to battle. It was rich from manufacturing, and its formidable factories were now churning out weapons, battle ships, aircraft and bombs.

Washington could not meet MacArthur's demand for soldiers and supplies all at once, but it could give him a title. He was dubbed "Supreme Commander of Allied Forces in the Southwest Pacific Area."

Who is this military prodigy? He was born under the flag at an armory in Little Rock, Arkansas. His father was still fighting the Indian Wars and Douglas says the first sound he remembers was a bugle.

Just after the turn of the 20th Century, watched by his beloved mother, Pinky, he graduated with Outstanding Honors from West Point. He became an aide to President Teddy Roosevelt. By the end of WWI, he was a Brigadier General and the most decorated veteran in all America.

How ignominious, then, for the great warrior to be run out of the Philippines!

His ego survived and Australia encouraged him. Once on the continent, he thundered:

"I have come out of the Philippines – and I shall return!" It was a personal promise, and in spite of an abysmal lack of resources and years in the doing, MacArthur forged his iron plans.

Gradually, more US troops were sent his way. At the heyday of the New Guinea campaign, there were tens of thousands of our soldiers in Port Moresby. But in every toe-to-toe fight, the Japanese taught them hard lessons. The enemy had years to dig in. When our boys attacked, they met withering fire. The result was slow progress and high casualties. Tropical diseases like malaria and typhoid cut down more troops than enemy bullets.

But for MacArthur to keep his promise to the Philippines, he had to move on! It chafed him enormously to read how the US Navy carved victory after victory across other islands in the South Pacific. His arch rival, Admiral Nimitz, turned Guadalcanal and Iwo Jima into household names. His ships won the battles of Midway, the Coral Sea, and the Solomon Islands.

In order to break away from New Guinea, the Supreme Commander came up with a new plan he called "leapfrogging." No longer would he face the enemy in the steaming jungle. Instead, he would bypass him. That was how it came to be that MacArthur, using his own army aircraft, carried his men up the coast. Ironically, in the end, he was forced to rely on Nimitz's ships to ferry his soldiers back to the Philippines.

And it was in those very waters that the US Navy fought the last remnants of the enemy fleet and sent them to the bottom.

So it was, on October 20th 1944, Supreme Commander MacArthur waded ashore on Leyte Island. He had fulfilled his famous promise.

"I have returned! By the grace of Almighty God, our forces stand again on Philippine soil. Rally to me. Rise and strike! Let no heart be faint. Let every arm be steeled. The guidance of divine God points the way. Follow in His Name to the Holy Grail of righteous victory!"

The General is at his best as an inspiring leader, and our troops and the Filipinos did indeed rise to the challenge.

At the time of this writing, July of 1945, the United States controls our Philippine Territory.

Now the Supreme Commander glowers north. On to Japan! Only open ocean stands between him and his ultimate destination.

It is certain that this very year, General MacArthur's full army will land on the enemy homeland itself. After Pearl, that became our nation's destiny.

America will not rest until we have forced utter defeat on the Empire of Japan.

13

Johnny's most recent wound didn't come in New Guinea – it happened in Manila, once "the Jewel of the Orient." That was before the big guns tore it up.

Johnny had spent most of his war in New Guinea, then gone with General MacArthur to the Philippines. He was in the throng of soldiers landed at Leyte Island, so was there to see the general, surrounded by senior officers and Filipino dignitaries, wade ashore.

The Supreme Commander had kept his promise to return and liberate the islands. He made a rousing speech and then came down the line of men, chewing on his corncob pipe. He recognized one of his go-to snipers and paused.

"God's hand is on us, my boy," the general's voice boomed at Johnny and others turned to stare. "The eyes of the world are watching. I have returned, and we will prevail!"

It was vintage MacArthur and Johnny believed him. They would fight to the finish, whatever the cost.

The next time Johnny saw the commander was on the road to Manila. He was packed with other GIs in the back of a truck, part of the huge convoy wheeling through the Philippine towns. There was a festive feeling. Families lined the roads, cheering their liberators. Johnny saw a jeep come charging from the rear. It drew close and he recognized the peaked cap, hawk nose, and aviator sunglasses. General MacArthur towered up from his seat.

"Faster men!" he boomed, pointing ahead. "On to Manila!" A column of tanks rattled by along the embankment.

But the Philippines would not be a cakewalk for MacArthur. Four hundred and thirty thousand seasoned Japanese troops were on the islands, and they'd had years to dig in. Every GI who had fought them knew how fierce they were, often choosing death over surrender. And in the Philippines, the Japs were made even more fanatical by their terrible predicament. If they were beaten here, the Yankees' next stop was unthinkable, intolerable – their own sacred homeland.

Johnny rode toward Manila with a lightness in his spirit. After all these years, he was closing in on the vow he'd made as a sixteen-year-old boy.

But that was before an enemy bullet almost put the period at the end of his life story.

Manila had once been the Supreme Commander's headquarters and MacArthur wanted it back.

While the tanks were beginning to crunch over the barriers the enemy had flung up, the general was planning his victory parade. That proved to be premature by a month, and a lot of lives.

"The Nips," as MacArthur called them, were fanatical in their defense, and the battle raged street-by-street, foot-by-foot, every advance bought in blood.

The enemy gunned down everyone in the line of fire – man, woman and child. By the time it was over, a hundred thousand bodies rotted in the ruins, and the Japanese had added the Massacre of Manila to the Rape of Nanking, and a long list of war atrocities.

In the Philippines, as he had been in New Guinea, Johnny was a sniper. It was a job for which he'd received no special training, for the simple reason that the US Army had no such program. But Johnny had been raised in a military family where all of the men were hunters.

When he was seven, his father taught him to stalk rabbits with a .22 rifle. When he was twelve, he shot his first deer, an eight-point buck. At fourteen, Johnny was finally allowed to tag along on the men's annual big game trip. At a private reserve in the Sierra Nevada Mountains of California, he saw his father and grandfather each shoot a giant bull elk.

That first year, Johnny was only permitted to observe. He was to do what he was told, and keep his mouth shut. Still, he was in his element. He slept in the tents with the men and walked the pine needle trails. He listened to the way his father and granddad spoke with the guides and outfitters and soaked up their manner of speech. After being sent back to camp early one day for making too much noise in the blind, he learned to sit silently for long hours, no matter how restless he felt, making no complaint.

That turned out to be good training.

For his fifteenth birthday, Johnny's parents gave him what at once became his prized possession – a scope-mounted .30-06 Remington rifle.

In the fall of 1940, the boy killed a seven-hundred-pound bull with a huge rack. The last time he'd seen the mount, it was on the wall of his grandfather's study in San Diego. Where it was now, he did not know. His grandmother had passed away early in the war, and in December last year, he'd received the cable that told him the retired Rear Admiral had succumbed to a heart attack.

The attorney told Johnny the house would be sold, and his portion of the inheritance, held in trust, pending instructions. So far, Johnny had done nothing about it.

Not long after that hunting trip, Johnny's father received new orders, and the family transferred to Hawaii. A year later, with the world as he knew it in ruins and his country at war, Johnny returned to San Diego.

He did not stay long.

Contrary to his grandfather's order, Johnny ran away. The seventeen-year-old went into the nearest Army recruitment post, lied about his age, and signed up. The officer took his word for it. Tens of thousands of other boys were in the same boat. But even before he hit boot camp, the lad who barely shaved the fuzz off his lip was an expert shot.

Still, it was not until he got to New Guinea that he saw enemy infantry and killed his first man. During his initial day in battle, in fact, he dispatched five. He seemed to have a knack for it. At first it was horrific for the boy, overwhelming. But men dying, Japanese, American and Australian, quickly became the norm.

The Army made attack after attack in the equatorial jungle against an enemy that knew how to fight in this country. The Japanese built near-impregnable bunkers, and in the dense foliage, the GIs often did not make them out until they were on top of them. Then fighting was fierce, often with pistols, grenades and knives, and the slaughter was close-up and personal.

Most sad sacks hated New Guinea, but this was right where Johnny wanted to be. At first, he was just another GI on the front line.

But early on, his marksmanship brought him to the attention of the brass. They gave Johnny his niche. He became a specialist, a shooter reserved for the long-range kill. From one jungle battle to the next, a routine evolved. First, the regular troops went in. Field command came behind, Johnny with them.

When the front line got into trouble, pinned down by enemy riflemen and machine guns, the young sniper was ordered to the front.

Up where the men were dying, the teenager crept alone into the jungle. At first he was as frightened as any boy would be, but he learned to do his work. He came to welcome those times by himself. Then he was the lone wolf, the ambush predator, the hunter of hunters.

Without any manual to tell them what to do, he and the other crack shots evolved their own techniques. Some dug a hole and waited under a nest of branches. Others liked to stay on the move, ghosting from one cover to the next. Johnny preferred the high ground with an eagle-eye view of the enemy.

Sometimes he looked down from a hill on a Japanese encampment, but his favorite place was up a tree. These, he learned to pick carefully. They must have sufficient foliage to conceal him, while providing a view of the target. The trunk had to be stout enough to stop a bullet, and the branches spaced for climbing.

After a few close calls, he learned to ensure as well that each perch offered an escape route. After he fired two or three shots, the enemy guns would turn his way.

Patrols came at a run. By then, Johnny needed to have slipped down the blind side of the tree. Then he'd either be picking off the Japanese from another location, or gone entirely.

The teenager became a student of enemy behavior. He preferred to shoot officers, and he'd learned the strategy early in life. Johnny remembered a day when he was six and his father grabbed a chicken and took it and the boy to the woodpile. The man laid the squawking bird on the chopping stump. Down the axe swung. Whack! There went the head. His father set the body on its feet and Johnny was amazed to watch it run in a circle before it keeled over. The shock of the unexpected death made tears spring to the boy's eyes, but that turned to startled laughter when the headless chicken made its run.

"Remember, Johnny," his father told him, "cut off the head, and the body dies. When you take out the leader, the followers lose their way. That makes them easy game."

At the time, Johnny had been in a series of fistfights at school, and he'd taken beating after beating from an older boy. Johnny told his dad about it, but the man would not intervene. Instead, he explained there was a pecking order, "on the schoolyard and in life," and Johnny might as well find his place in it. But his Old Man did teach him how to use his fists, and his feet.

"Never show them you're afraid, even when you're being beaten," his dad said. "Don't pick fights, but never back down from one. Once you start running, you'll never stop." The next lesson had been the one with the chicken and the axe.

"You beat the ringleader" – his father said, scooping up the chicken – "and the others will back off. That applies to that coward at your school as well. Remember this. Any boy who bullies a smaller one is a coward and beneath contempt."

After that, Johnny never backed down from a fistfight. He had some wins and some losses. When he was small, there were always bigger boys. But he developed a reputation as a fierce fighter, and he learned to hide his hurts behind a scowl. His dad arranged hand-to-hand combat lessons from a Navy friend. Johnny's last schoolyard fight happened when he was fourteen. He won. After that, he was on the football team, as big as many and faster than most. The gridiron gave him a place where aggression was rewarded.

Years later, alone in the jungle against an enemy who would kill as soon as look at him, Johnny remembered the headless chicken.

Many a Japanese officer paid the price. Of course, picking off the leader was a practice of both sides. Smart commanders quickly learned to remove evidence of their rank. Johnny taught himself to watch body language. The Japanese had a hard time hiding their hierarchical nature. Even across the distance, he saw who gave the orders.

As a hunter of men, Johnny had a high rate of success. His reputation grew. Still, many of the GIs disdained snipers. But Johnny remembered his men-folk telling him about the American frontiersman with his long rifle hiding in the woods, knocking down British redcoats. They were patriots, his granddad said.

Johnny soon found he no longer wanted to know the names of the newcomers to the front. All too soon, many would disappear into the mud. He got a reputation as a loner and a hard case.

But there were times when he did get in another fellow's face. That was when the GI did something stupid that got soldiers hurt or killed. Then Johnny could not help giving the guilty party a piece of his mind.

Unfortunately for his career, this was true even when the other man was an officer. Johnny was a natural leader in battle, and he'd received a number of field promotions, but he couldn't hold onto them. He had what one offended superior called diarrhea of the mouth.

Truth was, Johnny didn't care. He did not want to get promoted out of the fight.

February of '45 found him still a private, still practicing his solitary craft, but this time, in an urban jungle. By then, MacArthur had transferred his army back to the Philippines, Johnny with them. The sniper trailed the front line through Manila, Springfield in hand, pockets bulging with ammo and rations. Often, he was away from base for days at a time, eating his meals cold, sleeping in the ruins. His high ground became the roofs and windows of shattered buildings. His goal was, *every shot a kill.* When the front moved, Johnny drifted behind it like an avenging spirit.

In his three weeks in Manila, he added sixty-three kills to his private count. Only two of those were confirmed. It was rare for other soldiers to witness his work. But the official tally meant nothing to Johnny. His score was personal.

Eventually, the Yanks drove the Japs back into "Intramuros," the ancient walled city-within-a-city. It had been constructed during the five centuries the islands belonged to Spain.

The very name of these islands was for King Felipe, the one-time Spanish monarch. Intramuros was a priceless colonial legacy.

When "the Nips" took refuge in Intramuros, General MacArthur had them cornered. Their backs to the literal wall, they would fight to extinction. Unwilling to expend more of his own soldiers against their desperation, MacArthur made the difficult decision to shell the ancient site.

By the time Johnny got there, edifices that had survived the centuries lay strewn in blocks. Ahead along a rubble-choked street, he saw the GIs holed up in one building, exchanging fire with the enemy across the way. Worn steps took him up a splinter of wall. He lay on the sun-warmed top and watched. Soon he pinpointed two enemy snipers in the blown-out windows.

Johnny tugged out a bandanna, folded it, and laid it on the wall's edge. He rested the barrel of his rifle on it. He found his first target in the cross-hairs, drew a breath and as he released it, he fired.

The shot was just one more in the melee. The enemy crumpled back into darkness. Johnny panned to the second man as his fingers reloaded. He found this one kneeling at the edge of broken flooring, his rifle aimed at the GIs below. Johnny felt the familiar icy anger and increased the pressure on his index finger.

This time, the Jap made the swan dive to the cobblestones, his rifle clattering down beside him. Johnny reloaded and went back to glassing the enemy buildings.

An American tank rumbled into the street, clanking over broken stone and bodies. As Japanese bullets pinged the turret, the big gun turned their way. The cannon boomed and walls imploded. Johnny picked off three more defenders when they tried to escape through a side door.

Fifteen minutes later, the building was another smoking hulk, and the GIs were on the move. Johnny descended and went after them, hugging the walls. Often, he paused to scan ahead, searching for enemy practitioners of his own dark trade.

He heard them before he saw them. In a sunken doorway, two children stood sobbing. A small boy and girl were beside another Filipina who Johnny guessed was eleven or twelve. She sat silently, legs splayed, staring at him with huge eyes.

Her hands were clutched over her midriff and Johnny saw the crimson stain spreading across her sundress.

Gut shot – going to die, the Hard Case said. Johnny crouched and ran across the road. He spoke quietly to the little ones to calm them as he slung his rifle over his shoulder.

Maybe it's too late but I'll try. I'll get her to a medic.

He turned to take one last scan of the street before he picked her up.

And that's when he was shot.

14

March 1945

Manila, the Philippine Islands

Johnny came to in a hospital bed, swaddled in bandages. It was several days before the sniper was coherent enough to learn what had happened. The enemy bullet had smashed a rib as it entered his upper chest, clipped the lung on the way through, broke two more ribs and shattered his scapula on exit.

One of the first things he noticed was his Springfield rifle standing in the corner. He felt a rush of relief. It had been with him so long, it was as important as one of his limbs. He learned from a nurse that it had come in with him. In his delirium he'd babbled about it. She opened the bedside table drawer and showed him his effects – the Zippo, the folding knife. Johnny was grateful.

"Those belonged to my dad. They're all I've got," Johnny muttered. The nurse smiled.

He never met the medics who had carried him in. Nor could he find out anything about the children, although he asked. In the scope of the devastation of Manila, three more lives were of little consequence.

The bullet nearly killed him, but he had youth on his side and Johnny began to heal – until tropical bacteria invaded the wound. Day by day, the boy grew sicker. Somehow, he clung to life, but he was not improving. March became April, and still he lay suffering.

From time to time, he was given newspapers. They were full of the action in Europe. American, Russian and British forces raced for Berlin. Late in the month, the headlines trumpeted shocking news. The bodies of Adolph Hitler and his mistress, Eva Braun, had been found burned in their Berlin bunker. The Nazi leader's vision of a thousand-year Reich ended with him eating a bullet from his own pistol.

With the architect of their misbegotten dream gone, the whole Nazi house of cards caved in. On May 8th, much of the world went wild, Manila included, with the news that Germany had signed the unconditional surrender.

But Private Johnny Willman was too gravely ill to enjoy the victory party. He stared at the ceiling day and night, too weak to move. The pain became worse – something that whispered he might never be whole again.

His physicians decided that the boy needed to be sent State-side on the next available ship. "It's the end of the war for you," they told the young man.

"Back home they've got the best equipment! New drugs! For sure, you don't need this heat. They'll get you well and give you your old life back."

Problem was, Johnny didn't want his old life back! And, un-like many of the men, he wasn't looking for a way out.

He hadn't fought from '42 to '45 only to miss the invasion of Japan. *The Big One!* He did his best to explain this to every doc who came by. They humored him, and kept his name at the top of the evacuation list.

It was only the young New Zealand doctor who really seemed to hear him. Johnny latched onto the Kiwi as his last, best hope. Every chance he got, he told Dr. Cowell he did not want to be sent Stateside. The physician heard him out, but Johnny could tell he wasn't convinced.

Johnny was forced to play his only ace.

In all his years of war, he had never told this to anyone. But dire circumstances called for desperate measures.

Next time Doc Cowell came by, Johnny hoarsely asked him to close the door. In blunt phrases, he blurted out the story. The doctor listened and his patient's suffering was so raw and real, a lump formed in his throat.

"That's why I have to keep fighting until the Japs are finished," Johnny wound up. "Understand? I made a promise."

Johnny stared into the Kiwi's eyes and saw he'd made an ally.

"I'll help if I can," Doc Cowell said, "but whatever happens, you need to stay under medical care. Otherwise you'll die. That's a fact, understand?"

"I hear you," Johnny said. Every heartbeat pumped pain, and he saw his physicians' faces when they peeled back his bandages.

The newspapers said tens of thousands of American troops were now on the ships, returning from Europe. For once, it looked like Washington would have more than enough battle-hardened soldiers to supply General MacArthur for the upcoming invasion.

"If they send me Stateside, I'm never coming back," Johnny said. "But if I were to end up in Australia, once I'm better, they'll have to return me to my unit. You see?"

The Kiwi did see, but Johnny's scheme was a very long shot. By early July, it looked like he was sunk. In a week's time, a ship was scheduled to take thousands of Americans to Los Angeles. Private John Willman would be on it.

Gloomily, Johnny contemplated defeat. But then, two days before he was scheduled to ship out, Doc Cowell came by with news. A British floating hospital had just put into Manila with a load of Aussies from the enemy P-O-W camps in Asia. Some two thousand men, sick and near starvation, were being transported home. The ship had stopped to take on the Aussies liberated during the Battle of Manila. A few were at this very hospital and would be transferred aboard tonight. The Kiwi and the Yank put their heads together.

Around 20-hundred hours, a motley collection of men, many emaciated, gathered at a gangway up a ship on the Manila docks. Some were able to walk on their own, while several were borne on stretchers. On deck, a knot of officers checked each of the Australian's papers.

One young soldier appeared to be unconscious. His records were in the envelope pinned to his chest, and the fellow's name was listed on the manifest. The stretcher was transferred from one set of hands to another and the patient was carried into a vast hold. Here, hundreds of men reclined on rows of metal beds.

The orderlies found a vacant one and transferred the young man to it. There was a bad moment when they saw an old rifle under the sheet. A sailor tried to remove it, but the soldier suddenly revived, grabbed onto it for dear life, and would not let go. A tug of war ensued.

The sick man jerked it away. He slid back the bolt, causing consternation, but simply showed that the chamber was empty – unloaded. He glared at the medics, tucked the rifle against his body again, and pulled over the sheet. Deliberately, he closed his eyes.

The orderlies still had much to do before the ship departed: these poor chaps had been through ordeals they could not even imagine.

And this was not the only firearm on the ward. Many of the P-O-Ws brought such things and other mementos they had collected. They moved on.

Johnny lay back, drenched from the exertion. He had not dared say a word, because if he had, the jig would be up.

Eventually the banks of lights were switched off and the men fell silent. His wound already suppurating through the fresh dressing Doc Cowell had applied, Johnny lay awake as the hours crawled by. At last he felt the vibrations that told him the huge engines had started up far below. An hour later, he felt the roll of the open ocean. Someone opened a window and the fresh salt air felt like liberation. Only then did he allow himself to drift into slumber.

The breakfast trolleys had come and gone and it was late morning before the British doctors came down Johnny's row. They finished with the malnourished man beside him and gathered around his bed. Again, the medical men checked his papers. Apparently there was some discrepancy between the injury described there, and the bandaged chest of the fellow before them. They unwrapped the dressing and exclaimed over what was obviously a badly infected bullet wound.

They peppered the patient with questions, and finally Johnny had to answer. As soon as they heard the Californian accent, the doctors knew this was not the corporal from Woolgoolga his documents claimed. Some terrible mix-up had occurred! They fussed over the lesion, doused it with antibiotic powder and made him swallow some pills. They bandaged the boy up and moved to the next case. An orderly was dispatched to the bridge to report the error, but the captain never even considered turning the ship around.

The sole Yank on board watched the gulls drift by the portholes against the heave of the South China Sea. He even managed a weak smile.

The floating hospital powered down the South Pacific and entered the Slot – the channel between New Guinea and the Solomon Sea. As it rounded the eastern tip of the big island and turned for Australia, an explosion rocked the ship. In spite of the crosses painted on her, it seemed she was under fire. The hull shuddered along its length and the ship began to sink. Fortunately, it was not the kind of direct hit that would send her plunging for the bottom, the fate of so many vessels in these waters during the war.

The officers on the bridge never even saw what hit them. It might have been a torpedo, or a rogue mine. What mattered was saving the lives of those on board. Listing heavily to starboard, all her pumps on full, the ship limped into the nearest harbor. The captain ran his command aground in the shallows. At low tide, welders would go to work on the old plates.

One urgent point of business was to get a dying soldier strapped to a stretcher and lowered over the side. The bumping on the way down did not bother the poor Yank. He'd been in a coma for two days. His wound, already septic, had turned gangrenous. The medics knew all too well the blackened flesh and stench of death. They pursed their lips and shook their heads.

The boy was manhandled from boat to ambulance and rushed to hospital. And that was how Johnny Willman, one foot in the grave, returned to Port Moresby, the place where he had arrived in New Guinea all those years before.

15

Johnny had rested by the harbor long enough. Even though his rib cage pounded, he stood, rubbed sweat from his eyes and took a few strides.

I've got that meeting at 9-hundred hours!

He forced himself into a jog, retracing his route.

Keep on point, the Hard Case ordered. *Say whatever they need to hear to get back in the fight!*

And that's the trouble with Gwyn, Johnny thought.

There's no room for her.

The sun beat on him and he wanted a shower, as cold as the water would get.

The natives stared as the tall man flew by, undershirt pasted to his chest.

Why do they do it? Why run in a circle, only to stop and walk away? The white man was a mystery.

Anyway, what do I have to offer a knockout like Gwyn? Johnny asked himself. The killer was heard from at once:

Nothing. You've got nothing but heartache to give her. If you do care for her, leave her alone.

Each breath burned and his heart hammered like a loose piston. And while Johnny knew the Hard Case was right, he still hoped he'd see her today.

16

Gwyn and Ruthie turned heads as they approached Acute Care. The pair of them stunned the men around the hospital. Gwyn was tall and willowy, her wide-set green eyes framed in chestnut curls cut in a bob. Then there was Ruthie with her voluptuous curves and merry blue eyes, the cap barely hanging onto the red riot of hair.

Neither young woman fully realized how, in this male domain, they shone like beacons of a better world. The medics drank in their passage with longing, and a pang of something like desperation.

Again, Gwyn found her thoughts racing away – *to him!*

Get a grip, she scolded herself. *You're the one who swore off soldiers! And all this one cares about is killing. Most guys have a one-track mind – but his is on the wrong one.*

Still, she found herself hoping she'd see him today.

The nurses pushed through the swinging doors of the vast Quonset hut, assailed by the odor of disinfectant and disease. Patients were laid out on forty beds. The newcomers ducked behind a partition to scrub in, sleeves up, forearms under hot water. They continued to the nurses' station and exchanged greetings with four Australian counterparts going off duty.

Gwyn scanned the ward. Doctors moved among the beds, doling out medicine and advice. Nurses were changing dressings, sheets and bedpans. The kitchen staff carried in the breakfast trays.

Once again, Gwyn was struck by the profound nature of her work. Some of those she served would die. Others would recover. All of them would count on her to help get through the next minute, the next hour. This day.

Her eyes were drawn to the unmistakable white curls of Doctor MacClure, Director of the Hospital and Head of Surgery, presiding over his realm. "Doc Mac" was seventy years old, and a formidable intellect. He was gruff with the careless, and did not bear fools lightly. In fact, he bore them not at all. Dressings-down by the Chief were legendary, and to be avoided.

Some feared him, but Gwyn had no issue with Doc Mac. If you did your job with care and competence, you had nothing to fear.

Gwyn saw that Doc invariably chose the sensible thing. When some poor soldier was beyond help, the physician moved out of his hearing and said so. The patient was given painkillers and every kindness, and the chaplain or priest was sent for.

But if a life could be saved, Doc Mac wasted no time. If surgery was required, off he went to the tents. Doc was a master of the deft amputation.

In addition, patients were treated for the gamut of tropical ailments. Many cases were complex. Men with infected wounds also suffered from a Pandora's box of fevers and ailments. Doc ordered his tests and commenced treatment. If one approach did not work, he tried another, and another, until the man either improved or succumbed.

Gwyn guessed that, once again, Doc Mac had spent the night on the ward. He owned a fine home in the Moresby hills, overlooking the harbor. She'd been there for a party. But more often than not, he simply ducked behind a curtain and slept on a cot.

Now, eyes tired but sharp, he waved Gwyn and Ruthie over and launched into a briefing on the night's developments. There had been a battle somewhere inland. At first light, aircraft had brought in eleven wounded soldiers. Doc departed to take off a crushed leg, and the nurses went about their duties.

Gwyn brought her mind to bear on her tasks. For the time being, all thoughts of other men were pushed away.

17

Doctor MacClure was one of the best medical minds Australia had produced. He had been head of surgery at the Royal Sydney Hospital. In 1940, at the age of sixty-five, he retired. A lifelong bachelor, he returned to his house on the river in Parramatta and tended his garden. He nursed his roses and cigar collection, and went on hikes to places like the Blue Mountains.

But in 1942 when it became clear that the Japanese were on their way, sights set on Australia, Doc Mac could not remain on the sidelines. In fact, the military authorities were grateful to get a man of his caliber. He was assigned to Port Moresby. Australia would do everything possible to halt the Japanese juggernaut on the island of New Guinea. It was the last geographical barrier before the southern continent itself.

The enemy did bomb Port Moresby and even north Australia. That began within two months of the devastating strike on the American fleet in Hawaii. Doc Mac called the aerial attack on Darwin, "Australia's Pearl Harbor." He liked to point out that more bombs had fallen on Darwin than had on Hawaii. In '42 and '43, the Japanese mounted a hundred raids against his homeland.

February of '42, the same month the enemy bombed Darwin, Doc Mac arrived in Port Moresby. He oversaw the unloading of his crates of medical equipment. He was shown around the tent camp that was the military hospital. He was dismayed, but he wasted no time complaining. Instead, Doc Mac met with those in command. He gained possession of every available shelter and Quonset hut in town.

A set of new edifices rose on the hospital compound. These would become his wards, surgeries, laboratories, X-ray clinic, kitchens and mess tents, and dormitories.

His labs were stocked with the equipment that he brought, and continued to arrive, courtesy of his network of contacts. A few microscopes were those captured from the enemy – the only Japanese medical item up to his standards.

Experienced as he was, Doc Mac found he had much to learn in the steaming tropics. The microbe invaders of his patients' bodies were exotic and voracious. The physician devised a number of combination therapies that saved limbs and lives.

In 1944, the treatment of Allied soldiers improved around the world with what Doc Mac heralded as "a high-point in human history."

In the 1930's, a Scotsman, Alexander Fleming, discovered that *Penicillium* mold stopped most bacteria in its tracks. But it was an Australian, Doc Mac emphasized – his colleague Howard Florey – who developed penicillin as a practical treatment for human infection.

America was the source of the miracle drug, all derived, Doc Mac heard, from green mold on a single papaya.

They grew it from there. But with the extraordinary demands of war, penicillin remained nearly impossible to come by. Doc Mac was determined to get his hands on some, and he mounted a letter campaign.

In March of 1945, a crate of hope – packed in sawdust and ice – arrived at the docks. It carried vials of penicillin, courtesy of his mate, Howard Florey. Doc Mac carefully pried up the lid. At last, he had a potent new weapon in his war against death. That was how it came to pass, when a dying soldier was rushed to him off a ship, Doc Mac was ready to do battle for the young man's life.

When the ambulance rolled up, Doc Mac discovered the patient was comatose, barely alive. Gwyn was the lead nurse that day. She took the man's temperature while he was still on the stretcher: 106°F.

Doc snipped through the soiled bandages and the stench made them gag, an automatic reflex. The entire chest, they saw, was red and swollen. Worse yet, around the open lesion in the upper left chest, the skin had turned black.

"Gangrene," Doc Mac said in a hollow voice. It sounded like the death sentence.

Gwyn helped Doc raise the soldier on his side. They saw the healed pucker on the shoulder blade where the bullet had exited. They rolled him on his back again, and Doc probed the chest wound.

Gwyn wiped the unnaturally white face with a cloth. She brushed a strand of black hair from his eyes. His forehead felt like cold clay, in spite of his fever. His eyelids fluttered and the cracked lips moved, but no sound emerged. He had a ragged beard, and Gwyn brushed away the bits of food caught in it.

She worried that Doc would pronounce him a hopeless case, but the words did not come.

At least, not yet.

"To surgery!" Doc Mac ordered. Native orderlies hoisted the stretcher and brought it at a trot after the surgeon and the nurse. They transferred the man to an operating table. Doing so, they found the rifle under the sheet that had come with him, and a bag holding personal items.

"Put those aside," Doc told an orderly. "Save them on the off-chance the patient makes it." Doc and Gwyn scrubbed up. The anesthesiologist joined them.

He could not use ether – too volatile in the tropics. Instead, he had sodium pentothal and nitrous oxide. But as long as the soldier remained unconscious, no drug was needed.

Doc chose his instruments while Gwyn prepared the chest. She took gauze in a clamp, dipped it in iodine, and swabbed the wound and pectoral muscle. She stood aside while Doc took a scalpel and smoothly carved a cone of diseased tissue. Gwyn and the other physician pinched away the curls of necrotic flesh.

"Wide edges, you see?" Doc said. "Less chance of gas gangrene." If that infected the tissue, the nurse knew, the patient was done for.

Gwyn employed a hand suction to remove the blood and they applied clamps to the severed vessels. The wound looked better now, but she saw with a sinking heart that the dead patches continued into the cavity.

"Move him to isolation," Doc ordered. "Leave the wound uncovered. Inject him with penicillin. I'll be back."

Gwyn got to work while Doc drove his car to his house. He strode through, exited onto the veranda and crossed the lawn. He approached an odd-looking shed. The roof was metal, but the walls were mosquito netting stretched around posts, with a door in one side. The sound of buzzing swelled, and he drew a breath and held it against the reek of rotting meat. He unlatched the door, slipped inside, and fastened it.

The place swarmed with green flies. On the table in the center of the room were nasty looking chunks that seemed to be moving. It was well-decayed pork, riddled with maggots.

Doc took a glass jar from a shelf, removed the lid, picked up a paintbrush, and swept a number of twitching larvae into the container. There were holes punched through the lid he screwed down. He rushed with it back to the hospital.

Gwyn was at the patient's bedside, arranging a mosquito net over him, when Doc Mac came in.

He ducked under and used two fingers on the patient's neck to feel the pulse. It was irregular, and dangerously fast.

Doc Mac unscrewed his jar and spilled the maggots into the wound. Even though Gwyn had seen him do this before, her stomach lurched. Still, she knew the purpose. These fly larvae ate only dead tissue and left the healthy alone. Doc ducked out again, took the clipboard hanging at the foot of the bed, and made a note.

"Maggot debridement begun," he said. He looked at Gwyn. "We'll know soon if our patient – what's his name?"

"John Willman," Gwyn answered, having read the letter sent with him from the ship. "Twenty years old. American."

"We'll know very soon if our young Yank, John Willman, will survive this crisis." He assigned Gwyn to the man's care, along with her regular duties.

As the day went by, the nurse was frequently at Willman's side, peering at the writhing grubs. It both fascinated and disturbed her to watch them feed. Already, the black patches were shrinking.

Every three hours, Gwyn administered another shot of penicillin. Part of the challenge with the miracle drug was how rapidly the body expelled it.

Finally, hours after her shift was officially over, she dragged herself home to bed. First thing in the morning, she stuck her head into the tent and noted that her patient remained insensate, but was breathing evenly. She took his pulse and found it had slowed to a hundred and twenty.

Best yet, the wound looked clean and pink. The maggots were lethargic, but still moving.

She gave the patient another shot and took his temperature: 104°.

Another day went by, and it was 101°, his pulse a mere ninety. She and the physician agreed that the man now stood a fighting chance.

Two mornings later, Gwyn arrived to find a squadron of shiny flies circling inside the mosquito net. She opened the tent door, lifted the netting, and shooed the insects out. After what they had done, giving them freedom was the least she could do.

When she turned around, the patient's eyes were open. They were a warm brown, and he was staring at her.

"I'm Private Willman," the boy rasped. "You can call me 'Johnny.'" His voice cracked and he coughed. Gwyn had placed a glass of water by the bed. Johnny tried to raise himself on an elbow, but fell back. Gwyn went to him. She sat on the bed, got an arm under his neck, and helped him drink. The patient drained the glass.

It struck her that, shaved and cleaned up, he might be a decent-looking fellow. Of course, he needed fattening up. He was all skin and bones.

"Are you an angel? Am I dead?"

"No..." she started to say, and saw the hint of a smile.

"Good. If you can joke, Johnny, you must be feeling better."

"What's your name?"

"Gwyndolyn," she told him. "But you can call me 'nurse.'"

She saw his eyes open wider and she laughed. It was a musical sound that seemed to brighten the day.

"Call me Gwyn," she smiled.

For some reason, Johnny found his pain easier to bear.

18

For the first month, the wounded soldier was too sick to do anything but lie still and obey orders.

His doctor had taken to calling him "Young Johnny." Doc Mac took a particular interest in the case. Many times he came by to change the bandages himself, even though other doctors were on rounds. But while the gangrene was gone, the stubborn infection lingered. The survival of Young Johnny remained touch and go, Doc Mac thought. But at least now, he dared to hope.

It was one of those nights when the heat clung like a fever and pain made sleep impossible. Johnny rolled in the sheets, muttering. That's when Doc Mac appeared. The medical man had exhausted his arsenal of drugs and techniques, and the boy remained on the brink of death. He clucked his tongue and asked Young Johnny a question.

"Do you believe in prayer?"

The soldier was nauseous, suffering from a recurrence of malaria on top of everything else. The question caught him off guard. He opened his mouth and then shut it, not knowing what to say.

"I was raised in church," he managed at last. "But during the war..." He tapered off.

Doc Mac had seen many a soldier in similar straits. They came from the front where chaos, violence and death were the norm.

"Young Johnny," he said, looking down from beside the bed, "let me ease your mind. God does not require your belief in order to exist." The soldier gazed without comprehension and the old man patted his arm.

"Don't make the mistake of thinking we doctors are in the God business! Of course, our patients dearly hope so.

"They want us to perform miracles. I see myself more as a gardener. I am particularly fond of roses. When one has a damaged limb, I cut it away. When mildew attacks, well, I can spray for that. But as for giving life – or causing flowers to blossom! My! Those things are far beyond my simple skills.

"Healing happens within you, through processes we barely understand. I don't mean to shock you, but science cannot even define life. We recognize it, of course, and can describe it by its symptoms. But I cannot tell you what a human life is. All I can say is that it is a miracle from a power greater than mine."

"What are you driving at, Doc?" Johnny grumbled.

"There's medicine, and then there is the spiritual. I'm suggesting you pray for your life, Young Johnny," the old man said. "I've seen it have a salubrious – a healthful – effect."

Fever shivered through Johnny's mind and he was too nauseous to reply. Doc Mac dipped a cloth in water, wrung it out, and laid it across his forehead.

"Don't complicate it. Just ask for your life. And if you can't manage that, try not to worry!"

Johnny's pain throbbed on. His thoughts shredded and the world stopped making sense.

Much later, he regained himself and found he felt a little better. It was dark, he was alone, and the doctor's voice echoed in his skull.

God does not require your belief in order to exist.

He did not fully grasp what it meant, but strangely, it seemed to let him off the hook.

In his childhood, Johnny had been secure at the center of

his world. There was a loving God who oversaw everything. There was the world of his parents and teachers, and then him. It had all made sense way-back-when. But this simple view had not survived the war.

For years now, Johnny's reality had become a torment devoid of any loving presence. Human life, he observed, was fragile and easily snuffed. He'd had brothers-in-arms who'd been slaughtered in a heartbeat. One minute, he was a living, breathing human with all his hopes and dreams – the next instant, a sack of decaying meat, already sinking into the mud. What was the ultimate meaning? Johnny could no longer see it. Soldiers were animals in a slaughterhouse.

A cold conviction seeped through the teenager. Their lives added up to zero, and their fate was also his. He was not going to make it.

He turned away from it at first, but once he accepted this truth, things became easier. If death was inevitable, why live in fear?

Before my number comes up, I'll take out as many Japs as I can.

Sleep still eluded him. It came to him that he was dying. His heart tolled like the somber church bells over the San Diego of his boyhood.

Ask for my life, Doc said. *What harm can it do?*

If you're out there, help. Heal me or let me die. I'm at the end of my rope.

That was all Johnny could manage. For a time he lay without thought. Then, again the chant rose from deep within:

Fight to live, live to fight!

It echoed through his fever, over and over. At some point, he lost consciousness. He floated in the bottomless depths. And for once, he was free from the nightmares of the living dead.

Next morning when Gwyn came in, she found her patient deeply asleep. His skin tone was better. With a thumb, she smoothed the furrow between his eyebrows. Her thermometer confirmed what she already knew.

Johnny's fever had broken.

Gwyn fetched a basin of warm water, soap and a safety razor, and shaved him. His eyes remained closed. She washed and dried his face, tilted the chin and studied the clean features. How much younger he looked! The sunken eyes were old, but he was still a boy. She went and gave Doc Mac the news.

Fifteen minutes later, she was helping Doc tape a fresh bandage over the wound. Afterwards, they stood looking down on the patient.

"Young Johnny," the old man said to the sleeping form, "I do believe you are on the mend."

19

Three weeks into his sojourn at the Port Moresby hospital, Johnny was transferred to the general ward. Soon all the nurses knew the Miracle Yank — the boy who beat gangrene. As for Gwyn, she missed the nights with him in the isolation tent. Now she preferred to come by in the middle of the night, when the lights were low and the other patients were asleep.

Johnny still had trouble sleeping. He often came awake in the dark hours. His face always brightened when he saw Gwyn approach.

The nights were stifling even under the fans. Gwyn washed

the sweat off the patient's face, turned his pillow, and pulled up a chair. They spoke in whispers, careful not to wake the sleepers. By tacit agreement, they steered clear of the war. Johnny loved to hear her talk about fishing with her father in the ice-cold streams of home.

"Where is that?" he asked one night.

"Peachland," she said, "in British Columbia."

"And where is that?"

"Canada, silly," she said. "You're from California?" Johnny nodded. "A hop, skip and a jump – north through Oregon, Washington, and there's BC. You've never seen the Peace Arch?"

"Never heard of it."

"It's on the border between the US and Canada. The arch says, 'Children of a Common Mother.' I picnicked there with friends from nursing school.

"Never heard of the Peace Arch! What did they teach you in school?" she teased.

"Not much," Johnny grumbled with a sheepish smile. He loved the outdoors too, he told her, and he was impressed to find a girl who knew how to land a trout. In turn, he described hunting deer and elk in California.

She noticed that he grew particularly enthused when he told her about surfing the enormous Pacific waves off Oahu. Then his eyes lit up! For those few moments, he was able to escape his sweaty bed, and the nurse knew that this was as good for him as medicine.

The nights after she left, Johnny lay wondering if she would still visit if he weren't wounded, if he wasn't her patient. Or how he would get by if she stopped.

Over the next weeks, Johnny's strength gradually returned. By the second month, it was clear Young Johnny was going to make it. His wound knitted into a raised scar. There came the day when Doc Mac announced the infection had been beaten for good.

Gwyn was delighted.

But the more Johnny's appetite and energy returned, the more he seemed to turn into another man. The nurse was surprised by the bitterness of her disappointment.

This emerging Johnny, she did not care for at all.

As soon as "the corner was truly turned," as Doc Mac put it, it was a feisty soldier who emerged. Johnny read every newspaper he could get his hands on, and what he saw there beat him like a whip. He began to berate the medical workers.

"Do more!" he insisted. "Do it faster! Get me out of here!"

He was restless and cantankerous, and it was for this fellow that Gwyn developed an aversion. He seemed set on being the squeaky wheel, and if so, she was equally determined not to be the grease. Now when she had time in the middle of the night, she did not gravitate to the Californian's bedside.

Yet, to her annoyance, she found herself thinking about him.

Caring too much for any soldier was against her rules. Early in the war, she'd learned that lesson. Now she threw up her hands. The sooner Johnny managed to talk himself out of here, the better for everyone. The less Gwyn came around, the more Johnny made life miserable for others. The nurses stopped smiling and did only what they had to.

In fact, it was his own infirmity that held Johnny back. Every time he forced himself to sit on the edge of his bed, and then stand up, he discovered just how compromised he had become. His schoolyard adversaries would have recognized that scowl. Johnny gritted his teeth and pushed through.

On the latest attempt to walk, having convinced the red-headed nurse to lend a hand, Johnny managed a few wobbling steps between the beds. But his vision went white, a foot twisted, and in spite of Ruthie's attempt to grab him, he fell hard on the floorboards. Pain scorched his chest, and Johnny hauled himself onto his feet. Fed up and ferocious, he let loose some words that tasted like soap.

As it happened, Doc Mac was in earshot. He strode over, put an arm around the Yank, and marched him back to bed. Ruthie stammered an apology.

Doc Mac told her it was not her fault and to be on her way. Once he had the patient lying down, no matter how woebegone the boy's face, the physician let him have it.

"Young Johnny, you will curb your tongue! You are intelligent enough to understand that abusing my staff hinders, and does not help, your cause! We have more than enough to do," Doc Mac barked, "without bearing the brunt of your personal war!"

To his credit, Johnny apologized at once.

"I'm sorry, Doc, but I need to get out of here! I'm better, I tell you! I want you to send me back to my unit!"

"Better?" the physician snorted. "I suppose that is why you cannot walk? If you have medical credentials, please show them to me. Otherwise, accept mine! I will be delighted to send you packing the minute you are fit. Until then, you *will* pull in your horns."

Shortly thereafter, Doc Mac reassigned Johnny to a ward with more mobile men. He redoubled his efforts to walk. His face was hard, but he was appalled by how wasted his body looked. He saw the thin legs and remembered them thick with muscle, guiding his surfboard through the churning waves. He tightened his jaw and forced himself to move!

In the new ward, he saw Gwyn less frequently, although he caught himself watching for her. But the few times she did make the effort, things quickly deteriorated. At first she looked pleased to see him. But then Johnny wanted to tell her his plans – how he'd be on a ship for the Philippines, and then, on to the Battle of Japan!

At that, her eyes would cloud over. She'd make some excuse or other and be gone. Staring at her retreating back, the Hard Case would curl his lip.

Why even bother to come by?

At least Johnny was eating well and getting stronger. But with replenished energy came rising exasperation with being cooped up. Every day, the soldier made himself spend longer on his feet. He came to know the hospital compound intimately.

A highlight of the week was Saturday nights when they showed a movie in the main mess. They'd strike the tables, line up the chairs, and stretch a sheet on the wall. The men gathered after sundown, and they'd start the 16mm projector and run the reels.

On one such evening, Johnny was in the seats with his tent mates when Gwyn made an appearance. She arrived with Ruthie and a group that included a couple of men in civvies. That gave Johnny a turn. She didn't even see him. He watched her lean toward a companion, listen, and laugh. There was a bitter taste in his mouth.

The lights went off to shouts and whistles. The show began with a newsreel. It featured recent action on Okinawa. Johnny forgot everything else as the battle scenes unfolded. The Japanese island was a battleground. The fight was costly, the announcer said – fully twelve thousand US servicemen killed in action, fifty thousand wounded.

Things had gone far worse for the Japanese. It was estimated that two hundred thousand troops and civilians were dead. Johnny puzzled it through.

Okinawa – that's where it's going to be! That's where General MacArthur will stage the Army for "Operation Downfall." I need to get back to the Philippines so I can transfer with my unit.

I've got to go!

20

The newsreel ended and the next reel rolled. It was an action flick called "Raiders of Ghost City." It starred Joe Sawyer in a cowboy hat as "Idaho Jones."

Johnny watched, barely able to concentrate. While the credits were still rolling, he slipped out into the night. It had nothing to do with not wanting to watch Gwyn leave with her friends! Or so he told himself.

Now John Willman truly went on the warpath.

The next day, he hitched a ride to Army HQ. He demanded of the sarg at the desk that he be allowed to see the commander.

An aide knocked on Colonel Chambers' door and told him a Purple Heart soldier wanted an audience, but Henry was up to his ears. The private was told he could wait if he wanted. Johnny sat in the reception area in the oppressive heat.

A clerk pounded on a typewriter. A fan stirred the sodden air. The minutes dragged by. Finally it was dinnertime and the colonel was getting ready to leave for the day. He was reminded that a man was still waiting to see him. Henry sighed and had the GI shown in.

He expected to take five minutes to shake the hand of a wounded boy and promise to send him home. Instead, he found himself confronted by an ornery soldier with an axe to grind.

"A slack rear-guard attitude!" Johnny railed. "That's the only reason I'm still in Port Moresby! I'm a sniper – and General MacArthur needs me in the invasion of Japan, believe me. Sir, I need to be shipped back to the Philippines – at once, Sir!"

Normally, Colonel Chambers did not trouble himself with the fate of one man. He was higher up the food chain than that. He explained bluntly that Private Willman would be released only when Doctor MacClure said so, and then he would get his orders through channels – like everyone else in this man's Army! He ordered the soldier back to hospital.

The officer walked the boy to the office door and told him not to show his face again without an explicit invitation. Johnny couldn't get in another word.

Once the troublemaker was gone, the colonel told an aide to find Willman's New Guinea record – it had to be in the warehouse.

The following day, it took the lieutenant hours to locate the file, but the army was thorough. When the commander came into possession of the dossier in the afternoon, he skimmed it and ended up both impressed and disturbed.

It was clear the soldier could fight, but Chambers was an old hand at reading Army-speak. He closed the file and sat back.

John Willman had a bad habit of shooting his mouth off to his superior officers. *Not the Army way! Cannot have the men questioning the chain of command!*

Still, there's no doubt about his courage, or his facility with a rifle. So will I return him to the general – or send him State-side?

In the meantime, the colonel was buried under his duties. He had all the preparations necessary to relinquish command in two weeks. On top of that, he had his own project to complete. He could not afford much time for the boy's desire.

Some officers – like Commander MacArthur – were born to action. Others, like Colonel Chambers himself, were better bureaucrats. Someone had to oversee the giant machine that was the US Army. Certainly, Henry was gifted in the role. His mission, to be completed by his successor, was to prepare all US holdings in the Territories to be handed over to the Australians.

Most of Henry's career had been spent on American soil. The highlight of the 1930's was his two years as a military attaché to the US Embassy in Tokyo. He had put in the required appearances at the formal receptions. At the same time, he had gone about his true assignment – the gathering of military intelligence for Washington.

Henry developed a fascination for the bellicose Nipponese Empire. He cultivated the acquaintance of prominent citizens, including members of the armed forces. Many would not talk to him – America was seen by Japan as the great impediment to their expansionist plans. There were a few, though, who appreciated free dinners at fine restaurants, and Chambers saw to it that the whiskey and sake flowed freely. Then some had much to impart about the Empire's rightful place as leader of Asia.

He attended demonstrations of their formidable martial arts, including hand-to-hand combat, and sparring with wooden swords and other implements.

He studied their history, heroes, art, and literature.

Chambers warned the Washington chiefs that war with Japan was inevitable. He was outraged, therefore, but not surprised by the Japanese attack on the Pacific fleet and airfields of Oahu of December 7, 1941. By then Henry was back in the States, and while he thought he might be granted a combat command, he was assigned to help train and outfit the legions of raw recruits. Again, it was important, if tedious, work.

Then, in 1944, when he was beyond the usual age of retirement, still in the game only due to the extraordinary demands of wartime, Henry received an offer. At once he perceived it to be the feather in the cap of his career. The US troops in the Allied effort in New Guinea needed a commanding officer. Colonel Chambers accepted.

By then, Henry knew it was not his destiny to command the heady days of battle as had his predecessor, General MacArthur. The colonel might walk in the great man's footsteps, but he would never fill his shoes.

Still, Henry was grateful for the commission. He had a passion for American military history, and he had been granted an opportunity to journey to one of the great fields of battle.

Upon arrival on the island, the colonel toured the US bases – in particular, what would be his headquarters in Port Moresby. Here he saw the usual offices, parade ground, and armories. Then he was shown through a great warehouse, full of shelving piled floor to ceiling with file boxes.

It dawned on Henry that he was looking at the raw paper record of the war in this theater.

Another man might have seen a paper avalanche that would bury him. Instead, Henry saw his mother lode. Part of his mandate was to go through all this. He had an entire staff devoted to the project. They would summarize the key facts and burn much of the rest. Anything marked "secret," along with records that were, in his opinion, of lasting value, he would catalog and ship Stateside.

In that quiet warehouse, a light seemed to illuminate Henry's road ahead into retirement. He got a vision of his book. It would be a popular history of the war, primarily on the island of New Guinea, focused on actions of the US Army.

With refreshed zeal, the colonel settled into his official duties. At the same time, he began his private obsession. He filled journal after journal with notes – dates, battles, numbers of troops assigned, movements, enemy positions, casualties, and more.

So far, he had seventeen legal-size ledgers filled with his longhand. These he would guard closely on the long journey home.

Henry thought there would be a thriving market for war memoirs. While the Army battles of the South Pacific were fascinating in themselves, his book would have additional appeal because of the key figure who would loom from its pages. This was no less a personage than five-star General Douglas MacArthur himself. Every time the commander opened his mouth, something quotable fell out. The news hounds ate it up, and the colonel had a thick file of newspaper clippings as well.

The general was a larger-than-life character, enormously popular with the American public. Chambers believed the warrior might very well run for President. Henry calculated that should MacArthur win or lose, his book would benefit.

Now, with his last days in Port Moresby ticking by, Henry was consumed with the awareness that, once he was gone, there would be no return.

Urgently, he called for more files. The boxes climbed his office walls, and piles of paper stacked his desk. Each night now, a light burned in the commander's window.

Therefore, shortly after Private Willman made his upsetting appearance, he all but faded from Henry's thoughts.

But then Johnny disobeyed the colonel's direct order.

It was the worst thing he could have done.

21

"WORLD WAR II IN THE SOUTH PACIFIC"
- BY COLONEL HENRY CHAMBERS III

The One Punch Fight

Dear Reader, for us to understand our enemy, a key to the art of war, we must first grasp Japan's warrior code, "Bushido."

In the 1930's, your Author lived in Tokyo for two years as a Military Attaché to our Embassy. There he had the opportunity to study firsthand this alien and yet refined civilization.

In Olde England, the knights conducted themselves by a code of Chivalry. So, too, did Japan possess a warrior class and the code of Bushido. In the land of Nippon, as the Japanese call it, their version of Camelot played out in the era of the Samurai – a golden age that lasted nearly a thousand years.

Bullets and gunpowder transformed the knight in shining armor into a target in a tin suit. So, too, did firearms destroy the Samurai. How can a swordsman win against a gun? While the age of the knight died in Europe, however, Bushido did not disappear from Japan. The descendants of the Samurai live on. Many a Japanese military family proudly traces its lineage back to the now-outlawed warrior caste.

To the Samurai, a much-admired tactic is the devastating opening strike – as we would call it, "the one-punch fight."

One evening in Tokyo, a Japanese military acquaintance recounted a tale over sake and sushi. He told of a mere boy who used only a stick to defeat a formidable master swordsman. The teenager won because of his sudden, unexpected attack. He delivered a fatal blow, and the master died of a crushed skull.

That boy was Miyamoto Musashi, the renowned 17th Century Samurai warrior and artist. (That combination is greatly admired in Nippon). Musashi was undefeated in more than sixty duels.

And the tactic of the sudden blow is still admired. A prime example is seen in the opening years of this 20th Century.

Russia, that great power, had long craved a warm water harbor. The Tsar negotiated a lease for Port Arthur on the Chinese mainland. At the time, Japan was just one voice in the Asian chorus, but it did not like the intrusion of the Bear. Nippon saw Russia's encroachment as a threat to its destiny as the rightful ruler of Asia.

In 1904, without any warning (let me emphasize, Dear Reader – without any warning), Japan attacked the Russians at Port Arthur. The strike earned Nippon a stunning triumph.

Only after the victory did Japan present the belated declaration of war to Moscow.

The Tsar was caught flat-footed and flabbergasted. A minor power had bested a major one, and while Russia tried desperately to regroup, Nippon heaped victory upon victory. In hindsight, the Tsar's weakness encouraged the revolutionaries, and aristocratic Russia was hammered into oblivion.

America watched that unfold. Indeed, President "Teddy" Roosevelt was an expert on these affairs. He won the Nobel Peace Prize for his efforts to negotiate a truce between the parties.

Now let us jump forward to Pearl Harbor.

The attack by Japan on our Pacific fleet at Hawaii outraged America and rallied us to war. December 7, 1941, will live forever as the "day of infamy" described by our recently demised war President, Franklin Delano Roosevelt. Again, only after the deed was done did Japan present a declaration of war to Washington.

Yet, no one can say the Japanese strategy of preemptive strike prior to declaration of war was unprecedented.

On the contrary. It was entirely in keeping with the warrior spirit of Nippon.

22

A row of wrecks edged the Port Moresby runway. Every serviceable flying machine had long departed with the general, ferrying his Army up the coast of New Guinea.

One of the relics had been dragged from the ragtag line. It was a Hudson light bomber, built by the Lockheed Corporation. Now, on a Saturday morning, six men swarmed over the battered fuselage.

The Hudson had served Australia before it had been added

to MacArthur's army. After it had been aerated by shot on several occasions, and had crash-landed twice, it was stripped of its guns and relegated to reconnaissance. On its final flight, enemy fighters had found it. With an engine shot apart, streaming black smoke, it had barely made it back to thump down on the Moresby tarmac.

A cursory inspection showed ragged holes blown all through the body, the worst now covered with metal patches. The nose had once been a glassed-in turret, but that was badly broken up and had been closed off.

On each side of the Hudson's fuselage, below the cockpit windows, remained a vestige of her former glory. Worked in paint by a talented hand was a reclining beauty. She had flowing yellow hair, a big smile and ruby-red lips, long legs, a tiny waist, and balloon breasts. On these were prominent nipples with a line of bullets shooting from each one. She was scantily clad in a tied-off blouse and short-shorts.

Beneath her was rendered in script, "Miss Nippon These."

But, after years of exposure to the tropical sun, she was now just a peeling, faded rose.

The brains of the salvage operation sat on one wing. He was an Australian of medium height and build, with sandy hair and a freckled nose. Straddling an engine, he wore nothing but filthy shorts, and was grease to the elbows. He was a one-time soldier, expert pilot, gifted mechanic, and jack-of-all-trades.

He'd been at work on the Hudson for the last three months. It was the centerpiece of his plan for an air cargo business. He'd combed the discarded wrecks for one he reckoned he could save, and had settled on the "Miss Nippon These."

He knew all the mechanics in town, rounded up the best, and paid them from his pocket. To date, the repairs had been substantial, if primitive.

The main challenge was, he had been able to get only one of the aircraft's two engines running. He had dropped the ruin of the hopelessly shot-up one and replaced it with the motor, prop and cowling from a different wreck. He was confident it would serve.

Yet, after all his labor, the replacement motor would sputter but not run. He was frustrated, because that was the main thing that kept him from getting this crate into the air. Still, he knew he was close.

The cowling was open. His legs spread to each side, the man reached with pliers into the innards. A mate sat in the cockpit, window open, his hands in the tangle of wires below the panel. He pulled out a strand, stripped the insulation with his teeth, and touched it to another wire. There was a puff of smoke.

"Bugga!"

He jerked the wires apart, pulled out another, and touched again. A light flared behind the instruments and he nodded and twisted the wires together.

"Give the motor another go," the wingman called.

"Righty-oh!"

The propeller cranked and the pilot pulled his legs back from the blades. The engine caught, ran unevenly while the mechanics cheered, then backfired and stopped. There was a flash of flame and a gush of oily smoke. The pilot was enveloped in the cloud and emerged coughing. Frantically, he slapped at a flame that singed the hair off his inner thighs. Fortunately, it went out.

"Bloody hell!" He booted the recalcitrant engine with his heels, and muttering darkly, reached down with a spanner and tightened a fuel line.

Two other mechanics stood beneath the wings, working on the landing gear. One set of wheels cocked out at a forty-five-degree angle, and a brace was broken. The welder tipped the mask over his face while his mate watched through a piece of smoked glass. Sparks sizzled.

"Reckon she's jake now," the pilot called. "Turn her over!"

The man in the cockpit complied. This time, the engine sputtered, ground over a few times, and at last roared to life. It climbed in pitch and began to howl, almost blowing the pilot off the wing. He made a frantic slicing motion across his throat and his mate cut the juice.

"Bloody brilliant!" the pilot crowed to a chorus of yells and whistles. He stood and stepped on bare feet to the ladder against the wing.

He climbed down and saw the worn leather ball there. He coaxed it onto his toes, tapped it to his knee, bounced it a few times, dropped it to his heel, popped it over to the other foot and kicked up. As it fell, he caught it neatly on his forehead, then dropped it to earth.

"I gotta go to town," he called. "You blokes carry on. Now we've got the bleedin' motor running, she'll be ready to take up later t'day. Whadda ya reckon?"

"Right you are," the man in the cockpit smiled. "And where are you off to?"

"Gotta see a bird," the pilot grinned.

"Who's that then?"

"Never you mind. I'll be back in two shakes of a lamb's tail. Oo-roo." He tugged on a pair of sandals, went to an ancient motorcycle with wide handlebars and climbed on.

He kicked it to life and sped away.

"No doubt he's off ta see that nurse, mate – the Canadian," one of the welders said. His partner shrugged.

"Let's finish with these wheels. We're almost there. Poor Footy has no luck with the sheilas."

"This one'll be different, mate," his partner said. They laughed.

23

Colonel Chambers frowned over the faded cursive at the end of the letter.

"Father Bastion warns to 'beware of a monstrous beast,'" Henry told Dingo. "He hasn't seen it himself, but the natives say it's a new arrival. In fact, it has not been seen in their lifetimes, but they know it from the old stories of their people.

"'They call it *Ka-him-ka* – the Father of the Crocodiles," Henry read. "'They say it is a god that lives forever. We have had a difficult time preventing them from worshiping it, particularly after it devoured five of the faithful,' the priest writes.

"'Before you scoff, I must tell you that we have seen things here in the heart of Creation that beggar description. I am reminded of Leviathan of the Old Testament, that piercing serpent,'" Henry continued, finger on the place.

"'Our people say they must return to the old rituals in order to appease it. The elders insist that all the calamities that have befallen us are because they have not performed the human sacrifices required.'" Colonel Chambers looked up.

"He calls it 'a test from God...'"

"...Or the devil," Dingo snorted. "Leviathan! On my oath! As

I said, Henry, if it is real and not just the usual *kanaka* superstition, I know what it has to be.

"One that size can only be your saltwater crocodile. Name's a bit misleading. They got it because we find these big brutes in the estuaries and on the open ocean. They can handle the salt, unlike their smaller cousins. But don't let that fool you. They are equally at home in the rivers. Unusual for one to be so far inland – but not unheard of. 'The Father!'

"The salties are a plague back in northern Aus," Dingo went on. "We lose people and livestock to 'em every year, Henry. A croc with that weight can take down a full-grown bull and drag it into the river.

"And it's worse in New Guinea. What are the locals' sticks and stones against such a monster? The people must live on the river, and they will lose some of their number to the crocodiles every year. They have a supernatural dread of the big ones. No wonder they worship it!"

"Beware of the river is right then," the colonel said.

"I'd like your full briefing on Kissim, and the Raub, Dingo – before we go in." He set the letter on the table and looked up expectantly.

"Before we go in?" Dingo obliged. "Well, major, I can't leave 'my dear fellow American' to the tender mercies of the Japs, or this crocodile, now can I? Our standing orders are to capture or eradicate the enemy where we find him. The good Lord knows, the Nips have not surrendered in New Guinea! There are hundreds of thousands of them still here."

"Too right, bloody menace," Dingo nodded. "It will take us years to round up all of the Yellow Peril."

"As you know, these are my last days in Moresby," the colonel went on.

"In two weeks I leave for the States. But I believe we have time to pull off a rescue before that!

"Nothing too grand," the colonel cautioned. "Let's say four men – commando types.

"We'll call it – oh – 'Operation Teeth,'" Henry added, displaying his own in a smile.

"Operation Teeth!" Dingo enthused. "Got bite to it, eh?"

Chambers grew serious. "It is a long shot. We know several in Kissim are already dead, including two of these priests. The stakes are high, but I believe it's worth the effort.

"Good on ya, Henry!"

Dingo had come up with a plan of his own.

24

Against Colonel Chambers' explicit order, Johnny showed up at Army HQ once more.

He knew he was risking insubordination, but he just couldn't sit around any longer. Again he badgered the staff until Chambers had enough. This time, it was a very frosty colonel who had the young man shown in. The commander left him standing at attention in front of his desk and continued writing in a large book.

Johnny stood stiffly for fifteen minutes. At last the colonel capped his fountain pen.

"Private Willman," he said in icy tones, "what in blazes are you doing here?"

"Sir," Johnny said, "I am fit for duty, Sir! I request to be returned to my unit, Sir!" The colonel stared him down.

"I told you – Private Willman – you would be released only on Doctor MacClure's say-so! Then, like everyone else in the Army, you will get your orders through channels!"

Johnny stared ahead and did not answer. The colonel sighed and let his anger dissipate. He was inclined to send the boy to the general, after all. The two deserved each other.

But Johnny did not know when to leave well enough alone.

"Sir, some men might be satisfied typing memos," he blurted, "but a real soldier has to be in the fight – that's where I belong, Sir!"

In fairness, Johnny had not intended to insult his commander, but his haymaker hit a nerve.

Who does the pup think he's talking to? I'll show him a choke chain!

"Private Willman, you will return to the hospital – at once!" Chambers thundered. He stood and slammed a fist on his desk. In the next room, his aides exchanged a nervous glance.

"There you will remain, bothering absolutely no one, until you get your walking papers! You question my orders again and I will have you court-martialed! Am I clear this time?"

"Yes Sir!" Johnny replied.

Thoroughly downcast, he returned to his hospital bed.

In fact, the outing had sapped Johnny's energy. But within minutes of stretching out, Doc Mac came storming in. The old man's bushy brows connected in a frown.

"Young Johnny, neither the world, nor my hospital, revolves around you!"

The other men were staring.

"I've heard from your colonel – again. I'm instructed to exert better control over you!" Doc snorted.

"Frankly, I am fed up with you. But that does not make you well! I will, however, have you out of my sight!"

Johnny was banished to a canvas structure on the outskirts of the hospital, to what he and his roommates dubbed "the halfway tent." Here they were expected to make their own beds, keep the place clean, and walk everywhere they needed to go.

Yet, exasperating as the boy could be, privately, Doc Mac approved of Young Johnny. There was no medical evidence to prove it, but time and again he'd observed that patients with a reason to live often did so, while others with less grievous injuries, succumbed.

Young Johnny was the first type. What did disturb Doc Mac was what motivated the lad. He seemed obsessed with killing. Still, who was a physician to judge? This was war, and perhaps Young Johnny was just the sort of chap they needed.

Doc had to admit to himself, he preferred the young man to the many snivelers who had slunk through his doors over the years. Some were pathetically grateful for their injury because it was their ticket home. Then there were poor blighters with damaged minds – the so-called "NP's," neuropsychiatric cases – men too battle-shocked and terrified to return to the front. The doctor understood that their predicament was real and he treated each one fairly, but that did not mean he respected them.

Young Johnny was not of their breed. Some time ago, Doc had given the young man back his personal possessions. He'd seen how delighted Johnny was to get the few things – an old lighter and a folding knife. He remembered there'd been a military rifle as well, and he had an orderly drop it off at the tent.

Long shot as it was, the boy might need it yet.

25

"Let me show you the place," the major said to the colonel. The two walked to a side table piled with papers, dominated by a large colored map that displayed the entire island of New Guinea. The major traced a finger along the northern coast and stopped.

"Here's the Raub River," Dingo said, tapping a blue squiggle. His finger followed it inland until it faded in the middle of the island.

"Somewhere here, near the headwaters, is Kissim where the Catholic mission is located.

"Here" – his finger moved slightly in the direction of the ocean – "here is all the trouble and strife.

"This is the notorious 'Valley of the Cannibals.' You've heard of it? Home of the Mambu nation – most bloodthirsty tribe in all New Guinea, Henry. And that's saying something. No white man's ever gone in there and come out, dead or alive."

"Do tell," the colonel said.

"You know I've knocked about New Guinea a few years?" Dingo asked as the men returned to their seats.

"So you've said," the colonel murmured. "So you have said."

The door banged and Hala swished in with a fresh pitcher. She still wore the grass skirt, but she'd pulled on an olive T-shirt stenciled "US Army" across the chest. It was far too tight.

Almost worse than naked, the colonel thought. She replaced the empty jug, flashed another smile, and departed. Chambers refilled the glasses.

"Seen some strange things in my years here, so I have," Dingo said, eyes absentmindedly following the girl. He focused back on Henry.

"You know of course that millions of New Guineans are cannibals."

"Disgusting practice!"

"Too bloody right," Dingo said. "But consider this. Our good Catholic priests – like these blokes on the Raub – offer communion to the faithful. The Lord's Supper. The priests teach that the bread and wine transform into the literal body and blood of Christ.

"It's no less than the eating of God, Henry! In some parts of the world, I imagine that would be a most difficult mystery to communicate. Not in New Guinea! Here they understand what it means to gain a person's power by consuming him. They do it all the time."

"What a place!" Henry shook his head.

"Now, as to the Mambu Nation in the Valley of the Cannibals. Extremely warlike lot, even by New Guinea standards. Worse than the notorious *Kukukuku* tribe, and that's going the distance. There are thousands of headhunters in that valley, deadly jealous of their territory.

"Nearest I've been, I flew over the place before the war. Some of those *kanakas* were shooting arrows at us, no word of a lie! The valley forms a long strip beside the Raub, flanked by steep mountains thick with jungle. The flatland was covered in veggie gardens. There were four, perhaps five, villages along the riverbank. The only way in and out would be the river gorges at each end."

"Could a company of soldiers get through?"

"Nigh impossible. You might blow the natives up with

bombs or artillery. Even then, our side would take casualties."

"What – bows and arrows against a hundred soldiers with firearms?" The colonel raised his eyebrows.

"Don't underestimate those blighters," Dingo said somberly. "The Mambu are not afraid of your white man, Henry. Our patrols learned that the hard way, simply running into their war parties along the Raub. I suspect they would have you for supper, if only to see what you taste like." He sucked his teeth and the colonel clicked his tongue.

"Then – as this priest writes – there are the crocs to contend with. The Raub is infested. In fact, the river is named for 'em."

"For the alligators?" the colonel asked. "Please explain."

"*Crocodiles*, Henry. It's named for the crocodiles."

26

Johnny turned onto the road that led to the hospital, sweat stinging his eyes. He really wanted that shower now – and he had the meeting coming up. He hoped he'd see Gwyn there. He hadn't spoken with her since Doc Mac banished him to the halfway tent.

She is drop-dead gorgeous! Finding a beauty like Gwyn in New Guinea had been a surprise. Perhaps it was the heat of the day, but suddenly he daydreamed he was back on Waikiki Beach. And wonder-of-wonders, Gwyn was with him, holding his hand! She was wearing a skimpy two-piece – like Rita Hayworth or Esther Williams! He could smell the suntan lotion.

Whoooeee!

Johnny was so dazzled, he stepped in a puddle that drowned his shoe. He stumbled and nearly face-planted in the gravel. A native guffawed, and Johnny felt foolish.

His walks had taken him on ever-widening circles through town. Dying for a change from the unremittingly canned and overcooked hospital food, Johnny had gone on the hunt for a half-decent restaurant. But Port Moresby provided slim pickings. The few eateries he sampled were in or near the hotels that catered to military people and other expats.

A week ago, on impulse, he'd gone looking for Gwyn. He found her on the main ward and again noted that glad-to-see-you look, tempered with wariness, in her sea-green eyes.

He asked her to have dinner with him.

"I don't date patients," she said, steering him away from the onlookers.

"It's not a date," he protested. "It's just a bite. Out. Together."

She gave him a look.

"It's a date," she said, "and I don't go out with patients – or soldiers. Or either."

He backed off and bided his time. He set himself the task of finding the best restaurant in the whole town. It turned out to be a seafood place in the Islander hotel, with an Aussie chef. It wasn't as good as some of the fine dining restaurants he'd been to with his parents in Honolulu, but at least the catch-of-the-day was fresh.

Johnny spruced up. His fatigues were freshly washed and he put on his best buttoned shirt. He shaved, splashed on Aqua Velva he bought in town, and brushed his hair back. He hung around outside the ward until he saw Gwyn come out. Then he caught up with her, acting like he'd just happened by.

Gwyn looked this transformed fellow up and down, while Johnny did his best to muster the old appeal that had won him hearts back in high school. Again, Johnny asked her out to dinner. This time he did not pretend it wouldn't be a date. But the nurse seemed to have no problem resisting his admittedly rusty charms. She smiled, looked at him like he was crazy, and said no.

He ended up going for seafood with the guys from the halfway tent. He drank too much Aussie beer, and wound up woozy, belly-full and heart-empty. For the first time in a long time, he began to wonder if he'd been cheated out of something.

Like any chance at a normal life!

Nor did any of it change the fact that he had a promise to keep. He did his best to push Gwyn out of his thoughts. Yet she remained an itch at the edges of his consciousness that would not go away.

Most of his memory of his ordeal at the hospital was lost forever, eaten by illness. But whispers kept fading in. He remembered a beautiful woman in a golden circle of light. It was Gwyn, seen through mosquito netting, lit by lantern. It would be the dead of night, and he would awake to find her by his bed. Usually she'd been reading a book.

Sometimes he tried to hide his awareness as he watched her through half-closed eyes. But somehow, she always knew. Soon her book would close and she would be gone.

In another time and place, Johnny would have made a serious run at Gwyn. But this was war, and it wasn't over – not by a long shot. He had no illusions about his place in the invasion of the Japanese islands. He'd watched enemy soldiers sacrifice their lives for a piece of forgettable jungle.

How much more fanatical would they be, fighting among their homes?

Still, Johnny wanted more than anything else to be part of the final fight. That should have put an end to this foolish mooning over a nurse. But in spite of his resolve, her image kept coming between him and his do-or-die plans.

Then, one night, Johnny had a new nightmare. In it, he was making love to Gwyn. He woke drenched in sweat – shocked at the vivid images. An instant later, he was furious. This was worse than the dead men!

The suffering cut him to the heart – Gwyn might be right there, but she was out of reach. He was pierced by longing. In his anguish, Johnny turned Gwyn over to the Hard Case. The order was clear.

Give her up! This only got started because she was your nurse. Fair enough – but it's game over. Let her go!

Still, some part of Johnny did not want to let her go, and he brooded on it.

Even if she liked me, the best I have to offer is a fling. That would hurt her, and hurting Gwyn is not on the table!

Johnny did not ask the nurse out again. He began to avoid the places he might see her. He redoubled his efforts to recover, because that was his ticket out of here. But he was helpless to stop his thoughts filling up with Gwyn, especially in his dreams.

Those hurt deep inside – worse than the dead men who usually invaded his nightmares.

27

"Crocodiles – of course," Henry said with a chuckle. "The 'gators are back where I come from."

"The salties are much, much bigger," Dingo said. "You can

tell the difference between them and your American alligator by the sharper snout, and a croc's teeth line the outside of it jaws. Not hidden like your gator.

"As for the river – 'Raub' is German. There was a time when the Hun was all over New Guinea. Still a few Lutheran missions hanging on.

"The bloody Kraut who named it was famous in his own way. Nineteenth Century explorer, one Otto Finsch. Also named the 'Bismarck Sea' for the Iron Chancellor. You've heard of Finschhaffen?" The colonel nodded.

"'Means Finsch's harbor. 'Raub' signifies 'predator' – something like that – not that I speak Gerry. But I can confirm that the banks crawl with the scaly bastards. You should see 'em scramble when an aircraft goes over! Lots of the freshwater variety upriver. Grow a mere twelve-foot or so. Still, they regularly dine on your native and his animals.

"But the enormous brutes are 'salties.' From the description, this 'Father' can only be one of 'em. Long way from his usual haunts, but a bugger like that goes where it bloody well wants! The biggest I ever heard about was thirty-foot. If this 'Father' is in that league, he will top four thousand pounds. Not that any of us will be asking it to climb on the scales," he grinned.

"Four thousand pounds!" the colonel exclaimed. "Imagine that coming at you in the water!"

"A submarine with teeth," Dingo nodded. "And they're strong swimmers. They can cross oceans.

"Your male salty is extremely territorial. They've been known to kill rivals and even females. And like the people, they are cannibals. A big salty will tear his freshwater cousin apart, and eat him.

"They even attack motorboats! Old Otto Finsch lost an entire canoe of his *kanakas* at the mouth of the Raub. Overturned their dugout and killed the men as they tried to swim away. Otto named it 'Raubfluss' – Predator River – and went on to easier things."

"Well – that's clear," the colonel said. "My men will stay away from the river!"

28

The bull was forty-four years old and in the prime of its life. It was the dominant predator on the Big River and surrounding ocean. Except when it indulged an occasional urge to copulate, it was a solitary creature, too aggressive to tolerate company. It even killed a female that came too close when it was not in the mood.

Alone as it preferred, the reptile spent much of its day lolling on the riverbank. It luxuriated in the warmth that soaked into its armor-plated body. It spread six-foot jaws to the sun. This normally revealed sixty-eight teeth, but one had broken recently on the skull of a boar. Already, the replacement bulged under the gum.

For many years after it grew to full size, the bull had been able to relax as it basked. No animal had dared to disturb the enormous patriarch.

But everything had changed in profound ways. Its reptilian brain had no way to categorize the ships, aircraft, artillery, and armed soldiers that invaded its realm. But it did see them, and reacted with territorial fury. Yet its anger was impotent – the interlopers remained far off. At times its unrequited aggression was so strong, all the muscles in its vast body tightened like cables.

Even after the strangers were gone, the beast fretted and could not rest. On several occasions, soldiers had seen the monster in the distance. They exclaimed and pointed. Inevitably, some shot it. They did this instinctively. If pressed, they would have said it was sport.

The bull knew it was under attack when blows slammed into its thick hide, followed by explosions like thunder. Sometimes it felt mere thumps, but at others, there were sharp needles of pain. Infuriated and alarmed, the reptile would bolt into the river.

When the stings were bad, the salty would whirl to confront its attacker, jaws agape, only to discover nothing there. Then the giant raised its head and bellowed its unrequited fury, to the horrified delight of the far-off soldiers.

The changes agitated the beast. Always now, the crocodile was uneasy, even in the heart of its territory.

It grew so aggravated, it could not remain where it was. It surged from the mouth of its river and crossed open sea. It navigated the enormous swells for many days, until it arrived at distant islands. It slid over the reef and lolled in the lagoon.

On shore, the crocodile observed, lived a herd of the two-legged prey. When a number were foolish enough to venture onto the water in a hollow tree, the predator rose to meet them. A swipe of its tail spilled them screaming into the water. One by one, the victims found themselves in a nightmare of flashing teeth.

Eventually, though, the Father felt the call of home. It began to cross the open ocean. But then, the crocodile heard a rumble overhead that turned into a howl. The swimmer shifted course and moved on.

The Zero fighter flashed over, and the pilot looked down at the dark shape in the blue.

The creature was so immense, the aviator banked around for a closer look. He saw the length of the brute – as long as his aircraft. He imagined finding himself in the water with it, and shuddered. Again, he put his fighter in a loop, swooped and opened up with his 7.7 mm machine guns.

The reptile heard the explosions, saw the strangely spurting water, and dove. Through transparent underwater eyelids, it watched the white spears come, and sank deeper. The bubbles passed overhead, and it felt a shower of pebbles on its back that spilled off into the deep.

The pilot cut another circle, but this time, saw only ocean. He gave up and returned to base.

The reptile swam submerged, fear and ire pumping through it. Only when it needed to did it come up for air, then dove again.

A day later, the crocodile tasted silt in the stream. Following the trail, it came to the mouth of its river. As it coursed between the banks, its smaller kin witnessed the return of the ferocious patriarch and bolted for their lives.

The crocodile cruised through the murk and lay among the reeds. It had hatched near this place, and knew every hole where the big fish finned. But even here, it could not find peace. Time and again, the thunder and punctures came from shore, and the predator was forced to turn tail and hide.

Ever stronger, an impulse rose within it. The crocodile turned into the current. It swung the massive tail and surged upriver. It traveled while the bright light crossed the sky, and in darkness continued, guided by the stream. When the light returned, the triangular scutes along its back transferred welcome heat into its body.

On it voyaged, night and day coming in their turns.

During its lifetime, the predator had made other excursions up its river. This was all its territory and it had no peer. Every other crocodile that saw it froze where it was, or fled for its life.

The bull swam by many nesting places of the two-legged animals. Long before it saw them, it smelled smoke, then waste and body odor. It drew closer, saw the succulent animals and heard their plaintive cries. Normally, as it had done many times, it would have remained, hunting and feeding until it was satiated.

But now, driven by something deeper, it swept by.

The villagers gathered along the shore to witness the passage of the fearsome spirit of the river. Each tribe, in its own language, identified it as the Father of the Crocodiles. Even brave warriors trembled as they pointed out the demigod to their young. The little ones had been frightened since birth by tales of the giant, but never before had they seen the dark deity itself.

Should the river god choose them, there was nothing they could do. Their sorcerers would perform all the rituals, but the *Papa of the Pukpuk* was a force far greater than they were!

Yet they must live on the river. It was their drink, life-giver to the gardens, home to fish, eels and freshwater shellfish. It was the highway they traveled by dugout canoe for trade, to visit relatives, battle their enemies, and hunt in the forest.

All they could do was fear and worship it. At the same time, it was inevitable that some of them would be hunted and consumed.

Now the Father himself appeared on the Big River and the people were appalled. But when it remained far out in deep water as it surged along, they went weak with relief.

The reptile swam through the low country and entered the highlands. It had seldom ventured this far, but these were novel times. Eventually, it penetrated the foothills of the mountain range. The country grew so wild, there were no longer nests of the two-legged ones.

Each day, the crocodile saw the mountains loom higher. The riverbanks drew close and the water ran clear. At times it churned in rapids the crocodile must climb, dragging its massive body over the stones. Then it came to limpid pools where it slid underwater and glided on.

The calamities that had disturbed it began to fade. Here, the impetus that had forced the long journey, eased.

At last, the swimmer discovered another dwelling place of the two-legged prey. The old hunger returned. From the water weeds, eyes raised, the hunter studied the prey. It noted each type of animal, where on the bank it came to drink, and at what light.

It chose its target. It knew when the male would approach. In darkness, the predator ghosted into ambush. It crouched under the mirrored surface. At the expected time, its meal approached.

The predator lunged. It was over in seconds. Once more, its teeth sank through the good flesh. The Father was satisfied and he rested.

29

"Let's get to the particulars of Operation Teeth," the colonel said.

"Fire away," Dingo said.

"I'll send four soldiers. We'll have to fly them in. I'll need your expertise there, Dingo. As you know, I have no aircraft at my disposal. I'll pay the charter. The plane can take the men in, and wait there until the job is done. I say we give it – how many days do you think?"

"Three days," the major said. "That should do it."

"Exactly, my thought as well," the colonel said. "Three days. The plan is simple. Rescue the two remaining priests. Secondary objective – knock out the enemy. Then the return. In and out, quick and simple."

"And the monster croc – and our beloved native brothers and sisters?"

"As I said, the men will avoid the river," the colonel replied. "As for the villagers – I am afraid they are not our concern."

"Not our concern – of course," Dingo nodded. "Right Henry. Well, I've a coupla ideas – if you'll allow."

"Go," the colonel said, sitting back.

"First – limit the team to two good men. More than that will only get in the way. Second, make this a proper Allied operation – one of yours, one of ours."

Henry pursed his lips.

"Makes sense," he said. "Anything else?"

"Yes," Dingo said. "I'll be the 'one of ours.' I'll lead 'Operation Teeth' – with your blessing, Henry. I'm the best choice, if I say so meself. I'm the only one with first-hand knowledge of the region. And I speak some of the languages. I know how to handle your native tribesmen. And I've conducted my fair share of battles against the Japs. How does that strike you?"

The colonel was thrilled. Putting "Operation Teeth" under an experienced jungle fighter like Major Hawsey was a virtual guarantee of success!

"Dingo, you have my full endorsement," he said. "Glad to have you, Major!"

"Truth is," Dingo said, "I could use a few days in the bush – get absolutely fed up in town! Now you have only one bloke to find, Henry."

"That helps," the colonel said. "The clock is running. The priest's letter is already dated, and I have two weeks before I go. I want to be here to welcome you back. Can you be on your way by Tuesday?"

"Leave Tuesday? Heaps of time – if we find a plane," Dingo said. "That'll put us back here in Moresby – let me see – Friday? We can tear a chop together at the officers' club that night – with the priests, we expect. And that still gives you a full week before you leave us."

"What about the aircraft?" the colonel asked.

"Leave that to me," the major smiled. "I know of one. Pilot's a mate." He stood up. "I'll suggest he fly us in, touch down, let me and your man jump out. The aircraft would be a sitting target on the strip otherwise. He'll return Friday morning to pick us up. In and out, and Bob's your uncle. Tell you what – I'll work out the wrinkles and report back. You can tell me who's along for the show."

"Sounds like a plan," the colonel said, walking Dingo to the door.

"Main point," the Aussie added. "I need your Yank to have experience fighting Japs in this jungle. I won't have time to hold anyone's hand."

"Count on it," the colonel said. Dingo departed. Henry saw him to the door and returned to his desk.

Now who can I send? A file caught his eye.

Henry opened it while he extracted a handkerchief from his pocket and mopped his face.

Insane heat! I won't miss it — or this primitive place. He would continue to write about New Guinea for some time, but as for actually being here, he was done. In less than a month he'd be halfway around the world on the family estate outside of Charleston, South Carolina.

I'd hate to be the one going in-country, he reflected. *But I won't abandon these priests. And it's only a three-day operation.* Again, he thought about his book and was encouraged.

I may yet get a story out of this — something for my foreword. I orchestrate a daring raid to snatch missionaries from the enemy's clutches!

But first things first.

30

"Operation Teeth" — it does have the ring of victory. But who do I have of Dingo's caliber?

Colonel Chambers sat mulling it over. The pickings were slim. Here in mid-1945, the battle had moved far from Port Moresby. Most American fighting men were long gone. Certainly, there remained hundreds of thousands of the enemy dug in across the vast island. The battles were ongoing, and it would be up to the colonel's successor, and most especially, the Australians, to deal with them.

Henry still found it hard to believe that Germany had surrendered a mere two months ago. "Operation Overlord" had crushed the Nazi beast at last. In May, a stunned peace had settled under the dust cloud over Europe. But here in the South Pacific, World War II beat on, hammer-and-tongs.

Still, the American forces were relentlessly driving the enemy from their strongholds across the Pacific, back towards the Japanese homeland.

At this very moment, the colonel reflected, General MacArthur was in his beloved Manila. At last, he had made good on his promise to liberate the Philippines. Henry pictured the general, face fierce as the eagle emblazoned on his cap, staring northward. The scuttlebutt was that the Supreme Commander's "Operation Downfall," the invasion of the Jap islands themselves, would begin any day.

He returned to the file. Its subject was as decorated a campaigner as he'd come across. But he was also a problem. He'd been promoted on several occasions for bravery in battle, only to be busted back to buck private each time.

He's my best choice. He's less than half Dingo's age, but has about as much experience fighting here as the major does.

That boy's hell-bent on getting back to MacArthur. He's young, but he's no rookie. He could have gone home a hero, but instead, he's a thorn in my side.

Operation Teeth is the answer. If he can complete the mission, I'll ship him to the general.

He thought about "Leviathan" the missionary had mentioned. That could be a wrench in the works.

Well – stay away from the river.

Henry called, and an aide entered from the side office.

"Sir?"

"Take my jeep to the hospital," Chambers ordered. "Find Doc Mac. Tell him I got his message. Have him send the man to me right away."

"Sir, yes Sir!" The Lieutenant was already on his way.

31

Johnny showered and shaved for his meeting. He made his way to the hospital mess and lined up for breakfast.

A man spooned scrambled eggs onto his metal tray and another slopped on potatoes and canned gravy. Johnny grabbed several slices of toast. He filled a mug with coffee from the urn and topped it with condensed milk.

Johnny saw some of the men from his tent and joined them at a long table packed with recovering soldiers, mostly Aussies. As he wolfed down his food, he kidded the others about sleeping all day – he'd already run around the harbor and been to market. He told them about the mission girls and they laughed.

Johnny was always hungry now. Normally his six-foot-one frame weighed two hundred pounds, but when he'd got on the scales here, he'd been dismayed to see the needle settle at one-seventy. Since then, he'd managed to gain twenty pounds, and that was a start.

He wiped his tray with a piece of toast and got another helping. After his third coffee, he still had time before the meeting. He returned to his tent and disassembled the Springfield rifle. He laid the parts on his cot, oiled and wiped each one, and assembled it again. And then it was time.

Nervous, ready for an argument but determined to stay calm, Johnny made for the Acute Care ward. He saw frantic activity around the front entrance. Stretchers were being hauled out of an ambulance truck, and doctors, nurses and other staff were crowded over them. There was a jeep nearby, engine running, driver behind the wheel. Johnny ducked around the corner where a small wooden office stood against the rounded flank of the Quonset hut.

He knocked and Doc Mac's voice said to enter. Johnny stepped into the office, pausing to let his eyes adjust. He saw the old man in a rumpled white jacket, clipboard in hand, and another nurse – Ruthie – who assisted the Chief today. He suppressed a stab of disappointment. Doc Mac was saying something and Johnny forced himself to focus.

"Sorry Doc – what's that?"

"Any pain in the chest?"

"No," Johnny lied. "I'm good." He grinned and rotated the shoulder, ignoring the spasm.

"Well then," Doc Mac said, making a note. The finality in his tone surprised Johnny. He realized the meeting was wrapping up. It had taken less than a minute.

"I have a busy morning. Young Johnny, we are done with you. It's official. You are no longer a resident of this hospital. I do wish you all the best."

Doc Mac smiled with real warmth and offered his hand. Johnny shook it.

"Keep eating, will you? You need the weight." Doc looked him over. "And may I ask you not to take the war quite so personally? It interferes with your health."

"Sure," Johnny said. "And Doc – I owe you my life, I know that. Well – thanks for everything. I'm sorry if I got out of line."

The surgeon was still staring at him.

"I'm not sure you know it, Young Johnny, but there is more to life than war. Will you consider that?"

"I'll do my best."

"Good man," Doc Mac said. "I have a message from your colonel. He wants to see you at once. His jeep is waiting."

Johnny's spirits leapt. *I'm headed back to the general!* The doctor departed. Johnny paused to say goodbye to Ruthie.

"I'll see you around," he said. "Sorry if I was a jerk. It's just – well, I didn't mean it. Tell Gwyn goodbye for me, will you?"

"I'm afraid you'll have to do that job yourself," Ruthie smiled. "Take care, Johnny-me-lad."

She offered her cheek and he kissed it. Then he was out the door, heading for the jeep. Fifteen minutes later, he was in front of Colonel Chambers again. But this time he'd been invited and that made all the difference.

"At ease," the commander said, looking up from his writing. "I understand Doc Mac has given you a clean bill of health." The officer laid down his pen, removed his reading glasses, and leaned back.

"Private Willman, I have an assignment for you. I'm sending you into the New Guinea interior. It's a simple three-day mission I've named 'Operation Teeth.' Show me you can handle this, and I'll send you back to General MacArthur."

"Yes Sir!" Johnny grinned so enthusiastically, the colonel could not help smiling. It was hard not to like the boy, even if he was a pain in the keester.

"I've decided to go out on a limb for you," Chambers said, rising and coming around the desk to face the GI.

"I'm promoting you to sergeant. This is an Allied mission and you represent the U.S. of A – although you will be under the command of a senior Australian officer." He looked up at the younger man's face.

"You will hang onto this one. That is an order!"

"Sir, yes Sir!"

Johnny's smile was ear to ear.

32

Footy Carmichael propped the motorbike against the wall of his house, went in and kicked off his stained shorts. He stood under the five-gallon bucket on the rope in the stall, twisted the showerhead, and cool water cascaded over him. He scrubbed hard on the blackened arms and fingernails, raked the suds through his short hair and rinsed off.

He dried himself, ran a hand over his stubbled chin, applied a little soap, and scraped the safety razor over it. He dug through his few clothes and pulled out the orange shirt with parrots on it. It had been a gift from his auntie – sister of the mother who had passed when he was a boy.

He was dressed in a flash and slid into his sandals. There was a bottle of Old Spice on the dresser and he splashed a little on his cheeks. On the way out the door he peered into the cracked truck mirror hung on a nail.

He felt an uncharacteristic twinge of anxiety and brushed it aside.

"Footy mate, you're God's gift to the sheilas," he crooned at his reflection.

"She's gonna love ya!" Soon he was on the motorbike, weaving through the crowd, on his way to see his sweetheart.

33

"You'll be under Major Hawsey's authority," the colonel told Johnny. He waved the sniper to the sofas. Once they were seated, he picked up a soiled envelope and handed it over.

"Read this. It's a letter from the priest in Kissim – Father Bastion, an American.

"'Operation Teeth' goes as follows. You have three days to find Bastion. He's your primary objective. There will be an Italian priest as well – it's all in the letter. Bring them back. You have my authority to eradicate any enemy soldiers you run across. Kill on sight. That's your secondary objective.

"Now hear me on this. Stay away from the river. As the letter explains, there may be a dangerous crocodile there.

"I have a lot of faith in Major Hawsey. He's the most able New Guinea hand I've ever met. Got it?"

"Sir, yes Sir!"

The colonel stared at the young man.

"I've studied your file, John. You've had more than your share of disciplinary problems. Apart from that, you've got an outstanding record." Johnny glanced away and said nothing.

"That's why I decided to take a chance on you. You are now Sergeant Willman – I've signed the papers. You'll get your stripes in due course."

"Thank you, Sir!"

"Don't let me down, and I'll return you to MacArthur's Army. Supply ship comes through in nine days, bound for Manila. I'll get you on it before I depart for the States."

The colonel sized him up.

"Sergeant, are you sure this is what you want? I can send you home. You've done your share." Johnny did not hesitate.

"Yes Sir! That's exactly what I want."

The colonel nodded. "Settled then. Now – equipment and supplies. One of my aides will take you to the depot and authorize what you need. Get enough food for you and your superior.

"Report here Monday at 0-9-hundred for your briefing with Major Hawsey. Wheels up Tuesday, return Friday. Clear?"

Soon Johnny was standing in a storeroom packed to the rafters with equipment.

"Looks like you're well stocked," he observed. The supply sarg, a middle-aged man with a substantial beer belly, grinned.

"Most of it's used, if you catch my drift."

Johnny chuckled, then rattled off what he wanted. He got a large army backpack, and in short order, a box of .30-06 cartridges for his Springfield, a 1911 .45 semi-automatic Colt pistol in its holster, with ammunition. From a pile of knives, he selected a machete and the knife-style bayonet he liked for his Springfield, both in sheaths. He chose a webbed belt with numerous canvas pockets, and threaded on the pistol, knives, and two canteens.

He got a first aid kit. Johnny checked it; bandages, sulfa powder, iodine, gauze, a roll of tape and cotton swabs. There were bottles of water purification tablets, which he would use, and the anti-malarial pills, Atabrine, which he would not. He already had malaria, and the bright yellow pills made him feel sick.

Johnny asked for morphine. The colonel's aide was taking notes and approved the requisition. The supply sarg said the narcotic was in lockup and went to get it.

Johnny found an M1 helmet with netting – used, but in acceptable condition – and added it to his pile. He selected a coil of rope, a mess kit nested together, metal plates and cutlery – he didn't know what the Australian was bringing. He grabbed a coffee pot, a one-burner kerosene stove, and a can of fuel. He stuffed everything in the backpack.

The sarg returned and handed over the morphine – three metal squeeze tubes called *syrettes* with needles under glass caps.

"That's one for each day you're gone," he said. "Should be plenty."

Johnny nodded. He'd used these many times during the fighting and packed them carefully.

"Find me a jungle hammock, will you?" he asked. "And a sheet." In his experience, the hanging bed with its waterproof roof and mosquito netted sides was the way to go. It kept you out of the mud and away from the biters and creepy-crawlies.

Johnny turned his attention to food. He needed enough for two men for three, max four days, but he decided to take a six-day supply, just to be safe. The sarg brought him two empty cartons and Johnny selected from the stacks of canned rations – hard tack biscuits, canned crackers, corned beef, stew, spaghetti, potatoes, tomatoes, various vegetables and baked beans. He selected a variety of canned fruit, applesauce and custard. He added bags of ground coffee, powdered milk and sugar. He decided he'd round up some loaves of bread at the mess on Tuesday morning.

"I'll take two cartons of cigarettes," he said, "unfiltered Camels." He didn't need matches. He'd fill his Zippo and that would be more than enough.

Johnny put the smokes in the top of the pack, secured the flap, and tied the hammock on top. He grabbed a shoulder strap and swung it up.

Right away, his chest let him know what a bad idea that was. Pain popped like flashbulbs and he dropped to one knee. He felt the eyes of the men on him, so he crammed the helmet on his head and took a deep breath.

It wouldn't do for the colonel to learn he couldn't even hoist his pack!

To give himself a moment, Johnny pulled out a cigarette, lit it, grinned through the hurt, and climbed onto his legs. He hoisted the pack with his other arm and managed to get it on.

"Can I get a ride?"

"Sure thing, Sergeant," the looey told him.

"Give me a hand with that box?"

Johnny scooped up one of the cartons, careful to use his un-injured arm, while the colonel's man hoisted the other. A short time later, the jeep was pulling up in front of the halfway tent.

And this, Johnny saw, was a day jam-packed with surprises.

She stood in her uniform, surrounded by an admiring cluster of his tent mates.

Johnny had his helmet on, knives and the pistol hanging off his belt. He jumped out and sauntered over, feeling self-conscious under those cool green eyes.

Gwyn, it seemed, had been waiting for him.

34

Dingo Hawsey drove the jeep to his house and put his swag together. Truth was, he was tickled by the prospect of action. The major was in his mid-40s, but in the physical condition of a younger man. He regularly visited the gym and threw the pig-iron around with the lads, and played tennis three times a week.

That said, it was clear his days in the field were numbered. His promotion to major meant a jump in pay grade, but had tied him to a desk. As a man who'd run his own plantations all his adult life, Dingo was a hands-on type of bloke. But now he was stuck in a Moresby office. The younger fellows might benefit from his steady hand, but the duty wearied him.

"Operation Teeth" gave him an increasingly rare chance for a scrap in the bush. It was only a three-day jaunt, of course. He'd be back in the office before most knew he was gone. He'd never tell the colonel in so many words, but the rescue mission might be a bit of serious fun.

Dingo was alone in the house. His wife, Alice, was back in Australia, staying with her parents near Tamworth. Their two girls – teenagers now – boarded at Calrossy School.

There were no equivalent schools in the Territories, so they'd stay in Aus and only visit over the Christmas hols. Maybe, when things were more settled, Alice would come back to Moresby. But not yet.

Dingo knocked the dust off his wood-framed rucksack, rolled up a light blanket, put in a square of mosquito netting for his face, balled up a change of clothes, and stuffed in cooking gear and the rest. He couldn't stop smiling. *Reminds me of the Kokoda Track!*

The enemy had attempted to invade Port Moresby by sea and failed. Capturing Port Moresby would have given them control of all New Guinea, and become the staging ground for the invasion of Australia. They crossed the Owen Stanley Range – an impressive undertaking. Dingo had fought them there, and only experienced soldiers like him had an idea of what they'd endured.

The blighters ended up sick and starving. Put an end to the myth of the Jap superman! He whistled while he fetched his rifle.

Still, they'd actually clapped eyes on Moresby before they'd been turned around.

It had been a fight under brutal conditions, but Dingo was a man who thrived in the bush.

Helps to walk like a native – been doing it long enough. Bare feet let you slip up quiet-like on a chap and pull your knife across his gullet before he knows you're there.

Dingo could sleep anywhere. Insects and animals didn't put him off. Getting enough to eat could be a bit of a problem. He preferred meat, and included croc on the menu.

Of course, you give the huge salties a wide birth – brutes like "the Father" this priest mentions. A bloke must know his limits. Still, I'd like to lay eyes on the bugger the natives blather on about, if it's real – from a very suitable distance.

Speaking of natives, Dingo *was* an old New Guinea hand, and he knew how things worked here. *The locals won't do what you say unless you shout and wave your arms a bit. If some of the bleeding-heart Yanks wanted to coddle up to them – well, they'd soon discover that was a mistake. There are only a few of us here on the edge of civilization, outnumbered ten thousand to one.*

No, in order to succeed, you must have clear rules and a hard hand. That is the only way to bring a bit of law and order to the bush. Anyone who says different, Dingo snorted to himself, *is blowing air through his arse.*

The major lifted his .303 Lee Enfield off its pegs. The rifle held a magazine of ten shells, inserted in clips or chargers of five shots each. The firearm was loaded, and Dingo dropped extra ammo in his kit.

He withdrew the Webley pistol from a drawer. It was a six-shooter, made so it opened like a shotgun and automatically ejected the spent cartridges. It, too, was loaded, and Dingo put a handful of ammo in a pocket of his pack.

From under his pillow he took out his one concession to Yank weaponry, a gigantic hunting knife. This he'd salvaged from a dead GI. *Not that the poor lad needed it any more.* The knife had a leather sheath worked in a scene of a stag's head against pines. He withdrew it and tested the edge with his thumb. The blade was a foot long, with a bone handle – *a real beaut!* From the first moment he'd hefted it, it belonged in his fist. The Yanks called it a "Bowie" – though what that meant, he did not know. He had bloodied it in close fighting uncounted times, and never went into the bush without it.

Dingo was ready. He bellowed for his native cook to bring lunch. He got a plate of cold mutton, a packet of Melba toast, and some pickles he fished from a jar. After that, he'd get in an hour of tennis. Tonight at the pub he'd bend his elbow with his mates.

I'll have a chinwag with Footy – sort the aircraft out. The bloke was a corporal Dingo had spent time with on the Track, and now he was a pilot in private business.

I wonder how Footy's Folly is coming along? Perhaps it's ready to go. If not, he'll know the whereabouts of every serviceable aircraft in the territory.

Come Monday, the major would meet the soldier the colonel assigned. Dingo liked Henry well enough, but privately, he was scornful of the American's ability to put a fight together. There was no question the man was good at admin – his garrison ran like a clock. But when it came to action in the bush, Henry had been forced to rely on old Dingo every time.

Whatever Yank he picks had better not be wet behind the ears – or he can guard camp while I sort things.

Dingo was packed and ready. He headed for his jeep.

35

He was troublesome. He was bull-headed. And – strike three – he was a soldier. Yet, here Gwyn stood, waiting for him.

In some ways, she knew Johnny as intimately as he did himself, but in others, he was a stranger. It was his body she knew best. She had taken care of him while he was comatose, his life in her hands. She had seen through his flesh to the bone. Countless times, she had washed his hair, shaved him, and sponged him from head to toe. In that regard, he had no secrets.

But what about the man himself? Early on, when he was unconscious, his battle reduced to simply fighting for the next breath, she had kept watch. When he wasn't out cold or raving, they'd spoken and she knew something of his past. Gradually she was forced to admit to herself – he was a manly man, and he attracted her.

But as he improved, the carping complainer came to the front, with his cracked-record plan to get back to the war. There was something bent in him, she decided, probably broken, and she doubted it could be fixed.

But here she found herself, waiting at his tent.

After Ruthie told her Johnny had been discharged, Gwyn had come looking for him. She hadn't spoken with her patient lately, but she knew where he bunked.

And here he came, like a proud little boy with all his gear on – but the lines around his mouth, the way he favored one side, told her another story. Her heart beat a little faster and she warned herself to stay neutral.

What am I doing here? she wondered for the hundredth time as Johnny's buddies unloaded the equipment.

I've come to wish him well, she answered herself. *After all, I am his nurse.*

Johnny had a final word with the driver and the vehicle sped away. He came over.

"Will you give us a few minutes?" he asked the men, and reluctantly, they retreated into the tent.

"Hello Gwyn."

"Hello Johnny. I heard Doc Mac released you. I came to say goodbye. Where are you going?"

"I've received my orders. It's a three-day mission into the interior. There are some priests that need rescuing. I'll be back Friday. Then the colonel says he'll get me on a ship for the Philippines."

"Just what you wanted," Gwyn said.

"What I want," Johnny smiled. She looked away, but then her eyes flashed back at him and she spoke with spirit.

"Is that all you can think about, Johnny Willman? More killing?"

He was startled by the vehemence.

"I'm a soldier, Gwyn," was all he could manage. *Lame!*

"I know that," she said. "I just wonder — when will it be enough?"

Never. It will never be enough for what they did.

"Gwyn, this is war," he replied. "It's over when we win."

"Funny — some guys find time for other things," Gwyn responded. "But you asked me out. I'd like to know why."

Again, Johnny was caught off guard.

"I like you, Gwyn," he managed. "I like you a lot. You're smart – and about the prettiest girl I've ever seen."

I think about you all the time, even when I don't want to.

"Well, thank you," she said. *He thinks I'm smart!*

Johnny stepped closer and took her hands.

"I'd like time with you," he said. "Away from..." he glanced around, "...away from this. But I'm not going to get the chance. I have this job, and then there's the ship."

Gwyn looked down and did not reply. He was still clutching her hands. At last she stared into his face.

"Johnny, what happened to you?" she asked softly. "I know you've been through hell – more than I can imagine. But all you talk about is the war. Killing and more killing.

"Do you have any heart left?"

Johnny opened his mouth to reply and then closed it. He frowned and thought about what she was asking.

Do I have a heart? Can I feel – really feel – anything any-more?

"I guess I don't know," he said finally and looked down.

"I'm sorry Gwyn. You're – something special." He looked back up into those green eyes and felt vertigo.

"And you deserve – well, you deserve much more than I've got." Frustrated, he dropped her hands and turned away. He felt a touch on his arm. For a heartbeat, their eyes locked.

"When are you back?"

"Friday."

"I'll save that night for you. We can go for dinner – if you still want to."

What am I saying? She was scaring herself.

"Yes!" Johnny said, brightening. "Dinner – Friday night!"

"But..."

"There's a 'but?'"

"But I want you to do something for me while you're gone. Will you?"

"Yes," Johnny said at once.

"Will you try and find what you've done with your heart?" She saw him frown and smiled to take the sting out.

"Not this." She touched a finger to his chest. "I'm talking about the place where you've hidden the best things."

"Like what?"

"Oh – how about hope? And laughter. Enjoying people, life. Being kind. You know – that heart."

Johnny thought about it. *When was the last time I laughed? I mean, really laughed?* He couldn't remember and he shook his head.

"Gwyn, a soldier can't go around *feeling* things! You're right – you have no idea what I've gone through. What I've done. But I will make you a promise. I'll think about what you said. Okay?"

"Friday night," she said. "You'll pick me up?"

"At six," Johnny said. "I'll come by. I know where you live."

He knows where I live? Gwyn felt a flutter of something that might have been excitement, or maybe it was worry.

"Okay," she said. "Take care of yourself, Johnny."

She turned to leave and he surprised them both by leaning in and trying to plant a kiss.

She was in mid-turn and his lips landed on the corner of her mouth. He got a glimpse of startled eyes and then she was walking away. It was a sight he'd seen far too often.

He willed her to turn around. And then, at the corner, just for an instant, she did so. Johnny saw her eyes and the blush on her cheeks. But then she spun and was gone.

There were whistles and catcalls from the tent. Johnny's buddies spilled out and surrounded him, calling him a lucky son-of-a-gun, and worse, while they helped drag his gear inside.

Gwyn walked fast, not sure where she was going. She could feel the place where his lips had touched her own.

Her face felt on fire.

What am I doing?

What have I done?

36

Johnny felt like he was walking on air. But if he'd seen what Gwyn got up to after she left, the euphoria would not have lasted.

Back at her quarters, Gwyn grabbed her sunhat and market bags. Then she went out to meet another man.

He was waiting at their usual spot. The two fell easily into their rhythm, trading laughter and light jabs. As they did most Saturdays, they wandered through the native market where Gwyn haggled for vegetables for the children.

It was late in the day. Some vendors had packed up and gone, but the place still buzzed. Gwyn filled her *bilums* and slung them over her shoulders. When they were done, they strolled the road by the harbor.

At a scenic spot, Footy stopped and turned to her. He took her hands – just as Johnny had hours earlier – and she didn't pull away.

He spoke for a time, earnest and steady. Gwyn listened without interrupting, eyes watching. When he finished, she replied, soft and serious.

At last she was done and her companion found he had nothing to say. He turned toward the sea, and for a moment, there was only the splash of waves and the people passing.

Then, if Johnny had been watching, he would have seen Gwyn kiss Footy.

True, it was just her lips on his cheek, but she reached up and stroked his face. It was the kind of caress a woman only gives someone she truly cares about. She said goodbye and walked away.

Footy stood for a minute, lost in thought. But soon his natural buoyancy returned, and with it came his trademark grin.

He stepped back into the crowd, joking in pidgin with the natives, and climbed on his motorbike. He kicked it to life and sped toward the airfield.

Today's going to be brilliant, mate!

Half an hour later, he was airborne, sitting in the pilot seat, two of his mates with him, watching over his shoulder.

Expertly, the pilot guided the patched-up bomber over the city. The long days of grease and sweat had paid off! She had full tanks of gas and Footy put her through her paces until he was sure she was fully operational.

Miss Nippon These soared on the air columns as if she were made for it – as indeed she was.

37

Tuesday, Johnny had an early breakfast with his buddies from the halfway tent. He wangled some loaves of bread from the cooks.

He was waiting outside his tent with his pile of gear when the colonel's aide pulled up. In the heat, Johnny wore Army trousers and an undershirt. He had a change of clothes in the pack. His belt bore canteens of water, the pistol, bayonet and machete. A coil of rope hung from his pack and he had his helmet on, rifle in hand.

His friends helped heave his gear and boxes of food into the jeep and said goodbye. Johnny climbed in the passenger seat, and in seconds, he'd left the hospital behind. The driver raced to the airport and headed across the tarmac.

There was a line of wrecks along the edge of the airstrip, and they cut towards a bomber standing alone on the runway. Johnny's first impression was of a piece of junk. The plane had metal patches all over, and the propellers didn't match. As they got close, he got a smile from the reclining beauty, "Miss Nippon These."

This can't be our ride! But it must be, because there was that Aussie officer, the one he'd met yesterday at the colonel's office.

Major Hawsey. What did he tell me to call him?

The mission leader was dressed in shorts and a shirt with the arms rolled up, displaying thick biceps. He wore what looked like a cowboy hat with the side hooked up. The man was barefoot, a pair of sandals in one hand.

The major was laughing with a smaller man dressed in tan shorts and a short-sleeve shirt. At least this one was wearing his sandals.

The jeep skidded up and Johnny got out and began to un-load. The two men came over to lend a hand.

"Morning, Johnny."

"Morning, Major."

"Now, we had that out," the officer smiled. "I'm in charge, but from here on, we're just a coupla mates in the bush. You call me Dingo like I told you."

"Right – Dingo."

They had Johnny's gear out and the jeep departed.

The major put a hand on the shoulder of the shorter man. "This is a good mate of mine, and our pilot – Glen Carmichael."

"G'day mate," the fellow grinned, extending a hand. "I hear you're a Yank, but we won't hold that against you."

"Thanks Glen," Johnny said dryly as he shook.

"Nah – call me 'Footy,'" the pilot said.

"Footy? As in – foot...?"

"Footy – as in football."

"Soccer to you Yanks," Dingo grinned. "Footy's a right rip-per on the field."

Johnny looked at the aircraft.

"Tell me we're not flying in this junker!"

"She might look jiggered, but she's jake," the pilot said, bri-dling. "I've fully tested her. She'll get us there and back – no worries."

"You guarantee that?" Johnny asked.

"Bloody right!"

"Johnny," Dingo put in, "if Footy says so, you can bet on it. Come on lads, we've got work to do! Let's get airborne!"

Dingo grabbed one of Johnny's cartons – his own gear was already aboard – and headed for the Hudson. Footy took the other one and went that way as well.

"Ah, let's not get off on the wrong foot, mate," he smiled as they reached the wooden steps propped against the open door-way.

"Up you go. We'll be hunky dory, you'll see."

"Okay," Johnny muttered as he climbed. "But I don't like it. I don't like it at all."

He stepped inside and saw it was all open metal ribs and wiring. There was a set of seats bolted to the floor. Dingo was there and helped Johnny stow his gear while the pilot went forward and disappeared into the cockpit.

"Good to see you brought the food like we agreed," the major said. "Tie everything down – we may get turbulence."

Johnny uncoiled his rope and lashed their gear. Dingo approved of the way the Yank whipped the knots together. Johnny wedged his helmet and rifle under the strands. The men sat and saw there were no seat-belts.

One engine roared to life, and then the other, coughing smoke. Soon both were yowling and the aircraft began to creak forward. A hairy spider the size of a man's hand climbed out of the fuselage overhead and dropped fast, legs wide. Dingo whipped off his hat and swatted it away. It scuttled across the floor and fell through a hole.

"Poisonous," the Australian said. "Makes your skin go bad!"

"Yeah – I know that kind," Johnny said.

The Hudson tore down the runway, picking up speed. Suddenly, the shuddering stopped and in the instant calm, the men watched through the windows as treetops gave way to clear blue.

Footy took the craft up in a steep climb. At seven thousand feet, he leveled off. There followed a long stretch with only the hum of the engines and the whistle of wind around the patches. The air grew cold and thin. Dingo gave Johnny a wink, pulled his hat over his eyes, and fell asleep.

From time to time, Johnny went to the windows and stared at the interminable green, bisected occasionally by a river. Here and there were villages along the banks. Eventually, he felt the plane's engines labor and knew they were climbing again. Looming close were near-vertical mountain ranges with snow on the peaks.

Johnny grew hungry, tore the end off a loaf and ate. It occurred to him that he was dipping into the supplies for the trip, but he wasn't worried. He'd packed double what they needed.

The Hudson shot into a cloud bank, and the windows went white. After a time, they exploded into blue again. Dingo dozed on and Johnny wandered from bench to windows. Beneath them now were rumpled clouds to the horizon, mountain heads poking through.

Johnny felt tiny as the bomber threaded between cumulus towers that boiled up a thousand feet. Within the storm heads were flashes that must be lightning.

Once more, the bomber banked around the same thunderhead and it came to Johnny they were flying in circles. He made his way to the cockpit and stuck in his head.

"What's going on?" he yelled over the engines. The pilot turned and Johnny saw worry on the man's face.

"Not good. Can't see the bloody ground, mate!" There was a hand-drawn map spread on the copilot's chair and the pilot squinted at it.

"Look," he said, "I know we're in the vicinity of the Raub. Get Dingo, would you?"

Johnny woke the major and they returned. Dingo pointed Johnny to the co-pilot's seat while he stood in the doorway, gripping the edges.

"I reckon the Raub's right below us," Footy said, "but it's socked in. The bloody usual in New Guinea. Reason they call this blasted place 'the pilot killer.'"

"What now?" Johnny asked.

"Find a way through," Dingo nodded.

Footy ran a hand over his face.

"I'll circle – but I need enough petrol for the flight home. We must find a way down in the next fifteen minutes or we have to call it. Put your eyeballs out there!"

The men stared down but saw only clouds. At last Footy tapped the fuel gauge.

"That's it, I'm afraid..."

"There!" Johnny yelled. He'd seen a flash of green, a hole in the white blanket.

Footy half-stood to look, then sat back.

"Hang on," he called. Johnny gripped his seat, and Dingo grabbed the door frame. The pilot turned the Hudson on a wing and dropped. Down the bomber screamed, an arrow through the clouds. The gap was no more than a smear of forest in the mist, disappearing fast.

Expertly, Footy threaded the hole. The light dimmed and rain splattered against the windscreen, blurring the view. Footy saw the river to one side and wrestled the craft that way.

On the ground, the drone of engines had been noticed for some time. Hostile eyes watched the bomber drop from the clouds. The roar grew louder as the plane careened their way along the river.

Japanese soldiers, carrying a machine gun and rifles, bolted for the only place an aircraft could land.

38

The bomber blasted over the river's surface. The men stared at land rushing by, treetops level with their wingtips.

"There!" Footy shouted. "Village!"

He squinted through the drops that quivered across the windows. The clearing came up fast and was below. Johnny made out fire-blackened circles, the remains of huts. Behind that was a strip of grass in the jungle, then a mountain flank that shot into the clouds. It was only a glimpse and they were by, forest below. Footy banked hard back over the river, leaving Johnny's stomach behind.

"Gotta be Kissim!" Dingo yelled from the doorway.

"I saw the airstrip!" Footy called.

The landing site the priest wrote about, Johnny realized.

They were back over the burned-out village. Johnny stared down but saw no one – no movement at all. The bomber turned inland and there was the field. The pilot made a pass over it and banked hard as they approached the mountain.

Footy brought the aircraft around, pressed a lever, and the landing gear clunked into place. They could see nothing but rain, mist, and waist-high *kunai* grass.

"Look okay?" Johnny called.

"Have to do," Footy said.

A crosswind shoved them sideways and rain drummed on the metal shell. Footy nudged the nose into the wind and the plane crabbed, dropping lower.

With a stutter of rupturing metal, shafts of light poured into the cockpit. Holes opened along the fuselage as Dingo stared back.

"Machine gun!" Dingo bellowed.

Footy fought the stick and the bomber yawed. There were clangs to Johnny's right, and he glanced along the wing and saw chunks of the engine flying off. The propeller froze, black billows behind it, and there was the sudden stench of gasoline. The aircraft dropped again.

"Bloody hell!" Footy gritted, fighting for control. The ruined engine exploded in an orange fireball as the grass rushed up to meet them.

Johnny watched three men burst into the waist-high *kunai* in front of them. He could see they were Japs. The first man carried a machine gun and the other two had rifles.

Johnny saw tracers come from the machine gun. The windshield exploded and bullets whined overhead and struck the bulkhead. Dingo dropped to the floor.

"Bloody, bloody hell," Footy shouted. "Hang on!"

The plane hit dirt and bounced. They struck again, bucked up, fell back, and this time, stayed down. The landing gear gave way in a scream of rending metal as the bomber slammed onto its belly. Now it was no more than twisted metal hurtling down the field.

Johnny kept his eyes on the soldiers who continued to fire, the bullets slamming through the bomber.

Shedding bits of itself, the Hudson bore down on the men. At last the shooters perceived their danger and leapt for their lives.

The Hudson slewed so Johnny had a ringside view through the side window. The wing dipped, mowing stalks.

The machine gunner ran first, another man on his heels.

The third one stumbled and the wingtip struck and plowed him under.

The bomber continued in a din of rending metal. The line of jungle loomed up, but before they could hit it, the wing smashed into a giant boulder. The fuselage drew a circle around it and ground to a stop.

In the comparative silence, there was only the pinging of metal and the roar of the gasoline fire.

Johnny glanced back. Dingo sat on the floor, bleeding from a cut on his cheek, but apparently okay.

"Get out!" Footy screamed, fumbling with his seat belt. "She's gonna blow!"

Johnny and Dingo threw themselves at their equipment. Johnny pulled his slipknots and the gear tumbled loose. He jammed on his helmet, got his rifle and pack over a shoulder, while Dingo hoisted his rucksack and a box of food.

Everything took too long.

Footy dashed by, threw open the door and leapt out. Dingo bailed next. Johnny tossed his things out and, holding his Springfield, jumped.

He hit hard and rolled, protecting his rifle. He felt the jolt all through his torso, but ignored it as he scooped spilled cans and bread back into his box.

The machine gun opened up again, and Johnny's team dove on their bellies in the tall grass. The *kunai* gave cover, but no protection.

Bullets slashed the vegetation, searching them out.

TEETH

Book 2

The River

*"Can you pull in leviathan with a fishhook
or tie down his tongue with a rope? ...
Who dares open the doors of his mouth
ringed about with his fearsome teeth? ...
Strength resides in his neck;
dismay goes before him...
He makes the depths churn like a boiling cauldron...
Nothing on Earth is his equal – a creature without fear."*

– Job 41

*"I had a vision...the phantom-bearers, the wild crowd
of obedient worshipers, the gloom of the forests,
the glitter of the reach between the murky bends,
the beat of the drum, regular and muffled
like the beating of a heart –
the heart of a conquering darkness."*

– Joseph Conrad, Heart of Darkness

*"A good plan, violently executed now,
is better than a perfect plan next week."*

– General George Patton

39

"WORLD WAR II IN THE SOUTH PACIFIC"
- BY COLONEL HENRY CHAMBERS III

The Most Warlike Place On Earth

Dear Reader, for tens of thousands of years, the New Guineans lived in the Stone Age, and most still do. The people never discovered the wheel on their own, let alone metallurgy. They live in huts with dirt floors, without running water. For most, the toilet is the nearest bush. Their enemy is the tribe just over the hill. Their technology may be primitive, but their societies are complex, infinitely varied, and highly evolved.

At puberty, the warriors initiate the boys into manhood through secret, often violent rites. These include the scarification of the body and piercing the nasal septum. The hole between their nostrils is often used to insert a pair of bound pig tusks, or other bones and teeth. Your author has seen some carry a pen this way.

Once the youngsters have been welcomed into the ranks of men, they join their elders in vendetta battles against their enemies. And in many cases, these tribal wars feed a grisly culinary practice abhorred in the civilized world.

Millions of these people are cannibals. Not only do they kill their neighbors – they eat them! Some tribes consume their own dead – mortuary cannibalism.

The New Guineans have lived this way for thousands of years. More than a million inhabitants of the rugged Highlands never clapped eyes on a white man until a handful of years ago. The interior is so mountainous, it was presumed by the outside world to be uninhabited.

And then, along came that 20th Century invention, the aircraft. For the first time, in the 1920's, planes soared over the mountains. In what were blank places on the map, the aviators saw villages beyond counting, surrounded by colorful patches of vegetable gardens.

In 1930, rough Australians braved the heights on foot. Armed with guns and guard dogs, they searched for gold. Here, they came face-to-face with Stone Age people. The result was a clash of cultures that reverberates to this day. Some villagers fainted at the sight of white skin. These must be the ghosts of their ancestors, returned from the spirit world! The foreigners carried amazing goods, or cargo, and were viewed by many as demigods.

But some tribal warriors were moved by other emotions. Envy of the white man's goods turned to violent acquisitiveness. The Australians had to demonstrate just what their guns could do. Warriors paid for it with their lives.

This was a profound occasion! And it was the final place on Earth that such a momentous event would take place.

This was the clash between the civilized world and a million Stone Age people.

The miners had more practical things in mind. Their way forward was trade. The Australians exchanged a knife for a pig, or a steel axe for the company of a native girl. Many tribes considered these relationships to be marriages, and they arranged them to cement their security with these powerful newcomers. And it was those young women who discovered that these were not gods, after all, but men made like every other.

Of course, once they had scoured an area for the yellow metal, most miners moved on, leaving a legacy.

The mixed-race children of those trysts live in the villages today. Interestingly, they are not usually despised by the people. On the contrary: they are honored.

To heap irony on irony, the introduction to "civilization" for millions of natives was World War II. In 1942, the Japanese war machine invaded the island. The Asians saw the people as inferior, and they killed or brutalized many as they advanced.

The invaders were fought first by the Australians, and finally, the Americans, after General MacArthur and our troops arrived. The Allies treated the natives with kindness and respect, and won the support of most tribes.

It is a fact that thousands of our soldiers owe their lives to the natives. These people carried our wounded to safety and earned the name given them by the Australians, "the Fuzzy Wuzzy Angels."

Yet, while these islanders marveled at our guns and mechanized warfare, they are no strangers to combat themselves. Their own tribal battles are frequent and brutal.

New Guinea may be the most warlike place on Earth.

40

The three men crawled away from the wreck as fast as they could while bullets struck around them. Then the blast came, flattening the grass. It was followed immediately by a louder boom as the second wing-tank exploded. There was a roar of flame and Johnny felt the fierce heat on his back. A shower of metal crashed around them.

Dingo wiggled into a shallow depression, shoving the box of food he'd grabbed. Footy slid in after him, while the machine gun mowed the grass. Johnny left his gear, and rifle in hand, crawled to the others. He motioned for them to stay put, wagged a finger toward the machine gun, then pointed to himself:

I'll take care of them! He slithered away.

Good on ya Johnny! Dingo thought. He and Footy tucked their heads as slugs struck in front of their hole.

Still in the *kunai*, Johnny stood, bent double and ran. The land sloped away. The enemy rifleman saw the undulating grass and tapped the machine gunner's shoulder.

A line of slugs chased Johnny across the field. He heard them biting at his heels and began to zigzag like the football pass receiver he'd been. At the tree line, he threw himself behind a trunk. Bullets slammed in and the wood shuddered. He kept the tree between himself and the enemy and climbed. The gunner lost sight of him and went back to probing the field with lead.

Full of adrenaline, Johnny hauled himself up, still favoring his shoulder.

Take the high ground! Fifteen feet in the air, he squatted on a limb and peered through the leaves. What he saw chilled him. The Japanese had fanned out and were walking fast through the grass, almost on the Aussies' hiding place – Johnny could see his trail coming away from them.

He grabbed the bark with his left hand and rested his rifle on it. He had both eyes open. One absorbed the scene – *the Japs walking in the rain, the burning hulk behind them.* With his other, he had a close view through the scope of the machine gunner.

He aimed center-mass and shot. The man dropped.

The one remaining enemy threw himself down. Johnny watched the patch of grass while he reloaded by feel – a much-practiced move. He fired and hit true. The shot Jap bobbed up and tried to run.

Dingo's head came up. The major leapt across the short distance, big knife raised. The blade flashed and the combatants locked and fell. Then Dingo stood and beckoned with the crimson Bowie. Johnny climbed down.

By the time he got there, Dingo and Footy had checked the enemy corpses and found they were almost out of ammunition. There was no point hanging onto their machine gun or rifle so they threw them into the burning bomber. Then they headed for the jungle. Johnny glanced back.

The Miss Nippon These flamed fiercely, smoke blending with the clouds and rain.

41

Johnny, Dingo and Footy sat under a lean-to hidden in the trees. They had tied a sapling across two trunks, propped more against it, then overlapped elephant ear leaves to make a roof.

The rain fell steadily and night came fast. They ate a cold meal out of cans, not willing to risk the stove without knowing where the enemy was.

Footy was particularly downcast. He'd lost his aircraft and everything he'd poured into it. Here he was, deep in the unknown wilderness, with only the clothes on his back. It was chilly in the rain, but not cold, and Dingo offered to spread his blanket as a bed for both himself and the pilot. Johnny unrolled his hammock, took out the sheet, and gave it to them.

It was almost dark by the time Johnny got his hammock

tied between two trees. He sharpened sticks and rigged the hammock roof to shed water. Mosquito netting formed the walls, and the bed was a double layer of cloth.

Johnny undid the brass zipper and slid in, then leaned out and wedged his muddy boots upside down through the string web near his head. The Aussies watched him go through his familiar routine, but neither commented. Dingo felt no need except for what he had, a bit of cover and a place to stretch out.

Yanks and their bloody equipment! Footy thought. *But at least Johnny shared.* He covered himself with the sheet and prepared to sleep.

Dingo took the first watch. He was disappointed by their situation, and felt especially sorry for Footy, but otherwise, he was reasonably satisfied. Killing three of the enemy right off was a positive step for Operation Teeth.

As he lay snug beneath the drumming rain, Johnny's thoughts went to Gwyn and their last conversation. *What did she mean, find your heart? Okay, I don't feel things like I did when I was young,* he admitted. *Not even like I did when I first got to New Guinea.*

The Hard Case had something to say about that.

That's a good thing. Feelings! They're worse than useless in war – they turn you stupid, and stupid gets shot.

Johnny thought about the enemy soldiers they'd taken out today and the familiar hatred welled up.

See? the killer observed. *You do have feelings – just not the kind a girl understands.*

Johnny fell asleep. He woke in deep blackness, his hammock shaking. *My watch.* He unzipped the netting, fumbled for his boots and slid in his feet. He got up and felt the light rain. It was letting up.

155

Johnny sat under the lean-to with his rifle across his knees. Dingo was soon breathing deeply. When Footy started snoring, Johnny nudged him. The pilot rolled over and fell silent. Three hours later, Johnny shook him awake and crawled back into bed.

When next he woke, it was in dismal gray light. The rain had stopped, but water trickled off the glistening leaves. Johnny got up again and rotated his shoulder. It was sore but functional. He nodded at Footy who was sitting bleary-eyed on the edge of the blanket, hair every which way. Dingo was asleep.

Johnny stepped behind a tree and relieved himself. *A cup of hot coffee would be great. Can we light the stove? No,* he answered. *Not with the Japs out there. I wonder where the Kissim natives are?*

It dawned on him that he was staring at one of them. A black man – no, it was just a kid – stood mostly hidden in the foliage. Johnny stepped fast, shot out his fist and took the boy by the throat. His other hand pulled the knife from his belt. The native shivered but did not cry out. The soldier checked that the boy carried no weapon.

Johnny steered the native around the tree.

Dingo was just sitting up. Johnny forced his captive down on his knees. The boy was maybe twelve or thirteen. He wore a faded red loincloth, a shell the size of a silver dollar tied on his forehead, and another bark string around his neck with an amulet on it. In the center of his chest were four wavy lines of raised scar tissue.

"Can you ask him where the priests are?" Johnny said.

Dingo tried two or three languages and at last the boy answered. After a minute, Dingo reported that he could not get him to say anything about the location of the priests. Johnny studied the carving on the native's necklace.

He reached and touched it.

"Crocodile," he said to the boy.

"Pukpuk," Dingo said.

"Ka-him-ka," the boy whispered.

"Father of the crocodiles," Dingo translated.

"Is it near?" Johnny asked. Dingo spoke, and the boy peered anxiously around, but said nothing. He turned to Dingo and whispered some words.

"We're to go with him," the major said. "He'll take us to his people."

42

They broke camp. Dingo handed his rifle to Footy, shrugged into his pack, and drew his revolver. He ordered the boy forward and walked behind him, one hand clamped on his shoulder. Footy went next, Lee Enfield in hand, hefting a box of food. Johnny came at the rear, pack on, the other carton under an arm, rifle ready.

The boy took them on a route that broke out among the burned huts. The men crept through the village and noticed the remains of two larger edifices. The major and the boy exchanged whispers.

"The priests' house and church," Dingo said low.

So much for the world of brotherly love, Johnny thought.

The boy was edgy, eyes darting everywhere, and the men walked with their fingers on the triggers. Then they were in the rainforest again, going single file between the towering trunks. Johnny admired the way Dingo stepped silently on bare feet.

He saw that Footy was at home on the jungle trails as well.

The boy stopped abruptly and the men halted. Native warriors stepped from behind the trees and surrounded them. They were armed with longbows, arrows drawn back. The white men aimed their firearms at them.

"Easy!" Dingo cautioned. The natives wore the same red loincloths as the boy, shells on their foreheads, with similarly scarred chests.

The teenager whispered fast, Dingo occasionally adding a phrase. An old man with a frizz of white hair stepped from the circle. He spoke, and the men let the tension off their bows. Johnny's group lowered their guns. The old one said another word, and the warriors slipped back into the forest. The boy remained. The elder motioned the newcomers to follow and limped away.

Ten minutes later, they came to a clearing. Weak light filtered from the dark sky. The men saw two mounds of fresh earth. In the gloom behind were two more hummocks, overgrown with weeds. All four had simple crosses at one end – peeled sticks tied together. The old man paused beside the nearest one and turned, his face pulled down by sadness.

"Papa Chris," he said. He pointed to the next. "Papa Bruno." He moved to the overgrown sites.

"Papa Sid. Papa Bob." He fell silent. The white men stared at one another.

"The four priests!" Dingo breathed. "All dead!"

"Hell's bells," Footy said. Johnny shook his head. The elder was moving again and they followed through a fringe of trees. They came to an open meadow along the river, spotted with graves.

There were at least thirty or forty, Johnny guessed. About a third had crosses, and the rest, branches strung with bones and amulets. The old man spoke in his language to Dingo.

"These are the Kissim people, most killed by the Japs. We got here too late," the major said. He sat on a rock and stared at the river.

"Okay," Johnny took a deep breath. "But we've still got work to do."

"Let's get the bastards who did this," Footy said in a tight voice.

"Right!" Johnny nodded at him. *Maybe I can learn to like the guy after all.*

"There is that," Dingo nodded. "Let's have a chinwag."

They went down on their haunches. Johnny passed cigarettes.

"I think we can risk it," he said.

"Right you are," Dingo agreed. He and Footy each took one and passed the box back. Johnny saw the old man watching and handed him the pack. The fellow spread his lips in a smile punctuated by dark stumps, took two cigarettes and gave one to the boy. He began to hand the box back and reconsidered. He extracted two more and stuck them behind his ears.

Johnny flicked his Zippo and the circle lit up. When they were all puffing, boy included, Dingo spoke.

"Operation Teeth is buggered beyond recognition. There'll be no aircraft to pick us up come Friday, because here's Footy — sitting with us."

"More's the ruddy shame," Footy said.

"By now they'll know in Moresby you didn't make it back, mate," Dingo told him. "They'll have sent word to my office — and to you Yanks as well," he nodded at Johnny.

"They won't forget us," Dingo went on. "They'll come looking. Of course, I'm the only one who knows where Kissim is," he said. Your colonel will only have the vaguest idea, I'm afraid," he said to Johnny.

"Then there's this filthy weather," Footy added, squinting up. "We're socked in, for who knows how long?"

"Okay," Johnny said. "So, they're going to search for us. We're too late to rescue the priests. So why don't we salvage what we can of our mission? Sir — I mean, Dingo — let's hunt some Japs!

"I read the priest's letter. There were seven hostiles when he wrote it. If they were all still alive when we got here, we took out three yesterday. That means four left."

"Four, Johnny — what I reckon as well," Dingo said.

"How do we find them?" Footy asked.

"That's the easy part, mate," Dingo told him. He nodded at the elder.

"He'll show us."

As it turned out, the native did know where the enemy camp was. The boy was sent to guide the white men as close as he dared.

They walked through the jungle for twenty minutes. The boy slowed as they approached a bald hill. Logs with gun slits marked a bunker, positioned to defend every approach. They stayed well back, hidden in the foliage.

"They picked their site well," Johnny said.

"You can count on your Jap for that," Dingo said.

"We could try sneaking up at night – but there's a better way."

"What do you reckon?"

"Ask the boy where they go for water," Johnny replied. Dingo did.

Their guide led them to another trail. They followed this and emerged at the river. The men stepped out cautiously and panned the place with their firearms, but saw nothing.

Johnny told them his plan. After all, he was the expert at ambush warfare. Dingo approved.

I like the way this Yank thinks!

43

It was the afternoon of their third day.

Johnny was thirty feet up a tree. He'd picked it for its clear view along the path, although the river itself remained out of sight beyond the rise of the bank. Dingo and Footy were hidden in the jungle below, also with views of the trail. So the three of them had waited each day.

It rained frequently and the cloud cover stayed low and heavy. There had been no sight or sound of aircraft.

This is Friday, it occurred to Johnny. *Tonight I've got a date with Gwyn! Does she even know I'm not back in Moresby? And maybe,* he thought, *I won't be – not for a long time.*

Hidden in his vantage point, he had lots of time to think.

He imagined lovely Gwyn in a pretty dress. He saw them together at the Islander restaurant. There were cocktails on a white tablecloth. Johnny felt a pang of regret and forced his thoughts in another direction.

The previous afternoon, he had seen the Japanese far off on another trail. He confirmed that there were four of them, armed with rifles. They moved cautiously, staring around. *Hunting for us.* He could have shot at least one – he tracked the man through his scope. But he did not want to have to deal with them one-by-one. First reason, he'd give away his perch. For another, killing them piecemeal would take too long.

Wait and get them all!

Last night, the team had eaten another meal at their latest camp, not far away – cold canned spaghetti on bread. Footy had voiced his impatience.

"Let's get on with it! Let's give this up and just go after the buggers."

But Johnny's years of working his craft made him disagree.

"That's a mistake. If we go looking for them, we could be bushwhacked ourselves. No – we've got a great spot. And they have to be running low on water by now."

"Johnny's right," Dingo said. "They know Kissim better than we do. Men and animals, Footy, they all have to drink."

"Another thing," Johnny said. "When the Japs do show up, let me take the first shot. Then you can fire at will."

"And why would we bloody do that?" Footy snapped. Dingo put a hand on his arm.

"Johnny has a point, mate. The colonel showed me his record. We'll give him first crack. You and me, we'll get our chance!" Footy frowned at Johnny, but let it go.

44

At dawn, the three took to their stakeout again and remained all day. High in his tree, Johnny sat close to the trunk, sitting on a branch. He'd rubbed mud on his face and undershirt. As usual, he'd tucked leaves through his helmet netting.

He sucked in breaths nearly as wet as rain. A bead of sweat trickled down his forehead and dripped to the end of his nose. It tickled, but he did not move. He knew to stay absolutely still.

Movement is the telltale. Many of his victims had made the fatal error of doing something that caught his eye.

The day dragged on and the hissing of the cicadas lulled him, but he would not drift off.

He was wedged so he would not fall, but he knew sleep was every soldier's Achilles' heel. Then even the most seasoned commando was as vulnerable as a baby.

Through years of practice, Johnny could slow his breathing and sit completely immobile for hours on end. In fact, this was his element.

He recalled last Saturday, less than a week ago, when Doc Mac had released him from the hospital. At that instant, the Philippines had seemed so close.

How did it all go wrong?

That question led him nowhere, so Johnny moved on to memories that he could ponder. It was a technique he'd perfected. The trick was to occupy his mind, while eyes and ears remained sharp. Sometimes he retold the story from a favorite book or movie. On other occasions, he called up an event from his life.

Johnny thought back to September of '42, his first days in New Guinea. He'd been seventeen, a green boy from California.

He'd shipped out of San Francisco with thousands of other soldiers of the 32nd Division. In Australia, they'd spent long days
tramping around the outback, apparently where the officers
thought the fighting would be.

And then there'd been an abrupt change of plan. The men
had been loaded into a ragtag fleet of aircraft and flown north
to New Guinea. In fact, it made sense: the Japs were already
here.

They landed in Moresby, and almost at once, the poorly prepared men were ordered to march. MacArthur's idea was simple and brutal: trek 130 miles over the KapaKapa Trail, cross
the Owen Stanley mountains, and engage the Japanese on the
north coast. The general badly underestimated the effect of brutal heat, rampant tropical diseases, and the nearly impossible
heights.

Within days, the trail reeked of sickness. Men jettisoned
tents, raincoats – later rifles and mortars – just to keep dragging their ravaged, starved bodies along. Fever and dysentery
sapped their morale, and their strength.

More than a month of desperate days crawled by. Johnny
hiked with his California buddy, a boy about his own age. Walt,
with his myopic eyes behind wire-rimmed glasses, was not doing well. He'd stopped making sense days ago, and Johnny's
own mind flashed with fever.

All the men were freezing by the time they scaled the 13,000
feet up "Ghost Mountain." The native porters were terrified of
this place, and one night, they all deserted. They simply
dropped their burdens and ran. The soldiers, already lacking
most of their gear, even guns, could not pick up the slack. They
moved on.

Walt needed Johnny's coaxing just to stumble down the far
slopes, back into the stinking jungle once more. Word came

down the line – after they had begun their ordeal, MacArthur had rounded up some ships. Thousands of GIs had been ferried around the island. Already, the word was, they were being slaughtered by the enemy near a place called Buna.

The next morning, the raving, skinny scarecrows of the 32nd, were marched to the front, right under the Japanese machine guns.

Johnny gripped Walt's shirt with one hand as he dragged him through black water. He moved to the edge of the pond, out of the line of sight of the Jap gunner. *Thump-thump-thump* it fired, and GIs fell and did not move again.

Johnny stepped as fast as he could. Slugs stitched his way. He saw a sergeant go down face-first. Johnny shoved Walt ahead of him, but another burst forced him to dive. He couldn't both help Walt and hold onto his M1 rifle. He dropped it underwater.

With both hands free, he hauled Walt up the bank, then behind a mangrove for cover. His stomach flipped when he saw a big crocodile eating there, first one he'd seen close up. It was munching on a soldier's corpse, body and uniform in fragments.

Johnny's first need was to rearm himself and he looked around. There, among his dead countrymen, he saw something that called to the hunter in him.

It was a rifle he knew intimately, a bolt-action Springfield 1903 equipped with a simple tube scope. His dad had possessed the twin of this, and Johnny had trained with it. He strode over, snatched it from dead hands, aimed at the croc, and shot it through the eye. It slammed back into the scrub. He took a moment to strip off the fallen soldier's ammo belt, strung it around his own waist, and withdrew the big blade that hung there.

He knew instantly what it was, a knife-style bayonet, the one Teddy Roosevelt had helped design.

Johnny fixed it to the muzzle of the gun. He'd left Walt standing in the clearing and now, armed again, he turned back.

A scream came from the jungle. Johnny whirled and saw an enemy soldier charge Walt, prong bayonet extended. Another first – a Jap at close range.

The man ran Walt through. The boy's glasses had been lost in the swamp, and all he could manage was to grab the enemy gun. The two did a macabre dance of death.

Johnny lunged with his new rifle and slashed the blade across the enemy neck. Two dead men crumpled together.

Rage burned steady now. Walt was beyond help, and he could hear the machine gun still firing at the GIs. There were a group of them behind him on the mudflat now, directionless. Johnny called for them to come with him and attack the gun. They stared like he was crazy.

"Better stay put and wait for orders," one said. There was a murmur of agreement. Johnny curled his lip and moved into the jungle. In short order, he was scrambling up a bank. At the top, he went on his belly and parted the foliage with his barrel.

He saw he'd flanked the machine gun trench. There was a three-man crew – the gunner, a man feeding metal bands of shells into it, and a third, stacking empties. He shot the gunner, then the other two in quick succession. There was sudden silence.

Johnny called over the swamp, it was now safe to come up. He didn't wait to see what happened. He moved deeper into the jungle, stepping over dead soldiers of both sides. He came to an area where a group of GIs was pinned down. Even as he watched, a sniper's bullet found yet another man. Across the yards, Johnny saw the light go out of his eyes.

Johnny took cover behind a log. *Look to the tree tops!* There was another shot and a scream. He saw the puff of smoke. Johnny searched with his scope and found the sniper hidden in the fronds of a tall palm. It was a good 150 yards, but this was not a long shot for the hunter.

He fired and a body dangled among the coconuts.

On his first day in battle, Johnny made five kills. Shooting men gave him a bad feeling in the pit of his gut, but he got used to it. Soon, seeing dead men, friend and foe, became normal.

And then it was humdrum.

Walt was long gone. All Johnny felt now was ice-cold anger. Yes, it was personal, but during his three years of war, he had come to understand the global picture. He did battle for his country, to win the desperate World War for freedom. It gave the brutal work a higher purpose.

The Springfield was his, and so was the job.

I am an ambush hunter, and I hunt men.

45

All these years later, and sniper Johnny waited in his tree beside the Raub River. His hands still cradled the rifle he had taken in that first gunfight.

You kill them before they kill you, the Hard Case told him.

Live to fight. Fight to live!

He blinked the sweat out of his eyes and scanned the terrain. He was thirsty but did nothing about it. He breathed softly through his nose and ignored the mosquito drilling his forehead.

I've been in a thousand firefights, he thought. *I've seen things a hundred times worse than I did that day. I wonder why Walt's death is so clear, and hundreds of others, I don't even recall?* He had no answer.

Then his mind buzzed back to Gwyn.

This is Friday and I have a date with her!

Of course, he was not going to make it.

Does she even know that we crash-landed?

The hypnotic sigh of the cicadas suddenly tapered off. All of Johnny's awareness came to focus.

Movement!

Towards the river, a bush shook, and then another.

Here they come!

The hunter looked through the scope and his finger went to the trigger. Through the crosshairs, he watched the foliage shudder. He made out brown patches through the greenery, and these resolved into men slinking through the trees.

They approached along a faint side trail. Adrenaline pumped through Johnny like an itch. He hoped Dingo and Footy were aware.

One by one, gazing warily around, four Japs stepped onto the broader path. Johnny willed them into the open. The soldiers were emaciated, he noted, uniforms in shreds and their feet bare. All held rifles, and two had canvas buckets hanging from the crooks of their arms.

The first man was short and squat, middle-aged, his face in a permanent scowl. His helmet was the typical Japanese type, but blackened. The sniper grinned inwardly.

He's been cooking in it! Fire made the metal brittle, useless to deflect a bullet.

The second man had a conical hat of woven reeds. The third wore a cap, and the last had a strip of cloth tied around his head.

Each is armed, and the one at the back also has a sword on his belt. Johnny was studying this one when the man whirled and stared in his direction.

He feels me looking at him. The sniper remained frozen. He'd observed this phenomenon many times. It was as if sight was not passive, but something that probed the world.

He dubbed this man, "Headband." The cloth had the faint image of a red sun on it. Johnny noted the sun-dark skin, the eyes in shadow.

The others continued walking away. In seconds, they'd be out of sight, over the riverbank. Johnny had his plan – he would shoot them front to back. That way, the fallen would block the trail, and the others would not know which way to go.

Helmet, Coolie, Cap, then Headband.

The three were already going up the bank. Headband jogged to catch up. Johnny centered the crosshairs on the first one. He aimed at the blackened helmet and squeezed. Helmet dropped in his tracks.

Johnny's eye found his next target while his fingers re-loaded. Coolie barely had time to flinch before Johnny squeezed again.

Chest shot. He reloaded.

The last two Japs went hyperactive. Cap leapt off the trail and crashed through the undergrowth. Headband jumped the corpses and raced for the river. A rifle coughed below.

A miss.

He stayed on plan, following the undulating shrubs. He could not see him, but he knew where the runner was.

He fired. The bush went still.

Then there was one.

Reloading, Johnny whip-panned to Headband and found him at the top of the bank. There was another clap from the Aussie rifle.

Another miss. The sniper's lip curled. But before he could shoot, the man disappeared down the far side.

Johnny hitched his rifle over his shoulder and climbed down fast. He saw Dingo run by, revolver in hand. On his heels was Footy with the rifle.

Johnny had to focus on his landing. When he looked toward the river again, the trail was empty. Johnny sprinted that way.

He heard shots as he ran – four, five of them.

He scrambled up the bank and froze.

Nothing in his life had prepared him for what was waiting beside the river.

46

Johnny took in the scene at a glance. Lying beside the river was a crocodile so enormous, he was stunned. In spite of what the priest's letter said, he had no idea it could be so gigantic. It looked long as a bus, dwarfing the three men along its flank.

The Father!

In the presence of their far more ancient foe, these had forgotten one another. The Jap, near the tail, shot with his rifle into the body. Footy, who had Dingo's rifle, fired at the flank. Dingo was beside the great head, revolver in one hand, Bowie knife in the other. He shot into the skull and a shudder shook the scaled body.

Even as the knowledge thrilled through Johnny, the crocodile turned and looked at him. The yellow eyes chilled with their predatory glare. He saw in hyper clarity that across one of them was a curve of puckered scales. He watched the skin fold on the neck as the head turned. The jaws were open and he took in the rows of long, stained teeth.

His hands brought up his rifle. He saw the ridged tail swing inland, but his focus remained on Dingo. The major was in terrible peril.

Dingo fired again as his feet backpedaled. But the Father was fast. The head turned sideways and the jaws slid around the man, taking him from chest to knees.

It crunched hard. Bones cracked. The air wheezed out of Dingo. The crocodile lifted the man as if he weighed nothing. Dingo's hat spun off and he dropped pistol and knife.

Time slowed. Johnny was still bringing the rifle to his shoulder when the tail struck the Jap. Man and rifle parted company. The firearm tumbled over the water and fell in. The enemy was thrown backwards, over the bank, and there came the crash of breaking branches.

The Father, Dingo drooping from its jaws, turned to the river. Its armored flank knocked Footy onto his back.

It had been mere seconds since Johnny arrived, and he had the crosshairs on the speckled eye. Dingo was right below that, between the jaws, but Johnny was an expert shot.

He squeezed the trigger just as the tail came to the end of its swing and bumped his legs. It was like being hit by a steel beam. Johnny flew sideways at the instant the bullet exploded from the muzzle.

The shot struck the crocodile's foreleg. The 150-grain slug ripped through scales and flesh, shattered bone, and tumbled on. The end of the Father's foot blew off. A gory mass of claws fell in the river.

The crocodile hissed in agony and swung its head to peer at its injury. It saw the shredded leg – and the creature standing behind it. A spear of pain ripped through its brain as it stared at the helmeted man.

The image seared into its mind – the ruined leg and the Smooth-headed man. Anguish welded the two together.

The Father sucked in a breath. The unique body scent of its torturer became part of the transfixed moment.

Johnny reloaded. The crocodile heard the metallic clicks and fear boiled through its suffering. For a moment the reptile vacillated, caught in the warring urges to attack or escape.

Then the prey between its teeth heaved and groaned.

Dingo is still alive! Johnny thought in horror.

The Father rushed into the water. As its body turned, the ridged tail swung again and Johnny barely managed to jump over it.

Footy rolled frantically to escape being crushed under the belly. A back leg as big as he was thudded down beside his head, webbed claws spread.

Johnny found his balance and fired from the hip. The bullet carved a groove up the scaled back. Then the reptile was submerged – a wavering darkness in the flow, moving fast.

Footy leaned back on his hands, blinking in the mud. Again Johnny reloaded, but there was nothing left to shoot.

"Bloody, bleedin', ruddy hell!" Footy moaned.

Johnny was first to come to his senses.

"It's over! Get Dingo's things. Let's go!"

He spun in search of the Jap.

47

Johnny climbed the riverbank and followed the broken shrubbery. He found the foe sprawled on his back. The Jap had banged his head and was just coming around. Johnny loomed over and put the barrel of the Springfield hard against his chest.

"Get up!"

The man climbed woozily to his feet. His shirt had no buttons, his trousers were rags, and he was barefoot. He'd lost his rifle, thanks to the croc, but he did have the sword in its wooden scabbard on his rope belt. Footy came up beside Johnny. He had Dingo's hat on, big knife through his belt, and was carrying the pistol and .303 rifle.

"Put your hands up!" Johnny told Headband. He indicated what he wanted with his free hand and the Jap slowly raised his arms.

"Get that sword off him," Johnny told Footy. He aimed at the Jap while Footy sidled towards him.

"Don't get between us," Johnny warned. The pilot nodded, tugged the loop on the man's rope belt, drew the scabbard off, and stepped away.

Footy pulled the blade out and held it to the sun. The men saw a curve of gleaming steel. A wavy line ran behind the cutting edge the entire length of the blade. It had a silver hilt and pommel, and the handle was ornately wrapped, if faded and worn.

"I'll be a platypus's second cousin!" Footy exclaimed. "This is an old one! Proper Samurai antique I reckon – not the usual factory rubbish. I claim it – it's mine."

"Take it," Johnny said. "Okay, you, Jap, you can put your hands down." He watched closely to see what would happen. The man's pants were sliding down and he made a grab for them. He re-tied the rope-belt, while he kept wary eyes on the helmeted soldier.

He could tell by the accent the man was a Yankee. He observed those cold eyes and knew in his bones, this was the one who had just murdered his countrymen. It came to him that his own life hung by a thread.

Yes! The thought went through him. *Kill me!* The shame of being captured was unbearable.

After all these terrible years – this! He felt the urge to rush the man. Of course he would be shot, but then he would be free of this shame and torment.

But that is suicide and I cannot do it. My religion forbids it! So I will live and watch. When I get the chance, I will kill these enemies – even if I die trying.

"You speak English?" Johnny asked. The captive stared back and said nothing.

"Jap, you want to try to run, do it now. Otherwise, you're my prisoner. Even twitch the wrong way," Johnny told him, "and I'll kill you." He nodded at Footy. "He will too – you can count on it.

"So what's it going to be?"

"Give it up, mate! The bloody fool doesn't understand a word!" Footy said. "Why waste your breath?" Johnny shrugged, eyes fixed on the enemy.

"Let's go." Johnny pointed with his rifle and the prisoner rose to his feet. He staggered, still dizzy, then pushed through the foliage. He put a hand to the angry knot rising on his head and looked at the blood on his fingers. Johnny came close behind, rifle barrel to the Jap's back. Footy followed, pistol in his belt, sword and rifle in his hands.

They approached two bodies in a heap on the trail. The captive glanced down at the older man whose helmet had a hole in it, and the other with the woven hat. His face betrayed nothing as he stepped over.

They went by the place where the third corpse sprawled in the undergrowth. Johnny drove the prisoner that way and they looked. The enemy had been shot through the chest. Footy joined them and realized that Johnny had made the shot blind. He was impressed with the Yank, in spite of himself.

At camp, Johnny cut a few feet of his rope and tied the prisoner's hands behind his back. He forced the man to sit against a tree and lashed him to it. Johnny was the son of a Navy man, and he'd been taught all the sailing knots at an early age. He could tie a dozen types before most boys could get their shoelaces in a bow. In short order, he had the prisoner trussed so that escape was impossible.

For the first time since they'd come to Kissim, the men cooked a hot meal and brewed a pot of coffee. No need to be careful about noise or a campfire now! They tucked into plates piled with beef stew, mopped up with chunks of bread.

Johnny was deeply disturbed by Dingo's killing, but he'd seen too much during the war to allow it to affect his judgment.

175

He was encouraged by their triumph against the enemy, and both awestruck and fascinated by the colossal croc.

He and Footy talked over the death of the major. The pilot was distraught about the loss of his mate, with whom he'd shared so many battles and good times over the years. It was dawning on both of them that Dingo's demise could be their own death sentence. After all, the major had been the only one who had seen the Raub all the way to the coast, who knew something of the tribes, and had at least a nodding acquaintance with the languages.

Johnny saw Footy's hands tremble as he lit a cigarette. He realized he was quivering as well – it had been a lot to go through for someone just out of hospital!

He poured the rest of the coffee in their mugs and raised his own.

"Here's to the major," Johnny said.

"Right, mate. To Dingo – a bloody good bloke and the best of mates. Blast that friggin' lizard to hell!"

They raised their mugs and drank, then talked things over. Operation Teeth had taken a truly bizarre twist. Their leader was dead – killed by the beast they had been told to avoid. Now they were on their own, short of supplies, deep in uncharted territory.

"The priest warned about that croc," Johnny said. "He said it was huge, but I didn't have any idea!"

"Struth! That's the bloody Father for shore," Footy exclaimed.

"For sure," Johnny agreed. "Did you see the scar on its eye?"

"Yes mate! I've seen salties in Queensland, but never one

like that! Blimey! The biggest I ever saw was half its bleedin' size, and that was a brute!"

"So much for staying away from the river," Johnny said.

Footy noticed the prisoner's eyes on him.

"You – Jap!" he called. "What the bloody hell you looking at?" He turned to Johnny. "Think the bugger understands what we're saying?"

"Maybe," Johnny said. "Some of the ones we captured said they learned English at school. A lot more than we learned their language, that's for sure! But what does it matter?" He shrugged.

"We're all in the same boat now."

They continued to mull over their options. The upshot was, they would wait in Kissim for three more days. If no aircraft showed up, they'd move on. Thanks to Johnny's foresight, they had food for that time and a little longer, but they both agreed, they would not sit in Kissim and starve to death.

"This is Friday," Johnny said. "If no rescue comes by Monday, we go. Our only hope is to follow the river to the coast. There, at least we'll have a fighting chance. On the ocean, we'll be able to signal a passing plane or ship."

"I see your point," Footy said, "but you've forgotten something. What about the bloody 'Valley of the Cannibals' poor Dingo went on about?"

"The Mambu," Johnny muttered. "The priests were afraid of them."

"We could try another route," Footy said. "Didn't the letter say the Japs came through the mountains further up?"

"Too risky, and they had guides. Plus, no one will even think of looking for us in that direction.

"The Raub is our best bet. No rescue by Monday, and we follow it to the coast."

Johnny saw that the prisoner seemed to be listening.

48

Johnny and Footy left the P-O-W tied to the tree and went to see if they could find anything to salvage from the Kissim gardens. As soon as they were out of sight, the captive struggled furiously in his bonds, but made no headway.

The Yankee is too good with a rope!

Johnny and Footy went through the dugout vegetable mounds, but did not turn up even one bug-eaten yam. They were surprised not to see a single native.

Footy wanted to take another look at the airstrip. He was preoccupied by the thought that the wreck of his aircraft compromised any rescuers' ability to land.

They passed through the burned-out village and approached the *kunai* strip. There, they gazed at the blackened hulk of the Hudson, blocking the field.

"No bloody good," Footy said. "No plane can land, even if they find us."

"Worse," Johnny said. "If they see that, they're going to think we died in the crash."

"Crikey!" Footy said. "If we're here, of course, we can wave." The cloud cover had lifted a little. Johnny saw movement and stared up the mountain.

"Look! The villagers!" There were about forty men, women and children, strung along the trail hundreds of feet up.

"They're leaving," Footy said. At the end of the line, they made out the old man, leaning on the boy.

"Cooeeee!" the pilot called through cupped hands. The pair turned and the teenager pointed. The old man raised a hand in farewell, and they resumed toiling behind the others. Johnny and Footy watched until all were lost in the clouds.

"Nothing left for them here," Footy said.

"Just the Father," Johnny said.

The men returned to camp and found the prisoner where they'd left him. Johnny noticed again how starved he looked. He opened a can of baked beans, wiped his spoon on his shirt, and fed it to the man, who gulped it down. Johnny gave him some water from his canteen.

Footy sorted through the major's pack. *All I have is what Dingo brought. It has to do until we're rescued, or we make it to the coast. If we make it to the coast!*

The sheath and holster had gone with Dingo to his death, but at least Footy had the giant knife, the revolver and the rifle. In addition, there was Dingo's rucksack with ammunition, the bedroll, some clothing that would be big on the pilot, and the hat. That would be a blessing in the sun. The pilot's eyes watered and he turned his back.

The mood in camp was somber. Neither Johnny nor Footy said what they were thinking. In all likelihood, there was a perilous journey to come that they were unlikely to survive.

Now they had an added burden – the Jap. Neither said it, but both thought about doing away with him.

No one would ever know. In numerous battles in the jungle, with no ability to keep prisoners, soldiers on both sides had made that ruthless choice.

That night, Johnny and Footy divided the watch. It looked like they were alone in a deserted village, but they would take no chances. Johnny adjusted the prisoner's bonds so he could lie on the ground, hands lashed to the tree. It was not a comfortable arrangement, but as it turned out, the enemy was the only one to get a full night's sleep.

The next three days were long and dreary as the men waited. It rained a good deal of the time, a deluge that soaked everything and dampened their spirits.

There was no sign of an aircraft.

The following morning – Johnny was keeping track of the days and he reminded himself it was Tuesday – they broke camp and prepared to hike. He was already fed up spoon-feeding the captive. Footy made it scornfully clear he would not help. Johnny untied the prisoner's hands and told him to feed himself. He gave the man the same thing they had for breakfast, a plate of warm hash and the crust of their last loaf of bread. Footy glared daggers with every bite the prisoner took.

"We don't have enough food to go around, Johnny," he complained. "Now we've got to trek all the way down the bloody Raub with this Jap? You must be joking! I say we shoot him and be done with it. He's just one more that got shot, that's all we say – if we say anything."

"I hear you," Johnny said, "but I've never executed a man who surrendered."

"You don't mind shooting them in the back," Footy jeered. "I saw you do it!"

"That's different," Johnny said. "That is battle. This is a new situation. He's a prisoner of war. There are rules for P-O-W's that I've never broken."

"If you can't do it, I will," Footy said.

"Are you going to stop me?" He pulled Dingo's revolver, aimed it at the man's head, and cocked the hammer. The Japanese stared back at him.

"That's not right," Johnny said. "But I won't stop you, or report you later. Do it right now – or he comes with us."

He returned to roping his hammock onto his pack. Footy's arm was straight, finger on the trigger. The Japanese stared into the barrel of the gun and Footy got the strange feeling the bastard wanted the bullet. After a long moment, the Aussie scowled and dropped his arm.

"Sod me," he said. "I can't shoot an unarmed man!"

"We'll take him then," Johnny said. "Let's vamoose."

"And when we get to the bleedin' cannibals?" Footy asked. "No man's ever gone that way and – well, you know. And here we come, Jap and all!"

"We've got our guns," Johnny said, "and surprise will be on our side. Dingo said they've never even seen a white man in their valley? We'll march in like we own the joint, and bluff our way through."

"What – two men against a thousand bloody cannibals?" Footy wondered. He brightened.

"Perhaps we can trade the Jap – our lives for his."

"Could work," Johnny said.

"All right," Footy shrugged.

"But I don't like it. I don't like it at all."

49

Footy's mates gave it until Wednesday morning, but when there was still no sign of the "Miss Nippon These," they took the news to Australian HQ. Promptly, word was sent to the US Garrison.

When Colonel Chambers heard it, he got a sinking feeling. But he resolved to wait at least another day or two before he did anything precipitous.

Chambers told himself it would work out. *Dingo, Johnny, and the pilot – what was his name, Booty? – know the jungle better than anyone.*

New Guinea was notorious for abrupt weather changes. Many a pilot had been forced to put down and sit it out. Henry would bet, dollars to donuts, that Operation Teeth would show up.

But then, come Friday afternoon with no sign, Henry's alarm ballooned. His main concern was the safety of the men, of course, but he had not mentioned this spur-of-the-moment action to the brass in Australia. The colonel did not relish having to explain an unapproved operation gone wrong. Much better to bring it up once the thing had resolved itself, which he fully expected it would.

The problem was, he had no aircraft to send looking for them. The only planes that showed up in Port Moresby these days were privately owned, or under higher orders.

Gradually it dawned on the colonel that he had only a very sketchy idea of where Kissim was. Sure, Dingo had shown him on the map, but the major's fingertip could cover hundreds of miles.

How did I get tangled in this?

182

50

Friday afternoon, Gwyn showered, put on a summer dress she'd purchased in London, carefully pulled on her single pair of stockings – they were hard to come by with the war shortages – and slipped on shoes. She dabbed a little "Evening in Paris" on her throat and behind her ears. It had been a gift from her mother and she used it sparingly. Ruthie came home, changed, and headed out to meet her boyfriend. 6 o'clock turned into 8:00, and still no Johnny.

By then, Gwyn knew he wasn't coming. But still she waited.

At midnight, as she stripped off her dress and washed her face, she found herself absolutely fed up – not just with Johnny, but with herself.

Once again, she'd gone out on a limb for a military man!

Gwyn blew out the lantern and lay on her bed, but sleep would not come. She was still awake when she heard her friend let herself in at 2 a.m.

At 8 o'clock Saturday morning, Gwyn roused a sleepy Ruthie, cajoled her into throwing on some clothes, gave her a cup of strong tea, and dragged her out the door. Thirty minutes later, they were at US Army Headquarters.

Gwyn demanded of the sergeant at the desk that she be allowed to see the commander, at once. Chambers had them shown in. They found the colonel behind a desk stacked with papers, file boxes all around. He greeted them cordially enough and showed them to the sofas.

Yes, Operation Teeth was overdue – there was no question. But the men involved were more than competent. Did anything in New Guinea ever happen on time? Chambers chuckled, and assured the women that he was personally on top of this one.

Soon he would send another aircraft to reconnoiter the location. In the meantime, he expected them – *fully* expected them – to show up at any minute! The nurses should not be overly worried.

His aides came in carrying more papers for his signature.

"The burdens of command," the colonel sighed. He stood and escorted the young women to the front entrance and had his driver take them home.

"It will turn out fine," he called as the jeep was about to leave. "Then we'll wonder what the fuss was about! I don't depart for Australia for another week. I expect we'll have our happy ending long before that."

Still unhappy, Gwyn and Ruthie departed. Only then did the colonel admit to himself how concerned he was.

The minute his vehicle returned, he had it take him to Australian HQ. There he corralled Dingo's Number Two and went over the situation. They agreed they would both do everything they could to find another plane to send to the Raub.

"But don't fret yet, Colonel," the Australian said. "No one's better in the bush than the major. I'd like to see the thing that Dingo can't handle!"

With all Henry had to do, the intervening days passed in a whirlwind. He had his feelers out, but it wasn't until the following Wednesday that a suitable aircraft arrived – a privately owned DC-3 on a freight run from Cairns.

By then, the colonel knew something was very wrong. He drove to the airport and stuck his neck out by commandeering the craft. As it turned out, the pilot was sympathetic: Footy Carmichael was a mate. He would, of course, need a formal requisition for his bosses back in Aus.

"There will be an account to pay," he warned.

"But then, you Yanks are made of money!"

The colonel snorted. This was a common misconception among the Australians. They had no idea about the bean counters who combed through his expense reports. But he agreed to everything. What choice did he have?

At first light the following morning, the DC-3 lifted off. On board were three of Dingo's most experienced patrol officers. None of them had been up the Raub overland – who had? But as it developed, the point was moot. The entire region was smothered in clouds. The aircraft circled as long as fuel held, and returned to Port Moresby.

Colonel Chambers had a truck standing by to bring the rescued men to his office, but it was only the pilot and Australian officers who turned up. Henry told the aviator he would not force him to stay, but the US Army would count it a great favor if he would make arrangements.

"Talk to your owners and tell them this is a life-and-death situation." The colonel gave the man the run of his own radio room.

The pilot was able to get through and shortly had his answer. He could stay on for another two days, but no more. After that, contracts would be broken and the cost would become prohibitive. He quoted a figure that gave Henry heartburn.

Still, the colonel cabled his superiors and requested authorization for the unusual expenditure. Within the hour, the general himself was on the radio from Brisbane, demanding a conversation. The price for two additional days of aircraft charter would be covered, Henry was informed, but that was the limit. As it was, he would be called on the carpet when he landed in Australia. He would be expected to give a full account of what the general now referred to as "the incident."

What's the worst they can do, Henry sniffed, *fire me?* Of course, he would do everything he could for the men of Operation Teeth, and take the consequences. But Saturday, come hell or high water, he and his aides would be on that flight to Australia, and then, on to the States.

If he was anything, he was Army to the core, and orders were orders.

Friday morning, Henry pushed everything aside and joined the men aboard the DC-3 for its final run. Operation Teeth was a full week overdue. This time, the weather cooperated. The pilot was able to dodge the clouds and locate the headwaters of the Raub River. Flying visual, the aviator followed the stream. At last, running close to the halfway mark on fuel, they passed over a burned village.

The patrol officers agreed, it had to be Kissim.

But their relief was soon dashed. They circled the burned bomber on the airstrip.

"That's Footy's Folly, for shore," the pilot shouted.

The Hudson must have crashed on landing. One wing wrapped around a rock, and everything was twisted and burned. The chances were slim or nil that anyone survived the impact and the fire. The DC-3 could not land with the wreck in the way. The pilot was getting concerned about fuel, but Henry insisted he make a few more passes. The observers craned through the windows, but saw not a soul – not even an animal. At last, the pilot shook his head, climbed through the clouds, and set course for Port Moresby.

It was a somber flight home.

51

It was Friday afternoon when the colonel got back to his office. He glanced around and saw a room that was anonymous once more. His personal things, including the Japanese dagger that had been a gift from the men when he got here, were already packed.

Soon Henry would leave HQ for the last time.

He and his aides had a final task. They went through the short stack of the most important papers Chambers had prepared for his successor.

Colonel Waters would arrive on Monday and these would be the first issues to deal with. Henry lifted the sheet off the top – his report on Operation Teeth. He hand-wrote a few sentences summarizing the day's events, put it back on the pile and that was that.

He asked his men to give him a moment alone. One final time, he went to the window and gazed across the Port Moresby harbor. Then he exited the office and pulled the door shut.

It took another half hour to say goodbye to the staff. By now, he should be in his quarters. At his house, his suitcases stood ready beside a stack of trunks and crates. He had put together a collection of tribal artifacts, the lids nailed down over longbows and assorted arrows, stone axes, and some fine carved spirit masks. The most prized item was a real headhunter skull that Dingo had given him.

This evening, the officers had scheduled a farewell drink and send-off at the club. *Dingo should be there,* Henry thought. *But there's no use dwelling on that!* He had hoped to enjoy his last night in New Guinea, but first, there was a chore he did not want to delegate.

He drove himself to the hospital, got directions to the Canadian nurse's house, and continued. As it happened, he caught both Gwyn and Ruthie at home. The colonel accepted a seat at the kitchen table, declined the offer of refreshment, and launched in.

"I'm sorry to be the one to tell you," he said, and Gwyn got a bad feeling of déjà vu. "Just this afternoon, I have listed Major Dingo Hawsey, Sergeant John Willman, and their pilot, Glen Carmichael, as M.I.A."

"Missing?" Gwyn's hand went to her throat.

"Is it true?" Ruthie chimed in.

"Unfortunately, yes," the colonel said. "Today I personally flew with Dingo's men to Kissim. I saw their landing site. I hate to tell you that their plane was wrecked. There had been a fire. We flew over several times and saw no sign of survivors. I am sorry to bring you bad news." The women's faces blanched and he soldiered on.

"I must leave first thing tomorrow – orders. But we're not giving up! Dingo, Johnny and – ahh..."

"Footy," Gwyn snapped.

"Footy, yes," the colonel said. "It is possible – no, likely – they are alive," he said in a hearty tone he did not feel. "If anyone can survive New Guinea, it is those three.

"The effort to locate them will continue. I have prepared a report for my replacement. I gave your name, Gwyn, and asked him to contact you, or Doc MacClure at the hospital, the minute we have news."

The colonel glanced at his watch and stood.

"I'm afraid I must go." He shook hands with the women and departed.

There's still time for dinner and a drink at the club — I owe that to the fellows who have served me so well.

Sharp at 7-hundred hours the following morning, the colonel and his retinue boarded their military transport, and soon were airborne, on the first leg of the long journey back to the States.

That same morning, Gwyn packed the last of her things in her steamer trunk and moved to the Good Shepherd. The day had come at last. Before she was out the door, Ruthie's boyfriend arrived. He helped load the trunk into Doc Mac's sedan. The physician had volunteered to drive her over.

Gwyn gave Ruthie a hug and both wiped away a tear. They would see each other nearly every day at the hospital, of course, and they would visit, but it was the end of something that had begun two years ago in London.

Doc drove some minutes and turned into the driveway of the ramshackled house. As the car crunched up the gravel, a group of waiting children scampered eagerly alongside.

Auntie Gwyn had come to stay!

Once her trunk was in her room, she left the orphans under Doc Mac's care. While Gwyn unpacked, he took the opportunity to check their teeth, peer into their ears, and dress minor scrapes.

Doc Mac stayed for a lunch of cucumber sandwiches and lemonade, served on the lawn. Once he departed, Gwyn found herself with all of Saturday afternoon stretched out. She had nervous energy to burn, and she threw herself into the endless tasks required to care for a large house and sixteen children.

They spent the afternoon tidying the place, and there was time for a game of "rounders" in the yard, played with a tennis racquet and ball, and five bases.

Women of the native staff had been busy all day in the laundry house, working the gasoline-powered washing machine. There were rows of sheets and children's clothing billowing on the lines. The young ones' best set of clothes would be laid out for church tomorrow. Afterwards, Gwyn had promised an afternoon in the country, and a rare treat – ice-cream cones from a shop.

In fact, she was already looking for a new and more permanent location for her orphanage. The drive would provide a chance to explore. The house she had was on loan and wouldn't do forever. She might even build something: she did have her inheritance from the sale of her parents' house back in Canada. She had started to think about moving out of town, preferably on the coast – somewhere safe where children could play outdoors. She wanted to see the nearby village where two of the women working for her came from.

Come Monday, she'd be back at the hospital, and on it would go. She could fill every minute of her time, and still have more to do.

But as the hours grew into a day, and then another, underneath all the business was a growing level of anxiety.

Where were Johnny, Footy and Dingo? She did not want to contemplate it, but she must.

Are they even alive?

52

Monday morning at the US Garrison, Hala entered the corner office. There was a lot of excitement about a new boss-man arriving! She brought a broom to make a final sweep, as she'd been instructed.

The old boss with all the rules was *gone-finish,* and the men of the garrison did not seem to mind when she forgot her one and only T-shirt. She despised the constriction, and could not begin to comprehend the terrible harnesses the white women bound themselves with. A woman's *susu* should be as Papa-God made them – free!

Hala had been taught how to turn on the overhead fan, although the lesson was short. The room was closed up and stifling. She turned the dial. A breeze stirred the air and Hala began to whisk the floor. But the blades spun faster and faster and began to howl. The wind sent the stacked papers flying.

The young woman watched in dismay. She might lose her job, and then there would be no precious money to send home! Hala was terrified of being yelled at by these foreign men. She rushed to the control knob and turned it off. The typhoon subsided – but papers were everywhere. She froze in panic.

What would a white man do? The answer came and a smile lit Hala's pretty face. She dropped her broom and gathered the errant sheets to her chest. She went to the cabinets where she had seen the men put these things, and yanked open drawer after drawer. They were full! She went on. Finally, she found one half-empty, spilled everything in, and slammed it shut.

There, she thought with satisfaction. The room was tidy again. Her heart slowed to its normal rate.

She returned to her broom while she hummed her happy song.

53

Three men walked the path beside the river. Johnny wore his pack, helmet back on his neck, and rifle over his shoulder on the strap. The Jap came next, bound hands behind him. Then there was Footy, Dingo's hat and pack on, the Samurai sword waving from the top. He carried the Lee Enfield over a shoulder, the revolver and knife through his belt.

The first half-day's walk out of Kissim took them beside the village cemetery, and then along a defined trail. But by mid-afternoon, they had entered less traveled territory. The jungle had reclaimed entire sections of the footpath, and Johnny had to shoulder aside vines and slash with his machete. Mosquitoes whined in clouds.

Johnny remembered that Father Bastion's letter said the Mambu headhunters had not ventured this far upriver during the years the priests resided in Kissim. But battle experience told Johnny: *trust nothing*. Warriors could be mere feet away, hidden in the bush. There could even be armed Japanese.

They were in uncharted territory and anything could happen.

There were deadly creatures as well, like the Death Adder. Its bite was fatal. Once its fangs broke skin, a man lived just long enough to know what had killed him.

To his growing irritation, Footy's view was the prisoner's back. With his hands tied, the enemy could not ward off the canes that whipped back from Johnny's passage. The Aussie took some satisfaction in seeing the man take a beating.

At one point, a writhing centipede dropped on the prisoner's head. The Jap exclaimed and twitched it off, and Footy crunched it under a sandal.

The bugger was lucky that time. The sting of the jungle

192

centipede would put a man in agony for hours.

Footy's shoulders hurt from the pack and he hitched it up. The sword rattled, and inside the pack, the end poked his hip. He resented the weight – *but it's a real Jap sword and I will have it!*

At midday, the men came to an open place in the forest. A betel-nut palm grew there, branches loaded with lime-size nuts. Clear water pooled near the roots.

"Watch the Jap," Johnny told the pilot. He knelt, washed his face, and brought up a handful of water to taste. It was sweet and he drank his fill. He took the canteens off his belt, spilled out the dregs and refilled them. Then he made way for Footy, who drank deeply and replenished the bottle that had been Dingo's. He soaked the hat in the water, put it back on, and stood up. Johnny spoke to the Asian.

"Drink."

The prisoner sank on his haunches. He extended his bound hands behind him and looked at the American. Johnny did nothing, so the man put his face to the water and sucked. He choked and reared back. Again, he stared at the Yankee and thrust out his hands. Johnny sighed.

"Untie him," he told Footy, "I'll cover you." Footy sniffed. *Who does the bleedin' Yank think he's giving orders to?* But he did it. The P-O-W rubbed his chafed wrists, cupped his hands and drank. He splashed water over his face, pulled the soiled headband off, rinsed it and tied it back on.

Then, with a quick glance at the others, he stripped off his ragged shirt and splashed water on his chest and underarms. Footy grew impatient.

"Here!" he called. "What's this, the bloody Cairns Hotel? We haven't got all bloody day!"

The Jap held his shirt in one hand and pinched his nose with the other. Johnny laughed and even Footy snorted.

"True," the Aussie said, "you are number-one stinky!"

Johnny dug the bar of soap out of his pack and handed it over. The prisoner soaped up his head and body, scrubbed and rinsed his shirt and struggled back into it.

"Tie his hands," Johnny told Footy.

"You do it, mate," Footy replied, picking up his rifle and aiming at the captive. "I've seen your knots."

The Jap put his wrists in front together and held them out.

"Half a mo' – behind your back!" Footy called, but the captive stared at the Yankee.

"Why not," Johnny gave in. He tied the rope.

"What are you doing?" Footy protested.

"If he tries anything, shoot him," Johnny said. "Let's march."

"Who made you bloody king of the bush?" Footy muttered as Johnny strode off. It did go easier for the captive now, with his arms up against the foliage.

Late in the afternoon, the pilot called for a rest.

"Oy, hold up, mate. I'm tuckered. Ciggy break?"

Johnny leaned back, pack against a tree, took the box from his pocket and lit two. He handed one to the Aussie. When he'd smoked his down, Johnny threw the butt on the ground. He would have stamped on it, but the captive scooped it up and took a few quick drags.

Johnny chuckled. He took a slug from his canteen and offered it to the P-O-W. The man accepted with bound hands and drank.

"Okay," Johnny told him. "If you're going to drink, you're going to carry." He took off his second canteen and hooked it on the man's belt. They hiked on.

Sunset came and the trail grew dim. The river ran beside them through a series of rapids, mist cooling the air. While night fell, they made camp. The crocodile was on their minds, and Johnny picked a place fifty yards from the water. He made the prisoner lie down by a tree and once again, tied his hands and ankles and roped him to the trunk. He hung his hammock while Footy spread his blanket. Over dinner of canned hotdogs, green beans, and potatoes, the pilot said they must have already descended a thousand feet in altitude.

Again, the two took turns on watch while the captive slept. In the morning, Johnny opened cans of stew and warmed them on the kerosene stove. He opened peach slices and distributed the food on three plates. Afterwards Footy gathered the dishes and went to the river. He studied it apprehensively as he approached. He picked up stones and threw them here and there in the shallows. When he was sure no big predator lay in wait, he washed up.

They hit the trail again. Sometimes the path disappeared entirely and Johnny had to cut a way through.

We can't go too wrong, he thought, *as long as we keep the river in sight.*

But not too close!

Not with the Father out there.

54

Two more days passed as the men trekked out of the mountains. The Raub River alternated between frothing rapids and stretches of fast water that tumbled from the high country toward the plains.

To his surprise, Johnny was coming to enjoy the journey. His legs were getting stronger and his chest hurt less each day. It was tough eating everything from cans. He craved fresh meat and greens, but it was sweet to be done with the endless days in bed.

At times, a pack strap pressed his scar and made it ache. Then he grasped the straps in his hands and gave his shoulders a rest.

He distracted himself by looking at the countryside. This was pristine wilderness, and spectacular Birds of Paradise and flocks of parrots brought the jungle alive.

Orchids and giant fungi grew on fallen trees. The insects were legion. There were butterflies in rainbow colors and beetles with great horned heads. He saw a Walking Stick on a branch, eighteen-inches long.

On the afternoon of the third day out of Kissim, the men's spirits soared when they heard an unmistakable hum.

"A plane!" Johnny shouted.

"DC-3, I swear," Footy called.

They raced to the river with the prisoner in tow. They stared up, straining to be the first to see the silver flash that heralded their rescue. But the rumble became a drone, and then it faded altogether. Still the men waited, staring anxiously skyward.

"Let's face it. It's gone," Johnny said.

Footy let loose a flamboyant string of words. He threw himself down and put his head in his hands. Even the prisoner slumped on a boulder.

"Let's just camp here," Footy muttered.

"You want to cuddle up to that croc?"

"Aww yeah," the pilot muttered. "Let's move off – much farther off!"

For dinner, they had more canned food. Afterwards, they smoked. When he was down to an inch of unfiltered Camel, Johnny handed it to the prisoner. The man sucked it greedily until he scorched his fingers.

"Johnny, you've gone soft, mate!" Footy scoffed. "Do you forget, we're at war?"

"I never forget," Johnny said.

They did an inventory of their remaining food. The bread was gone, and they had enough hard biscuits for one more day. There was half a bag of ground coffee, but no powdered milk, and no sugar. They had a single can of corned beef, another of baked beans and two more stews. There were two cans of fruit, and that was it.

"It's enough for one more day – two, if we go a little hungry," Johnny said.

"I'm already starved. We have to find some gardens," Footy said.

"Sure," Johnny agreed. "But gardens mean natives – and you know the rest."

"Bleedin' Valley of the ruddy Cannibals, mate," Footy nodded. "Big bloody problem."

Johnny tied the captive for the night, then wandered back to the river to spend a little time on his own. He sat – not too close – staring at the hypnotic flow. Again, he thought about Gwyn.

She probably thinks I'm dead. He pictured himself surprising her.

I'm back! He'd take her in his arms and kiss her on the lips.

Where did that come from?

What a crock, the Hard Case jeered. *Have you got the fever? Think about getting off this river and on to Japan!*

Besides, she doesn't even like you.

Oh yeah? Something in Johnny rebelled. *Then why did she want to have dinner with me?*

The retort came at once. *Forget it! Find the enemy – make him pay!*

Johnny sighed and turned his thoughts toward General MacArthur.

I figure it is the first of August already! Has my unit left for Japan without me? He was flooded with urgency.

If this three-day mission had gone right, I'd be on a ship to Manila!

Something splashed out on the river and Johnny's heart thumped. In the deepening twilight, the surface heaved. A whirlpool spun out there, and something heavy moved in it.

Johnny jumped to his feet. But then a leafy branch splashed up and he realized there was a fallen tree in the spiral.

Where's that monster croc right now? He'd seen death-by-crocodile a number of times in New Guinea.

Once, he and his squad were fording a swamp. The GI beside him was dragged under. One second he was there, the next, nothing but bubbles and blood on the surface.

That time, death came fast. But the Father took Dingo on land, and Johnny figured the major must have known what was happening.

Eaten alive! Johnny shivered. Again, the man saw the stare the crocodile gave him after he shot its leg.

I hope it bleeds to death!

But don't count on it, the Hard Case warned. *Do not count on that!*

Night was coming on. He went back to camp, made sure the prisoner's bonds were secure, and strung his hammock. In pitch black now, he sat on a fallen log for the first watch. Footy rolled in his blanket and was snoring in seconds. The prisoner snuffled as well. Pretty soon, they had a frog duet going.

Johnny let them sleep.

55

On the fifth morning since Kissim, they found evidence that the Valley of the Cannibals could not be far away.

They had descended out of the high mountains into the foothills and the river was a hundred yards across now. They had a quick breakfast and returned to the trail. By mid-morning, they knew that thousands of natives had gone this way. The footpath was worn smooth and lined with crimson.

Spit from the mouths of cannibals!

Johnny cautioned the others to keep quiet and he and Footy walked with rifles ready.

By the afternoon, the cliffs towered overhead and they realized they were entering the river gorge. Late in the day their trail dead-ended into an even wider path. Johnny held up a hand and the others stopped. The new trail was more than a yard across, packed hard by the passage of countless feet.

Rifle at his shoulder, Johnny stepped out and whirled each way. No one. He waved the others forward.

"Bloody *kanaka* highway!" Footy whispered. Johnny nodded and continued downriver. The rosy light of sunset spilled through the woods. He quickened his pace. Danger was all around, and they had to find a hiding place for the night.

Twilight came on. Ahead, the trees thinned out. Johnny led the way off the path into the undergrowth. He put a finger to his lips and motioned the others to get down. On his belly, he crawled the last few feet. He parted the vegetation and gazed out.

Spread before him was the Valley of the Cannibals. Hundreds of natives moved across the landscape. He was looking down a grassy slope to the river, sixty yards off. Stretching away was a long canyon between steep mountain flanks, the river cutting through rougher terrain on the far side.

Everywhere were the people of the Mambu nation. Warriors stood in groups. Women were leaving the gardens. Hundreds congregated on the footpaths, presumably returning to the villages for the night.

There are thousands of them!

Back in Kissim, Johnny had been certain that following the Raub was their best hope. But now he was full of doubt. He motioned Footy and the Jap forward and they surveyed the valley. The river flowed wide on the far side, and all the land between was garden plots. These ended abruptly at the nearby craggy border, thick with jungle.

What did Dingo say? "Impossible to pass through the mountains."

Johnny counted five villages along the valley, each under a pall of smoke. The largest was near the end of the canyon, where the peaks closed together again.

Footy gave his arm an urgent squeeze and Johnny looked where he pointed. A squad of warriors was coming towards them along the edge of the forest. Johnny counted eleven men, armed with bows and clubs. They were naked except for the long gourds over their genitals.

Border patrol!

The warriors stared all around with keen eyes. The three in the foliage froze in place. The patrol passed within thirty feet and continued towards the river. Johnny's group remained prone behind the trees while the sky turned dusky and faded to charcoal. They did not move until the first stars flickered over the peaks.

They worked their way backwards until they could stand. Johnny led them into thick scrub.

"We sleep here. No stove."

"Not even a ciggy," Footy whispered. Johnny untied the prisoner's hands. Footy opened a can of beans and another of stew and the two men ate this cold, leaving some in the bottom for the captive. They remained hungry, but all they had left was one can of fruit cocktail, and that would be their breakfast.

Not only do we have to get through this place, but we're going to have to beg or steal food from the cannibals! It seemed impossible and Johnny pushed the thought out of his mind.

He tied the Jap for the night. He would not string his hammock – he'd sleep on the ground. *We may need to be up in an instant, fighting for our lives.*

It was Footy's turn to take first watch.

"The valley is huge," Johnny whispered as he lay down in the dark. "Five villages and thousands of cannibals. It will probably take all day to cross."

"*If* we get across," Footy said. "Dingo said no one's ever..."

"Yeah, yeah," Johnny interrupted. "At least we've got surprise going for us. We'll march straight through. If we have to, we'll shoot the ringleaders and run for it."

"And that's your plan?" Footy complained.

Johnny didn't reply. Footy sat with his guns ready. The captive fell asleep and Johnny envied him. He just couldn't get there. He knew he needed a clear head for the day to come. He kept his eyes shut, but the minutes lumbered by.

At long last he drifted off – only to be shaken.

It was time for his watch.

56

A mile away, a Mambu sentry stared at the river. Every night, the warriors guarded each end of the valley. These were the vulnerable points through which any enemy must enter. Once more tonight, he did his duty.

The *Mambu-Ato* had issued his orders, and his elite guards came by regularly to ensure they were followed.

Twice a day, he and his kinsmen patrolled the perimeter of their territory. Every night, they watched the river. If a sentry fell asleep and the chief's guards found him, he would pay with his life.

The warrior stimulated himself with *buai*. His uncles, brothers and cousins slept beside him. It was shaping up to be another quiet night, but these were unusual times.

And then, far out on the face of the river, something moved!

The sentry leapt to his feet and stared. It was difficult to see by starlight, but something huge disturbed the current! He roused his kinsmen.

Then all of them saw it: a monstrous, living shape broke surface. This was no enemy canoe, and far too big for the usual *pukpuk*. Strong magic stirred the river! The men were terrified of the spirit world, and there had been alarming signs in recent times.

Come morning, they must journey to the war chief's village and report.

Three moons ago, an elder-woman had seen the dark river god in her dreams. Her familiar spirits awakened her and led her through the sleeping nation. There on the riverbank, beneath the face of the full moon, she witnessed a portentous event.

When it was over, she scurried to the war chief's *Haus Tambaran* and roused the guards. While she waited outside, they woke the *Mambu-Ato*. Respected as the elder was, if she had dared to set foot in the realm of the warriors, she would have been cut down. As it was, her life was at stake. The chief was notoriously cranky when his sleep was disturbed.

His advisors spilled out of the house like angry ants, carrying the wooden chair from which Bumay held court. Its back was a carved arch of crocodiles that reached up, snouts touching at the top.

The sorcerers and warriors arranged themselves by rank around it. At last Chief Bumay, the *Mambu-Ato* himself, came out yawning and threw himself in his seat. He was a powerfully built young man, sulky and half awake. He adjusted the gourd that pinched a testicle, raised his leg and scratched a bite. He called for *buai* and began to chew.

One of Bumay's brothers, a thickset older man with a raspy voice, commanded the crone to speak. How dare she disturb the warriors? Bumay squirted spittle on the ground and stared at her.

The woman spoke: the Papa of the *pukpuk* had come to the nation once more. For many years, it had not been seen. But on this night, the Father of the Crocodiles cruised by, going up-river.

It was the *Mambu-matu* itself.

The Chief was wide-awake now, his petulance forgotten in the face of stupendous news.

"What is your advice?" he asked his sorcerers. They replied, human sacrifices must be made to the Father. If not, the dark power would consume the Mambu people. The Father was not like other crocodiles. For one, it was the biggest ever seen and it had come and gone as it pleased as long as anyone remembered. When this one burst from the water, even if they had a chance to run, it was faster than they were. They knew from the past, when the Father was in their stretch of the river, it would feed on the people at will – until they worked the magic to send it away.

Bumay's shamans were in agreement. Human prisoners were needed for the first round of river sacrifices to the god. The warriors must do it at once!

Bumay ordered the action. By first light, a war party of his best fighters gathered in front of the great spirit house.

While the sorcerers beat drums and cast spells for success in the manhunt, the cannibals readied themselves. They rubbed their bodies with blackened pig grease and painted each other in bold patterns. They donned towering egret headdresses and chose their fighting weapons.

The *Mambu-Ato* himself led them through the palisade at the downriver side of the valley. Bumay's army streamed along the river gorge. The chief felt the killing lust rise and he broke into an eager trot.

They were headed toward their age-old, favorite enemy.

Two days later, Bumay and his warriors were back, dragging four captives. Often, they brought only dead men, but the rituals to placate the Father required live sacrifices. Three prisoners were the expected members of the downriver tribe. But they brought something unusual, an exotic captive, with straight black hair and yellowish skin. He was skinny and haggard, but he might give them powerful juju.

In a costumed ceremony attended by the entire nation, the four men were sacrificed outside the spirit house. Chief Bumay himself took off the yellow man's head with a blow of his fighting axe. His warriors made quick work of the others.

The heads were mounted on spears set in the riverbank.

Bumay oversaw the cutting of the victims' testicles. These, they pierced with sticks and roasted over the coals. He popped a chewy morsel in his mouth, and so took the warrior's power as his own. He distributed the other nuggets to his current favorites, a great honor.

The priests carved the meat and passed the cuts to the people. Many wanted to try the exotic man's flesh. They found it spicy, but too stringy.

The ceremony concluded with a grand *singsing* at the village gathering area beside the Big River. The remains of the carcasses were floated on banana log rafts into the stream, their gift to the *Mambu-matu*.

Several days later, the sorcerers reported success. The sacrifices had pleased the river god and the Father had moved on.

But now, as the sentries witnessed, the *Mambu-matu* was revisiting the nation.

57

Johnny came awake with Footy shaking him.

He remembered. Today they must confront the headhunters in the Valley of the Cannibals. Dingo had been clear, the Mambu were some of the fiercest fighters in New Guinea, and the only way forward was to cross their territory.

Dawn filtered through the forest canopy.

There's a good chance you won't see sunset, the Hard Case said. *But this is as good a day to die as any.*

Johnny crawled to the prisoner and untied him.

Footy opened the can of fruit and ate the first third. Johnny went next, then handed it to the captive. The Jap slurped it down and wiped up every drop of syrup with his fingers.

Johnny tied the man's hands in front again.

He and Footy double-checked their firearms. Rifles and pistols were loaded, ammo handy in their pockets. When they had their packs and gear on, Johnny pulled out the cigarettes. He put one between his lips, gave another to Footy, and on impulse, handed one to the prisoner. Surprised, the P-O-W accepted it in bound hands. Johnny lit them up.

"It might be our last smoke."

That done, he put on a savage grin and led them into the open.

"Keep moving," he said over his shoulder. "Don't stop for anything!"

They came to the edge of the trees and went down, scanning the valley. It was daybreak and quiet, a few people in the distance. Johnny lengthened his stride and the others scrambled to keep up.

The trail took them through vegetable gardens and into a grove of banana trees. Johnny rounded a corner – and bumped right into the Mambu.

An elderly couple stood there. The man was using a bamboo knife to cut down a bunch of red bananas while the woman held an open *bilum*. They were bickering as they attempted the insertion.

Then the couple saw the strangers. Their mouths fell open and everything tumbled from their hands. The old man clutched his chest and fell back while the woman fetched up against a tree. Babbling, the man lurched for Johnny and grabbed his arm.

"The stories are true," he gasped in his language. *"Our ancestors can return from the land of the dead!"*

He reached a quaking hand and rubbed Johnny's cheek, then looked to see if the white came off.

"They are spirits!" he cried. It was the greatest shock of his life, and he began to sob. The old woman crept forward, lips in a grimace as she stared into Footy's face. Tears ran into the folds of her cheeks.

"You see?" she quavered, *"here is my uncle Fumay!"*

Her fingers stroked the blonde hair on the Aussie's arm and he grinned at her.

"What are you on about, Mum?"

"They have forgotten how to talk," the old man observed. The woman reached for Footy's sandy hair sticking out under his hat and tugged.

"Ouch!"

Footy took a pinch of her own stiff curls and gave a playful pull. The woman jerked back and squinted at him. Footy laughed and went to the fallen bananas.

"I'm bloody starving – may I?" He tore one off, peeled it and shoved it in his mouth. Johnny leaned his rifle against his leg and broke off a few, stripped the skin from one, and ate it in two bites. He tossed the peel and attacked another. The couple stared as the two men wolfed down a hand each.

"Good!" Footy said to the old folks, rubbing his stomach.

"Our relatives still like the bananas," the woman observed.

The Jap tugged Johnny's elbow. Johnny peeled one for him and put it in his hands. The man shoved it in. Johnny fed him four in a row. The elders came close, the native man shorter than the prisoner. He touched the skin, sniffed, and stared into the slanted eyes.

"This one is different," he said. *"He is like the foreigners they kill downriver. You remember the taste?"* He put a gnarled finger on the rope that tied the Japanese's wrists.

"I do not think this one is a ghost," he said doubtfully.

"Perhaps our ancestors brought him for food?"

"Struth!" Footy exclaimed. "Their eyeballs are popping!"

"They must think we're aliens from another planet," Johnny said. He slung his pack down, and began to load it with fruit. Footy did the same.

"I reckon the stories about these bloody Mambu are exaggerated," the pilot said hopefully.

"If the buggers are all like this, we just might survive. "

"Don't count on it," Johnny said. "Let's go!"

The trio moved off and the old ones hurried to keep up. The man hung off Johnny's arm while the woman hobbled beside Footy, grinning at him while she recounted everything that had happened since he, her mother's brother, had gone to the spirit world.

"What are you on about?" Footy grinned. "Are you completely daft?"

The men strode the path among the gardens and a clutch of women carrying digging sticks saw them coming. At once they broke into shrill cries and came running, heavy bark skirts swinging, breasts bouncing on rounded bellies. Soon there were some twenty women surrounding the travelers, all reaching to touch their skin and hair. Johnny pushed through, batting away hands that fingered his pockets.

"Smile!" he called, grinning around. Footy pasted one on and even the Japanese bobbed his head and exposed his teeth.

The crowd swelled with each step and Johnny had to shove to get through. The body odor was ripe.

"We're friends!" Johnny called as he bulled on. Natives pressed from all sides. The Japanese in particular did not like that. He crept close behind Johnny and ducked his head.

"Friends!" Footy shouted in a jovial voice. "Bloody good mates!"

He smirked at a man, then had to shoulder aside a heavy woman in his path.

"Top of the morning, you great bloody cow! A lovely day, isn't it? Yes, we are all best mates here, you bloody, horrible savages!" The noise grew deafening as more Mambu jogged up, every one hollering at the top of his lungs.

They arrived at the palisade fence around the first village. The path continued beside it and they took that. A flood of dark-skinned people with rugged features spilled from the huts and rushed to join the commotion.

But more and more, it was armed Mambu warriors who came at a run. These included the sentries who had witnessed the return of the Father of the crocodiles in the night.

This is what the deity's visitation signified – the coming of invaders! They shouldered through the throng.

This was a marvelous event, unlike any in their lifetime, and there was sure to be some killing!

Every man was naked, Johnny saw, except for the genital coverings. He'd heard about penis gourds in New Guinea, but he'd never seen them until the Mambu valley. These were the color of yellow squash, but from man to man, the shape varied. Some were short and simple – others, long and twisted. They were held around the waist by a string, and some men had another around the chest to keep the tip up. Hanging down their backsides were long leaves that more or less covered the crack.

Most men wore a circlet of bound pig tusks through their noses. Some had large shells hanging on their chests. They carried arrows and spears with fire-hardened points, axes and knives of stone.

The throng hampered Johnny. More and more, those in his way were agitated warriors.

At last, facing a wall of bristling points, he had to stop. The Mambu harangued the strangers, screaming in their faces. Johnny's group did not understand a word, but they read violence in the gestures.

The old couple remained at their sides, clinging to their arms. They talked garrulously until warriors pulled them off.

This is it, the Hard Case said. *We're surrounded and outnumbered.*

We can't shoot them all, but we can die fighting.

"Get ready to fire!" Johnny called.

The Mambu headhunters continued to whip up the killing frenzy.

58

The warriors were hopping up and down in their fervor to attack. Johnny thrust his rifle into the air and fired. The explosion cracked across the valley and the mountains clapped back. Some Mambu fainted dead away. Men recoiled, pricking themselves on other spears.

Hundreds of natives cowered as Johnny reloaded. A native grabbed the spent brass and singed his fingers.

Instantly, the headhunters' fear boiled into anger. Their razor points hovered inches from the strangers' skin. Johnny saw that an attack was imminent and played for time.

"Take us to the chief!"

"Big chief!" Footy picked the shout up and tried it in the trade language.

"Mepella go long Luluai!"

The shock of their voices gave the crowd pause, but then the growl came back. Footy, too, fired his rifle. In the ringing silence, he called again:

"Luluai!"

Johnny knew the word and he took it up.

"Loo-loo-eye! Loo-loo-eye!" This was the trade language term for leader, but it meant nothing in Mambu. However, one of their traders had heard it downriver. He was a thickset older man, the brother of Chief Bumay. This was the first thing the strangers had said that made sense.

"Luluai!" he repeated in his hoarse voice and then said it in his language.

"Mambu-Ato!"

"Mambu-Ato," voices chorused. The hoarse warrior continued.

"Bumay!" He shook his spear and repeated his brother's name, stamping his feet. *"Mambu-Ato – Bumay!"*

The people took up the chant. *"Bumay, Bumay!"*

"The dog-strangers call for my brother! We will take them to him!" the warrior cried. But the head of another clan disagreed.

"No! Kill them now," he screamed. *"They have broken taboo! The invaders trespass on our land and you know the penalty. Death!"* A hundred voices joined in, each with a different opinion.

"Hear me!" The hoarse warrior gained dominance by sheer volume.

"The dog-strangers call for my brother, and this is the law. Their lives are forfeit to the Mambu-Ato – to him alone!"

The assembly considered this – out loud, and all at once. Johnny's group watched the debate without comprehension. At last it seemed the warriors reached a consensus. They began to wave at the village in the far distance.

The crowd surged that way, pressing Johnny's group forward. The Mambu danced as they walked, shaking their weapons and chanting.

"*Bumay! Bumay! Bumay!*"

"We're shagged now mate," Footy hissed.

"We bought some time," Johnny responded. "Stay ready!"

It was a long trek, pressed upon as they were by their escort, dragging a tail of hundreds more. They passed village after village, and the throng swelled enormously. After hours under the broiling sun, with nothing to eat, at last they approached the final and biggest village. The crowd nearly crushed them against the fence.

About a half-mile beyond, Johnny saw, was the end of the valley.

In order to enter the village, everyone had to negotiate a gap in the fence. In the opening stood a stump. Each one must step up, then down on the far side. It was an ingenious way to prevent an attack in numbers.

The squad led by the chief's brother went first. Johnny was next and came down among more people, yapping dogs, pigs, chickens and screeching children. It was bedlam.

Once the strangers were over, the procession surged through the Mambu town. Those from the other villages were slowed by the bottleneck. Johnny's group was forced between the huts where the crush grew worse.

To their consternation, Johnny and Footy were forced apart. They used the stocks of their rifles to push back together, one on each side of the prisoner.

There were two types of native buildings – peaked-roof longhouses from which men spilled out, and round huts buzzing with women and children. Through the dark doorways, they saw fires glowing. There were no chimneys, and smoke seeped through the thatch.

For the Mambu, the arrival of the outlandish invaders was a once-in-a-lifetime event. That these aliens would dare to intrude on their valley was beyond belief! Every member of the nation rushed to be part of the occasion. There would be bloody slaughter, and then – exotic meat.

As the three strangers moved within the phalanx, spear points began to prick their backs. After a painful jab, Johnny spun and caught the young man in the act. He knocked the spear aside with his rifle, then used the butt to hit the man in the jaw. The warrior tumbled back and fell hard. Some of his companions laughed and the fellow – about Johnny's age – jumped to his feet screaming. He drew his spear back to stab.

Johnny leaned into his face:

"Bumay!" he shouted. The crowd took up the chant again, and they surged past the aggressor.

The crowd burst onto the open area on the riverbank. It was surrounded on three sides by village huts. Johnny guessed this must be the village gathering place. You could put a thousand people here, he figured.

It did give a great view of the Raub River. Across it he saw dozens of dugouts, all paddling their way. His attention went to the biggest building. It was a rectangular men's house with a high point at each end of the sloping roof, but twice as high and several times as large as any other they'd seen.

"Haus Tambaran," Footy nodded. "Must be bloody Bumay's royal castle."

The tallest peak of the A-frame faced them. Like the other buildings, it had an open timber-framed entrance, but no door. They saw a fire flickering in the gloom. The front wall appeared to be made from flattened bark, covered with paintings of totem animals and mythical figures. At the top was a rendering of a giant crocodile with a yellow crescent moon over one eye. The toothy jaws formed a peak.

On each side of the door frame stood a pyramid seven or eight feet tall. Johnny thought at first, they were stacks of stone, but something made him look closer. He raised his rifle and used the scope. He found himself staring into dark eyes and nose holes above permanently grinning teeth.

"Skulls!" Johnny said.

"Bloody headhunters!" Footy spat. The prisoner stared wide-eyed.

The upper heads were white bone, some with patches of hair attached. Those nearer the bottom were yellow ivory.

Elderly men surrounded the big house. Some sat cross-legged, scraping at skulls in their laps. When these old ones saw the strangers, many dumped their work and hobbled over to gawk. Again, a multi-voiced exchange took place. Meanwhile, Mambu continued to press into the meeting area. The place was packed with people of all ages.

The banana pickers they'd first met pushed through to the pale spirits. They came weeping, and now embraced Johnny and Footy like old friends. They shouted to the crowd, and some people nodded, while others seemed to scoff.

"Bloody drama!" Footy said. "Whadda ya reckon they're on about?"

"No idea," Johnny said. "But let's get some food."

"Right mate," Footy said. *"Kaukau,"* he yelled, using a hand to mimic putting food in his mouth.

"Kaukau!" Johnny echoed. Hundreds of heads spun their way and mouths dropped open.

"Kaukau," said Mambu voices. Others repeated the word in their own tongue, and a roar erupted.

"They want sweet potatoes!"

Women reached into their *bilums*, pulled out roasted tubers, and passed them from hand to hand.

Johnny and Footy ate one-handed, holding their rifles. Mouths full, they grinned at the natives. A startled laugh went up. An animated discussion took place, and women scurried to the huts. The Japanese nudged Johnny.

"Okay, okay," Johnny said. He gave the man a potato and watched it disappear in ravenous bites. More food kept coming. Shortly there were piles on the ground.

A chunk of cooked pork was thrust into Johnny's hands. He felt his mouth water and bit in. A roasted chicken was handed to Footy, bits of burnt feathers still on it. He tore a leg off and chewed. Another chunk of pork was handed to the prisoner. He gorged himself.

"Save some," Johnny said. He went on a knee beside his pack, rifle against his side, and put his hands out. The natives passed him more *kaukau* and meat. He shoved this on top of the bananas. Footy filled his pack as well.

The Japanese ate like there was no tomorrow. *And maybe he's right,* Johnny thought. With some provision for a future that did not include their heads being taken, the men ate at a more leisurely pace. The food continued to flow.

While he chewed, Johnny studied the far side of the village. He was looking for the best way out. Beyond the chief's house were more rows of huts, and over those he could see the end of the valley. He was craning at the paths between the huts when another cooked joint was put in his hand. He was about to bite when the Japanese struck his arm with bound fists.

The meat tumbled in the dirt and Johnny glared at the prisoner. Urgently, the Jap pointed down and his face got Johnny's attention. He eyeballed the dropped piece and realized what it was – *a fire-blackened human forearm, elbow to wrist, all veins and crisp skin.*

"Dear God!" Johnny gasped. He felt the urge to vomit. Footy's eyes went wide.

"Damned cannibals," he choked. "May they rot in hell!"

The Mambu warriors laughed. They knew revulsion when they saw it. Their neighboring tribes did not eat humans, so they liked to terrorize captives by showing them man-meat, before the victims joined the larder.

A village mutt rushed between the legs and snatched up the arm. But before it could turn, the hoarse warrior stabbed it with his spear, skewering the dog to the earth. He picked up the arm and waved it. The people roared approval. The chief's brother grinned, brought the flesh to his mouth, and tore off a strip. He chewed heartily, reveling in the outrage on the invaders' faces. The crowd cawed with enjoyment.

"Let's get the hell out of here!" Johnny growled. While the people were occupied by the warrior's antics, Johnny and Footy donned their packs. They hooked arms with the prisoner and muscled forward.

They had no choice but to push aside warriors who whirled on them. Like a cloud coming over the sun, the mob's mood turned. Mirth became sneering cruelty, and the blood lust rose.

217

The brother tossed the gnawed arm into the crowd. A woman caught it and cackled at her good fortune. The warrior who had skewered the dog pulled out his spear and leveled it at Johnny.

A shout erupted from the old men by the big house. All eyes turned and saw a group of thirty young warriors come from the far side. Their near-naked bodies shone black, decorated in whirls of red, white and yellow. Each wore a yellow penis gourd, white feather headdress, with pig tusks in the nose, turned up.

They were strong men who carried weapons wet with blood. Those at the back dragged burdens the watchers could not make out.

War party, Johnny knew. Talking exuberantly, the warriors broke off when they saw the vast gathering and especially, the three aliens at the front.

Johnny picked out Bumay at once. The heavily muscled young man led the way. His headdress was the most magnificent, his penis gourd, the longest. On his chest he wore a magnificent shell the size of a dinner plate. In one hand he hefted an enormous black spear, in the other, a stone axe, both bloody. The warriors around Johnny formed an aisle.

"Bumay, Bumay, Bumay!" a thousand voices chanted. The *Mambu-Ato* stretched scarlet lips to expose the ebony teeth. He strutted along the riverbank and stopped fifteen feet from Johnny, fury on his face.

"We asked for the chief – now we've got him," Johnny muttered.

"Too right mate," Footy said.

"We're in the deep poo now."

59

Johnny's group faced the haughty chief. Bumay made a comment to his warriors and guffawed. It was a theatrical laugh that irritated Johnny. The war chief passed his axe to another man, grasped his spear in both hands, and leveled it at Johnny's chest.

Do something or die! the Hard Case urged.

"Bumay!" Johnny yelled in his deepest voice. He had the satisfaction of seeing the chief's eyes widen at hearing his name from foreign lips. Johnny took a step.

"Greetings from President Harry Truman of the United States of America! And it's not important what I say as long as it's loud!" he bellowed. Out of the corner of his eye he saw Footy staring at him.

Chief Bumay let loose a string of words Johnny didn't understand. He accompanied this with stabbing motions of his spear, which Johnny did get. His warriors menaced the intruders with axes and clubs, while bowmen put arrows to strings and drew them taut.

The hoarse warrior stepped to Johnny's side and spoke to his brother in a voice intended for the assembly. Bumay cocked his head, nodding, while his eyes went from Johnny to Footy, to the prisoner, and back again.

When the oration was done, the old couple pushed between Bumay and their spirit-ancestors. They raised their hands and told their tale. After a few words, the chief sneered and interrupted. His warriors manhandled the old ones into the crowd.

Deliberately, eyes on Johnny, Bumay threw back his head and laughed again. He swaggered toward the tall man and pressed his spear point to the white man's chest.

The point went through Johnny's undershirt and drew blood. Johnny pointed his rifle at the man and it took all his self-control not to blow him away.

While he was so preoccupied, the young warrior he'd knocked down snuck up behind and flipped Johnny's helmet off his head. It tumbled at Bumay. The chief trapped it under a foot and picked it up. He turned it this way and that, studying the lining and straps.

He spoke, and a warrior stepped to each side. They un-pinned the egret headdress and removed it. The chief grinned at Johnny as he pulled the helmet over his own springy curls. He held his spear at arm's length and struck a regal pose. The crowd shrieked with delight: what a splendid man was their *Mambu-Ato!* Johnny knew he was being ridiculed and scowled.

Bumay thumped the butt of his spear on the ground and shouted over a shoulder. Men came forward, dragging their loads. Bumay stepped aside and his warriors dumped three corpses on the clay. They were also native men, Johnny saw, but outfitted very differently from the Mambu. They wore cloth *laplaps* around their waists, and on their heads were bamboo circlets with bark strips on springy stalks. Their torsos were painted in bands of yellow and white around their pectoral muscles.

It was clear the three were fresh kills. One had an arm hacked off. A Mambu dragged it nonchalantly by the hand. The other two were spiked with arrows.

Bumay watched the visitors for reaction. Johnny heard the intake of breath from Footy, but kept his own face hard, staring at the chief with his chin out.

Again, Bumay thumped and warriors dragged up two more carcasses. Johnny saw uniforms and thought for a second they were GIs, but then made out the Asian hair and realized they were Japanese. The bearers dropped these with the others. They, too, had arrows in them and slashes in the flesh. Johnny glanced at the prisoner and saw him fixated on his countrymen. Johnny's gaze went back to Bumay and his insufferable grin, and the fighting rage rose in him.

Bumay pointed with his spear at the prisoner and made a comment. His warriors chortled. Again, Johnny wanted to shoot Bumay, but kept a grip. There were too many Mambu! He needed an escape plan.

Show them what rifles can do!

Johnny picked a target near the spirit house and pulled the trigger. The report cracked like a whip across the river, and a pile of skulls tumbled with a sound like dry wood. Johnny watched Bumay while his hands reloaded. He was pleased to see the headhunter flinch.

Bumay was not thrown for long. He had witnessed the foreigner's magic sticks in action down the river, and while he feared them greatly, that had not stopped him from setting ambushes and slaughtering their bearers.

Bumay had not been born *Mambu-Ato*. He had earned the position in single-handed combat with the most formidable warriors of his nation. In the previous year, he had challenged and killed the reigning war chief. Two others, his nearest rivals, he had also speared in front of the gathered nation. At a lavish feast, the clans confirmed Bumay as their undisputed leader. He accepted their tribute of virgin wives, pigs and prime gardens, including a fine grove of betel trees.

Bumay stood in the Mambu heartland, beside his grand *Haus Tambaran*, surrounded by the most feared army of warriors on the entire Big River. The intruders were already dead men.

Yes, these were the hairy foreigners with the killing sticks and steel knives. The third was their captive, of no consequence. But two men against the nation? It was no contest!

Johnny saw the emotions play over Bumay's face and knew he was getting ready to kill them. Urgently, he spoke to Footy.

"Aim at another pile of skulls. Wait for my word!"

"Right!" The muzzle of the Lee Enfield swung around.

"Bumay!" Johnny called again and the chief's stare swung on him. He raised his arm and dropped it.

"Fire!"

There was the crash of Footy's shot and a second pyramid exploded. Skulls bounced across the dirt. A gasp went up from the crowd. Warriors picked up the orbs of bone and stared.

Bumay was livid. The invaders had committed sacrilege! He fixed his scowl on the tall one and the urge to kill swelled. He felt fear as well because of their strong magic, and that made him even more enraged. He made another show of laughing.

"I will spear that one and lap his heart-blood," he howled in the language. His muscles bunched in anticipation. *"Now these will die!"*

"Get ready to run!" Johnny snarled to Footy. "I'll take Bumay. You get the brother, then fire at will. Run for the far side!"

"Roger," Footy said, lining up the shot. His barrel almost touched his target.

A skull had rolled near Bumay and he kicked it in fury. It spun away, spewing teeth. He shook his spear and screamed.

"Are we dead men?"

"No!" the warriors roared.

"We are Mambu – the only true people! These invaders have broken our law. What is the penalty?"

"Death, death, death!" the shout came.

"We will kill them now!" Bumay promised.

Johnny was in his killer mind and it no longer mattered if he lived or died. His eyes flashed to the pilot.

Rifle up, good man. He glanced at the Japanese and saw he was calm and alert, even with his hands tied. Johnny felt a flash of respect.

Johnny flexed his knees and his gaze returned to Bumay. His helmet was still on the chief's head, and he glanced at it, then back to the dark eyes. Bumay saw the rage on the foreign face. Satisfaction flooded him, sweet as wild honey.

"The tall one is mine!" he thundered. "Kill the others! Attack!"

What happened next took the space of heartbeats. Bumay jerked his spear back to stab Johnny, who aimed his rifle at the chief, but there were warriors in the way. Johnny got a clear glimpse of the chief's shoulder and that would have to do. He fired. The bullet struck true and shattered the joint. Bumay spun like a top and went down, dropping his spear.

Footy shot the hoarse warrior so close that powder scorched the curls on the man's chest. The bullet tore through the heart and blasted through two men who stood behind. All three fell, knocking others over.

Footy fired fast, working through the magazine. More natives bit dirt. Johnny was only a little slower, having to reload between shots. The Mambu closest to the strangers lurched back, even while those further away pressed to attack.

Abruptly the P-O-W moved. His bound hands flew to Footy's pack and he grabbed and jerked up. There was a flash of steel and his sword was in his hands once more. He felt a rush of elation.

If this is the time to die, let it come!

He swept the blade in a semicircle. Tips of arrows and spears fell in a rain of fingers. Mambu brought bloody stumps before incredulous eyes.

The warriors pressed too close! Johnny swung the butt of his rifle again, driving them back. Again, the sword flashed across the sun, and a warrior's head leapt from his shoulders, into the crowd. There was a collective scream.

Johnny put his rifle against a man's jaw and fired, getting drenched in the hot spray. Footy's rifle spat again and again. Shot warriors released arrows as they fell, skewering their fellows.

Two Mambu managed to grab the barrel of Johnny's rifle. He kept a grip on it while his other hand drew his pistol and shot.

His rifle came free.

The Jap carved them more elbow room.

A warrior swung his axe at the prisoner's head. Johnny shot the Mambu through the ear and the blade whistled overhead and struck another headhunter across the eyes. This one screamed and staggered away, trying to tug the stone out of his face. The prisoner's eyes met Johnny's and he gave a nod.

A thickset warrior rushed Footy, took him in a bear hug and began to squeeze.

"Help!" the pilot cried. Johnny put his pistol to the Mambu's temple and scrambled his brains.

Suddenly, the three men found space around them. Warriors recoiled from the ring of death, leaving the ground thick with their fallen.

Their departure revealed Bumay, still on his knees.

It had only been a space of breaths since the chief ordered the attack. Now his left arm dangled useless, but his strong right arm was sound. Bumay clutched his war spear and sprang up. He threw back his head and howled his legendary war cry.

At the sound, his men felt their courage flow back into their veins. They rallied around the *Mambu-Ato*, as they had done countless times before.

Hundreds of cannibal warriors faced the three invaders.

They would overwhelm them in a rush.

60

The Father dove with the two-legged prey in its teeth, trying to swim away from the sharp noises and pain.

It surged underwater and the prey stopped twitching, but the reptile was too overwrought to be hungry. It opened its jaws and let the current sweep the carcass away. Then it flailed downstream, trying to outrun the agony of its exploded leg and the puncture wounds to its head and body.

It came to a place where the water turned shallow and boiled over rocks. As the crocodile bumped over them, its foreleg was battered and the suffering was terrible. It hissed and writhed its way down the Big River.

The Father continued as darkness and light passed in their turn. It swam with the throbbing limb held stiff. Infection bloomed. The leg swelled and the skin was too tight.

The misery was relentless, and the Father grew more desperate by the hour. Its teeth chattered and it felt the shudder all through its skull.

Its distress became one with the Smooth-headed man. Each beat of its great heart pulsed with urge to kill.

At last, the rapids were behind. The river grew wide and smooth. In darkness, the reptile approached another well-known nesting ground of the two-legged prey. It glided underwater to a bank where it had hunted before and waited for the light. The sun rose and the day grew hot as the Father crouched beneath the surface.

But then the thundering explosions came once more. The reptile's old fear spiked. Its agony and rage mounted until it could bear no more.

The Father threw up its gargantuan head in a great splash. The stench of gunsmoke flew up its nostrils, straight into its brain. It stared at the throng of jostling animals along the shore.

And then, through the fray, it perceived the very source of its torment.

The Smooth-headed man!

At once, the vast body convulsed and the crocodile charged. Each stabbing shock from its leg added to its fury. The wide body crested the riverbank and launched into the mob, sending warriors flying like bowling pins.

It was in the midst of the greatest crowd of prey it had ever seen. It paused, long tail swishing, instantly sending more Mambu to the spirit world. It spread wide its huge jaws and growled so long and low, the people's bones shook.

A thousand Mambu spun to the sound and were dumbstruck. The very *Mambu-Matu* itself had magically materialized among them!

The river god stood in the multitude, sunlight outlining its monstrous glory. Water poured from ten thousand scales. For an instant under the malevolent gaze of the divinity, the natives turned from the battle with the invaders. Their consternation peaked at the sight of the grotesquely swollen, bleeding stump. In their legends, the *Mambu-Matu* was all-powerful. What magic could have hurt the river god?

The Father peered into the crowd, questing with its eyes. Then it bellowed and their bowels turned to water. The beast ran among them, crushing more under its mass.

The predator had a single interest: dead ahead was its target. It rushed him.

The old woman who had seen the deity in her dreams stood in the way. She raised her arms and screamed.

"Mambu-Matu!"

The river god trampled its handmaiden. People scattered on all sides.

Johnny, Footy and the Jap were fighting for their lives, ears ringing from the gunfire. They did not see the crocodile explode from the river, but they did hear the bellow. The hair stood up on their necks.

Another warrior rushed them, axe swinging. The sword unzipped his belly.

The colossus parted the people. Johnny whirled and in the sudden gap, saw the Father come at a run, shoulder dipping. His eyes flew to the bloody stump and he knew he was the focus of the reptile's fury.

Bumay witnessed the advent of the deity and was filled with awe. He might be *Mambu-Ato,* the War Chief, but here came the *Mambu-Matu,* the very Chief of Chiefs!

The prisoner took advantage of the confusion. He ran toward the corpses of his countrymen. Beside them stood the two warriors who had dragged them here. The sword chopped one neck. The other man tried to jump away, but the blade flew fast, parting the torso until it struck spine. Two bodies went down in a shambles.

"It's the blasted Father!" Footy choked. In desperation, the warriors struck at it, but wood and stone did not dent the armored scales.

There was only one thing left to do.

"Run!" Johnny shouted. He knocked the wall of natives aside with the butt of his rifle and bolted. Footy did the same and came on his heels.

Bumay, still wearing the GI helmet, saw the tall enemy go. With his good right arm, he turned to spear him through the back.

The Father charged the Smooth-headed man. Jaws wide, it turned its head, took the prey in, and put all its ferocity into the bite. The teeth crushed Bumay's pelvis and cracked the spine off like a twig. The spear dropped from the chief's hand and tumbled under the Father's foreleg. Its full weight came down, the shaft splintered, and two feet of fire-hardened wood jammed into the reptile's flayed limb. The Father reared up, hissing in horror with the man in its jaws.

The death scream squeezed from Bumay's throat. The crocodile shook its head and the body tossed, coming apart. The steel helmet sprang off Bumay's curls and rattled away.

Johnny had only managed a few steps when he heard the shriek. He glanced back to see Bumay torn between the teeth — and then the helmet bounced his way. Still running, he scooped it up and jammed it on. He and Footy raced for their lives.

The fresh stab in its leg caused the Father to gag and drop the body. It bellowed pure anguish and the Mambu fell back on all sides. Its jaws slammed shut and the predator blinked in confusion. The blood of its tormentor still gurgled down its throat – but there, running away, was the Smooth-headed man.

Johnny and Footy were neck-and-neck at the longhouse, then between the huts. Ahead, they saw the final palisade fence. They aimed for the gap.

The Father went after its enemy, but each step was searing. The great longhouse was nearby, and it limped that far, but could not continue. It gave a pain-filled rumble and lashed its tail. It smashed elders against the wall, but the appendage did not stop. It broke through bark and woven reeds and struck the posts that held the edifice up.

There was a boom like a bomb going off. The *Haus Tam-baran* shook to the roof and imploded. Splintered tree trunks and thatch tumbled down on the central hearth.

The Father dragged itself back toward the river. The entire clearing had emptied, the prey cowering among the huts.

The beast approached a mangled body. Bumay was alive, but barely. The reptile parted its jaws and took him in. The throat opened wide.

The nation watched their *Mambu-Ato* slide into the deity's gullet. The man's eyes were open and his hands embraced the snout of the god as his body disappeared into it. The scaled neck rippled and Bumay was gone.

The Father hauled itself to the bank, fell on its belly, and slid into the opaque water, leaving a scarlet swirl.

But the river's wrath was not yet done with the people.

61

The chief's mansion had been spacious. Outside it, Bumay had sat on his throne in judgment over his subjects. Inside, he arranged the festivals, many involving the consumption of human flesh.

His edifice had been home to his elite clan warriors. Here they planned the tribal wars. Chains of rattan looped from the rafters, a link added for each skull taken

The floor above was even more rarefied. Only the *Mambu-Ato* and most trusted confidants, could ascend. It was here that rituals were performed with fresh heads in order to appease the malevolent ghosts. The upper floor also stored the fetishes and spirit masks. Here, too, were the instruments – the bull-roarers, drums and flutes that gave voice to the spirit realm.

When the Father of the Crocodiles knocked down the *Mambu-Ato's* house, all the precious artifacts rained down as well. Eagerly, flames leapt to embrace them. Smoke billowed, and the inferno consumed it all. In mounting panic, the people watched the seat of the political and religious power of the Mambu nation burn to ash. Soon the edifice crumbled to a heap of glowing coals.

Then, out on the face of the river where the deity had disappeared, a gust of wind arose. It rippled across the surface, coming toward the village. At the shore, it transformed into a dust devil. It spun across the clearing, gaining strength. Almost playfully, it danced into the conflagration. Feeding on the heat, it grew stronger. Now a column of fire, it picked up bundles of grass, fanned them red-hot, and threw them into the sky.

All around, the torches floated down on the grass roofs of the surrounding huts.

62

Johnny jumped through the gap in the fence and sprinted for the gorge. He did not have to look back to know Footy followed. He could hear the footfalls and ragged breaths.

He pelted on until there were at least three hundred yards between him and the Mambu village. Ahead, the river dropped into the jungle and he could hear the rumble of falling water. Johnny's heart was a jackhammer and he went down on a knee. Footy collapsed beside him, panting like a dog.

"Hell's bloody bells," the Aussie gasped, leaning on his pack.

Johnny looked toward the village and saw someone coming. He raised his rifle and put the scope on the runner.

The Jap!

The prisoner raced at them with the bloodstained sword in his still-tied hands. He got close.

"Stop right there!"

The man gasped for air. He chanced a look back, saw no one coming, and sank on his knees.

"Put down the sword!" Johnny ordered. The man stared at him.

"Put – it – down!"

And then the Japanese spoke.

"Must clean first!" he croaked.

Footy sat bolt upright.

"Well I'll be stuffed!" he crowed.

"The Jap speaks English!'"

The prisoner kept one eye on Johnny as he wedged the handle of the sword between his bare feet. With his roped hands, he pulled up grass, wrapped it around the blade and wiped, hilt to tip.

Johnny alternated between watching him and darting glances back at the village. His attention went to the cloud of smoke that suddenly billowed up. The Japanese discarded the grass and repeated the process, then wiped the blade on the tail of his shirt.

He knelt, placed the sword across the path and backed away.

"Footy," Johnny said, "go get it."

"Crikey!" Footy said. "Shoot him if he even twitches!"

Clutching his side, the Aussie walked warily toward the Asian. He snatched up the sword and moved back behind Johnny.

"What the bugger can do with this thing!" he exclaimed. "Struth, mate!"

"And with his hands tied," Johnny said. Footy slung his pack down and slid the sword into its scabbard once more.

Shouts came from the village. In the distance, a group of warriors arrived at the fence and a few came over. Behind them, thick smoke stained the sky.

"Fire in the village!" Johnny said. "And here comes the posse. We've got to run some more. You – get behind me," he told the Japanese. The prisoner went to stand with Footy.

"All this time, you speak the King's English," Footy accused him. The man shrugged.

Johnny lay down and rested on his elbows. He held his rifle steady and put the scope on the lead runner. The warrior raced at them, spear high. Six or seven more strung out behind him.

Johnny shot. The leader's arms flew up and he tumbled. Another went down behind him, shot by the same bullet.

The next runner faltered, but then jumped over his fallen comrade and kept coming, axe high. Johnny jacked in another shell. He squeezed and watched the man somersault.

The rest of the string pulled up, then turned and ran. They leapt back through the fence and stood on the far side. They might think that meant they were safe, but Johnny knew better. He smiled without mirth and sent a slug their way. Another warrior joined the ancestors.

That did it. The Mambu scuttled for the village, but pulled up as a wall of fire burst from the row of huts.

Johnny watched the smoke boil against the blue sky and it came to him, this was a good day. His shoulder pulsed, his lungs were raw – and it was sweet to be alive. He grinned at Footy and the Jap.

"Hey! We made it through! Way to fight, both of you!" He got to his feet.

"You," he said to the prisoner, "You go first! Then you, Footy. They're stopped for now, but who knows for how long!

"Let's go!"

The three charged along the trail between cliffs. They sprinted down the gorge while the river cascaded nearby and the forest closed over their heads.

The path led to a drop-off. They stared down the steep rock scree and saw the native trail in switchbacks across it. The jungle canopy spread a hundred feet below.

The prisoner led off and Footy fell in behind him. Johnny watched them descend and then decided to take a shortcut.

233

Half running, half falling, he went straight down. He skidded by the other men in a slide of stones. The Jap and Footy watched him go by and then took his example, the prisoner having to scamper on bare feet. At the bottom, Johnny slammed to earth and stood aside while the others landed in a rattle of rocks. They jogged off again.

And so, the trio left the Valley of the Cannibals behind.

63

The mountains spread apart as the path descended through the rainforest. The river dropped in rapids beside them, echoing through the jungle. Sometimes the path was soggy, and at others, the men clambered over slick rock. The smell of fungus filled the air and orange shelves grew on trees and deadfalls.

An hour later, they came to a meadow and risked a break. After they caught their breath, Johnny and Footy were anxious to take stock of their ammunition.

Footy found he had only ten shots left for the Lee Enfield, and he loaded them all into the magazine. Johnny had a scant six cartridges for his .30-06, including the one in the chamber. The clip in his .45 was empty and he fed his last five into it. Footy broke open the Webley, and six spent casings flew out. He put in the final four from Dingo's supply.

"We're very low," the pilot muttered.

"Right," Johnny said. "That battle ate up almost everything we had. From now on, we have to make each shot count."

They ate sweet potatoes from their haul in the valley and set off again. They walked until nightfall and camped beside a clearer stream that joined the river here.

As usual, Johnny and Footy took turns on watch. The

Mambu could catch up with them at any minute, and who knew whose territory they were in now?

In the morning, they breakfasted on the old folks' bananas.

"For shore they'd never clapped eyes on a white man before," Footy said. "Crikey, I thought they'd have a heart attack."

"But they acted like they knew us," Johnny said. "What were they thinking?"

The men walked all day, refilling their bottles when they found fresh water. They crossed rolling hills, and the path alternated between wooded and grassy land.

The river continued beside them, and from time to time, they startled crocodiles that went thrashing into the water, but these were all of the freshwater variety.

At last the jungle gave way to *kunai* grassland. This provided respite from the mosquitoes, but the sun beat on them relentlessly. Johnny was grateful when the jungle took over again, even though it was sweltering as a sauna.

At mid-afternoon, the men came to a pretty place of low grass among spread out trees. A spring burbled from the stones. The bushes were smothered in fragrant flowers, and hundreds of tiny yellow butterflies filled the air. The men sat to drink and wash. Johnny broke out the cigarettes and passed them around, including the prisoner. Footy glowered but said nothing.

The Jap smoked his down to an ember and stubbed it in the grass. When he looked up, his eyes went wide. He pointed over the other men's shoulders. The two whirled and saw a line of native warriors.

Eight men stood with longbows drawn, arrows back on the strings.

They knew at once these were not Mambu. They looked like the victims they'd seen in Bumay's valley – same *laplaps* and headdresses.

Johnny slid his hand towards his rifle, but the biggest of the warriors stepped close, a barbed arrow aimed at Johnny's chest.

"I wouldn't touch that roiful," he said in a broad Australian accent. "Me boys are a bit nervy, ya see. You don't want an arra in ya, do ya?"

"No," Johnny said, retrieving his hand.

"That's betta," the man nodded. "You sit easy and we'll talk."

"Blimey!" Footy exclaimed, "Where in hell did you come from?"

"Well, not hell, mate," the warrior said, letting some tension off his bow, although his men remained poised. He smiled, displaying ruby inner lips and blackened teeth, and picked between the front ones with a sharp fingernail.

"This here is about as close to heaven you gonna get."

64

"Who are you?" Johnny asked.

"My name is Mulakuwapatawny."

"Wow," Johnny said.

"Cor blimey!"

"This here Uhuli land," the man said. "The betta question is, who are *you*, and where are *you* from?"

Johnny stood slowly, showing empty hands.

"I'm Johnny Willman," he said, "Sergeant, US Army. This is Glen Carmichael – Australian."

"Ahh, I like you Aussies," the warrior grinned. "And you Yanks. Allies!"

"Call me 'Footy,'" the Australian said. "Your name again?"

"Mula-kuwapa-tawny," the man said with relish.

"Hold on!" Footy said.

"That's a jawbreaker," Johnny added.

"Ahhh – call me Mula," the warrior grinned, enjoying the moment.

"Mula," Johnny said gratefully.

"Mula, mate, where'd you learn such bloody good English?" Footy asked.

"In Australia, mate. At school in Adelaide."

"Adelaide?" Footy asked.

"Adelaide."

Mula looked at the Jap and he scowled again.

"And this bugga?"

"Our prisoner," Johnny said. Mula narrowed his eyes at the man, then looked to Johnny.

"How you come to be on our land?"

"We've come from Mambu territory," Footy said. "Bloody Valley of the Cannibals, mate."

"Do you know a chief called 'Bumay'?" Johnny asked.

Mula couldn't have looked more surprised if he'd been slapped. He spat a string of red juice.

"The brutha of Satan," he said, licking his lips. "Wot about Bumay?"

"Glad you think that..." Footy said.

"...because Bumay is dead," Johnny continued. "And maybe thirty of his men."

"Or more," Footy added. "Maybe fifty. We didn't stop to count."

"And when did this bloody miracle take place?" Mula asked.

"Yesterday," Footy said. Mula spoke rapid-fire over his shoulder. The Uhuli crowded around, all talking at once. They unbent their bows, but kept their circle intact.

"Nothin' personal," Mula said at last, "but we find this ratha hard to believe! No one comes outta the Mambu valley, not evva! I've lived here all me life, and I've nevva seen it! You go in there, the only way you come out is *pekpek*." He roared with laughter and slapped his leg. He retold his joke to his men and they all howled.

"*Pekpek* is..." Footy explained. "I know – it's crap," Johnny said.

"Well, we did it," he told Mula, "and we're not *pekpek* yet – as you can see."

"This fella Bumay," Mula went on. "He's killed a lot of me people, mate. You lot couldn't fight 'im yestaday, b'cause, see, he was here. He killed three of me *wantoks*. We hunting them sons-a-Satan t'day."

"This is the truth," Johnny said. "We saw his war party arrive with your dead brothers. I shot Bumay – but then a monster crocodile attacked and ate the chief."

Mula stared at the soldier in absolute astonishment.

238

"This Jap here," Johnny pressed on, realizing how strange it all sounded, "we captured him at Kissim, up the river."

"Kissim – aww yeah? Nevva been that far," Mula said. He stepped to the Japanese, put his broad face close and smiled in a nasty way.

"We don't like these fellas," he said. "We hunt 'em. Bad fellas. They killed Masta Billy – me missionary. An' Missis Sarah, they carry her off."

"When was this?" Johnny asked. Mula scratched his head and spat *buai*. Again, he conversed with his men.

"Two Christmases," he said.

"Two years," Footy said.

"You men got quite a yarn," Mula said. "Me missionary, he had some yarns. But yours – it takes the bloody cake!

"Now. We gotta find out if wot you say is true. You come with us. You stay in my village. You get to see the Lighthouse Mission!" Johnny and Footy glanced at each other.

"Look," Johnny said, "we need to keep going." "We've got to get to the coast, mate," Footy put in.

"The way I see it," Mula said, "you lot are on my land. You *say* you been in the Mambu valley. I've lived here all me life, and I've nevva done that.

"But you two – and 'im..." he nodded at the prisoner, "...you go through. You fight Bumay an' his boys – in the Mambu valley! You get help from a *pukpuk*! You kill a lotta Mambu and you come outta the valley! That is a lot for us to eat, mates."

"A lot to swallow," Footy suggested.

"Yeah," Mula said, "a lot ta bloody eat and swalla!"

65

"I gotta tell ya," the Uhuli chief continued, "some of me boys, they think you're pulling our foots. They say we kill you now."

Johnny and Footy had been sitting while Mula talked, but now they rose, rifles in hand. Mula grinned.

"Aw, yes, you got roifuls," he said. He shouted a command and his men bent back their bows, arrows steady. Mula smiled his black smile.

"Now – if wot you say is true, you got no worries," he said. "I hope wot you say is true, as Papa God is my witness!" Mula looked up and clasped his hands around his bow. He stared back at the white men.

"But if you lyin'," he said, "well, that is bad for you. You see that?" His smile flashed again.

"But mates, if wot you say is true, then we'll have a *singsing* – big bloody party, mate! We'll kill some of me pigs, have a dance. We hate them Mambu! So ya see, you really our guests. That's how to look at it." Johnny and Footy shared another glance.

"Okay," Johnny said, "but you say you can't go into the Mambu valley. How are you going to verify the facts?"

"Berrify defects," Mula repeated. "That's good, I like that one." He thought for a moment. "Wot does it mean?"

"Verify the facts," Footy repeated. "It means, how will you find out what we say is true, mate?"

Mula conferred with his men. While he was doing that, Footy dug in his backpack and extracted a hand of bananas. He passed some to Johnny, who shared with the captive, and they

240

began to eat. Mula's warriors saw what they were doing and began to mutter. The Uhuli chief looked up.

"Aw, that's bad form, mates!" he hissed. "Don't eat without sharin'! The boys don't like that!"

"Sorry," Johnny said.

"We didn't know," Footy added. They dug in their packs and passed out more bananas and *kaukau*. These went hand-to-hand around the group. The warriors sank on their haunches, weapons at hand.

Johnny drew a chunk of meat from his pack and eyed it suspiciously.

"We took this from the Mambu," he said to Mula. "Know what it is?" He gave it to the native, who sniffed, and bit in.

"This is pig, mate," he said with his mouth full. "Bloody good pig!" Mula ripped the meat in two and offered a piece back.

"No, that's okay," Johnny said hastily. "You go right ahead."

Mula grinned and passed the portion to his men. Johnny and Footy dug out all the meat they had and handed it over. There was a good deal of smacking of lips and grunts of pleasure. When the repast was done, Mula wiped his fingers on his chest and stood up.

"Nothing as good as the food of ya enemies," he sighed.

"Awlright then, here's what we're gonna do. Anda here," he pointed to a young warrior with stringy curls, "he got himself a sweethaht near the Mambu valley. I tell him he's *longlong* – crazy. He's gonna get himself killed – but he's a young bloke." Mula shrugged and said a few words in his language and the men chortled and nudged one another.

241

"I'll send 'im to talk to his sweethaht. Tonight he'll find out wot's wot. You blokes come to the Uhuli village. You can hang onta your roifles, your pistols, your knives – bloke's gotta keep his weapons. But you havta stay till we find out wot's wot. Right by you?"

Johnny and Footy knew there was no way around it. They had to go through the Uhuli lands. They'd shared all their food and had to get more, hopefully from Mula's people.

"Okay," Johnny said.

"Right by me," Footy said. Mula looked at the prisoner.

"One more thing. Can me boys have your Jap?" Johnny saw the prisoner's eyes narrow.

"When you say *have him*," Footy asked, "you mean...?" he drew his thumb across his neck.

"Could be," Mula nodded. "That could very well be! The boys came for blood t'day, didn't they, mate? It'd do 'em good. Consida it a fava to me."

"Yes mate," Footy said thoughtfully.

"I reckon we can work something out."

66

Johnny mulled over Mula's request and Footy's willingness to go along. He looked at the Jap and found him staring back.

"Sorry, no can do," he said to Mula. "He's our Prisoner of War. And remember, he did kill your enemies yesterday."

"Fair dinkum," Footy admitted. "He went chop-chop on the Mambu, that's for shore."

The chief considered this and nodded.

"Awlright," he said. "The boys'll listen to me. But you watch him," he warned, wagging a finger at the prisoner. "We have a score to settle with them Japs! The blood of our families and our missionary is on 'em."

He grasped his bow and arrows and stood, greased muscles catching the sun.

"Let's be off, shall we?"

He had a last word with Anda, who watched his kin and foreigners go out of sight. Then the young warrior turned on the trail and trotted back toward the Valley of the Cannibals.

Mula's entourage followed the river downstream. The chief peppered them with questions – the purpose of their journey, their experiences in Kissim, and with the Mambu. Every time he spoke the name of the hated enemy, the chief spat red.

Johnny and Footy told him what he wanted to know. The Uhuli chief kept returning to the confrontation with Bumay.

When they came to telling about the corpses the Mambu warriors dragged into their village, Mula exclaimed and had them describe each in detail, and identified the fallen by name.

"Those are me scouts," he said sadly. "I sent 'em ahead yestaday. Them sons-a-Satan musta surprised 'em. Time we got there, all we found is blood." He spoke to his men. Groans turned to sobs. Mula was also interested to learn of the dead Japs.

"They a few here an' there in the bush," he said. "We hunt 'em when we find 'em, but we don't bloody eat 'em!" Again, he spat.

Late in the day, the forest opened onto a broad *kunai* plain. Beyond this were fields of gardens, ripe with vegetables – all Uhuli, Mula explained proudly.

As they walked, his men cut stalks of purple-skinned sugar cane. The chief handed lengths to Johnny, Footy and even the Jap. Like the natives, they peeled the tough outer layer with their teeth. The inside was white and fibrous, loaded with juice. They bit off chunks and crushed these between their teeth. They sucked the sweet sugar and spat the pulp.

Chewing and spitting, the group continued. Finally, they saw the Uhuli village in the distance, a collection of edifices in the trees along the riverbank.

"Home!" Mula sang in a happy chorus with the other men's voices. The village mongrels came out to greet them. Running behind them came dozens of warriors. Shouts echoed across the distance. By the time Mula's party reached the others, women and children had joined as well. There was a grand reunion. The chief turned to Johnny.

"Now I gotta tell them about me dead bruthas," he said sadly. He called in his language and the people went quiet. Then a woman screamed, others began to wail, and all the people gave way to grief. The newcomers were surprised to see Mula and his warriors openly sobbing, tears spilling down their cheeks.

The procession moved on, arms around one another.

They came to a wall of piled dirt and rocks with logs across the gaps. Warriors removed these so they could climb through. They passed sentries, and were absorbed into the larger gathering on the far side.

Soon they were parading by Uhuli houses. These were different than any the travelers had seen so far. They sat high on pole stilts, sunk in the clay. There were forty or more along the mudflat.

Simple staircases, tree trunks with notches for steps, leaned through holes in the floors. Natives ran nimbly up and down, and a woman with a bundle of firewood balanced on her head, carried it into her dwelling.

Mula led to a low hill. On top of it was a large square structure under a corrugated metal roof. On one side stood a steel water tank on posts, and an outhouse. The walls were cement panels, inset with windows and doors. They drew close and stopped.

"This a happy time," Mula said, "we like visitas like you! But this a sad time. We gotta say goodbye to our dead bruthas. T'morra – if Anda fartyfy your fack, we gonna feel betta! But tonight, I gotta send me dead *wantoks* to heaven. The people gotta get ready."

The crowd ground to a halt and Mula spoke. Again, the women set up a high-pitched keening. Then the Uhuli dispersed.

Mula led his guests to the door in the nearest wall. He swung it open on rusty hinges and made a grand gesture to enter.

"Welcome to da Lighthouse Missin!"

67

Johnny went first into the gloom. It took some seconds for his eyes to adjust, and he realized they were in a room that served as kitchen, dining and living rooms. Afternoon sun slanted through dirty louvered glass, some panes missing. Mosquitoes and flies droned through the shafts of light.

Mula entered last and set his bow and arrows with a collection of weapons against a wall. These included two rifles, Johnny noticed – a rusted relic and a current Japanese model. The chief saw where he looked.

"Yes mate, I got roifles — but no bullits. I need bullits," he added hopefully.

"After the fight with the Mambu, we're low on ammo ourselves," Johnny added. Mula sighed.

"I need bullits," he repeated, "and many utha things."

The kitchen was dominated by a cast iron stove. Beside it was a counter built of planks on two-by-four legs. A metal sink emptied through a pipe over a hole in the floorboards. A bucket of water stood nearby. Dirty plates and cutlery were piled everywhere.

The table was plywood on posts, ringed by factory-made chairs. In the gloom, a sagging sofa faced a cable spool repurposed as a table.

In the nearest wall, a door hung by one hinge. Through it, the men saw a mattress on the floor. A native young woman was rising from the tangle of sheets. She cradled a baby, while another child sprawled beside her.

"'Ello love," Mula called. "I'm 'ome!"

He turned to the men. "This is where me missionaries lived. I keep it good, till we get a new one.

"'Ave a seat." He gestured toward the chairs. Johnny and Footy took off their packs and leaned them and their rifles against the wall. They sat at the table with Mula and the prisoner.

The young woman approached. She wore a cloth skirt in a floral pattern gone gray with grime. The baby suckled a breast and another boy, naked except for the string around his waist, trailed her, knuckling his eyes.

"This is me wife, Makamalingatopa," the chief said. He saw the concern on his guests' faces again and grinned. He loved his little joke, honed back when the missionaries first arrived.

"Da Masta and Missis, they called her 'Miriam,'" he went on. "Call her Miriam. They called me 'Mark,' but well – now I'm Mula again. These here me sons. Luke, he's got six Christmas – and the baby, he's George for the King – one Christmas."

"Welcome to de Lit Hass Missin," Miriam said. Her smile would have been pretty if not for the blackened teeth.

"Would you like some tea?"

"Oooo, tea? Right! Good on ya, Miriam," Footy said.

"She don't know what she sayin'," Mula said, shaking his head. "No tea, not for a long time now." He said something in his language. Miriam looked downcast.

"Aww, no worries," Footy said, heartbroken.

"We got water!"

"Water, sure," Johnny said. Miriam dipped an assortment of chipped glasses and cups into a bucket and passed them around. Mula spoke in the language as she worked, apparently telling her about his trip. He began to cry again, and she sobbed as well. Then he cheered up and was laughing between his sentences, pointing to the white men.

They heard the words, "Bumay" and "Mambu."

"I tell her about our dead bruthas," he said. "And ya good yarn – killing Bumay and them sons-a-Satan!" He hawked and spat a gob of red *buai* that tumbled through the air and almost hit the hole under the sink.

"Sorry," he said shamefacedly. "We don't spit in the house!" He scowled at the prisoner. "Now I tell you why I don't like these yella fellas! When his lot come to me village – many times – we hide in the bush. Me missionaries hide with us. But one time them Japs come early – in a motorboat.

247

"There's a lotta them – a lotta guns. They come in and grab me Masta outa bed." Mula pointed to the room. "They drag 'im outside. I see it all. They shoot him – my dear Billy!" Tears filled Mula's eyes and spilled down his cheeks.

"Wickid bloody Japs!" he howled at the prisoner. The man dropped his eyes and stared at the table.

"Me an' me boys – we watch – but they got the guns. The Masta an' Missis – they good people. They send me to Australia, ya know, before the war."

"Yes," Footy murmured, "Adelaide."

"Adelaide," Mula nodded. "The Lighthouse Church. I learn bloody good English in Adelaide.

"But them Japs – they keep Missis Sarah inside the house. She scream a long time. They bring her out. She got blood on her legs. She see 'er poor husband lyin' there – *dead-finish!*"

Mula shook his head while more tears fell. Miriam sobbed as well, and the boy, Luke, cried with her. Eventually the chief wiped his nose on his arm.

"The Japs, they drag her to the boat. Then, you sons-a-Satan buggas!" Mula shouted at the Jap, who flinched. "You grab our women – six women! You find our pigs! Seventeen pigs!" The prisoner stared away while Mula glared.

"They rob our gardens – take all we got! Then they go."

"What happened to Sarah?" Footy asked. Mula shrugged.

"She *dead-finish* by now," he said sadly.

"We take me missionary, we – ahhh – we plant 'im in the groun'. Then we go afta them Japs. We look a long time. But them Japs – they gone." He looked as if a great weight pressed on his shoulders.

"We know some Japs still 'round. They hide inna jungle. A lotta them go downriver – long-time finish."

Mula went from anger to deep sadness again. At last, he squeezed his eyes with his thumbs and spoke.

"Now you tell me why I don't kill this fella?"

"Believe me, the Japs are our enemies," Johnny told him. "But this man surrendered. You know what that means?"

"Yeah shore," Mula said. "He give up to you. You kill him if you want."

"No," Johnny said. "That's not how it goes. He's a prisoner of war. We have to take him back. We've got rules. The Aussies will lock him up."

"Bloody right," Footy agreed. Mula frowned, then noticed the near-horizontal angle of the sunset through the windows.

"Well – time for the news," he announced, scraping back his chair.

"The news?" Johnny and the others were dumbfounded.

68

"What are you bloody on about?" Footy asked.

"I got a wireless!" Mula grinned. "News from Sydney – that's Australia, mate! Them Germans finished in Eeew-rope. They say the Japs finish quick-time now.

"Come on, let's 'ave a listen!"

The men stood, and Johnny motioned for the prisoner to come. Mula lit the wick of an old hurricane lantern with a twig from the stove, and led them past the bedroom to another door, back in the gloom.

"The mission office," he explained as the yellow glow revealed the interior. They saw a desk and office chair, with four more like the ones in the kitchen lined up against the wall. A portable typewriter sat on the desk, although there was no paper in sight.

Beside it stood a radio in a carved wooden cabinet. Johnny whistled.

"The Masta, he make us hide it from them Japs inna jungle," Mula said. "But now – no Japs."

He raised the lantern to display a curious contraption. It was a bicycle, front wheel removed, bolted to sawhorses. The metal rim of the rear wheel spun a rubber belt, which turned a contraption fastened to the wall. Wires ran to the radio.

"This how we gen-rate the juice. You want a go?"

"Sure," Johnny said. He climbed on and began to pedal.

Mula set the lantern on the desk and clicked a knob. Light faded up behind glass inscribed with lines and numbers. A wave of static rose and Mula turned a dial.

Music filled the room – the strains of a swinging orchestra. The native made a fine adjustment and the whistling lessened. There was a crescendo of horns and rolling timpani, and it faded into the clacking of a machine. The dispassionate voice of an Australian announcer came on.

"Good evening. This is the World News from Sydney, New South Wales. It is Monday, August the sixth, 1945.

"The Allied leaders who attended the historic Potsdam Conference near Berlin in Allied-occupied Germany are returning home.

"One of those in attendance – President Harry Truman of the United States – met with King George at Plymouth. The

American leader is now *en route* to his nation by sea.

"As announced by the Potsdam Declaration, Germany will lose every nation it took by force since Adolph Hitler's Nazis came to power. In addition, Germany will be stripped of a further twenty-five percent of the land it possessed prior to the outbreak of hostilities in 1937.

"Efforts are underway to carry out the Potsdam requirement for the demilitarization and denazification of Germany, and for the prosecution of the Nazi war criminals.

"The Potsdam Declaration also demands 'the immediate and unconditional surrender of Japan.' We now have the response from Tokyo. Premier Suzuki has released an official statement. The enemy nation, he said, 'will take no notice of the Allied demands.'

"In that case, the Potsdam declaration promises the prompt and utter destruction of Japan. The United States announces it has escalated the bombing of the nation. In the last two weeks alone, tens of thousands of tons of bombs have been dropped on more than thirty cities. This is reported to have resulted in widespread destruction and loss of life.

"Furthermore, the American Navy has completed its mission to drop mines in every enemy port, sealing off the nation.

"From Allied Supreme Commander, General Douglas MacArthur in the Philippines: the mop-up of Japanese troops on the island of Mindanao is almost complete. President Truman has expanded the commander's authority to include the Japanese Ryukyu Islands – most famously, Okinawa.

"From Burma: the rout of the enemy by Allied forces continues. It is estimated that more than twenty thousand Japanese troops were killed last week.

"From New Guinea: the remnants of the Japanese Eighteenth Army are surrounded at Numbogua, with reports of heavy enemy casualties."

The broadcast continued while the small audience in the Lighthouse Mission hung on every word. When the news concluded, music once again warbled into the room. Mula turned off the radio and Johnny quit pedaling.

Footy wheeled on the Japanese.

"See? You're about to lose the war!" he gloated. The prisoner stared at him a long minute and shrugged.

"It is impossible," he said.

Even though Johnny and Footy now knew he could speak English, it was a shock to hear it.

"What?" Johnny retorted. "You heard the news!"

"That is one man. We know these tricks. It is impossible," the Japanese said slowly. "The Empire of Nippon has never been defeated for two thousand years."

"Well, get ready," Johnny said hard. "You're going down — and I'm going to be there to help make it happen!" There was a pause.

"It will not happen," the prisoner gritted. "We will fight to the death — every one. Old people. Women. Children. No foreigners will conquer us."

"Who's this 'we' and 'us' you're going on about?" Footy asked. "You don't mean *you*, do you? You won't be there. You'll be rotting in our prisons!" The Japanese went silent.

"But I *will* be there — in Japan," Johnny told him. He turned to Mula. "You heard the news! You heard them say 'General MacArthur'? I'm his soldier! Mula, I have to go!"

"No worries," the chief told him. "Anda will be back t'night. We'll have our *singsing* tomorra – we'll give you food for your trip. Then you lot can go – *if* your yarn is true."

"Okay," Johnny told Mula. "It's been a long couple of days. I'm beat. Where can we put him for the night?" He nodded at the captive.

"This way," Mula said. He led through the living room to a door in the back wall. The men stepped into what was clearly the building's largest room.

"This the mission church and school," Mula explained. His face fell again. "But no church – no school – for a long time now. Not since me missionary go to heaven."

Along the far wall was a row of tall, narrow windows with the glass broken out. To their right was the main entrance, two heavy doors standing open in the weeds. The floor of the room was hard-packed clay, and on it were arranged benches of planks nailed to stumps.

Lounging on these were Uhuli warriors, some they recognized from the trail. These munched *kaukau* while they continued removing their fighting gear. Others sat plucking one another's sparse facial and chest hair with bamboo tweezers.

At the other end of the room was a pulpit or lectern – a pole with a square of wood nailed to it. On the wall they had come through, sheets of black-painted plywood were nailed on each side of the door. The faded alphabet and English words were scrawled in chalk.

Through the windows, the men noticed a tall tree alive with movement. It was inhabited by a colony of the big fruit bats called "flying foxes." They hung upside down, bickering noisily, and jostling one another as they came awake for the evening feed. They began to drop off and flap away.

Fair exchange, Footy thought. The bats would eat some of the villagers' bananas – and the people, in turn, would eat some of the bats.

Mula spoke to his men and turned to his guests:

"Your Jap can sleep here. I've told me *wantoks* not to hurt 'im – unless he makes a run for it. Then they can have him. Awlright?"

"You hear?" Johnny asked the prisoner and the man nodded.

"Now," Mula said, "suppa time! We got a special treat – come see!"

His smile made a comeback.

69

A week had passed since Gwyn's last fruitless visit to Army HQ – and though she kept busy, the silence gnawed at her. She'd heard Colonel Chambers was gone, replaced by a new officer. For days, Gwyn tried to get answers – but met only shrugs and silence. At last, unable to bear any more, she went to find Doc Mac.

Not long after, it was the doctor's car that pulled up at the US Garrison. Gwyn and the hospital administrator were ushered in to see the new commander, a Colonel Waters. He invited them into what had been Chambers' office and asked how he could be of service.

"What has become of the rescue for the men of Operation Teeth?" Gwyn asked. Colonel Waters looked mystified.

"I'm sorry," he said. "I'm new here. 'Operation Teeth?' Please explain."

By the time it was sorted out, it had been nearly three weeks since Johnny, Dingo and Footy had left Port Moresby.

That night, after the children were asleep, Gwyn lay in bed and wondered about all the responsibilities she had taken on. She mulled over the roundabout way she had wound up in New Guinea, and the vow she'd made in England never to get involved with a military man again.

Yet here she found herself, losing sleep over a couple of soldiers!

Gwyn had graduated from the School of Nursing in Vancouver, British Columbia, in the spring of 1942. With the coming of war, the Motherland's dire need of medical personnel had been in the news, and Gwyn had volunteered.

It had been years since her mother passed away, and her father had died the year before, while she'd been at college. She'd gone inland for the funeral, held in the church where she'd attended Sunday School. She was surprised by how it had shrunk, and how dowdy it looked. Of course, in Vancouver, she'd gone to Christchurch Cathedral and the grand First Baptist church downtown.

Still, she made the rounds. She saw old friends and discovered to her dismay that she'd grown apart from most of them. Many were married with babies.

Gwyn instructed the family solicitor to put the house up for sale, and returned to her studies. She had her inheritance deposited in an account at the Royal Bank, and invested much of it in Victory Bonds to aid the war effort.

Now she met with her banker to find out how to transfer funds overseas, if and when she so instructed. She withdrew sufficient cash for her travels, and used the first of it to purchase a new wardrobe at the Timothy Eaton Store. She also bought a stout steamer trunk from the Hudson's Bay Company.

The day came when she boarded the train at the False Creek terminal. From here, the western terminus of the Canadian Pacific Railway, it would take the better part of a week to cross the continent. She was grateful she'd treated herself to a private sleeper. While others endured the nights as best they could in general seating, she was able to retreat to the privacy of her small room.

The train departed in the evening. In darkness, it climbed through the dry sagebrush interior. As morning dawned, she saw a landscape out of a Wild West movie. Eventually, they wound their way into the stunning Rocky Mountains.

Gwyn marveled at the snowy peaks, but the equally plunging depths frightened her. Then the train thundered and swayed across flimsy-looking wooden trestles, and Gwyn shrank back from windows that hung over thousand-foot drops.

Through Banff and another night, they descended the foothills onto the prairies. There were endless farms, horse and cattle ranches, and towns where passengers boarded and departed, many in uniform.

Gwyn enjoyed the dining car with its linen and china, gracious service and decent meals, in spite of the war shortages. Other times, she wandered the aisles and conversed with fellow travelers, or sat in her berth and wrote in her new diary. This was a leather-bound book with a strap she could lock. She strung the tiny key on the gold necklace that had been her mother's.

In the vast Province of Ontario, the train rolled through forested hills inset with the bluest of lakes. They chuffed on, and at last arrived in the eastern Maritime provinces. She had crossed the continent from the Pacific to the Atlantic Ocean.

In Halifax, she met up with other nurses on the same journey. There were eleven who boarded the twenty-thousand-ton liner-come-troopship, the SS Duchess of Bedford. They discovered that thousands of soldiers were also aboard, all bound for the UK. Smoke churned from the checkered stacks, the hawsers were thrown off, and tugs pulled the ship from the quay. As the mournful horn echoed across the harbor, Gwyn stood in the crush at the back rail and waved to well-wishers she did not know.

For a young woman on her first great adventure, it was thrilling. She remained at the rail and watched North America recede into the past, and then they were on the blustery open Atlantic.

The nurses shared adjoining cabins and spent much of their time there. It was a rough crossing, and most were seasick, but not Gwyn. Often, to avoid the smell, she buttoned herself into her tweed coat and paced the deck.

There, she discovered, the eager young soldiers were more of a bother than a plague of Okanagan mosquitoes! No matter how many she swatted down, more kept coming. No doubt the odds were to blame: males outnumbered females three hundred to one.

Many of the Canucks were raw-faced prairie boys who'd never been off the farm. So far, their war had been an exciting cross-Canada tour, and then a voyage on a one-time luxury liner. They were a goodhearted bunch, no doubt, but all pimples and hormones. Their boisterous energy was too much for the nurse.

Reveling in her own adventure, Gwyn had no interest in a romantic entanglement. When her countrymen's overtures got to be too much, she retreated to her cabin. There she passed the hours playing card games like hearts and euchre with the other nurses, writing letters, and adding entries to her diary.

Months later, she wished she remembered more of the men when the news reported their slaughter. More than half of these Canadians were killed or captured by the Germans at an obscure French port named Dieppe.

At last, she saw England for the first time – a landmass under dark clouds. The ship docked at the industrial City of Liverpool. There, the nurses and the soldiers separated.

The nurses took the train to London. Staring at tall buildings through sooty windows, Gwyn could hardly believe she was in the homeland her parents had reminisced about all those years.

Eventually, she stepped down into the one-time heart of the British Empire – still the hub of the United Kingdom. To Gwyn, it was like being in a storybook. Even the gray drizzle could not dampen her spirits. She had her "brolly," her umbrella, and needed it as frequently as she had in Vancouver.

At a government office, she and the other nurses were given their postings. They would be dispersed across the British Isles, some going to Europe and even Africa.

Gwyn was assigned to London. Goodbyes and promises to write were exchanged with her new friends, and she was on her own.

She found the rooming house a teacher back home had recommended. Then she reported to the hospital.

The closer she came to the hulking Victorian edifice, the more nervous she was. The place was forbidding, like some medieval castle. Suddenly Gwyn felt small and ill-prepared.

She took a deep breath and forged on. Inside, warrens of hallways led in every direction. A legion of staff and patients marched about, but Gwyn kept getting lost. At last, she arrived at the office of the Matron of Nursing.

There in the waiting room, she encountered another nurse. Gwyn first noticed the mass of red curls and pretty smile.

She introduced herself and learned this was Ruthie, from Ireland – a newcomer like herself. The two chatted up a storm, relieved to find a friendly face in the massive facility.

They were ushered in to see the Matron together. They were briefed, assigned their duties, and handed off to another nurse for a tour of the hospital.

Over the next days, whenever they could, the young women got together. They were the same age – kindred spirits, they decided. While they put a brave face on it, they both felt like colonial hicks in the grand, if bomb-cratered city.

A week later, they decided to room together. They found a flat not far from the hospital, and Gwyn felt quite mature, negotiating the rent and putting down the deposit.

It had only one bedroom, for which they flipped a shilling. Gwyn lost. She ended up on the couch in the sitting room. Here, she split her clothes between her trunk and a box.

The arrangement offered little privacy, but had the advantage of being close to the single coal burner. But even when they found fuel to buy, or scrounged lumps along the railroad tracks, the place remained frigid. Gwyn's homeland might be the distant colonies, but at least Canada had central heating – an amenity the Motherland did not seem to have discovered.

When they both happened to be home and awake at the same time, the girls bundled up, put their feet to the brazier, and got to know each other.

Gwyn described her hometown, Peachland, on a vast lake in the interior of British Columbia. Like Loch Ness, she confided to Ruthie, Lake Okanagan even had its own monster! It was no lie! "Ogopogo" was a gigantic, if shy, marine creature.

"Get away! You're having me on. And I suppose you've seen this 'Oo-goo-poo-goo' with your own eyes?"

"Ogopogo," Gwyn said. "No, I did not see it, but I've seen pictures." But many had seen it, she insisted. There were photos and even films. Ogopogo had an enormous body, flippers, a long neck, and a smallish head. The creature's existence had even been confirmed by the Vancouver Sun newspaper.

Gwyn described going for sundaes and sodas with girl-friends as they watched the boys on the beach. Those were summer nights that stayed light well past 9 p.m. In the winter, it was home early with her parents in front of a fire, while the snow piled against the windows.

Gwyn sometimes told stories about fly-fishing for trout with her father, but learned that Ruthie had little interest in such "tomboy tomfoolery."

"Your turn then," Gwyn said, "where are you from?" The lass flashed a grin, hair a halo in the fire glow.

"Me?" she said, "Well darlin', I'm from nowhere, really — a wee farm with one milk cow, an hour's walk from Pallas Grean."

"And where's that?"

"Along the road between Limerick and Tipperary," Ruthie smiled. "Blink and you'll miss it."

Ruthie's stories revolved around boys, the ones she met at school, at church, or in town. Boys who showed up late at night and tapped on the glass. Ruthie giggled as she admitted to putting a coat over her nightie and climbing out. Gwyn heard about Paddy, Pete and Rolly.

Then, Ruthie said, she'd left for nursing school in Belfast and had really spread her wings. She gave her Canadian friend a wink. In truth, Gwyn was mildly scandalized, but she enjoyed her friend's laughter and generous heart.

In spite of the ongoing German bombing of London, Gwyn and Ruthie managed outings. They dodged the damaged streets and skirted ruined buildings

Together they stared through the gates at Buckingham Palace, disappointed not to catch even a glimpse of the King. Gwyn snapped photos with the Brownie camera that had been her father's.

Other trips took them to the Tower of London, Westminster Abbey, and Trafalgar Square.

Afterwards, they searched out pubs where they might get a meat pie – or Gwyn's favorite – steaming fish and chips in cones of newspaper, sprinkled with malt vinegar and eaten with the fingers.

Wherever they went, as always, they had to ward off men in uniform. At this, Gwyn proved more diligent than Ruthie, but they sometimes let the eager lads stand them a glass. Gwyn learned the differences between lager, pilsner, ale, bitter, porter and stout. The girls enjoyed a laugh and sank a pint or two.

They did not bring boys back to the flat. This was a pact Gwyn had insisted on from the beginning. And so it was that sometimes she returned home alone, while Ruthie made herself scarce for a day or two.

But then, in spite of herself, Gwyn fell totally, hopelessly, dangerously in love.

"Arse over teakettle," as Ruthie put it.

70

Anda, spear in hand, jogged through the jungle. Rapidly, he climbed into the high country. It grew too dark to see anything but the faintest outlines, and still he pressed on. When the moon rose, he was able to go faster. He went silently, alert for enemies, but saw none.

In the early hours of morning he slowed, searching for a particular boulder by the path. He found it, got down on all fours, and crawled through dense foliage. Eventually he was able to stand again, and jogged along a faint trail for another hour. He crested a ridge and dropped into a hidden canyon. Below, a brook trickled past huts outlined against the stars.

Six armed men surrounded him. Anda spoke a word of greeting and they said his name. The men squatted and passed a thin cigar as long as an arm.

These people were Mambu, but only distantly related to the inhabitants of the great valley. Even their language was a dialect. The intermarried clan that inhabited the five huts had garden patches scattered in the jungle. They maintained an uneasy truce with both the Mambu nation and Anda's Uhuli, based on a complex set of favors done and debts owed.

By chance, Anda had encountered one of their teenage women while hunting wild boar in the hills. His courtship of her was at first tolerated, then encouraged, because it strengthened the clan's ties to Mula's Uhuli. At the same time, Anda was warned, the relationship must be kept secret from the Mambu nation, or the people would suffer murderous reprisals.

Yesterday, two of their men had trekked to Bumay's valley to barter Birds of Paradise feathers and *buai,* for *kaukau* and other produce. But they returned early, without making a trade. Instead, they carried a burden of frightening news.

They told their tale under the wheeling stars. When the men finished their story, they disappeared in their homes. The young warrior waited expectantly.

The girl emerged from a doorway. With quickening pulse, Anda saw the starlight outline her shoulders and plump breasts. She carried food she had cooked for him.

Anda took her by the hand and led her to a place among the roots of a forest grandfather. In anticipation of his visit, she had lined it with dry moss. He laid her down, parted her skirt, and they joined. She moved with him, watching his head against the stars.

A few minutes later, the girl stole back to her hut. Her mother saw her enter from the bed of skins where she lay with her husband. The young woman spooned into the warmth of her siblings, and the family slept again.

Anda carried the bag of *kaukau* across a shoulder, spear in hand as he retraced the path in the ghostly light. He ate as he went, careful not to drop anything that would betray his passage. After what he had learned this night, he did not expect to encounter Mambu, but his life depended on vigilance.

On the main path at last, Anda ran hour after hour, anxious to share his astounding news.

71

Mula led his guests to the kitchen table and they sat. Johnny untied the captive's wrists. The Jap was distant, morose. *The news,* Johnny thought. Miriam brought plates piled with baked sweet potatoes. These she'd cut open and smothered in tomatoes and green beans. Also on each plate were chunks of meat, swimming in their juices. Johnny poked suspiciously at the meat.

"What's this?"

Mula grinned. "Me *wantoks* dragged this outta the rivva. *Pukpuk*, mates! You evva try it? Croc is good eating – give it a go!"

"Are you sure?" Johnny asked. "That it's croc I mean?"

It was Mula's turn to look perplexed.

"Look, I don't want to be eating any person," Johnny told him bluntly. "We don't eat humans, Mula."

The Uhuli chief took offense.

"We don't eat no 'ooman beans here! We are not bloody cannibal, mate! I'm hurt, I am, that you think that."

"Don't take it wrong," Johnny said, "but in the Mambu valley they gave us human flesh."

"Bloody cannibals!" Mula shouted and banged his fork on the table. "Them sons-a-Satan! They eat us Uhuli, why do you think we hate 'em? But we, the Uhuli – we the only real people – we not eat no 'ooman beans."

"Aw yeah!" Footy said, "that's what they all say, mate! That's the old story in New Guinea. 'It's them, not us!' 'Til you find yourself chewing on a bit of arm or leg. 'The long pig' some tribes call it."

Footy eyeballed his plate. The prisoner did not touch his helping. Mula speared some flesh, popped it in his mouth, chewed with relish and swallowed.

"'The long pig' – good 'un! I like that one! Nevva heard it 'roun here. But *no*! Eating 'ooman beans, that bloody primitive, mate!" he said as he loaded another forkful. "We Uhuli, we not eat people. Nevva did, even in the old days." He filled his mouth again.

"Naw. We headhunter!" he went on proudly. "That's what me missionary call us. Headhunter, mate — not cannibal."

"What's the bloody difference?" Footy asked.

"Big bloody difference," Mula insisted. "Headhunter — we take your head. Cannibal — he eat you mate. See?"

"Mula, you swear this is croc?" Johnny asked, studying the chunk on the prongs of his fork. His stomach growled.

"I swear onna Bible," Mula said. Johnny decided to trust him. He put the meat in his mouth and it was tasty — nearest thing to steak he'd had in a long time now. Footy watched the Yank, then forked up a bit, sniffed, and ate. The Jap waited for the other men. When he saw them swallow, he decided to brave it.

"'Course I've eaten *pukpuk* — back in Aus," Footy said as he chewed. "And here in the Territories. But in this country, you want to bloody well make sure what's what!"

The meat was firm, Johnny found, whiter than beef, more like pork. There was nothing fishy about it.

"This is *pukpuk* like I told ya!" Mula grinned as he helped himself to more.

"We Uhuli gotta fight, same as you blokes, to protect ourselves. Sometime we kill Mambu to even the score. An eye for an eye, a tooth for a tooth, the Good Book say.

"That the Uhuli way! We like that. But we add one: 'and a head for a head.'" The chief brayed laughter and pounded the table with his fist.

"A head for a head!"

Even Johnny and Footy had to chuckle, and the Jap cracked a smile.

"We usta take Mambu heads," the chief went on. "We put 'em in our *Haus Tambaran*. But me missionary explain the erra of our ways, mate. Now we don't bring no 'ooman heads inta this village no more.

"We good Christian now. The missionary, he take us in the rivva. He baptide us. We burn down the spirit house and all them heads. And we had some good 'uns – even one *Mambu-Ato* from the old days. "Now, with the Masta *dead-finish*, some of me *wantoks*, they go back to the old ways. Some take heads, hide 'em inna jungle. But I don't allow no heads in this village! Things not easy with me missionary gone. But..." he slapped the table, "...we Uhuli are *not* cannibal mate! The real people are Christian!"

"Well, good to know," Johnny said, finishing his portion. Miriam had a chair at the table and was eating as well, baby asleep on one arm. Luke climbed on her knee and ate from her plate.

"Good dinner, Miriam," Johnny said. "Thank you." She dazzled them with her dark smile. The men all had seconds. When they were done at last, nothing left in the pots, Miriam took the plates and scraped them out the door. There were excited snorts, growls, yips and clucks.

"Now sleep," Mula said, standing and stretching. He took a lantern and led them to the bedroom door. "You can have me room," he offered. The men peered at the stained mattress piled with grubby sheets.

"No, no," Johnny said, "We couldn't put you out, Mula! We'll bunk in the living room."

"Couldn't take your bed, mate," Footy chimed in. The Aussie spread his blanket on the sofa while Johnny and Mula walked the Japanese to the church. They got the prisoner settled on a bench, and Johnny said he'd get the rope.

"No need," Mula told him. "You," he spoke directly to the Jap, "you run – if you like." He grinned and said a few words to his men that brought a laugh. The prisoner stretched out.

In the living room, Johnny roped his hammock from the poles. Footy was on his side on the couch. He could feel every spring, but it was better than the hard ground he'd been on. Mosquitoes whined around his ears and he arranged Dingo's square of netting over his head.

Johnny lay in his hammock and heard Footy snore. He was exhausted, and it felt more than physical. He pondered why, and it came to him that he was bone-weary from all the killing.

After three years of war, he had entered strange new territory. It wasn't just about the Japanese anymore. In the Valley of the Cannibals, he had slaughtered natives. That was a first. Complicating it, his sworn enemy had fought by his side. It had never occurred to Johnny that something so strange could happen.

Killing those Mambu was self-defense, he reminded himself, but remained uneasy. *Sure, they're cannibals – but this is their country. What beef do I have with them?*

In mid-thought, Johnny fell asleep. Neither he nor Footy saw the moonlight spill through the windows. In the church, the prisoner slept like the dead, and did not hear sounds the warriors made when they came to stare down at him.

72

Mula posted the guard, and the rest of the men accompanied him, with Miriam and the children, back to the village gathering place. Here, the people were assembled. Men threw wood on the fires, and the Uhuli prepared to mourn their dead.

The five wives of the three fallen men sat together, ashes smeared over their bodies. They began to keen, and their mothers, sisters, and all the women took up the ritualized, warbling wail.

Two of the wives worked themselves into a frenzy of grief and called for hatchets. They splayed the fingers of one hand on the ground while they raised the hatchets in the other. The crying of the entire group became hysterical. While their friends held them upright, first one, and then the other, swung her axe.

Each one chopped off a finger at the knuckle. They screamed and writhed in agony while their companions held them down and staunched the blood with ashes.

When the first wave of grief had ebbed, Mula addressed the group. He described each man's life and pointed out his relationship to dozens present. These connections, the kinship lines, were of paramount importance in village life. That done, he said a prayer to Papa God, asking him to take the souls of the dead into heaven, repeating as much as he could recall of what the missionary had said on similar occasions.

Then, feeling guilty because the missionary had tried to stop such practices, Mula called for the fallen men's possessions. The wives had come prepared with weapons and other items of their *bilas*, their tribal dress. These were placed before the chief, and he and others each picked one up.

Some grabbed flaming branches to light the way. Arm-in-arm, the weeping community walked upriver. Mula assigned warriors to ensure they were not being followed, while he led the people into thick jungle.

They approached the secret place – a grove of trees with an enormous ancient one at the center. This was the Uhuli Tree of the Dead.

None of the tribespeople had breathed a word of this to the

missionaries! To do so was strictly taboo. Furthermore, the elders agreed anxiously, their white man would wage an endless campaign against the tree, as he had against so many of their customs.

Even as they gradually adopted the faith in the spirit God, and his man-son, Jesus, under cover of darkness, they continued the secret death rites among the remains of their ancestors.

With the people circling the broad trunk, Mula ordered the dead men's clan brothers into the tree. He did not look up. He feared what – or who – was waiting there.

Putting on a brave show, but inwardly quaking at the supernatural forces swirling in the darkness, the kinsmen prepared to climb. They hoisted the deceased's belongings, along with *bilums* of food and gourds of water, and climbed swiftly. They hung their burdens on the branches while the bones clattered around them. Then, hearts pounding, they scampered down.

For all time, this had been the Uhuli way to launch the perished on their journey to the spirit world. It was imperative that this be done in the correct manner; for if not, the dead would be unable to depart. The souls would be tethered to earth, and their anger at their kin would turn malevolent. The ghosts would haunt the living, causing calamity and disease.

Mula was deeply distressed that they had not found even a portion of the bodies of the lost men. At least a part of the corpse must be lodged in the tree, or the ghost was unlikely to find its way through the final crossing. This added a special sadness to what they did here tonight.

On numerous occasions, the missionary had explained to Mula – kindly, but with steel in his eyes – that the old and new ways could not mix.

But without the white man to guide him, Mula was mired in complex tribal situations, torn between the worlds.

As he stood beneath the limbs of the great tree, listening to the bones, at last Mula forced himself to raise his head and peer into the spiraling blackness. The branches formed grotesque shapes, strung as they were with gourds, bags and bones. The leaves fluttered as his eyes fastened on what he knew waited there, but did not want to see.

Perched on a tree limb, surrounded by the assembled Uhuli dead, sat the carcass of Masta Billy himself.

The chief saw a skeleton in a rotting shirt and shorts stained by tatters of flesh. The skull wore a leather hat, with a fringe of reddish hair. The eye sockets glowered at Mula, and he coughed and looked down, shivering violently.

Yes, there was a grave back at the mission with a cross of posts. If any white man should ask, the missionary was buried there. But every Uhuli knew the truth.

After the white man's death, the elders counseled Mula that the man had gone through the ceremony that made him Uhuli. Since he was a member of the tribe, they could not put him alone in the dirt! His spirit would wander aimlessly through the ghostly realm. And so, out of their love for him, they had brought him here to be with the people.

Their duty at the tree was done and they could leave. The people were watching Mula.

He took a deep breath, squared his shoulders, and forced himself to walk slowly towards the village. In fact, part of him was terrified, and his instinct was to run like a wild pig through the jungle.

The Uhuli returned to the village and stirred up the fires. For several hours, one after another, they rose to tell stories about the murdered men. Acts of prowess, exploits in battle, and kindnesses to kin, were all described.

The tales were already taking on mythic proportions. The recollections were interrupted ever more frequently by angry outbursts from the younger warriors. Their sorrow gave way to rage. A man would leap up and swear that he would not rest until he had avenged his uncle or brother. The Mambu would pay in heads! On and on it went, until, spent at long last, the people stumbled to bed.

Mula led his family to the mission bedroom, got them settled, and padded into the church to be with his men. They kept an eye on the sleeping prisoner while they talked through the momentous events of the last days. They discussed the white men's fabulous yarn from every angle, and voiced the hope that it was all true – that the demon *Mambu-Ato* and his hated cannibals had been destroyed.

A particularly intense discussion centered on the *pukpuk*, the legendary Father of the Crocodiles. Before the missionary came, the Uhuli had worshiped the beast.

They had grown up believing that it had lived since the dawn of time, and several of the elders argued that the old rituals of appeasement must be revived. If not, they warned, the Papa would punish them by feeding on the Uhuli.

But on this point, Mula would not be swayed. There would be no revival of the crocodile worship and sacrifices.

They had been shown the way. The Uhuli were special – they were children of Papa God. They learned that God gave them the world and they were in charge, not victims.

Mula hammered his point home. They would pray to Papa God to save them, not the crocodile.

At last, the chief crept through the house where his guests slumbered. He crawled into the sheets with his wife and sons, wrapped them in his arms, and passed out.

73

The east was golden when Anda entered the village. The dogs scented him and barked – but only a little, because they knew who approached. The sentries heard the tone and prepared for his arrival.

Cocks had been prematurely announcing dawn for hours.

Anda approached the mission building. The guards watched him come, and an elder crept into Mula's room to wake him. Miriam and the boys stirred, but fell back asleep. Mula joined his warriors. The prisoner cracked one eye open, saw the movement, then dozed again.

Mula handed Anda a slab of cold *pukpuk* steak. The young man chewed as he spoke, recounting his tale. Mula stripped a betel nut with his teeth and took it in his mouth. A gourd of lime powder was passed. He dipped, sucked, chewed, and spat a red jet onto the dirt. Yes, he felt guilty. The missionary had been strict: no spitting in the church! But these days, Mula was one of the worst offenders, and the dirt bore the stains.

Anda's story took some time, drawn out by questions. At last it was told. Mula took a moment to think, then gave a series of sharp orders. Warriors departed.

In the living room, Johnny awoke to the shaking of his hammock.

"Time to get up and shine," Mula grinned through the netting.

"I got bloody big news!"

Johnny had slept in his pants. He swung down from the hammock. Mula wore his broad, black smile.

"Anda's back, mate!"

Johnny smelled coffee and saw Footy in the kitchen, chatting with Miriam.

He went to get the prisoner. The Jap was awake. Johnny said, "come eat." On the way to breakfast, he greeted Anda and the other warriors with a cheerful, "Good morning."

They beamed and chorused, *"Goodpella morning tru!"*

Johnny and the prisoner joined the family at the table. Breakfast was sweet potato and crocodile stew. Mula sliced yellow papaya – what Footy called "pawpaw." The pilot passed around mugs of strong black coffee, though there was no sugar. Mula talked between bites.

"You'll be glad ta know – Anda done, ahh, fortafy da fats."

"Verify the facts," Johnny murmured.

"Right," Mula nodded. "Bumay village is burn down – *gone-finish!*"

The chief threw back his head, held his belly, and laughed. Miriam and Luke giggled and even the baby cooed.

"Anda, he hear a lotta white fellas come outta the sky and fight the Mambu. These fellas got big magic – they kill plenty Mambu! Anda's mates, they seen a lotta dead men. Meebe fifty, meebe a hundred – all dead! Dead!"

Again, Mula laughed.

"They say a big yella man..." Mula looked doubtfully at the prisoner, "...he gotta magic knife and he cut a lotta Mambu head. They say one bloody *bigpella pukpuk* spirit come outta the river and fight along-side them white men.

"This what they call the *Mambu-Matu*, mates! This the Papa-god of them sons-a-Satan! The *pukpuk* eat Bumay, their numba-one *pekpek*-head!"

Again, Mula guffawed, delight transforming his features.

"They say the *Mambu-Matu* burn down the bloody village! Ahhh, wotta day, wotta day!

"These magic fellas," Mula looked doubtfully at the unwashed men at his table: "This you lot – for shore?"

"That's us," Johnny grinned, mimicking aiming a rifle. "Big magic men from the sky."

"Bloody right," Footy said. *"Bigpella fight tru!"*

Mula gazed at them fondly.

"The Mambu – they got a lot ta do now," he said. "First, they gotta make magic to find out why they been punish. Find out why Papa *pukpuk* fight them – kill them – eat that bloody Bumay.

"Then – for shore, mates – them Mambu, they gonna find someone ta blame. Oh yeah! That the Mambu way! And who they gonna blame?" He slapped his chest.

"The Uhuli! That's who! Why? They always do! Then they gonna come this way – in four, five days, I reckon. An' we gonna wait for 'em – back in the bush. I got me *wantoks* watchin' the track now. When they come, we gonna get 'em. We gonna cut a lotta Mambu head!"

Johnny and the others had finished eating and sat back, drinking coffee.

"Tell me more about da croc," Mula went on. "He the *pukpuk* with this mark..." he cupped a hand and placed it over his eye "...like this?"

"That's him!" Footy said.

"You know the Father?" Johnny asked.

"Aw yeah, mate," Mula said.

"Everybody on the Big River know the Father! He the Papa of all the *pukpuk,* that for shore. He got strong magic, that one.

"Me missionary, he not like us to call 'im 'Father.' He say, we got only one spirit Father up in heaven. But I say, this *pukpuk*, he a demon Papa, come ta eat the people. And pigs. And dogs." Mula paused and thought again.

"What I wanna know – what the Papa *pukpuk* do, helpin' you blokes fight the Mambu? Why the Papa eat that *pekpek-*head? Tell me this, Joe-nee."

"Mula, the Father's a crocodile," Johnny said. "Just a croco-dile. It's a big one, for sure. But I shot its foot off. It's flesh and blood, like any animal."

"Not magic, mate," Footy agreed, "though that is the biggest bloody croc I ever clapped eyes on. And believe you me, I've seen the sodding brutes back in Aus. Johnny here bloody well did blow its foot off," he continued. "The Father's no devil – but I do believe it is hunting this Yank." Johnny shrugged and laughed.

"Naw, naw, don't laugh," Mula went serious. "It could be, could very well be. That the *pukpuk* way. A croc want a fella, it watch him. Once a *pukpuk* pick a fella, it get him by-n-by.

"If this *pukpuk* hunt you, Joe-nee, you watch out. Mebee you gotta big problem, going down his rivva."

"Well, maybe," Johnny acknowledged. "Now," Mula said, "your yarn, it prove true! This a big day! Tonight we gonna make one big *singsing*. We gonna eat, we gonna dance! Our en-emy Bumay *die-finish!* Many Mambu *die-finish!* I say tank-ya – all Uhuli say tank-ya!" Mula looked at the prisoner.

"You, Jap – you my enemy," Mula spoke to him directly, "but you kill a lotta Mambu! For that, we not gonna kill you, awlright? You now a friend of the Uhuli."

Mula grinned at the man and the prisoner searched his face, then nodded. "Tonight we dance. Tomorrow, you go your way along the rivva. Me – I'm bloody happy!"

Mula leapt to his feet and performed an impromptu dance, singing at the top of his lungs. From outside the door, warriors joined in. The chief grabbed a battle-axe and shook it in the air.

The boy, Luke, a finger in his mouth, gazed wide-eyed at his father. Miriam looked on contentedly, the baby asleep on her shoulder.

74

After breakfast, Johnny told Mula they needed to wash – themselves and their clothes. Mula said he'd show them where.

Johnny and Footy gathered all their dirty things. They brought these with Johnny's towel and bar of soap. Mula led them to the riverbank.

"Hold on," Footy said, hanging back from the muddy water.

"What about the Father – or any croc?" Johnny asked.

"We *washwash* inna rivva all-a-time, mate," Mula said with a grin. "We look for *pukpuk* – most times, no croc." He shrugged.

"How 'bout someplace else," Johnny said. "Somewhere with clean water?"

Mula thought a moment. "I know a spot. The Masta, he *washwash* inna rivva. But da Missis, she no like it. She like the place I take you." He spoke to the villagers, and soon it became clear, there was an outing in the making. Mula posted guards, then led the procession into the bush. Today, Johnny didn't tie the prisoner's hands.

A crowd of warriors with Miriam, other women, and children, followed. They walked through the gardens and into the forest.

Half an hour later, they arrived at a grassy bank where a brook gurgled over smooth rocks. Butterflies drifted on the air. Green parrots chatted overhead. Dragonflies touched their tails to the stream. Johnny noticed the prisoner watching with real delight.

Miriam and the women volunteered to handle the laundry. Johnny and Footy stripped to their underwear and handed over the rest. The Japanese removed his shirt but kept his trousers – all he had.

The women went to work, soaping, scrubbing, and beating the clothes on rocks. They rinsed and spread them in the sun.

Johnny, Footy, and the prisoner eased into the stream. They found a deep pool upstream and dunked themselves with sighs of relief. The chill water washed away the jungle's grime and sweat.

Johnny called for the soap. It was tossed to him. He lathered and passed it on. Footy scrubbed, then gave it to the prisoner, who did the same. The villagers pointed and laughed. Kids splashed in the shallows around them.

Johnny called to Mula. "Are you coming in?"

The chief folded his arms, grinning. "I already *washwash* this moon."

Eventually, the men climbed out and sat to dry. A few warriors stood guard at the jungle's edge. Most others, like Mula, sprawled in the shade.

Eventually the people meandered back to the mission. Mula said he had things to do, and left with Miriam and the children.

The prisoner sat at the kitchen table while Johnny and Footy reorganized their packs. Afterwards, Footy stretched on the couch and napped. The prisoner lay on the floor, head on his hands, and did the same.

Johnny had noticed there were photos on the living room wall. With daylight at its brightest, he took a closer look. The frames were thick with dust and fingerprints, and the photographs were faded.

Johnny made out a young couple in white, she in a wedding gown and he in dress shorts and shirt. *The missionaries.* He moved to the next frame. There was the man with his arm around a gray-haired couple. Other frames displayed various family portraits.

The final one showed a group of men and women in front of a building. Written across the bottom was: "Bible School, December 1938."

Why would this Australian couple leave their homes and come to this remote land? Why pick New Guinea?

Most of the soldiers Johnny had known couldn't wait to get out of the place.

Johnny got a strong sense of the Australians in this room. He imagined them sharing a meal at the kitchen table, the place new, all clean and tidy, with curtains on the windows. Here they had lived, with music on the radio and news from Australia to ease their homesickness. The couple had spent months, maybe years, right here, helping one another cope with the alien world waiting outside the door.

Johnny thought about their bad end, when the man lay shot and dying. *Did he know his wife was being raped? Did he wish then that he'd never heard of New Guinea? Did he believe God had deserted them – or did he see himself as a martyr, rushing to his reward?*

Once more Johnny found his thoughts going to Gwyn. *What would she say?* He wished she were here. He'd have new things to talk about instead of going on endlessly about Japan! But that was like wishing his parents were still alive.

When Mula returned, his guests were seated at the table. Johnny and Footy were cleaning their firearms.

The chief had to duck to make his impressive entrance. On his hair perched a spectacular headdress of springy bark decorations featuring a magnificent eagle plume. His forehead was painted with a white cross, rays around it. Bold lines of white and yellow were drawn across his face, and outlined his prominent pectoral muscles. His chest was plucked of hair, and his whole skin glistened with pig fat. He wore a *laplap* of brilliant yellow tied around his waist.

Johnny was drawn to Mula's necklace of big conical teeth. The chief sat and Johnny leaned closer to examine it.

"*Pukpuk*," Mula explained. "I killed the crocs meself."

"Now, you blokes wanna see the place for the *singsing*?"

He and his guests strolled through the village. Everywhere, Uhuli were painting one another and putting on their *bilas*.

Mula led to a wide-open space. In it was a pit about ten feet long and four feet across, the dirt piled beside it. Piled in it was a row of hog carcasses. These were packed all round with *kaukau* and leaf-wrapped vegetables.

"This the *mumu*," Mula said.

Five pigs had been slaughtered that day, a rare and special event. Early in the afternoon, a large fire had been built in the pit, the chief explained. Special stones were laid on it – ones that would not explode in the extreme heat. When the wood burned down, the rocks glowed red. On these, a layer of banana leaves had been spread, and then food arranged on top.

They watched men wedge hollow bamboo tubes between the stones. Women covered the mound of food with another blanket of banana leaves. Then men used wooden shovels to cover the entire mound with dirt.

Other men came with bamboo containers of clear water from the stream, and poured this into the standing poles. There was a hiss as the water hit the super-heated rocks. Tendrils of steam came through the earth. It was this, Mula explained, that did the cooking.

"You wait," he smiled. "The Uhuli *mumu* the best you evva taste!" He glanced at the sunset.

"Time for the news."

"Right!" Johnny said.

75

The men returned to the Mission office, and this time it was Footy who climbed on the bicycle generator. A song Johnny hadn't heard before filled the room, although the women's voices were familiar. It ended, and a cheerful Aussie spoke.

"That's the latest from America's Andrews Sisters," he said. "It's called 'Along the Navajo Trail.'"

He pronounced it "Nava-joe," and Johnny grinned.

"And now, time for the news." There came the clacking of a machine, and the news announcer spoke.

"Good evening. It is six o'clock. This is the World News from Sydney, New South Wales. It is Tuesday, August the 7th, 1945.

"American President Harry Truman has announced that a new type of bomb – an atom bomb – has been dropped by the

United States on the Japanese City of Hiroshima." The prisoner's breath hissed in.

"What...?" Footy asked.

"Listen!" Johnny said.

"President Truman announced this from the mid-Atlantic, where he is aboard the USS Augusta. The American leader is returning from the historic Potsdam Conference.

"President Truman said the atomic bomb was more than two thousand times more powerful than the largest bomb ever used to date.

"An assessment of the damage caused to the City of Hiroshima has been impossible, due to the huge cloud of impenetrable dust over the target.

"The atom bomb was dropped from an American B-29 Superfortress, known as Enola Gay, at 8:15 a.m. local time. The plane's crew reported a column of smoke rising and intense fires springing up.

"President Truman said the atomic bomb heralded 'the harnessing of the basic power of the universe.' The President went on to say that this marked a victory over the Germans in the race to be first to develop a weapon using atomic energy.

"President Truman warned the Japanese that America has completely destroyed their ability to make war. I quote; 'This is the last chance for Japan to avoid utter destruction.'

"President Truman said: 'If they do not now accept our terms, they may expect a rain of ruin from the air the like of which has never been seen on Earth. Behind this air attack will follow, by sea and land, forces in such number and power as they have not yet seen – but with fighting skill of which they are already aware.'

"In other news..." the announcer continued with lesser events of the day. When it was over, Mula turned down the volume.

"Have you ever heard of an atom bomb?" Johnny asked Footy.

"No mate," Footy said. "What is it? It must be a bloody big bomb."

"Can one bomb destroy a city?" the Jap broke in, startling the other men. "Is this a trick?"

"This is no bloody trick!" Footy snapped. "This is real, mate!"

"You heard what they said," Johnny joined in. "If President Truman said it, it's true." Something occurred to him.

"Is that where you're from?" he asked. "What was the city?"

"I am not from Hiroshima," the P-O-W said shortly.

"Is it possible one bomb can wipe out a city?" Johnny echoed the question. No one knew the answer. Mula's eyes went from face to face. He was very impressed that the white men were so shocked.

"Mula, we've got to leave!" Johnny said urgently. "First thing tomorrow! You heard what they said – the invasion of Japan! I've got to be there!"

"Shore, mate," Mula said. "You're free ta go. This big news – this Adam bomb?"

"Atom, atom," Footy said. "And it's bloody big news!"

"Who is this Atom?" Mula asked.

"It's not a person – it's a tiny thing," Johnny said, "so small you can't see it. That's what I've heard."

"And this tiny thing makes a big bomb?" Mula asked dubiously. "Are you pulling my foot?"

"No!" Johnny barked. "Mula, I can't explain this bomb. It's a new thing!" He looked at the Jap. "But it's the end for Japan."

"Why so important for you to be there, for the end of Japan?" the prisoner asked Johnny, his voice raw. "Why?"

Johnny didn't answer. He stared hard at the Jap for a minute, their eyes locked. On the radio, the lighthearted announcer came on and Mula turned the sound up.

"The very best news! They've turned up the heat on the Japs! This must be the beginning of the end of the war. And now we continue with our musical entertainment. Sit back, relax, and hoist a cold one to the blessed Yanks!" The strains of a big band gushed out of the speaker. Mula turned the radio off and Footy dismounted the bike.

"What does it mean?" the pilot wondered.

"Beats me." Johnny shook his head.

"Well mate, nothin' we can do about any bloody big atta-bomb," Mula said. "We gotta *singsing!* This a cel-bration over them sons-a-Satan Mambu.

"You blokes come along now. You the guests of honna!"

76

At Mula's urging, Johnny and Footy left their rifles at the mission. The chief assured them his sentries were on guard. They kept their pistols and knives on their belts, as they were used to. The prisoner pulled Johnny aside: he did not want to go.

His expression was so strained that Johnny had a quiet word with Mula. The two agreed — the prisoner would stay under guard in the church.

Mula led Johnny and Footy into the village.

Night had fallen and torches lit the pathways. The chief carried his longbow and a prized man-killing arrow — its thirty-inch hardwood head was barbed, dyed, and tasseled. He also bore his best battleaxe with a green stone head.

As they walked, more villagers in their finest *bilas* joined them. The crowd swelled until they reached the central clearing. Bonfires flickered, casting light across hundreds of Uhuli.

Near the cooking pit, Miriam appeared. Her skin gleamed with oil, and intricate patterns were painted across her chest, back, and legs. She wore a bright grass skirt, necklaces of colored beads, and flowers in her hair. Luke stood beside her, painted like his father and clutching a small spear.

Mula shouted greetings. The crowd quieted as their leader stepped into the firelight. He launched into a speech in Uhuli, his voice ringing out. Laughter came in waves, then moments of solemn reflection. He gestured often toward Johnny and Footy.

At his signal, drummers stepped forward. Hourglass-shaped drums beat out a rhythm, and the unmarried girls lined up. They wore layered grass skirts to widen their hips and had painted spirals on their torsos. They sang and clapped, moving in time.

The boys took their place, Luke with them. The drums beat faster and the little men shouted and waved their spears. They were followed by girls about their age, waists encircled in strings of flowers, blossoms in their hair. Then the married women gathered, including Miriam. They danced in a circle, following one another, each holding the waist of the woman before her.

It was the teenage warriors' turn. The boys wore a white feather in their headbands. Mula explained that at the time the boys' voices changed, he and the mature warriors held the ceremonies that made them men. It was at this time they were honored with the feather. Each man-boy would wear it until he either killed a *pukpuk* or battled the Mambu. Then he earned his eagle feather.

The teenage men finished dancing, and it was time for Mula and the warriors. The chief strode to the dance area, his bow and arrow in one hand, axe in the other. He called and his men gathered around him.

For the first time, big drums joined the handheld ones. These were hollow logs with slits, pounded with cudgels. Bass notes thumped beneath the others. The warriors faced the people and stamped their feet to the rhythm. Mula sang phrases, each one taken up and repeated by his companions. They shook their weapons and shouted battle cries.

That done, Mula called them to the *mumu*. The women had been busy while the men danced, and Johnny and Footy followed to the pit. The dirt and top layer of banana leaves had been removed. Rising steam carried a mouth-watering aroma.

Women jumped into the pit and sliced up the pigs. Others waited with stacks of cut banana leaves. On each square, the servers piled juicy pork, sweet potatoes, and a variety of vegetables. Elderly men crowded around and provided much advice, largely ignored.

At last, Mula called in a loud voice. Silence descended and all eyes turned his way. The chief handed his weapons to a warrior, glanced at Johnny and Footy and smiled.

"Let's pray, mates." He pressed his hands together and the assembly followed suit. Even the serving women paused and squeezed their eyes shut.

"Tank you true, Papa-God, for bringin' us togetha!" Mula shouted. "Tanks for killing them bloody Mambu – for new mates and good food." He translated into Uhuli and then bawled, "let's eat!"

Women passed out the laden leaves. Miriam brought the first serving to Mula. On her heels came two unmarried girls, who smiled shyly as they handed helpings to Johnny and Footy. On his square of banana leaf, each man had a generous slab of pork, soft bamboo shoots, yellow and orange sweet potatoes, beans in edible pods, and whole tomatoes. The men sat in the firelight, while the sky blazed with stars. They ate with their fingers.

When everyone was full, and many, including Johnny and Footy, had second helpings, the *singsing* continued. Dance followed dance. Johnny's eyes stung from the smoke and Footy's head began to nod. They asked Mula for permission to leave – and food for the prisoner. The two returned to the mission.

Johnny took the leaf-plate to the captive, found him asleep, and woke him. The man looked at him with dull eyes. Johnny set the food down and went back to the living room. Footy was already on the couch. Johnny climbed into his hammock. Within minutes, both men were out.

The *singsing* went on and the hours wore away. None of the Uhuli saw the disturbance far across the river, in the shadows beneath the bank. A *cuscus* was the only witness. The possum was asleep on a branch when it was blasted awake. An exhalation through huge nostrils fanned its fur. Terrified, nocturnal eyes bulging, it stared down and saw something massive move. It squealed in fright and scampered to the very highest twigs.

There it curled again, complaining into its soft belly as it covered its eyes with its paws.

The Father stared across the river, saw light flickering on the prey animals, and smelled smoke. But its flayed leg throbbed, its bones ached, and it was not hungry. It sucked in a deep breath, submerged, and swam downstream. Pushed by the current, aided by sweeps of its tail, the *Papa pukpuk* passed by the place where the Smooth-headed man slumbered.

Mula and his warriors continued to dance. Only when shafts of morning light probed the sky did the last drumbeats fade, and the diehards reel away.

The chief returned to the mission. He changed the guard and he and his *wantoks* stripped off their *bilas*.

They lay down on the benches and conked out.

77

Johnny woke with morning streaming through the windows. He saw Footy, up early again, alone in the kitchen. The Aussie had lit a fire in the stove. Johnny slid out of his hammock, untied it, and rolled it up.

We leave today. He greeted Footy, accepted a cup of coffee, and said they'd be on their way shortly.

Johnny went through the door into the church and woke the prisoner. He saw Mula nearby, out cold among his comrades, and did not disturb him. Johnny and the Jap went to the kitchen. Footy had been outside and returned with his hands full of eggs.

"Look – cackleberries! I've been watching where the chooks were laying."

"I cook," the prisoner said. Footy shot him a look.

"Go on then."

There was a cast iron skillet on the stove and the Jap threw in a pork rind. When the fat was sizzling, he cracked in the eggs. He chopped roast *kaukau* from a pile and dropped that in as well. Shortly, he was sliding plates in front of the others.

Breakfast done, Johnny told the prisoner he would tie his hands for the trail. Listlessly, the man held them out and Johnny used the rope. Johnny and Footy were putting the last things in their packs when Mula entered, yawning and scratching.

"Top o' the mornin'," he said, voice raw. "Time to be off, is it?"

"Yes," Johnny said. "That was quite the party."

"Yes, ta. That was interesting. Looks like you went all night, mate," Footy added.

"Too right," Mula agreed, pinching red eyes. "Gotta stay with your *wantoks* at a *singsing.*"

Uhuli warriors followed, arms loaded with rolled leaf packages they piled on the table.

"Food for you lot," Mula smiled. They stuffed the cooked pork and vegetables into their packs, then slung up their loads and picked up their rifles.

Miriam shuffled out of the bedroom, the children still asleep. Johnny and Footy thanked her. Then, to the others' surprise, the Jap went to her, said thank you, and made a small bow.

Outside waited an escort of ten warriors. The group set off, Mula and his men yawning hugely.

It was a fine morning, the breeze off the river carrying a hint of coolness. Johnny gazed across the swirling surface.

Where is the Father? Well, one thing you can count on, the Hard Case said. *It's out there, and it seems to be hunting you.*

Mist rose from the reed beds. The men walked for an hour and came to a sapling fence along the jungle.

"The end of my land," Mula said. "Me *wantoks* stop here, but I come with you blokes, show you where to go. *Long-way likilik.*"

"'A little bit of a long way,'" Footy grinned.

"Yes, mate," Mula said. "We go into Taifora land. They strange ones, the Taifora. They friend of the Uhuli, and not hurt you – prob'ly not – but best if I'm with you. Got their own ideas, this lot. I take you by 'em."

Johnny's group shook hands with the line of warriors. The Uhuli said goodbye to the foreigners who had killed the cannibal demon Bumay and made an ally of the Father of the Crocodiles.

They watched their chief disappear into the forest with his new friends.

78

"What did you call the tribe?" Footy asked.

"Taifora, mate," Mula said. "Had their own missionary, *long time-finish*, but the Mambu got him early on. That was before the Masta and Missis come to the Uhuli. The Taifora, they got some Christian, some of they own ideas.

"'Misguide,' that's what me missionary call 'em."

"Misguided? How?" Johnny asked.

"You see for yourself," Mula shrugged, "soon enough."

They hiked the morning away and ate a cold lunch of *mumu* food. They moved on and began to hear drums echoing through the forest.

"Awlright," Mula said, "no more talk."

A few minutes later, he ducked around a tree and the others followed. They found themselves going up a jungle-covered hill. From the top, Johnny paused to look back, and there was the Raub, winding into the distance. The men continued along the spine of the ridge and the drumming grew louder.

Mula motioned for the men to get down. They slid on their bellies to the edge of a cliff. Johnny found he was looking onto a field thirty yards below. Behind it in the trees was a village, but it was the activity on the grass that commanded attention.

A line of twenty drummers stood along the far side, facing his way. Each of them beat on the now-familiar hand drums. They wore headdresses of glossy parrot feathers, and were painted from head to toe in green with bands of yellow. Around their hips were short skirts of the same plumage.

On the near side of the field was a tower of four tall poles. Perched on top, not far below the watchers, was an open-sided thatched hut. Two men stood under the roof, staring away.

They had hands cupped around their eyes, and appeared to be looking for something.

A pole stood beside the field. From it, long streamers fluttered. On the opposite side, midway down the line of drummers, was a homemade table of saplings and vines.

Behind it stood two men, the most outlandish of the lot. They had bleached white crocodile skulls tied onto their heads.

"Priests!" Mula whispered.

The two were busy with a small box on the table, also made of sticks. A vine ran from it to a woven ball one held. One of the croc-heads spoke words into it, then passed it to the next shaman, who did likewise.

The drums beat faster, and the line of warriors began to hum in deep voices. Johnny realized something was moving in the forest. A shape emerged that looked like an airplane. The effigy was cleverly made of saplings bent into a frame, covered with painted bark cloth. Six natives walked inside, heads poking through holes. The "aircraft" was complete with wings and a tail, and had a propeller of bark that spun in the breeze.

The contraption drifted down the field. The humming grew louder, a sound like engines. The thing stopped in front of the priests' table and, as the drums beat faster, the men inside lifted it off and laid it on the grass.

The drums were at fever pitch and the warriors broke into frenzied vocals. All at once, they all looked up. Johnny thought at first his party had been seen, but realized the Taifora were peering into the sky. The priests were gyrating and shrieking like men possessed. Johnny felt a touch – Mula wanted them to leave.

They backed into the jungle and descended the hill. Half an hour later, they emerged on the riverbank once more.

"What in the world was that?" Johnny asked.

"The missionaries call it 'Cargo Cult,'" Mula said.

"Aw, yeah," Footy said. "I've heard of that, but first I've seen of it. It's all across New Guinea they say. There are a lot of different versions."

"What's the Cargo Cult?" Johnny asked.

"Right, mate," Mula said. "I'll have a go. Some people believe you lot – you whites – are their dead family come back to
life."

"Okay," Johnny said. He thought of the old Mambu folks.

"I saw a plane," Footy said.

"Yes mate," Mula said. "It go like this. God have a son who
die for everyone – that's wot they say, right? The son go to
heaven and make big houses, plenty big houses for all the people, right?"

"I guess so," Johnny said. "Something like that."

"We see you fellas. You come along, cut a path in the bush.
You talk to a magic box. I know it's a wireless, I'm educate. But
these fellas, they bloody primitive! Then a *baloose* – a plane – it
come! And all the cargo come out. Big magic! These Taifora,
they want the cargo! Right mate?"

"Right mate," Footy said.

"So what does that have to do with God?" Johnny asked.

"Ahh," Mula said. "Where does the cargo come from? From
big houses far away, the white men say. Jesus go to heaven and
to make big houses for his children. He make lots of good
things! But the white man, he get there first! He gets the cargo.
He don't wanna share!"

"Whoa!" Johnny said. "That's not how it goes!" Mula
shrugged.

"These Taifora, they make the magic, but the *baloose*
doesn't come. How do they explain that?" Footy asked.

"Ahh, they don't get the magic right – yet," Mula said.
"Soon, they gonna get it."

"That is so nuts, it almost makes sense," Johnny said.

"More like, the most buggered story ever told," Footy added.

"Mula, if the Taifora put half that effort into real work, they could buy the cargo!"

Mula rounded on Johnny and stared at him.

"Is that right, Joe-nee? What you mean, work?"

"Here's how," Johnny said. "You grow coffee, tea and coconuts. Or you get croc skins. You'll sell that and get paid – good money."

"That true, Joe-nee?" Mula asked. "I don't know 'bout those utha things, but *pukpuk* skins, I can get. We trade 'em for cargo?"

"That's how it's done," Johnny said. "Right, Footy?"

"Bloody right, mate," Footy grinned. "Take the skins, scrape all the meat off, and rub 'em in salt. Dry 'em in the sun. You sell for money, and money buys cargo. That's the Australian way."

"Japanese way," the prisoner nodded. The others stared at him. He'd hardly opened his mouth all day.

"I think 'bout that," Mula nodded. "Thank you to verify the facts." He grinned proudly.

"Now this is where I stop. You got *a long way likilik* to the big saltwater. Maybe five days, maybe ten. I don't know, mate – nevva been there, but that's wot I hear." The travelers readied themselves to leave.

"You tell 'em when you get back," Mula went on, "the Uhuli need anotha missionary! We keep the missin nice for 'im. We need guns and bullits, clothes, knives, axes. We like them motors for our canoes – an' petrol! You be shore to tell 'em that!"

"Yes, yes," Footy said.

"You get your croc skins," Johnny smiled. He offered his hand and Mula pumped it vigorously.

"And thanks, Mula. You're one of the good guys."

"One of the good guys!" Mula smiled broadly. "I like that! You lot friends of the Uhuli now. You come back. Thank you for killin' that *pekpek*-head and those sons-a-Satan. Joe-nee, you watch out for the demon Father! Don't let him eat ya!" Johnny waved and headed along the trail.

"Nice guy, that Mula," he said.

"Yes mate," Footy said.

"But crikey, he likes to talk!"

79

The three men walked for hours. At a spring, they drank, refilled their canteens, and kept going. The water tasted a little strange, but Johnny had gone through his treatment tablets long ago. They had no choice.

All three were subdued, the darkening day dragging them lower. They'd left the friendly Uhuli behind and were in unknown territory once more. Rain clouds gathered ahead, and they heard the boom of thunder.

They toiled through the forest and emerged beside more gardens. Women were digging in the distance, but when they saw the aliens, they fled into the jungle.

Whenever the path drew close to the river, the men paused and scanned the banks for crocodiles. Several times they passed a mudslide and noticed fresh dung. They saw eyes watching from the reeds, but none with a span wide enough to be the Father.

At midday, they slumped on rocks to eat. They were all sweat-soaked. Johnny untied the prisoner while Footy dug out *mumu*. The Jap ate robotically. Johnny wasn't hungry – his head throbbed and stomach churned. *Malaria?* He hoped not. When Johnny retied the prisoner's hands, he asked how he was doing. He got an eyebrow twitch as a response.

As they took to the trail, the last patch of sunlight disappeared and the whole sky went dark. The trio pressed on while thunderheads piled overhead. Over the river, a shaft of lightning flashed and thunder ripped the sky. Another arc zapped to earth, accompanied by an explosion, and at once, they smelled rain.

The first fat drops splashed on them and Johnny pulled his helmet over his eyes and walked into the oncoming storm. The trail led them into another clump of jungle and the men ducked under the branches. The creatures had gone silent, and the only sound was drops striking leaves.

There came the roar of approaching rain and then it struck in earnest. The canopy absorbed the first barrage, but the water licked over branches and everything ran. Instantly, the men were soaked and the path melted into mud. Johnny and Footy's foot-gear pulled up clods. Now the captive's bare feet were an advantage.

After a time, they emerged from the trees and slogged in torrential rain through a cane field. The sullen river ran forty yards off, the surface pocked by drops. The rain drummed off Johnny's helmet and sluiced down his collar. A sheet washed in front of his eyes and he could barely see his feet splash through deepening puddles. The flashes and booms were like battle.

Johnny's skull hurt. His thoughts fixated on the Father. He peered ahead and his heart hammered.

There it is! The monster rode the lurid lightning. It rushed at him through the deluge, as massive as it had been when it killed Dingo.

Johnny saw the scar, puckered scales cupping one eye. Its mouth was wide and he smelled putrid decay that made him want to heave.

The beast opened its jaws and thunder erupted from its belly. The sound vibrated through Johnny's body. Deep within him, something turned. Lightning shot from the yellow eyes and blinded him. He shivered from head to foot, spots of light danced, and all his skin rose in goose-flesh.

His guts twisted again, and here came an army of the gruesome dead. Some had been his brothers-in-arms, and he saw them shot and dying, blown up and dying. They came side by side with the snarling Japs he had shot, blood dripping from their terrible wounds. *It's my nightmare!* But it was wrong. The dead only haunted his sleep – yet here he was awake beside the river.

And then he saw Chief Bumay coming and his blood turned to ice. The cannibal drifted his way across the flooded plain, but only half a man, legs gone and loops of guts dragging through the puddles. The warrior had his great black spear in one hand, held back to throw.

He smiled his ebony smile that crackled with lightning, and he aimed the spear at Johnny's heart.

80

With all his will, Johnny braced himself for the blow. Bumay ran him through and came after the spear. Johnny felt him pass, the guts tugging at his own. Drums pounded, rising into whistling static.

A cheerful Aussie voice called out: *an Adam bomb went off this morning – a bloody big bomb went off!*

The rain cut him like broken glass. Far below, boots knocked together. Fear shot up his legs. He scraped together the tatters of his awareness and staggered on.

Footy was thoroughly wretched. When the rain began, he unhooked the brim of the hat, but the water poured off and drenched him. The mud sucked his sandals. All he could see was the back of the prisoner and the great flood.

When he could peer beyond the Jap, he made out the Yank, grinding on. He forced himself out of the stupor he'd fallen into and looked around. The path went by a cane field, and then they skidded into a lower area. He squinted through the driving rain as the swollen river surged over the bank.

Dark water swept their way and drowned the path.

And then he saw Johnny stumble, almost fall, and grind to a swaying stop. The Jap, head down, ran into him. The Yank reeled like a drunk.

"Oyyy!" Footy called. "Johnny! Hold up, mate!" The Yank's face turned, white and slack. The prisoner froze as well, and his gaze spun to Footy.

"You, Jap!" the Aussie snapped. "Go by the sergeant! Then wait." The man sidled around Johnny and turned. Footy splashed to the Yank's side and grasped his bicep.

"Mate, you're ill," Footy said urgently. Johnny felt the pinch on his arm while another hand reached inside him and pulled.

"Sick!" Johnny said. The word banged in his head and did not find his mouth.

"Let's find shelter," Footy said. He stared around.

Ahead through the flooded field he saw a hill. Now it was an island in the storm, crowned by a tree. At least that would give some protection.

"Go there!" the Aussie barked at the P-O-W, pointing with his rifle.

The man led off while Footy guided Johnny through knee-deep water. They reached the slope and scrambled up.

"Sit!" Footy ordered the prisoner, motioning to the tree. The man put his back to the trunk and slid down.

Johnny groaned and thrust his rifle to Footy. There was a boulder standing in the rain and he stumbled to it, got his pants down and sat, pack still on. His body began to convulse and he moaned in distress. The sound and the smell were atrocious and Footy, standing beneath the tree, felt a wave of nausea – *from the stink.*

He stood fretting.

Of all the times!

The thunderstorm bellowed and crashed, and the whole sky became falling water. One second it was garishly lit, then twilight. The flood expanded until it filled the world.

Johnny turned his face up to see what was hitting him. Drops fell out of a black sky and struck his eyeballs. He dropped his chin to his chest and sat panting while the spasms worked through him.

Footy was leaden with fatigue. Clutching a rifle in each hand, he sat on a buttress root. He felt a prickle of danger and swung his head to look at the prisoner. The Jap was staring back.

Then the pilot felt the first cramp tear his own belly.

Johnny's eyelids crashed down. Outwardly, he appeared

unconscious, but within, the nightmare raged full force.

The cannibal chief stood before the Mambu nation, yelling in a loud voice. Johnny raised his rifle and shot at his head, but the bullet curved in flight and slammed the chief's shoulder. There was a noise like breaking glass and Bumay lifted off the ground, legs gone and intestines hanging. And there was the croc, waiting below. It lunged up.

The Father! It bites the guts and drags Bumay down.

Johnny tasted the man-flesh and vomited. Thunder rattled his bones and he hurt everywhere. Lightning lit up the inside of his head. His skull split open and his mind shot up in a blaze of light.

The prisoner sat, back against the tree, and knew the Yankee was finished. During his years in New Guinea, he had suffered from the belly sickness many times, and he had watched his countrymen die that way. He felt a hint of compassion and rejected it.

Pity is weakness! – his Father's voice. He focused on his duty.

I will kill my enemies and escape. Yes, he thought, *but not yet.*

Footy had his rifle up, aimed at him. He saw a scowl on the white face, knew it masked fear, and was encouraged.

The storm raved on, and the Japanese made himself relax. He closed his eyes and thought about the atom bomb. The news had set off a war inside him. People had spoken of such a thing for years, but it was thought to be an impossible theory. Yet it was important not to lie to himself in his deepest thoughts.

The destruction of Hiroshima – is it true? His captors, he could tell, believed it absolutely.

If it was so, the Empire of Nippon was finished, for who could fight such a thing? He felt desperate.

But there was another possibility and it rose like steel within his disgrace.

It is a trick – the enemy is a master liar. All we did was take the land and resources my people need to live. Along that path, we found weaker, lesser people, and we conquered them.

In spite of our setbacks, I believe in the Empire! I live to serve the sacred homeland. There is no such thing as a single bomb that destroys millions of people!

These feelings were so strong, they made him nauseous. It reminded him of how many times he'd been sick in these night-mare jungles. He felt unmoored in the terrible storm.

Do not think too much. Do your duty!

He opened his eyes and found himself staring down the dark barrel of the rifle, the pilot still watching him.

It was not yet time and he rested.

81

The Australian groaned as the cramps milked his own belly. Footy knew he was in terrible trouble and he glanced at Johnny. *No help there.* He flashed another look at the Jap. Lightning flickered and he saw the black eyes.

"Just breathe wrong and I'll shoot!" Footy hissed.

He kept the prisoner covered while his other hand fumbled with his shorts. He barely got them down in time. On and on it went, wave after wave, and he grew faint and panicked.

Shoot the Jap while you still can!

He ordered himself to pull the trigger, but discovered the rifle muzzle was in the mud. With all his might, he hauled it up, but it was heavy.

Again, Katsu gazed down the barrel and wondered which heartbeat would be his last.

Footy's vision went white. A roar filled his ears, and from far away, he realized he was falling.

Katsu watched the enemy topple and the rifle drop.

Now act!

Yes, he had fought beside these *gaijin*, but that was self-preservation.

These were the enemy, and this was war.

He rose to kill them.

82

The Father drifted in profound darkness, throbbing foreleg held out, and let the current bear it along. Only when it had to breathe did it rise. Its head broke the surface. It unsealed ears, eyes and nostrils, and sipped the air. It observed a dull day and felt the beat of raindrops on its skull.

Forked lightning struck a tree by the river. It went up in a fireball. The reptile flinched at the sound, so like the attacks it hated. It sank into liquid silence and drifted underwater with the scent of the rain in its lungs.

When the Father rose again, there were no more explosions, but the downpour continued. It swam close to the bank and saw that the land was flooding. The current swirled across a wide new territory.

The predator floated in. As it went over the bank, it struck its foreleg and hissed in pain. Then it was coursing through the shallows.

Since its injury, the healing process had begun. In the reptilian way, its body attempted to regrow the limb, but the damage had been profound. Still, it had formed a clubbed stump.

But then, the wound had been brutalized again. Something had plunged deep inside, and with each movement, this probed the joint. The torment never ceased.

Both suffering and healing consumed energy. The infection often made the crocodile nauseous, but at this moment, it was famished.

Across the muddy shallows, it perceived a hump of land. Its senses prickled when it saw a two-legged animal. The Father sped at it.

The man stared across the flood, wondering when it would subside so he could depart. At once, he was alarmed. Coming across the water were ripples! It could be an uprooted tree, but no – it moved against the current.

The wake stopped at his feet. Before he could move, a gigantic head burst from the water. The jaws flew open, and the teeth took him in a brutal embrace. All his flesh quivered and came apart.

His companions woke to find hideous death stalking among them.

83

The Asian stood up on the island. At last, the moment he had waited for had come. Fever had conquered his enemies – now it would be easy. The two had treated him well enough, but war was war. He would give them one last gift – a swift cut across the neck.

He stepped towards the Australian, bound hands reaching for his *katana* in the pack. But agony sliced him in two. He was knocked to his knees. He vomited and filth blasted into his trousers.

I am sick as well!

Still, he was Samurai and an officer of the Empire. He forced his body to crawl, but again, weakness betrayed him. The spasms were torture. He fell on his side as the inner storm shook his bones.

He came to in the black of night. Again, he willed his limbs to move, but they would not obey. He lay hyperventilating, mustering his strength. Lightning flickered and he saw the Australian with his eyes closed, lying in the mud beside the rifle.

With supreme effort, the soldier raised himself, but as his arms went up, they seemed to draw a sword through his own guts. He fell back and rolled down the slope, into the water.

Rise! Do your duty!

He tried to obey, but he lay half submerged in the flood and lost consciousness.

Three men sprawled on the flood-made island, half buried in mud.

They were undone, exposed to whatever came their way.

84

December, 1942

Near Buna, North Coast

Sheets of rain lash the jungle and a dismal patch of mud by the swamp. The black water is putrid with floating corpses. Water swirls where crocodiles feed.

On the sodden shore is a pile of dead GIs, dragged there by the thirty or so of their countrymen who cling to life in this place. These are young men in their late teens and early twenties who have strung tents and tarps against the tropical downpour. Their uniforms are so ripped and filthy, they are almost unidentifiable.

Some gather around a sputtering fire that sends clouds of smoke into the mist. To keep it going, they shave wet sticks and dry these in the flames. A dozen more soldiers huddle under a tarp roped to mangroves, playing poker with a dog-eared deck. Even though this is the equator, most shiver with fever. Around the clearing's edges, GIs squat in the foliage, groaning as dysentery rumbles through their guts. Elsewhere, men sprawl in pup tents – sick and unconscious.

Near the edge of the clearing, one of the bearded scarecrows lies on a muddy blanket under branches, helmet for a pillow. The only indication that he lives is the slow rise and fall of his chest.

On the jungle side, there is a trail pocked by boots and strewn with more American dead.

A machine gun deep in the forest shatters the stillness. Along the footpath, slugs kick up mud and make the corpses jump. Rounds whip through the foliage over the GIs' heads. Branches crack and leaves flutter. A few men spit or curse. Most don't even glance up – they've seen too much of this.

A man deals the cards again. After a few minutes, the big gun quits.

In the sudden silence, two men stride from another direction into the clearing, one after the other.

"Ten-shun!" one yells.

The GIs do not move, but their eyes turn wearily to the voice. They see an American officer, a lieutenant, standing there. He wears a clean uniform, spattered on the shoulders by rain.

Someone comes striding behind him. The men stare at an older man in a khaki uniform, wearing cap and raincoat. In disbelief, they take in the two silver stars on each collar point.

This means he is a general of the U.S. Army, by far the highest-ranking officer they have seen at this sorry, disease-ridden front. He strides to the center of the mudflat and gazes contemptuously at the men. Most now struggle to stand, although it is a pitiful display.

"As you were," he says in a scornful voice. The GIs sink to the mud again.

"Listen up! I am General Bob Eichelberger – your new commander. I'm here under Supreme Commander General Douglas MacArthur's direct order to take this place! I have relieved General Harding of duty. I am here to change things."

He waits, but the men simply stare dully back.

"What are you doing here?" General Eichelberger asks.

Again, nothing.

"Who is in charge?"

There is a pause.

"I guess I am now, Sir," a man with sergeant stripes says.

305

"We are – were – a platoon, K Company. The Lieutenant took most of the men that way –" he nods towards the trail, "– yesterday."

"Where are they now?"

"They didn't come back, Sir. There's a Jap machine gun. We're pinned down."

The general takes a step closer.

"You've been sitting here since yesterday?" he asks, incredulous. "You didn't go to help them? Didn't move?

"You've got to take that gun emplacement! Wipe it out!"

The dejected soldiers look at each other and back to the ground. One snickers hysterically.

"We're sick, sir..." a GI begins. Eichelberger cuts him off.

"I will personally decorate any man, right now, who will attack the Japs down that trail!"

He waits a full minute, but no one will meet his eye.

"Anyone who volunteers to lead the way – I will promote you to captain, right now!"

The GIs have run out of places to look. The general glowers but realizes, if he gives the order now, he will face open mutiny. The rain begins to fall heavily.

"I could order you down that trail," he says in a milder voice, "but I know you men have been through a lot and I will cut you some slack. I'll send you hot chow and medics, but prepare yourselves for battle! Commander MacArthur ordered me to take this place or not come back. That's right! That's how important this is. And now I'm the one giving orders. You are American soldiers and you will fight! Grow some backbone!"

Again, there is silence, and the general's aide speaks.

"We need to get back to the jeep, Sir."

General Eichelberger takes the time to stare at each man in that sodden place. No one will meet his gaze. Then, from the edge of the clearing, a bearded scarecrow lifts his head and looks directly at him. The commander acknowledges the eye contact with a slight nod. He stares back at the platoon.

"Next time you are told to attack, any man who does not jump to it will be court-martialed. Am I clear?"

"Yay," someone mutters in a sarcastic voice.

The general snorts and shakes his head. He spins on his heel and he and the looey exit the way they came.

The GIs go back to the poker game and stirring up the fire.

Beneath the foliage, the scarecrow sits up.

"I'll go."

His voice is a croak that no one hears. He knocks the mud off his helmet and puts it on. He picks up his rifle, leaves the blanket and pack, and walks toward the trail. His knees give out and he almost goes down, but manages to stumble on.

"Private!" the sergeant calls. "Sit back! Don't be stupid."

The man sways and mutters. The sarg shrugs and turns back to the game.

A palm frond lies in the mud, a coconut attached. The scarecrow picks it up, stands on one side of the trail, and holds it into the open.

The machine gun thumps. Bushes come apart and the coconut explodes, splashing milk. The scarecrow drops the frond and returns across the mudflat to the trail the general just took – the opposite direction from the gun emplacement.

"Where you goin', fool?" someone asks. The GI looks around.

"Gotta go back to go forward," he says.

"You're outa your blasted mind," the sarg tells him. "Best you wait."

The scarecrow rolls bloodshot eyes his way.

"Wait for what?"

There is no answer.

Johnny continues to stand for a moment while his teeth chatter. He clamps his jaw and slings his rifle over a shoulder. He gets down on his knees and crawls into the scrub.

Behind his back a few men laugh – a hopeless, mirthless sound.

85

Seventeen-year-old Johnny is alone in the jungle. His mind buzzes like angry wasps. In the mangroves, he freezes as a snake slithers across the trail. Its scales seem to glow from within. The soldier lets it pass and keeps going. He arrives at the place he was aiming for, a bend in the trail. He takes a breath, runs across the path in a crouch, and dives into the foliage.

The machine gun pounds and dirt dances behind him.

He lays flat while slugs cut branches. The scarecrow hasn't made it far, but already, his heart is banging against his ribs. He sits and gasps. He looks up and catches raindrops on his tongue and swallows.

Eventually, he can move again. Staying under cover, he parallels the trail through the undergrowth, heading in the direction of the enemy gun. Whenever he glimpses the path, he sees the corpses strewn along it. This is the bad ending for some of the men he hiked with across the island.

Johnny finds a trickle of water dripping through the foliage. He puts his lips to it and drinks. He takes the canteen off his belt and fills it.

He moves on. A fever wave hits – buzzing ears, eyeballs vibrating. He curls up and waits.

He awakes in darkness. The rain has stopped. Slowly, he remembers where he is. Under cover of night, he returns to the path. He crawls over bodies. On one side in the gloom, he hears a heavy body slide and then the crunch of breaking bones. He moves on.

At last Johnny is beyond the dead and still he crawls. It takes forever. The sky clears and there is the faint luster of the moon.

He pauses when the trail turns again. His hands find a log wall that looms before him.

A bunker! The Japs!

Johnny ghosts around it. From inside, he hears a faint snore. When he guesses he's past the gun emplacement, he crawls back into the jungle. He stays there, waiting for dawn. He will not let himself doze off, even though every breath aches for sleep.

Eventually, first light comes. Johnny's nerves hum. He hears Japanese voices speaking softly, smells smoke, and then, boiling rice. Someone laughs. The light intensifies. Johnny finds he is staring into the open bunker. It is a simple structure, three walls of stacked tree trunks, with an open back.

He sees two Japs crouched by their bedding with a small fire going. There's the machine gun, trained through a slit down the trail he navigated in the night. He wonders what to do. Will the sound of a shot bring more Japs on the run? Then he thinks that gunfire from this location will be expected.

An enemy stands and Johnny shoots him. The Jap flails back against the logs and falls. The other one scrambles for his rifle, gets a hand on it, but Johnny fires again.

He reloads as he steps into the place. A pot of steaming rice stands beside the coals. He picks some up with his fingers, blows on it, and feeds himself until it is gone.

He goes to the machine gun and turns it on its mount until it is pointed his way. He scrapes up handfuls of pebbles and mud and stuffs this into the barrel. There's a cleaning rod against the wall and he uses it to jam in the stones. He wipes the outside of the barrel with his shirt and points the gun down the trail once more.

Johnny drags the dead men into the brush. The effort wears him out and he sits to recover. When he has breath again, he re-takes the trail, continuing deeper into enemy territory.

Fifteen minutes later, he hears boots tramping and Japanese voices. He slides into the jungle and goes still. A six-man squad passes. Johnny reemerges and walks on, rifle ready. Eventually, there's more marching and he hides again. Another patrol goes by.

In the distance, he hears shouted orders and many voices. The path has become a dirt road. He even hears a horse whinny.

Johnny enters a stand of tall trees. When he is deep among them, he pauses. The sounds from the enemy encampment grow louder.

Johnny finds a forest giant he likes. The tree has low limbs he can haul himself up on. He dips fingers in mud and smears camouflage on his already dirty face. Then he climbs. The trunk is broad and provides protection. Up a dozen feet, he rests. He picks leafy twigs and threads them through the netting on his helmet. He pulls down a vine and loosely wraps the barrel of his rifle.

By midday, judging by dim light through the clouds, Johnny has worked his way up fifty feet. Now he rests in a fork. There's an opening in the foliage and the view is breathtaking.

For the first time since getting to the north coast, Johnny is looking at the wide South Pacific Ocean. Blue waves dance to the horizon. His hunter eye tells him it is two hundred yards to the water. Between him and that is a wide-open area, and moving across it are hundreds, maybe thousands, of Japanese soldiers.

The enemy stronghold!

On one side are native vegetable gardens, and behind those, sunlight glitters on black water among the mangroves.

Near the beach stand three western-style buildings. From the peak of the largest flies the Japanese army flag. Curiously, it is nailed to a cross. This is the first time Johnny has seen one in real life – a white rectangle, with a red sun and rays.

In a circle on the edges of the clearing are a series of half-buried bunkers, some facing the ocean, others, inland. They are camouflaged by palm fronds. He sees the dark gun slits and earth-covered roofs. There is no way to approach by land, swamp or sea, without facing those guns. From his vantage, he makes out a network of trenches connecting the buildings.

Johnny takes time to study the place. He makes mental notes as best he can, so he can report later. He fights a wave of fever and concentrates. He counts the bunkers and the directions they face, and makes a mental map.

He has no other plan. In fact, he cannot remember how he ended up here. He thinks for a time and recalls the visit by the general. *A general at the front?* He must have been hallucinating. He does remember killing the machine gunners.

He thinks he will wait until nightfall and then sneak back to his men: he'll find an officer and report. Maybe with the big gun gone, they'll follow orders and attack again.

But while he is watching, something so extraordinary happens, it changes everything. Between the buildings near the ocean, a white horse prances into view. Across hundreds of yards, Johnny sees the animal toss its head.

On it is a uniformed rider wearing a cap. The GI gazes as the horseman brings his mount to a canter and circles the compound.

Johnny observes that the foot-soldiers clear the way and incline their heads.

The boy remembers his father and the chicken. This target is irresistible. Hidden in the foliage, Johnny raises the rifle and tracks the man through the scope. Sometimes the officer is hidden behind buildings and the hunter waits. Then the rider comes into view once more.

Johnny sits in his tree and breathes. He puts the crosshairs on the enemy and tracks. The hunter compensates slightly for trajectory and movement, and aims for center body mass.

Johnny breathes in, lets it out and gently squeezes.

There's the eruption of the shot and the rifle thumps his shoulder. He sees the rider sling sideways in the saddle and the horse spring into full gallop.

Now Johnny cannot see the man, but the horse runs strangely, something hanging from it. Johnny guesses the officer's foot is caught in the stirrup. The horse careens among the foot soldiers, knocking some down.

Johnny continues to watch. A Jap with a strip of cloth tied around his head runs at the animal and grabs its bridle. The horse rears and the man is lifted off his feet, but hangs on. He gets control of the horse. The rider comes loose and crumples in a pile. Johnny watches, but the fallen officer does not move again.

Every fiber of Johnny's being tells him it is time to go. Even now, soldiers are yelling and pointing in his direction. Carrying rifles, some dash his way.

His own Springfield slung on his back, Johnny swings down from branch to branch. He hits the ground running, keeping the trees between himself and the pursuit. Another fifty yards, and, lungs screaming, he goes to earth in thick brush. He lays in a hollow under dense foliage and pulls fallen branches over himself. He sneaks a drink from his canteen, keeps the rifle ready on his chest, and goes as still as death.

All through the afternoon, he hears the enemy patrols pass. Sometimes they call to one another far away. Sometimes, they come so close, he smells them. Once the thump of boots goes right by him. A bayonet stabs through the bush, inches from his head.

The man goes on, and Johnny lays there.

In late afternoon, the day grows dark and rain begins to fall. Johnny eases his helmet over his face and keeps his place.

Night comes, and finally, there are no more patrols. Johnny sits up and rubs his cramped legs until they can move. He stands and hobbles back the way he came.

He realizes he is approaching the machine gun bunker once more. He is too exhausted to continue, so he crawls into the jungle and lies down.

He is soaking wet, wrung out, and he sleeps a little. He wakes before dawn and waits for sufficient light. When it comes, he emerges behind the bunker.

In the twilight, prepared to shoot, the sight heartens him. The machine gun is tipped up on its stand, the barrel split and peeled back.

On the ground is a body. He watches for a minute but it does not move. He pulls his bayonet knife and creeps closer. Flies buzz over another dead enemy.

Johnny steps to the man and sees the deadly wounds. His machine gun booby trap worked! A smile too grim for a seventeen-year-old creases his face. He continues along the trail, back towards his men. He is surprised by how short the distance is, given how much trouble he had going the other way.

When he is close to his camp, he gives a call.

"Don't shoot! I'm American!"

"Identify yourself," a voice calls.

"It's me – Private Johnny Willman! I'm one of you!"

"Come on then!"

Johnny slings his rifle and steps onto the mud bank, both hands high. The pitiful remnants of his platoon are there, as he left them. A few guns point his way. When they see that the scarecrow truly is one of theirs, they lower them.

The men are gathered outside the largest tarp, serving something onto metal plates from a big pot. The scent is delicious, overwhelming, and his stomach whines.

"Johnny?" It's the sarg.

"Johnny," he agrees.

"The general sent us turkey stew!" The man grins.

"Merry Christmas, Johnny!"

"Christmas?" The boy is stunned.

"Christmas, 1942," a GI calls. "Hell of a hellhole, but come and git it!"

"Now Johnny," the sarg says, handing over a steaming plate:

"Where the devil have you been?

86

The Raub River, 1945

The river, and Johnny's consciousness, drifted through pain and time. By degrees, he came to. For some reason, he was thinking about Christmas. His stomach complained. The stench hit him, wretched and thick, but there was nothing to do but breathe through his mouth.

Sheets of rain continued to fall. It came to him that it was late afternoon, night was coming on, and he had been lying on a rock for a very long time. His whole side was numb. He stretched out his legs and felt the painful prickle of returning sensation. At last, he was able to sit up. His pack lay in the sludge. He stared up at black tree limbs against a bruised sky, and then at the muddy lake all around.

Slowly, Johnny recalled what had happened. He saw Footy lying in a fetal position among the tree roots. The pilot had his pack on, the two rifles beside him.

The Jap!

Anxiety shot through Johnny and he stared around the knoll, but the prisoner was gone. The day grew darker and Johnny watched the Aussie fight for consciousness.

315

Eventually Footy's eyes flicked open, and he groaned and struggled to rise. He managed to shrug out of his pack and then keeled over, cheek to the mud, and began to snore.

Johnny forced himself to stand. He reeled to the water, crouched, and rinsed himself and his clothes. He rose, got his sodden pants fastened, wobbled to Footy, and slumped beside him.

Johnny fumbled up the rifles and propped them against the tree. He sat stunned while night came on. Eventually the Aussie cracked a bloodshot eye and squinted at him.

"Bleedin' hell. It's you. Reckon I blew me bum off." He wrinkled his nose. "What a pong! Who died – was it me?"

He got on all fours, crawled to the water, sluiced out his shorts and scrubbed himself, then crawled back and lay shivering under the tree.

"That was ghastly," he muttered. "I'd rather have Christmas with the nuns than do that again." His eyes fluttered shut and he slept.

Johnny forced himself to crawl to his pack. He got it up against the trunk and propped Footy's beside it.

There was something clamoring in his mind and he tried to recall what it was, but it would not come. He slid lower as the rain poured down on the now-black lagoon.

Johnny realized his belly was caved in, but the strength to dig into his pack for something to eat was beyond him. His head felt swollen and he thought he'd take off the helmet, but his hands would not obey.

Then the night crept up and stole his mind.

87

Johnny awoke in a dismal morning and gazed across a field of mud.

Where am I? After a few minutes, it came back – the diarrhea, the rain, the island. He turned and saw Footy asleep, face in the dirt.

At last Johnny remembered – *the Jap is gone!* His eyes darted over the island that had become a hill again, but there was no prisoner. Panic jolted him and he checked the rifles – *both against the tree.* That was a relief. He forced himself to stand and looked around.

He was on a hump of muddy grass in a sea of sludge. Fifty yards off, under a leaden sky, the river muttered between its banks once more. Johnny forced himself to walk a circle. *No Jap.* He was anxious and his tender stomach did flip-flops. He knelt and went through his things – *pistol and knives here. Everything is in my pack!* He went to check Footy's gear as well.

The sword! Johnny saw it standing in the rucksack, and again, relief flooded through.

But the prisoner wouldn't leave without that – no way – or our guns! Why did he let us live? That's the question.

He pondered it every which way, but nothing made sense. Johnny shook Footy.

"Come on buddy! Wake up!" At last Footy opened crusted eyes.

"Bloody hell! You still here?"

"Listen!" Johnny said. "The Jap is gone."

"Ooo, I've been through the wringer," the pilot groaned, propping himself up. "What do you mean – gone?" He pulled his hat off and knocked the clods of mud against the tree.

"Gone. As in scrammed, vamoosed, skedaddled."

"You mean – gone?" Footy worked his way to his feet and wobbled to the edge of the mudflat.

"Why didn't he kill us or take his bloody sword? Or guns?

"Or the food?" Johnny asked. "But he didn't."

Footy scratched a bite in his whiskers and suddenly sucked in his breath.

"Blimey! Company!" He pointed and Johnny looked, but saw nothing. Then the mud shifted, and he made out the crocodile. It slithered a few steps in their direction and froze again, and Johnny saw the alien eyes staring at him. He noticed a motion in different direction – another croc.

"Look!"

"Struth!" Footy was pointing as well. There were at least a dozen predators coming from all sides, intent on the men.

"We better go!" Johnny said.

"How? Where?"

Johnny pointed to the ribbon of puddles that had been the path, and then, across the field, to the place it climbed into the jungle.

"There!" He stepped to his pack and hauled it up, noticing that the illness had made him feeble. Footy grunted into his own load and the men snatched up their rifles.

"River crocs," the Aussie wheezed. "Not giants like the Father, but any of these bastards can do us in."

"We could try and shoot our way out," Johnny said.

"But there are too many."

"No good," Footy agreed. "And we're short on ammo. We cannot wander the bloody bush unarmed!" The men went to the edge of the knoll, ready to run. But they'd have to negotiate deep mud and the flooded sections. And now there were four crocs between them and the path.

"They'll be on us faster 'n a dingo on a duck," Footy said.

Johnny strode to the top of the hill to stare down the other side. The predators came from that direction as well. The first was a big brute that had just reached the slope. It rushed up at Johnny. He jumped back and whirled to look at the tree. The attacker rumbled and waddled closer.

"Climb!" Johnny called. He slung his rifle on his shoulder, sprang to the tree and swung up. Footy turned to do the same. Johnny got his hands around a branch just as the big male arrived below. It was ten feet long and thick as a barrel. Johnny pulled up and the croc lunged. Its steel-hard jaw ground his boot against the trunk. He got his butt on the wood, but his pack jammed under the next limb and his legs dangled.

The croc fell and jumped again, jaws open. Johnny jerked his legs up and teeth crunched into the branch just below his hind end. The reptile hung a few seconds, then belly-flopped to earth. Johnny wrenched his pack free and stood.

Where's Footy?

The Aussie had skidded to a stop when the bull came between him and the tree. Now another croc slunk close behind.

"Come on!" Johnny yelled, trying to balance himself and get his rifle ready to shoot, but it was tangled in the branches.

The big one faced Footy, saw its prey was trapped, and grunted. Reptiles slithered onto the knoll from all sides. The Aussie froze.

319

"Footy, get up here!" Johnny shouted.

The Aussie stared at the circle of death, the crocs slid closer, and Johnny could not free his rifle.

Then Footy did something that looked like suicide.

88

The pilot slung down his pack as five scaled brutes came at him. He stuffed a hand inside, rummaged, hauled out a leaf packet and pulled it open. Bamboo shoots spilled.

"Sod it!" He shoved his arm back in as the crocs stepped closer – the snouts were almost to him. This time, he came up with a chunk of pork.

"Take it, ya slimy bastards!"

He lobbed the meat between two crocs and they hissed at each other and turned for it. Johnny was still wrestling his rifle loose. Footy dug in his pack again and came up with more meat. He heaved it in another direction and three predators spun in pursuit.

But in the meantime, six more crocs were on the hill, climbing fast.

Footy probed deep and came up with his last roast. He peeled off the leaf and tossed it in his hand as he stared at the bull between him and the tree. Its head bobbed up and down, following the bouncing pork.

Footy dropped the meatball and kicked hard. It struck the croc between the eyes, and flew – right into the foul-smelling pile he'd deposited in his illness.

The croc didn't seem to mind. Its head went sideways and it scooped up meat and muck together. Footy grabbed his pack in one hand, rifle in the other, and ran directly at it. The bull spread brown-stained jaws to welcome him. The Aussie made a wild leap, cleared the snout, landed a sandal behind the head, and used it to springboard up.

Two more crocs raced at the man, one from each side. He jumped and they leaped. Footy managed to get his pack and an arm over the branch. With his other hand, he shoved his rifle at the Yank.

"Help!"

Johnny grabbed the barrel in his free hand and pulled, dragging the Aussie with it. The leaping crocs just missed his legs and, jaws wide, slammed together. Teeth clashed and they fell on the big male.

Footy let go of the rifle, got both arms around the branch and clung. With the weight suddenly gone, Johnny stumbled backwards along the branch, a rifle in each hand. He would have fallen if his back had not thudded against the trunk. The big croc twisted and snapped at the two on top of it, and they backed away.

Footy managed to climb and reclaim his rifle. The quarters were close as Johnny wrestled his pack off. With a hand, he shoved it onto a higher branch. He went after it and continued until he found a good limb to sit on. Footy perched on the one below. The two stared down at their scaly reception party.

"Strike me pink!" Footy panted. "I was nearly a *pukpuk* sandwich."

"So that's what happened to the Jap," Johnny said.

"Struth! One of these buggers got him!"

"Only way he'd leave his sword and our stuff," Johnny said. "But now what?"

"I never liked him, but that's a terrible way to go. Yes, mate – now what?"

The men considered their options while fifteen crocodiles milled below. The big male growled at each one that came too close. These edged away, pushing others. Soon they were positioned around the trunk like spokes in a wheel.

Footy looked down and hooted like a monkey. The reptiles cocked their heads. Johnny drank from his canteen. Footy took a swig from his own.

Weak from the illness and jittery with adrenaline, Johnny felt a strange giddiness overtake him.

"Looks like we're stuck here," he said. "Might as well have lunch! Or I'll have a bite. You got any food left?" He put a hand into his pack and pulled out some wrapped pork. He let the leaf flutter down and took a big bite. Below, the reptiles snatched for the scrap.

"Mula was right – their *mumu* is the best!" Johnny said. Footy watched the Yank anxiously.

"Don't play silly buggers," he said. "Not the time, mate! Give us a bite, would you?"

Johnny chuckled and took another mouthful.

"Don't be a bleedin' wanker!" Footy shouted.

"Okay, I'll share my food. But only if you say 'please Johnny.'"

"Up yours with barbed wire – sideways!" Footy whined.

Johnny finished the meat and extracted some green beans, which he forked in with his fingers.

"Bloody hell!" Footy snapped. "You're a right bugga, you know that? All right Johnny, give me a bloody bite to eat.

Please!"

"Now, was that so hard?" Johnny asked. "Catch!" He extracted another lump of pork, held it out – and let it tumble.

"Crikey!" Footy lunged for it. He swayed, but caught it while the crocs craned up. In order to keep from sliding off his branch, Footy had to stuff the meat in his mouth and grab on. The big bull clawed up the tree.

Johnny chuckled and dropped a packet of veggies. With meat protruding from his teeth, Footy barely managed to snatch it. Eyes bulging, he glared up at the Yank.

Johnny stared at the filthy face, the hat back and the hair every which way, the bizarre pork tongue hanging out. He chortled wildly and had to hug the trunk. Footy watched the Yank gasping, the whole tree shaking, and the sheer silliness struck him. He launched into spasms of high-pitched laughter around his mouthful, eyes wild.

The crocodiles watched intensely, and understood only that their prey was trapped.

Finally, the men chuffed to a ragged stop and ate in silence. After that, there was nothing to do but wait. An hour passed, and then another. This was going nowhere.

"You know about crocs," Johnny said. "Do they eat their own kind?"

"Shore," Footy said. "Bloody cannibals, the lot of them."

"Nice," Johnny observed. "Right at home here! I count nineteen now. We can't shoot that many! How 'bout this?"

He outlined what he had in mind.

"Hardly counts as a plan at all," the Aussie complained.

"Got a better one?"

"Not at the mo'."

"Well then..."

"Right."

Johnny swung down beside Footy. They helped one another get their packs on. The crocodiles saw movement and stirred.

Johnny and Footy aimed their rifles.

"Ready?" Johnny asked.

"Ready."

"Fire!"

89

Two rifles clapped together. On each side of the big bull's tail, close to its back legs, chunks blew out. The wounded croc bellowed and whipped around at its injuries. Its kin flinched away at the explosions, then instantly snapped back on the tang of blood. Eagerly, they snuffled for the source.

The injured croc bolted for the river, dragging its broken tail. At once, the others were after it. They slid down the slope and ran or paddled across the mud flat. Johnny and Footy reloaded and prepared to jump.

The bull was slowed by the dead weight. The nearest pursuer caught up and bit into the wound. The male arched skyward in agony, twisted as it fell, and snapped at the attacker. The two locked and rolled across the field. They came to a stop with the injured one belly up. It struggled to roll over, but more crocs rushed in and one slammed teeth into the neck.

The wounded croc's jaws flapped upside down, while others bit into its body. The hide ripped and blood gushed.

The men lost sight of the shot male under the scrum. But it heaved up and made a last-ditch rush for the river. The rest scrambled after. It reached the bank, slid in, and tried to lash away. But now only the stump swung, the tail dangling useless. It was marooned in the shallows. Its kin piled on and a free-for-all erupted. Another bite tore the appendage clean off.

The bull's wide head went under and its last breath burbled up. Tan water turned burgundy.

"Go!" Johnny whispered. He and Footy jumped, skidded down the muddy bank, splashed through a puddle, and dashed for the trail.

As they went by the carnivore picnic, they were spotted. A twelve-footer took the lead. It came at a gallop – faster than Johnny thought possible. It closed and Johnny sprang to one side while Footy leaped to the other. The croc jumped, its head between them, jaws spread. It belly-flopped and skidded and the men bounded on.

Johnny's boots were heavy with clods and he had spots pinging in front of his eyes. Footy got ahead, intent on the path into the jungle.

Two more crocs raced to cut him off.

Johnny lengthened his stride, hit a patch of clay, and went airborne. He slammed down full-length and all his wind was knocked out. For agonizing heartbeats, he lay unable to move, while the Hard Case shouted to get up, on the double! At last, he managed to struggle onto all fours, but could not breathe.

A crocodile caught up with Footy. It charged, he jumped, and teeth snagged his shirt and ripped it as they went by. The flank clipped his legs and the Aussie did a cartwheel.

The reptile swung its head to take him.

Johnny still could not get air, but his Springfield was in his hands. He was almost blinded by mud as he got on a knee, sure Footy was done-for. But somehow the Aussie got up and ran, the croc on his heels. Footy was dodging from one side to the other and Johnny waited a second until he was sure he would not hit the man.

Johnny shot the croc just behind the head. *Spine shot!* The animal crashed down. Footy flew the last few yards and bounded up the trail into the forest.

Johnny's diaphragm convulsed, but he could not draw air. He forced himself to stand, knuckled slime from his eyes, and ran. He went by the downed croc and saw its eyes track him, but it was paralyzed.

But now another big brute skidded onto the path in front of Johnny. It faced him, tail twitching. Johnny, still breathless, had to pull up. He glanced back and saw a dozen more crocs coming.

His rifle was empty and he was out of time. The croc took a step toward him and bared its teeth.

Then its head jolted as if struck by a sledgehammer. Johnny heard the clap and glimpsed Footy in the foliage, rifle smoking. The predator ripped a terrible burp into the soldier's face and dropped. Johnny backed up a couple of feet, counted three as he ran, as he had practiced doing the long jump at school, and leaped high. He sailed over the croc's head and caught a glimpse of the hole oozing blood. He landed on a boot, jumped, and came down on the trail. On he sprinted.

He splashed through the last puddle and flew up the trail. At the top of the rise, he fell on his knees, his vision going white. He was about to pass out when, at long last, he was able to suck in a lungful. It felt like heaven. He panted for a minute and his sight cleared.

And there was filthy Footy, leaning on his rifle.

"G'day, Yank," the Aussie said. "Good of you to come. But the lizards are still on the move. I suggest we shake a leg."

Johnny nodded weakly and hauled himself up. Footy jogged ahead, and Johnny followed into the rainforest.

Overhead, a white cockatoo flared its crest and shrieked at them.

They knew crocs could run, but not for long. They kept the pace until they were sure the brutes were far behind, then slowed.

They paused to catch their breath. Johnny saw the Aussie was caked head to toe in dripping brown sludge.

"You're a mess."

"So are you," the pilot puffed.

"You look dipped in *pukpuk pekpek*."

90

The men climbed a promontory that fell away in mudslides, then followed the path into the rainforest. Still recovering from the belly sickness, they were slow and had to pause frequently to catch their breath. They drained their water bottles. They were grateful when they approached the top and the slope leveled off.

They came to a gushing spring. They paused to slurp water and fill their canteens. They stripped, again washed the mud off themselves and their clothes, and spread the things over branches to dry.

Again, they talked about their ammo. Both had shot twice, so now Johnny had only four cartridges, and Footy, eight.

Both men were starving – a good sign, they agreed. They must be on the mend. They watched steam rise from their clothes while they lay back and smoked.

"Blimey I'm hungry," Footy said. "I could eat a kangaroo."

"You do that?" Johnny asked.

"Shore mate," Footy said. "A 'roo is good meat – strong flavor, best with a sauce."

"Never thought about eating kangaroo!" Johnny said. "Me, I'd go for a T-bone steak, seared on the outside, red in the middle." His mouth watered.

"Aww, put a sock in it!" Footy moaned. "I'm so hungry I could turn cannibal meself."

"Don't look at me when you say that," Johnny said. Footy chuckled and they lay quiet in the sun.

"What made us sick?" Johnny wondered.

"Who knows in this bloody place?" Footy grouched. "Water we drank – maybe something died in it. But it could have been anything..."

"...the food in the village. A mosquito bite." Johnny paused. "I've got malaria."

"Me too," Footy said, "who bloody doesn't?

"You still reckon a croc got the Jap?"

"What else?" Johnny said. "Makes sense."

"Too right," Footy said. "One of those lizards comes along, pulls him in the water..." He raised his eyebrows.

"You see how many there were?" Johnny said as he dressed

328

himself.

"Must have been an entire *pukpuk* tribe." Footy struggled into his clothes as well.

"We should have put him out of our misery long ago."

"Maybe," Johnny conceded. "But the P-O-W was all that was left of our mission. Now we've got nothing. We better high-tail it for the coast and get the heck out of Dodge." They hiked down the far side of the ridge. Darkness came while they were at it and they had to camp. They ate the last of their food – cold sweet potatoes – and slept by the trail.

In the morning, they pushed on. At least the storm had knocked the humidity out of the air. There was nothing for breakfast except a smoke. An hour later, they skidded down the last incline and emerged beside the river.

They hiked on, and at last, late in the afternoon, they found a native garden. They had no idea whose lands they were on, and they approached with rifles ready, but the place was deserted. They pulled up mounds of sweet potatoes and knocked off the dirt. They discarded the ones riddled by insects. They found beans in hairy pods and stripped handfuls of these as well.

They camped right there and lit a fire. They boiled the beans and wolfed them down while the sweet potatoes roasted. When done, they speared them with knives. They ate until they were stuffed, and saved some for the following day.

In the twilight, Johnny slung his hammock between trees and Footy spread his blanket.

Even though they had seen no natives, they agreed they must stand watch. They took turns, Johnny first. He found it strange not to have to feed the prisoner or truss him up, but it did make things easier.

Shortly after sunrise, they set off, eating leftovers as they went. Both men were still weak, but their stomachs felt better. They stayed by the river, passing ever more frequent trails that led inland. These, and more gardens, should mean natives, but they saw no one, and this was disturbing.

In midafternoon, they approached another mudflat along the river. They paused at the edge and gazed uneasily across. It was very much like the site where they'd been attacked by crocodiles. Johnny panned the place through his scope, but saw no predators. The two men held rifles ready as they began to pick their way through. Ahead was a low hill with a tree on it.

Like the one where we got sick and the crocs took the Jap, Johnny thought. Carrion birds circled and they approached cautiously. They had to work their way around grassy tussocks. When they came around the last one, Johnny grunted in surprise. There in the mud was the perfect imprint of a massive scaled body. They felt dwarfed just looking at it.

"The Father!" Johnny said.

"The bloody same, mate."

Their hair on end, the men panned the field with their rifles, but nothing moved. They continued by the imprint, and Johnny paced it, counting steps. Footy paused to marvel at the dent made by a massive foot. It came to him that this was the one that had nearly crushed him back in Kissim.

Johnny continued by the flooded boat of the belly. He came to a hole left by a foreleg and realized there were no claw marks.

"Look at that! No doubt about it."

"Where you shot it," the pilot said.

Johnny went on until he was at the tip of the snout.

"Ten full paces," he said. "Thirty feet!"

"Cor blimey!" Footy said. "That's three times the length of the bloody lizard we shot back at the tree!"

The men approached the hillock and stared up. It was not big enough to hide a monster like the Father, but they could see raw earth torn up.

"He left his calling card," Johnny said.

Strewn among the shrubs were dark-skinned corpses in pieces. The hikers climbed. Raptors took flight at their approach, and they saw native heads with the eyes plucked out.

"The birds wouldn't feed if the croc was close," Footy said.

"So says you," Johnny muttered.

The men worked their way up, turning frequently with rifles ready. They passed shrubs splashed with blood. Footy stumbled over a head and part of a shoulder in the grass.

Johnny found a leg. Blowflies buzzed, and the stench of ripped guts made them gag.

They moved to the upwind side of the knoll and skirted the carcass of another victim. They approached the tree. Beneath it, the ground was thick with body parts. Johnny did a literal head count. There were five.

"They're from a tribe we haven't seen," he said. He studied a face. The hair was in dreadlocks, woven with white beads.

"Job's tears," Footy commented.

"What?"

"The beads – we call 'em Job's tears, because they grow by the thousands."

"These guys found a lot more trouble than even old Job did," Johnny said.

From the top of the hill, he looked at the mudflat again.

331

Now they could see the trail made by the giant reptile. It was one-way, going back to the river.

"Look," Johnny said. "I'd say it swam in on the flood, had breakfast, and walked out."

"I reckon so," Footy said.

"We need to watch out. Crocs usually stay near their kill."

91

"Right," Johnny said. "Let's keep going and try to stay back from the river."

Again, they held rifles ready as they traversed the muddy field. They breathed easier in the forest again. As fast as they could, they put several miles between themselves and the massacre.

They came out of the jungle on a grassy riverbank. Again, they studied the landscape but saw no sign of their pursuer, or any natives, and walked on.

This stretch of the river had a wild beauty. Storks, egrets and other waterfowl hunted the shallows, while ducks careened overhead. Johnny would have liked to shoot a couple for dinner, but knew they could not spare the ammunition.

At least they would not go hungry. They wandered through deserted gardens, interspersed with groves of papaya and banana trees. They pulled off two football-size "pawpaws." These they sliced in half, scraped out the glistening black seeds, and gorged on the orange fruit. They added several more to their packs, along with bananas.

They hiked on and the land grew flatter. The Raub remained swollen, and in several places, it still spilled into the jungle. They had to wade through, one man covering the other in case a croc – or *the* croc – showed up.

Now they were truly in the tropical lowlands. It was a steam bath. They mopped the sweat from their eyes.

The path became a wide band of well-worn clay. It was clear they approached another settlement. At last, they made out the silhouette of a village and stole closer.

"No one here," Johnny whispered.

"No dogs or animals," Footy breathed.

"No smoke."

They arrived at the first huts and went between them. They stuck their heads through doorways and found them vacant. Johnny ducked into one, put his fingers to the fire ash, and sniffed.

"Stale. No one here for a long time," he said in a normal voice.

Just then, a dog began to howl. The men went looking for it and the keening grew louder. They approached another hovel when a dog appeared in the doorway. Its muzzle was gray and ribs stood out. Its eyes were misty marbles.

"Blind," Footy said.

"Left behind," Johnny said. The men exited the village. A path took them between chest-high boulders crowned with old human skulls.

There was a thicket, and they emerged beyond in a peaceful, grassy clearing. It was dominated by the ruin of a giant A-frame structure, much like Bumay's house.

"The wreck of another *Haus Tambaran*," Footy said.

It was obvious that some catastrophe had occurred here.

Only the massive upright poles remained in the earth. The rest of the building was down around them, a jumble of splintered beams and the great ridgepole, woven walls and thatching. Footy put a hand on the trunk towering beside him.

"Look!" he exclaimed. "Bullet holes. Big caliber!"

Johnny stuck a finger in one of the puncture marks and studied the angle.

"The shots came from above. This place was strafed by fighters."

"Why would anyone waste ammo on a spirit house?"

"Let's take a look," Johnny said. They entered the ruin and he raised a piece of matting.

"Here!" he called and Footy scrambled over. They were staring at the remains of a man – no native. The bones wore a Japanese helmet and faded uniform, black holes across the torso.

"What's a Jap doing here?" Footy asked.

"Let's see if there are more," Johnny said.

Half an hour later, they'd counted thirty-four enemy corpses and six natives. The tally was complicated by hundreds of smoke-darkened skulls also in the wreckage – headhunter trophies, they decided.

"Looks like the Japs were hiding here and our guys found out," Johnny said.

"Fish in a barrel," Footy said. "But bad magic for the bloody natives."

"Maybe that's why they're gone," Johnny said.

"Let's hope this is the end of the bleedin' Japs on the Raub."

The men returned through the village. Even the dog had

gone quiet, and the silence was eerie.

"I don't fancy this," Footy said uneasily.

"Feels like a cemetery," Johnny said.

They came by the last huts and stared out. A glare was on the river as clumps of storm-torn weeds floated by.

"Let's push on to the coast," Johnny said. "I'm itching to get out of here."

"Too bloody right, mate," Footy said, slapping at mosquitoes. "I reckon we're through the worst of the drama now." The men did not return to the trail along the river, but chose a path directly into the jungle.

The instant they disappeared, a swath of floating vegetation rose into the air and spilled off, revealing a massive head with water coursing off it. The Father looked after the prey and there was the Smooth-headed man. Its belly was full and it was not hungry, but it was intensely focused.

The predator was now in hunting grounds it knew well. As the superb ambush hunter it was, it got an image of a site downstream where the game trail came to the water's edge.

Many times over its long life, it had slaughtered the two-legged animals there.

It submerged and swam fast. It would get to the place first, and the Smooth-headed man would walk right into its jaws.

92

After it had eaten at the island, the Father rested. When it surged out of the water and took the first man, it aggravated its wound. The pain enraged it and it rushed up the hill and killed everything it found.

The great reptile bolted down some of the meal. Then it slid down the slope into the flood once more. The water lifted the weight off the pulsing foreleg and gave it some relief. Darkness descended and the Father dozed. As the hours passed, it felt the flood subside. Dawn found it stretched on a bed of mud beside the hill where its prey was scattered.

With the first light, carrion birds rode the death scent and began to circle. Their sharp eyes noted the predator and they did not land.

Welcome heat scorched the crocodile's back, but the raw leg made it cranky. The Father lifted its head and let out a guttural grunt that made crows veer in flight.

The infection was mounting a new assault, and the reptile no longer cared to eat. It half-walked, half-dragged itself to the river and eased in. Always now, it watched the path of the two-legged animals, seeking the one prey it desired. Only this killing would satisfy its strange new hunger.

It drifted with the detritus of the flood. With every bend of the river, the predator entered increasingly familiar haunts. Again, the sky burned as the Father followed the course. Eventually, the world disappeared in darkness once more.

Poison seeped into the crocodile from its foreleg, while points of light glittered and jumped. With hypersensitivity, it felt every place in its hide where the thunder-strikes had hurt it. It shivered along its great length, making waves slap. Sensations popped and crackled along its spine and into its brain.

The monster grew bilious. It retched, spewing man-flesh into the water. Sunk in distress, the swimmer stopped heeding its surroundings.

Its suffering a discordant jangle, the Father and all things bumped together through the liquid black. Eventually, the light came again. Now the hunter observed a landscape it knew.

Nearby was another nesting site of the two-legged animals. The crocodile was floating among the storm-torn waterweeds when all its senses sharpened.

There, a distance away overland, it saw the Smooth-headed man! The usual companion animal was with it. It readied itself to attack, but the one-prey did not come to the river. It went another way and disappeared among the trees.

Again, the predator considered its favorite hunting places along the river. One image dominated – the point where the two-legged animals congregated in such numbers, they had worn the vegetation away.

Once, in a single rush, the Father had knocked five into the water and drowned them all. It had dragged the corpses to its larder places, allowed them to rot, and consumed the soft flesh at its leisure.

The Father dove and swam strongly to outrun the prey. The site it sought was a bay – a shelf in the river, thick with rushes. The crocodile approached underwater from the open river, and swam towards shore.

One minute, the bay was a sleepy place where reed heads nodded at the sun. The next, there were eruptions all across it, as the giant's smaller cousins sensed its presence and arrowed away from mortal danger.

The Father nosed to the bank and settled. The water was shallow. Its eyes broke surface and water trickled down the moon scar. Sharp eyes fixed on the game trail. The hunter hid among the bullrushes and went still as death.

93

Katsu regained consciousness when his head went under water. He choked, jerked up and suffered a coughing fit. He was no more than a pinprick of awareness – merely something that fought to breathe, that was all. He attempted to puzzle it out, but only straws of nonsense drifted by.

Time passed and he remained in the void.

Gradually, he came to simple distinctions. There was air – his head was in it. There was water – it surrounded his body. And there was mud – he lay in it. Gradually a word coalesced.

Nigero! (Escape!)

Again the thought came:

Nigero!

But from what – to where? His head burned and yet he shivered. He groaned and, like a drowning man, he grasped the only thing he could.

Nigero!

He tried to move but did not. At last, he rediscovered arms and legs and got on his knees. Shivering and panting, he raised a hand to wipe his eyes. Both arms rose bound together. He could see nothing, but he forced himself onto his feet. He stood tottering in darkness as rain drummed his head and shoulders.

The next thing he knew, he was floundering through water that came to his belly. He moved awkwardly, legs tangled. He plunged his hands down and they snagged something that became trousers. He pulled them up and knotted the rope belt.

On he stumbled. Abstract patterns swam in front of his eyes. He attempted to marshal his thoughts, but they would not obey.

He fell, swallowed earthy water, came up hacking, and forged on.

When the flood spilled across the field, the she-crocodile remained in the reeds and watched. She had not fed in weeks and she was urgent with hunger.

Darkness came, and with it, the desire to explore her expanded territory in search of drowned animals. She nosed through the shallows and then heard it – frantic splashing. All her senses told her it was a land creature in distress. She launched in pursuit.

The man blundered on. His toes stubbed dirt and he climbed up through thorns. He crawled on, tearing face and hands.

The female heard the animal leave the water and surged after it. She encountered the slope and rushed up, pushing aside brambles with her iron head.

She smelled the animal now and knew what it was. She had eaten this kind many times.

It was close.

The man ran into a rough wall. His hands explored the surface of a fallen tree and found a splintered branch. He grabbed and climbed, tearing fingernails. He teetered at the top and fell headlong down the other side. Instinctively, he broke his fall with his hands, losing skin. For a moment he lay panting, then struggled on.

The crocodile rushed up and slammed her snout against the tree. She could hear the prey very near, but on the other side. She reared to climb, but it was too high. She ran one way and met impassible branches. She went the other and at last got around the roots. But the prey was gone, and she knew she would not catch it now.

She slunk back to the water in search of an easier dinner.

The man careened through the night, flayed by unseen whips. Eventually, he was pinned on all sides. He dropped and crawled so long through gnarled roots, he wore the skin off elbows and knees.

At last, his hands found cool, smooth columns that seemed to reach up forever. They felt like home and soothed his torn mind.

He grasped them like a drowning sailor clutches anything that floats, and lost consciousness.

He awoke in profound blindness, but with knowledge like a temple bell tolling through his mind.

I am Takano Katsu. I am in a bamboo grove.

It was coherent – something to hang onto.

Then he dropped like a stone through the lake of oblivion.

94

The day Katsu arrived in New Guinea had been a proud one! He had come with the absolute conviction that the Imperial Army would rapidly conquer the enormous island. It was a belief he had in common with his commander, General Taro Yazawa, the flamboyant officer who rode his personal war-stallion into battle. The two men shared an even deeper, unspoken connection.

Both were Samurai.

The caste had been Nippon's warrior elite for nearly a thousand years. Then firearms and the modern age rendered them obsolete. In the 1870's, the Samurai were stripped of their elevated standing by the supreme leader, the Shogun himself.

Then they were outlawed. But that did not stop Samurai families from remembering their roots and taking pride in their heritage.

General Yazawa had a love of the golden age of the Samurai and cultivated the pride and discipline of the ancient warriors. On his white warhorse he had appeared invincible, but he had soon been proven mortal. Katsu had been there, early on, when the general was shot out of his saddle by an enemy sniper. In fact, with his own experience with horses, it had been Katsu who grabbed the reins of the terrified animal.

Katsu had learned that day that it was foolish pride to bring attention to oneself as General Yazawa had done. Since then, he had served under many other officers, in far-flung places. At first, victory had seemed close. But the years dragged on, and the jungle devoured them. Diseases in this terrible place killed many of his countrymen. The daily struggle was simply to survive.

No one spoke of triumph any more.

At last, Katsu had been among the tens of thousands of his fellow soldiers near the coastal town of Wewak. From there, he was assigned to the Sepik River. Katsu and three hundred infantrymen were put under a *Rikugun Chūsa*, a lieutenant colonel, one Yuudai Matsui. Their assignment was to advance up the mighty Sepik and secure an area that gave them control over all who passed.

They conquered seven villages and set up their base. Months passed, but there was no word from command. Neither the promised relief nor supplies arrived. A squad was sent downriver for orders, but never returned.

What could it mean? What made the predicament more difficult for Katsu was that he did not get along with his superior.

More accurately, Colonel Matsui found frequent reason to bait Katsu.

And it was all because of the sword.

Katsu's family, the Takano clan, had been Samurai for five centuries. His father, a high-ranking officer, had given his son the *katana* to take into battle. It was a great honor.

Yuudai Matsui, on the other hand, came from a wealthy family, but of lowly merchant lineage. He found a thousand ways to make it clear that he despised his junior officer and his precious sword! At every opportunity, he tormented the captain.

What little rice they had left, the colonel reserved for himself and the officers. Katsu was one of them, but he found this offensive when the foot soldiers were starving.

He led the men to scavenge the native gardens, but these were soon decimated. For meat, they killed every village pig and chicken, and then the dogs.

Now and then, they were able to shoot a crocodile, but the aquatic reptiles were clever and difficult to kill.

There was never enough to eat, and the troops began to die. Starvation was abetted by malaria, chronic diarrhea and a host of fevers, and men succumbed every day.

Then, just when it seemed things could not get worse, the enemy found them.

Fighters screamed from the sky and strafed them. Gunboats sped up the river, guns blazing. The Japanese who could still run, scattered into the jungle.

Matsui ordered the captain to round up the able-bodied soldiers. Katsu gathered nine men. The colonel said they needed guides, and they took five locals at gunpoint. The villagers, starving and petrified themselves, refused. Matsui shot one, and the rest fell into line.

Matsui would not go downriver where Allied forces had apparently taken control. Instead, they followed the Sepik upstream, robbing village gardens wherever they could. Each night, Katsu's responsibilities included posting guards over the guides, or they would have run off.

But the enemy followed them. Time after time, Katsu's squad was forced to dive into the jungle as another patrol boat came at them, or a fighter screamed out of the sky. On occasion, they heard the guns hammer and men shriek, and knew more of their countrymen were gone. It was clear that their enemy's plan was to hunt them to extinction. Hatred on both sides was deep and bitter.

In desperation, the colonel ordered the guides away from the river, into unmapped territory. Now their defense was merely their guns and dwindling ammunition. With only the food they had scrounged from the natives, they found themselves deep in unknown mountains.

It took days to climb the passes, and they were starving and increasingly desperate. Finally, they encountered a stream that grew into a river and they followed it. At least they could wash, and they would not die of thirst. Even the guides did not know this place, and the Japanese herded them forward at gunpoint.

Then, in the distance, they saw a village.

95

The squad's urgent priority was food and they went in search of gardens. They found them – but also stumbled upon *gaijin*, two white men, with a group of natives. That was a surprise, so deep inland. The colonel knew his underling spoke English and ordered him to interrogate the enemy.

They were Australian, Katsu informed the colonel, Christian priests. Matsui listened with his habitual scowl. He did not care! They were the enemy and they would be executed.

He bellowed an order. The soldiers seized the foreigners and forced them to their knees.

"Now you, my precious Samurai," the colonel said with venom. "Draw your *katana*! Prove it's still a weapon – or you will dig my latrine with it!"

One soldier, a farmer with buckteeth, guffawed. Katsu shot him such a look that the man ducked his head and went quiet.

Katsu did not like to draw the sword unless he intended to use it. It was certainly not for showing off. Now, under a direct order, he withdrew the blade from the scabbard. The band of steel came into sight. Even under these appalling conditions, Katsu kept it oiled, sharp, and free of rust. None of these men, including the senior officer, had even held a priceless heirloom such as this.

"How beautiful!" sighed one of them.

"Yes, beautiful," the colonel sneered. "A beautiful relic from an outlawed caste. Where was it made?"

"Bizen."

"And you, Takano – I expect you know *kendo*?"

Katsu had trained in the martial art since he was a boy, two hours a day, six days a week.

"Yes, honored Lieutenant Colonel Matsui," he replied with exaggerated courtesy.

"What *dan* are you?"

"I have been fortunate enough to achieve the fifth level."

"Impressive, Captain," the commander spat.

"No doubt you are also a master of *iaido?*"

This was the art of the sword. While *kendo* involved sparring with fists, bodies and wooden swords, in *iaido* there was only solitary practice. *Katana* were far too deadly for sparring.

"I am third *dan.*"

"Again, impressive." The colonel forced his lips into a semblance of a smile.

"Well, Takano. Let us see if that *katana* can do something besides inflate your self-importance. I command you! Behead these enemies!"

The priests stared at the Japanese in terror, understanding nothing as the conversation went on. They did understand the sword and they gazed at the one holding it. Katsu looked back at them. They wore threadbare clothes and sandals. One of them was younger, bald on top. He began to pray in a panicked voice, begging God to save them.

The older one had a head of shaggy gray hair. He told his companion to calm himself.

"Pray with me," he said. He held his hands together and closed his eyes.

"Our Father, who art in heaven..." The younger priest took a breath and joined in.

"Hallowed be thy name. Thy kingdom come, thy will be done...."

Katsu found himself in an impossible dilemma. He was a career officer from a renowned military family. Orders were to be obeyed at once, without question!

Yet it was clear to him that the *gaijin* were who they claimed to be. Never in his wildest imagination had he contemplated that he would be forced to kill monks of any kind – Christian, Buddhist, Shinto or Taoist!

For the first time ever, he faltered at obeying a direct order.

"I am sorry, honored Lieutenant Colonel Matsui, but anyone can see that these men are civilians. Priests will not harm us and in fact..."

"Silence, Takano!" the commander bellowed. "Do not show insubordination, or reveal yourself a coward before the men! There will be immediate consequences!

"Obey at once – or give me the sword!"

"...lead us not into temptation but deliver us from evil..." the priests went on.

Katsu saw the entire fate of his career, and the honor of his family, hang on these seconds.

He came to a decision.

Abruptly, he reversed the sword, offering the handle to his superior. Matsui swelled like a toad.

"Just as I thought! You are a coward – worse than useless!"

The older man grabbed the *katana*. He pulled so hard, it would have taken off Katsu's fingers if he had not jerked away. The colonel clutched the weapon and raised it in the air. Katsu knew by his grip that he was a clumsy amateur.

Matsui spun and slashed at the young priest's neck. The blade chopped the flesh, but it was a shallow cut. The man screamed and the older one cried out in horror. Soldiers wrestled the injured man into place and stretched his neck.

The colonel raised the sword and hacked again. This time he cut deeper, but it was an ugly blow. The man fell on his side and writhed in torment. He choked for long minutes and it was a relief when he died.

Katsu felt a new emotion surge – blazing contempt.

The lieutenant colonel turned to the remaining white man and he raised the dripping sword.

"Lord help me!" the priest cried, and Katsu found he was moving. He ran at Matsui, put a hand over his superior's own and squeezed. The colonel tried to break loose but could not. In fury, he even tried to cut the captain, but Katsu held him like a vice.

"Please relinquish my *katana* and step aside, honored Commander Matsui!"

The colonel felt his fingers bend most painfully, on the verge of snapping. He was in grave danger of losing what remained of his authority, and he took a different tack.

"Well, Takano. Take it then. But my order stands!"

Matsui let his subordinate reclaim the sword. Katsu glared at the colonel, then turned to his repugnant task. He raised the blade in his two-handed grip and the old priest looked up at him.

"One blow, son," he said, "by all that is holy!"

"Yes Father," Katsu said in English. "Forgive me."

"May God forgive you," the man replied and bent his neck.

The sword flew. The priest's gray head tumbled from his shoulders. The soldiers holding the body let it drop.

"A passable stroke, Captain," the commander said in his smug tone. "Perhaps you are not totally useless after all."

Katsu faced the older man, the crimson long knife easy in his grip.

"Please do not speak to me just now, honored Lieutenant Colonel!" he barked.

The colonel stared back at this upstart vagabond in his rags. But he could not help seeing the muscles corded in his arms and chest, and the way the hands held the sword.

Most clearly, he saw his own death in those shining eyes. He bit off the insulting retort he'd been about to make.

"Yes, well..."

Hastily, he took a few steps away and turned as if to look at the river.

Katsu forced himself to breathe and regained control.

Local natives and the Sepik guides had watched the slaughter of the white men in mounting horror. Now one of the women shrieked and they all shouted and began to run.

"Shoot them!" Matsui screamed.

Soldiers raised rifles and brought the runners down.

Mere minutes after they had arrived in Kissim, corpses lay scattered across the landscape.

The nine-man Japanese squad took control of a nearby hill. On top of it, they built a bunker of logs. Here, they lived and kept watch. Here, they were reasonably safe. But still, they must go for water and scrounge for food, and then they were vulnerable.

Indeed, a patrol was ambushed. Two of the soldiers were killed with arrows.

It was a terrible way to die, Katsu thought, studying the spiked bodies. He ordered the men to set traps of their own. They captured a native and brought him before the colonel.

As it turned out, this prisoner knew a smattering of *tok pisin*, the trade language.

The colonel revealed a talent for torture. He sharpened bamboo slivers and went to work on the captive's hands, sliding spikes beneath the fingernails. Within minutes, he knew there were two more white men hiding with the villagers. The commander ordered the native to take them to the place. The fellow balked.

Matsui had his men untie the loincloth while he sharpened another wedge of bamboo. Again, within minutes, the victim was hobbling through the jungle, on his way to betray his people.

Katsu did not approve of the colonel's method of interrogation, but he was in agreement with the decision. If they allowed the slaughter of their men to go unpunished, they would all die. They were outnumbered, short of ammunition, and they must respond with strength.

Over the next days, they hunted down and shot the remaining white men and every villager they could find. After that, a troubled peace settled over Kissim.

But then the aircraft landed, bringing enemy soldiers. These were not harmless priests, but seasoned jungle fighters. In mere days, they slaughtered all the Japanese, including Lieutenant Colonel Matsui.

Except one.

Katsu was the last of his crew.

Yes, you are disgraced, his father's voice came again, *but you can redeem yourself. Whatever the cost, find the enemies of Nippon and kill them.*

This is the way of the warrior.

96

Johnny and Footy scrambled down a wooded hill and emerged on the open riverbank. Before them stretched vegetable patches. They looked carefully, but saw no natives.

The main river, still swollen from the rain, flowed out beyond a wide bay, thick with rushes. Johnny watched a heron with a six-foot wingspan glide in and splash down. It froze on one leg, dagger beak poised.

"Look," Footy pointed. "I reckon that's where the locals go to wash and get water." He pointed to a bald head of clay surrounded by shallows.

"But where are the bloody natives?"

Johnny shook his head. He, too, studied the path that led to the much-trodden point, the ground splattered with betel. Beyond, the riverside trail continued beside the gardens.

Johnny shrugged and strode towards the water. Footy trailed a few yards back. They were almost to the river when the pilot heard something. He stopped and cocked his head inland. For a few seconds he heard nothing and was about to go on when the reedy sound came again.

It was so unearthly – so out of place – his skin prickled.

"Mate – hold up!" he called.

Johnny paused, mere paces from the river.

"Listen!"

Through the reeds, the crocodile stared at the Smooth-headed man – not yet within reach, but all its muscles tightened in anticipation of the charge.

Johnny heard nothing and looked back towards the bay.

"Bloody wait and listen!" Footy urged.

"What is it?" Johnny turned to face him.

"In the trees – over there!" the pilot pointed with his chin.

"Struth mate, someone's singing!"

Johnny took another step, a hand cupped to his ear. Now he heard it too. The voice was faint, off in the distance, but there was no mistaking it.

"It's a woman!" Johnny exclaimed.

Footy nodded and trotted that way and Johnny went after him.

In frozen anticipation, the predator watched the One-Prey retreat. The Father remained poised where it was.

Footy cut across the gardens and Johnny caught up. The breeze shifted their way and both men stopped in astonishment.

"It's bloody English!" Footy breathed.

Johnny put a finger to his lips and unstrung his rifle. Footy pulled the Lee Enfield off his shoulder.

Rifles in hand, the men moved across the *kaukau* mounds, hunting the singer.

97

The two men worked their way from the gardens into a band of trees and slowed down. The song came from somewhere beyond. They stole to the edge of the woods and peered out. They saw a sun-drenched meadow, and at the center was a woman, sitting on a log. She was naked except for strands of blossoms looped around her hips. She was in profile, and her long hair hung in honey-colored waves down her back. Her skin was dark gold but the watchers could see she was a white woman.

The song came from her:

"Oh, where have you been Billy boy, Billy boy,
Oh, where have you been charming Billy?
I have been to see my wife,
She's the darling of my life,
She's a young thing and cannot leave her mother."

On either side of the singer stood a young native woman. They, too, were in a state of near nudity, and were drawing bamboo combs through the blonde tresses. The hidden men drank in the bare bodies, loins barely covered with flower chains.

The woman sang and the men crept closer. Johnny counted four more dusky nymphs lying in the long grass, stringing blossoms.

"Struth!" Footy blurted. Johnny raised a warning finger – too late.

The woman's song broke off and she stared into the forest. Johnny's gaze locked on her – the long, lovely body, in spite of the angry scar across her chest. She was looking right at him and he saw wide gray eyes in a striking face. There was something eager in her gaze – not surprise, but expectation, as if she had been waiting. His heart beat raggedly and he glanced at Footy and saw the Aussie's jaw hanging open.

"They've seen us," Johnny said in a normal voice.

"Yes mate," Footy agreed, still staring.

The singer said something to her companions and they all turned towards the watchers in the woods. The women in the grass rose to their feet.

"We're friends!" Johnny called. "We're Allied soldiers!"

The singer spoke louder and the men heard a string of guttural sounds. Then she raised her voice and said in English: "We see you! You can come out now!" The men glanced at one another.

"What is this!" Footy rasped. "This looks like heaven!"

"Not heaven," the Hard Case growled. "But they're unarmed women. Let's not scare them any more than we have to."

He took off his helmet.

"Be careful. This is too weird! Let's stow our gear here, but stay armed! Keep your guard up!" He dumped his pack against a tree, leaned the machete and bayonet against it, and put his helmet on top. Footy did the same with his pack and big knife, and left his hat on the pile as well.

But they would not go unarmed. The men tucked pistols in their belts, behind their backs. Rifles in hand, they walked out of the trees. They stood outlined in light at the edge of the meadow, facing seven women in that sun-soaked place. It came to Johnny how rumpled and dirty they must look.

The women, by contrast, were clean and groomed. They wore blossoms in their hair, in addition to the flower strings around their hips. They were adorned with shell necklaces, bracelets and ankle-bands.

Johnny's gaze seemed to have a mind of its own. It followed the white woman's body from her bare breasts, down her belly, to her hips beneath the blossoms. Her eyes followed his own, and she laughed, an eerie sound.

"Come," she said.

98

The woman looked at Johnny and opened her arms.

"She's Australian," Footy rasped.

"I know it." Johnny ran fingers through his hair.

The woman spoke again in that other language and her six companions came smiling toward the men. They held their hands out, clearly unarmed.

Johnny and Footy were a few paces apart, and they clutched their rifles as three young native women approached each of them. The women saw the men's wide eyes and giggled. Hesitantly at first, they began to touch. Johnny felt soft hands on his arms and shivered. His nostrils filled with the scent of sun-warm skin. The women's lips glistened and their breasts grazed him, while gentle hands began to caress his arms and body.

In spite of their misgivings, Johnny and Footy relaxed into the attention like men dying of thirst would sink into cool water.

Johnny's gaze kept returning to the singer. She stared back with those gray eyes. Johnny licked his cracked lips.

"Something's off!" he croaked. He heard the Aussie grunt and looked over to see that a female had pried one of his hands from his rifle. She guided the fingers to cup her breast.

"What could possibly be wrong?" the Aussie crooned. He still had one hand on his Lee Enfield, while two girls stroked the arm. They coaxed Footy into the meadow.

Johnny felt a hand slip under his shirt and touch his chest and he shivered. He suddenly yearned to throw caution aside and succumb. His younger self might have done it, but not the soldier who'd survived three years of war.

Warm hands at his back urged him toward the woman on the log and his feet were moving like a sleep-walker. He glanced at Footy and saw the pilot's shirt off, the girls touching him.

"Footy!"

"What mate?" Footy asked in a dreamy voice – even as his rifle was tugged away. His free hand went to the twin of the breast he stroked.

"Come to me," Johnny heard again, and his attention returned to the bewitching singer. He was almost on her and as his eyes found hers, she arched her breasts and near-naked body to him.

Johnny gaped, hardly aware when one of his own hands was pried from his Springfield. His fingers went to the white woman's hip, and they both quivered at the touch.

"Who – who are you?" he gasped. A shadow passed over her face.

"We are the bridesmaids," she said, serene again.

"Those who are thirsty, come and drink."

The soldier voice shouted a protest in his mind, but Johnny's young body was swamped with desire. He found himself up against her, and the woman put her hands around his waist and pressed.

Her hand went behind his neck and she drew his face to hers, lips parted.

No! The shout was within. With supreme effort, he turned away and the woman's lips brushed his bearded cheek.

He saw Footy sinking into the grass. The women were all over him and the Aussie's arms were around one of them. Footy kissed her on the mouth.

"No!" Johnny called, aloud this time.

The singer put her hand on his chin and turned his face back to her. With her other hand, she pulled his shirt up and her breasts pressed his bare chest. It was excruciating pleasure. He was panting and he barely felt the tugging on the rifle he still held in one hand.

Fingers came from behind and worked to unbuckle his belt.

The singer let go of him and lay back on the log. She spread her knees and the flowers parted. The Hard Case protested, but as if from far away.

Johnny was not a virgin, but the war had ensured that he lacked much experience with women. He'd had a few trysts with high-school girlfriends in the back seats of cars, and rare encounters during the war, while on leave. But Johnny had never been with a woman who behaved like this in broad daylight.

She was acquiescent, flung back, hands up in her long hair.

"And the lion shall lay down with the lamb," she said in a throaty voice.

Somehow, Johnny still held his rifle, but now he groaned, set it down, but put his boot on it.

He pressed against the woman. He did not notice that two of the girls had moved behind the log. One remained behind him, hands busy.

The singer gazed into his face. It came to him how other-worldly her eyes were. Then a low chuckle escaped her lips. The sound was so unearthly, a shiver went up Johnny's spine. It was like being doused in cold water.

Johnny froze.

Gwyn's face rose in his mind and the contrast was profound – those thoughtful green eyes, and these eldritch gray ones.

Johnny stood upright, away from the singer.

But she rose with him, bringing up the hands that had trailed behind her. They held a spear with a knife lashed to it. She pressed the blade to his neck. Her smile disappeared in a scowl. Suddenly, she looked older.

Then Johnny felt more spears against his back.

He felt furious and foolish all at once. In an instant, the physical desire was gone and he wanted his rifle. The stock was under his foot, but he could not reach for it, not with her knife at his jugular.

"You are the lamb – I am the lion," she growled.

"And you're as nutty as a fruitcake," Johnny spat. He realized his belt was undone and he redid the buckle. Still looking at the woman, his hands patted frantically around his waist.

His pistol was gone. Cautiously, turning away from the spear, he looked in Footy's direction.

The pilot lay with a woman in the field, but two of them now loomed over him, spears raised.

"Footy!" Johnny yelled. The Aussie's flushed face turned and Footy absorbed Johnny's predicament. Then he craned over his shoulder and saw his own danger.

Johnny saw that all the females were momentarily focused on Footy. In one fluid movement, he pushed the spear from his neck, scooped up his rifle, and pressed the barrel hard between the naked tanned breasts. His finger curled around the trigger.

"Call off your friends!" Johnny snarled into her startled face. "Put down your weapons or I'll kill you." Her gray eyes rested on his face and she did not speak.

"I'll put a bullet through your heart!" he warned her. "Believe me."

She kept staring even as she deliberately brought her blade back to his neck. Then he felt steel against his spine.

"That's your pistol," the woman said. "My handmaiden knows how to use it."

Footy rolled away from the woman onto his back, and those with the spears re-positioned them over his throat and heart.

"Easy," he panted. "Easy!"

The one he'd been with scrambled up, found her own spear in the grass, and stood above the Australian. She frowned and poised the point over his genitals.

"No mate, not bloody that!" he moaned and cupped himself with his hands.

The singer spoke as calmly as if they were discussing the weather.

"Now – you shoot me, and my handmaidens will kill you."

She wants to die! Johnny thought. *Delay her – keep her talking!*

"My friend is Australian like you," he tried. "You don't want to kill us – we're Allies! We're on the same side!"

"He's a filthy little pig," the woman said. "And we are not on the same side because we are women and you are men."

Johnny searched her eyes and saw nothing he could read.

"What does that mean?"

"We were given Eden," the woman said, "But then men enter, and you – you bring the serpent. We were pure – you show us evil.

"We slay the snake by killing the man. You see?" She smiled again, but it was just a stretch of her lips.

"But I am finished talking," she said. "Let us make an end."

And all at once, Johnny knew who she was.

99

Evil creatures attacked Katsu. His skin was covered with biting things! He jumped up and beat frantically with his bound hands. There were big black ants all over him. They chewed everywhere, even inside his ears and beneath his trousers. He shouted as he brushed them away and had to reach inside his pants to pull off the ones that hung there.

His fingernails were cracked and filthy, but as he watched them pinch the torturers, it came to him again who he was. He even remembered part of how he happened to be here, alone in the jungle.

I am Katsu. It came in a rush – Kissim, the crocodile, the enemy soldiers, the trek. He pictured the fight with the fearsome cannibals, the Father's attack, and then Mula's village, and the news of the atom bomb. But the most recent event he could recall was the thunderstorm. He vaguely recollected that his captors had fallen ill – and after that, nothing.

How he came to be alone in this bamboo grove, tormented by ants, he did not know. Where his captors were, he had no idea. He realized he was starving when his stomach gave a high whine.

Katsu had no weapons and no food and he was hopelessly lost. He felt a prick of fear. At least with the enemy he had been fed! He tried to form a plan and the best he could think of was to free his hands and find the river. His mouth was parched and he needed water or he would die.

Katsu searched the forest floor until he found a sharp-edged rock. He sat and sawed at the rope, and though he chafed the skin raw, at last he cut through and peeled away the coils. He tried to leave the place, but found he was in foliage so dense he could make no headway. He was reduced to crawling on his belly over the roots, and then he knew this was how he had come, from the pain in elbows and knees. After suffering a long time beneath the bushes, faint from lack of water and food, he struggled into an open place. He crawled into a shaft of sunlight and fell unconscious again.

He did not hear the wild pigs. The boar sniffed around the man, snorted and trotted off, followed by his harem.

Katsu woke in darkness and his body was one huge itch. His tongue stuck to the roof of his mouth. His fingers searched out a pebble and he sucked it until a little moisture came. He could see nothing and he resigned himself to remaining there. The mosquitoes were a constant torment and so were his thirst and hunger. He tried to cheer himself up by thinking: *I am free – free of my captors, free to go where I will and do what I want!*

But the night dragged on and on and he could not stop the insects feeding. When he could bear no more, he slapped madly at himself and rubbed his head. Then he knew that somewhere, he had lost his shirt, but still wore the ragged trousers and there was the band of cloth around his head. It had been with him so long, it was his last comfort. At last he put his face against his knees and sheltered his scalp with his hands.

The night was eternal and sometime in it, he began to say to himself, *the enemy is a liar!* For years now, fighting in this foul jungle, he and his comrades had encouraged one another.

Nippon will win! We are the only civilized people, and we are the rightful head of Asia. The Empire will seize its divine destiny!

But now as he tried to muster the old bravado, the words rang hollow. Lost and alone, he was forced to admit the truth, at least to himself.

The news of the atomic bombing of Japan stabbed through him like a dagger. He felt the reality of it in his bones, and he knew that all Nippon's grand plans were undone. A voice like steel rang in his head.

The Empire is vanquished. Our enemies have won. We will be prisoners, even in our own land. The world has changed forever. It has become hell on Earth.

The man hated this voice that pierced the night. But he could not deny it. He was a weak boy, alone in a heartless universe. The weight of the infinite heavens pressed on him so he could not breathe. He felt he would crack like a bug. There came a stabbing pain in his chest and he thought he was dying. A sound rose in the forest. It was harsh, in waves, the essence of despair. His chest heaved and moisture he could not afford to lose spilled from his eyes.

He was utterly defeated, and he dropped his hands and let the mosquitoes feed unmolested.

Later in that boundless night he saw pinpricks of light. At first, he thought they were hallucinations born of illness.

But when they came close, he saw them reflected on leaves.

Fireflies! They lifted his spirit and he slept. He awoke to the voice in his head. *The world I knew is no more. My father, myself, and all soldiers of the Imperial Japanese Army – we have been duped.*

Our leaders let their pride convince them of the lie that we would win. And where did we go so willingly? To disaster. Our ships are sunk at the bottom of the ocean, our planes are shot from the skies. My countrymen lie dead by the millions all over Asia and the Pacific.

We despised each nation we conquered as "the defeated" – worthy only of abuse and contempt! But we have joined them. We have lost face before the entire world. Nothing prepared us for this humiliation!

I have become a stranger to my home. I am ashamed.

His mind was quiet for a time, but then another voice rose, and while it too was harsh, it retained human warmth.

Yet you live, my son. You are my child and we are Samurai – forever – whatever others say. This is wartime and you are a soldier! Harden yourself! Your self-pity is intolerable! This is weakness born of sickness. You will gather your life force and you will walk the warrior's path!

Katsu was grateful then for the discipline his father had, at times, beaten into him.

There remains only what I must do. He thought of his captors. *I will find them and I will seize my sword! I will wield it against my enemies, and if that is the end of my story, so be it.*

Gradually he distinguished branches against the sky. The sad, old world took form once more. He saw the shadowy legions of mosquitoes – legs splayed as they drank his blood. He crushed scores of them, and rubbed their bodies and his own blood on his tongue for nourishment.

He stood up, giddy for water. With no path, he crossed his arms in front of his face and pushed through. At last, he stumbled upon a trickle and he knelt and drank. He followed the rivulet until it became a puddle, and he splashed away a little of the itch and sweat. He followed the water, ducking under giant leaves and clambering over rocks. He caught a frog, pulled off its skin and ate its legs raw. That made him gag, but he kept it down.

The brook became a stream and, after many hours, it led him to a native path through the jungle. The sun was a mere bright spot in the forest canopy and he could not tell in which direction to go. He simply followed the trail and at last broke out of the trees and there was the Raub River. He realized at once he was moving upstream, in the wrong direction.

His captors might have died of their sickness, it occurred to him. They probably had. But if he lived, perhaps they did as well. And if they lived, what had they made of his disappearance? He hoped they thought he had been swept away by the flood – or eaten by crocodiles. This encouraged him, for if they believed he was dead, he could surprise them.

The sword known as "Katsumushi-maru" has sung in the hands of Takano warriors since it was forged centuries ago. I was named for the blade, and I will possess it again. With it, I will take my enemies' lives.

But that must wait. First, he needed food. He turned downriver on the trail. An hour later, he found a stream of clear water running into it. He drank and continued, moving faster.

Now I am the most dangerous of men – the one with nothing left to lose.

100

It came to Johnny in a flash.

"You're Sarah!"

The woman cried out as if he'd punched her. Her face contorted and she turned her head, as if listening to a sound far off.

"Sarah?" Her voice quavered.

"Your husband is Billy," Johnny said.

"Billy? Where is Billy?"

Johnny glanced at Footy and saw him still on his back, three spears ready to stab. Johnny returned his attention to the white woman and found her eyes wide with grief and remembrance.

"The Japs!" she exclaimed. "They came to the mission and..." She paused as memory flooded in and Johnny saw her flinch.

"Oh!" she gasped. "They murdered Billy!"

She sagged as if an internal cord had snapped. She began to sob and her spear drifted from Johnny's neck.

"He is dust," she raked a hand through her hair. "And I am ashes!" She was silent a moment.

"This is hell." She groaned like her heart was cracking.

"I'm sorry, Sarah," Johnny said. He felt a stab of pity, but far stronger was the need to get himself and Footy out of mortal danger. His mind raced.

How do you threaten a person who wants to die? And then it came to him: *you don't. What does she care about?*

Johnny swung the barrel of his rifle away from Sarah's

chest. He jammed it under the chin of the nearest native girl who cried out and dropped her spear. The singer raised her eyes in alarm.

"Esther!"

"Sarah," Johnny grated, "put your spear down. Right now! Order your women to drop theirs as well! Or I will blow Esther's brains out." He pushed the barrel up so the woman choked. Confusion, anger and fear played across the singer's face.

This is the moment of truth.

"Sarah," he barked, "I am a soldier and I have killed many, and I will kill Esther now – unless you do exactly what I say. On three." He tightened his finger and knew he would do it.

"One."

The women looked uneasily at one another.

"Two..."

"Stop!" Sarah cried. She opened her hands and let the spear fall. She spoke in a tremulous voice in the native language. The women stared at her and then at each other and began to withdraw. Johnny saw that the one with his pistol kept it pointed at him while she circled away. She joined the others gathered behind Sarah, but they did not put down their weapons.

The three over Footy backed off as well. A few feet from him, one handed her spear to a companion and plucked the Aussie's rifle and revolver from the grass.

She gave the handgun to another and checked the Lee Enfield in a way that told Johnny she knew how to use it. Walking backwards, guided by a friend, she kept it trained on the pilot's chest. The one with Dingo's revolver pointed it at him as well.

"Footy," Johnny called, "We can't fight this. Let's go!"

The Aussie got to his feet and secured his pants. He grabbed his shirt and then watched, fists clenched, as his guns departed in the women's hands.

A companion came to Sarah and helped her get up. Something about the way she did it made Johnny wonder who was really in charge – the mad woman or the natives? He had the Springfield still pressed under the chin of the one called Esther. Sarah grasped the barrel and pushed it aside. Johnny let her do it and she stared at him with grief-bruised eyes.

"The Japs raped me," she said. "Each one of us." She nodded at her companions. "We were their 'comfort station,' their *ianjo*. I fought back." Her fingers touched the livid scar across her chest. "But there were too many. I prayed to die. But I did not die." She wiped her eyes with her long hair.

"I forgot myself," she said. "I became a thing that lays under men." Her voice broke.

Johnny stared at her, appalled.

"But one day, there were less Japs." She looked at her friends, then back to Johnny.

"After that, we took sticks and rocks. Now we stopped the men who came at us. Then we had their guns. The killing got easier." She sneered and Johnny found nothing big enough to say.

Footy broke the silence.

"Come with us, Sarah."

"You!" she glowered at him. "Rooting little pig!"

Johnny shot a warning glance at Footy and saw the man look sheepish and defiant at the same time.

"Sarah, we will take you home!" Johnny said. For a moment there was a flicker of hope in the gray eyes.

"Home?" Sarah whispered.

"To Aus!" Footy said. "To your family!"

Sarah shuddered.

"My family! I cannot see my family! I am *ianfu* – unclean!" She looked to the native girls beside her and took their hands. "These are my family. They saved me."

She stood with the women and they joined the others. And then the group retreated to the far jungle. The three holding firearms shuffled backwards, still aiming at the men.

"Leave our guns!" Johnny called, raising his rifle and putting the cross-hairs on the one with Footy's Lee Enfield. But the women continued to move away.

"Johnny!" Footy shouted. "Save our guns!"

Johnny sighed and lowered the Springfield.

"I've never killed a woman and I'm not going to start now," he said.

The women melted into the forest and they heard Sarah call in a loud voice.

"Unclean! Unclean!"

There was silence for a time and then the voice came from further off.

"Unclean, unclean, unclean!"

"That's the bloody world for you," Footy said bitterly. "Whenever anything good comes along, it's usually too good to be true."

He stalked back into the forest.

101

Johnny followed the pilot to the place they'd left their gear.

Footy struggled into his shirt. A button came off and flew away. Footy cursed and took a quick look for it, but it was lost. He jammed on Dingo's hat, took the Bowie knife and shoved it through his belt, and heaved on his pack. The sword handle sticking out of it slapped his face.

"Bloody bloomin' bleedin' bastard!" Footy exploded. He stormed off. Johnny got his own gear on and went after him. The pilot took a shortcut directly across the gardens, Johnny on his heels. They passed well inland of the native washing place on the river. As they entered the jungle, Footy wheeled on Johnny.

"Look," Footy snapped. "Now we'll have to take turns with your rifle."

"Take turns?"

"You get it half the day," Footy said, "and I'll take it the other. Fair enough?"

"You're kidding!" Johnny shouted in his face. "Give my rifle to a man who let his be taken off him – by a girl?" He laughed angrily and shouldered by.

"And where's your own soddin' pistol?" Footy yelled after him. "You're going to play the bleedin' saint?"

Johnny shook his head and blitzed through the jungle and didn't care if the Aussie followed or not. His rifle was the main tool of his trade and he did not like anyone else to even touch it.

He strode fast for the next few hours and Footy fell far behind. Johnny stopped only when night was falling. He chose a campsite near some overgrown gardens. As the day had worn on, his rage had simmered to general exasperation. He was angry about the whole fiasco. He felt stupid for losing his pistol, but at least he'd kept himself under control.

Or so he told himself. *I've still got my Springfield, don't I!* Truth was, something deep within had wanted that woman, and this made him even more furious. Still, their predicament was sobering. To lose three of their firearms, with ammo, could be their death sentence.

Darkness fell while Johnny gathered wood. When Footy puffed up red-faced twenty minutes later, he was tending the fire and would not look at the pilot. The men moved separately into the nearby gardens, and dug sweet potatoes. They laid them on the coals without speaking. When these were cooked, they ate in silence. Footy spread his blanket, lay down, and muttered to the sky:

"No bloody point keeping guard without a bloody gun!" He turned away. Johnny wasn't going to argue with the fool. Instead of crawling into his hammock as he longed to do, he sat against a tree, rifle across his lap. From time to time, his fatigue overpowered him and he dozed, waking every few minutes.

Footy rolled on his back, snoring loudly. Johnny slapped at mosquitoes and thought he might put his boot in the man's mouth, but did nothing.

The night dragged by like a clock winding down.

102

From the river, the Father watched the man in the patch of light. The reptile had waited in its ambush place until it knew the One Prey had eluded it. Then the crocodile swam in pursuit. It spied the enemy in the distance and trailed along, quiet as a drifting log.

With darkness, the other animal came into view. The croco-dile waited, but it could not rest. Its leg throbbed and it knew instinctively it was too far away for an attack over land. It watched for most of the night, but in the way of its kind, the awareness arose that it needed a better stalking site.

On this reach of the river, the cliffs climbed and the game trail went along the top. The Father desired the Smooth-headed man beyond all else, but it knew this was not the place to take him. The better hunting grounds of its youth lay downstream.

While the stars were still strong in the sky, the hunter moved into the deep and swam with the current.

The One Prey would follow the water, and the Father would be waiting.

103

Johnny woke frequently that night and had trouble getting back to sleep. Daybreak found him tired and cranky. He lit the stove and boiled water from his canteen. They were low on cof-fee and out of almost everything else. Johnny felt like brewing a cup just for himself, but he made two and put one beside the sleeping pilot. He gulped his quickly and stuffed his things in his pack.

As he was getting it on his back, Footy sat up and rubbed his eyes. Even the way the man scratched his belly was aggra-vating. And when he hawked and spat, Johnny could have slugged him.

Johnny clenched his jaw and strode away.

Footy had to throw his things together and trot, just to keep the Yank in view. He carried his cup, but could barely get the coffee into his mouth. For his part, Footy observed a fine morning. His dreams had been laced with erotic images, and a guilty euphoria was still on him. He felt terrible about the loss of his firearms, but that was *his* problem – wasn't it? *The Yank should be over himself by now!*

The air was fresh, and the sun, a halo over the forest. The surface of the river traced intricate patterns. Water birds flew in abundance. Footy watched a kingfisher skim, dive, and come up with a fish.

Johnny peeled a cooked sweet potato as he walked and tossed the burned skin off the high bank into the river. Fish rose to feed, making rings. Eventually, he came to grasslands that gave way to scrub. All signs of human settlement were left behind.

Footy was well back and his anger grew with every step. *The bloody Yank's no better than me! I saw him all over that poor mad woman – and he lost his pistol. That's a fact. I saw him put down his rifle. Sheerest chance he got it back. Who the hell does he think he is, Mister High-and-Mighty!* He took some deep breaths to calm himself.

Not that I'm proud of meself. No, not the best thing you've ever done, Footy-me-lad. But it's not the Yank's bloody business!

The miles and the hours wore away and Footy went through a change of mind. He had to admit – only to himself – that he'd been stupid to lose his firearms! He might as well be naked out here in the bush!

But I don't need bloody-Johnny-come-lately to tell me! By midafternoon he had worked himself into a real rage.

Just like a bleedin' Yank – act like they run the world! Forget the ruddy Nazis, mate – it's the Yanks who believe they're the Master Race!

Footy glared at Johnny's helmeted head in the distance.

All right, if the wanker won't talk – I won't either. Fine with me, mate. Bloody fine with me!

The pilot deliberately let the American get out of sight as he stumped alone through the sullen heat.

I'll be glad when this is over. Glad when the Nips and Yanks all go back to whatever hellhole they crawled out of.

Up ahead, Johnny's thoughts circled like hornets.

That dipstick is going to get us killed! Why do I always have to be the responsible one? This is just like the war. Fine talk about "Allies," but it's the U.S. of A that gets the job done. We beat the Japs by land and sea, and were the Aussies grateful? Not nearly enough!

He knew Footy had fallen way back and he didn't care. He had his rifle and food – and the last cigarettes. If the runt couldn't keep up, that was his problem.

Late in the day, having covered a lot of distance, Johnny looked for another place for the night. It was mostly raw wilderness now, but he continued until he found a few *kaukau* mounds. He dug some roots and proceeded to camp.

By the time Footy came along and pulled up his own supper, Johnny had his hammock strung. Again, they did not speak while Footy unrolled his blanket.

They ranged out for firewood, moving around one another with the exaggerated courtesy men reserve for strangers.

104

Johnny lit the fire with his Zippo. The fuel had about dried out and it took several tries. *Something else to worry about!*

He'd asked Mula if he had any matches, but the chief told him, no, not for a long time. The villagers always kept a fire going.

The lack of even the whisper of a breeze made the evening oppressive. Mosquito squadrons attacked in force. The men placed *kaukau* on the coals and sat in the smoke in silence. An egg-shaped moon floated into the sky. When the tubers were ready, they speared them, each careful to take only his own.

After they'd eaten, Johnny pulled out two cigarettes. After several flicks of the Zippo he gave up, lit a piece of grass on the fire, drew on the smokes and passed one to Footy – all without a word.

"If you're going to be miles off all day, give us a few ciggies to carry!" Footy broke the silence.

"We're almost out," Johnny said. "And besides, how're you going to light them?"

"Why's that your bloomin' worry?" Footy snapped. "Trouble with you Yanks – think you run the bloody world!"

Instantly, Johnny regretted sharing his cigarettes and all the pent-up animosity boiled over.

"I don't know about the world, but we saved your bacon in the war!" he said hotly. "If not for us, you'd be getting your orders from Tokyo right now."

"You arrogant bugger," Footy choked. "You forget you're my guest here – of me and all Australians!"

"Oh yeah?" Johnny said. "Your guest! You ever hear about the 'Battle of Brisbane'? Don't tell me how you treat your guests!"

"Aw yeah," Footy said. "Yanks fighting us in our own country!"

"Then you know," Johnny said. "Thousands of you ganged up on every American soldier you could find. You were drunk. We had to barricade ourselves into our buildings and fight for our lives! It went on for days. Australian hospitality! What a sick joke!"

"We got tired of you bloody Yanks strutting around like you owned our country – abusing our women," Footy said.

"Your women? You, Footy? Huh! Don't make me laugh!"

"You know what they say back in Aus?" Footy said. "There's only three things wrong with you Yanks. You're overpaid – oversexed – and over here. At the end of it, it was one of our lads who lay murdered in the street. Shot and killed by a Yank in the poor bloke's own country! Yet not one bloody Yank died, did he?"

"Yeah? Well, I saw a lot of Americans die in this jungle," Johnny said, "and for what? For a bunch of losers who can't say thank you. Now I'm getting mad. You better shut up."

Footy flicked the butt of his cigarette to the ground in a shower of sparks and moved to his bedroll.

Johnny spoke to the pilot once more that night – at midnight when he shook him awake.

"Here," he said, thrusting his rifle at the man. "It's your watch. You take care of it or I'll know why. You and me, we're going to have to get along 'til we're out of here. It's loaded. I've got three more shells and we're out."

Johnny headed for his hammock. Footy sighed, roused himself and took the watch.

Both men were moving by first light. Johnny took his rifle back. With ill humor, the men threw their things together and hit the trail. The sun baked down and they dripped sweat.

At mid-morning, they came to a stream and replenished their canteens. The land was flat and the mountains were far behind – a blue ribbon under clouds. The Raub spread beside them, wide and sluggish, the banks all gone to mud. It looked like a wilderness unchanged since the dawn of time.

At midday, the river split into two branches that diverged across the silt. The men had no choice but to follow the outer arm. Another hour, and Johnny felt his hopes surge when the first seagull drifted overhead, but his spirits sank again when he saw the mangrove forest in the distance.

It seemed to take forever to arrive at the swamp. Stagnant water flooded the place, choked with stands of many-legged mangroves.

This is a crocodile's dream, Johnny thought. *But if we're going to reach the South Pacific, we've got to go through it.*

He and Footy stood at the water's edge, gathering the will to enter. There were ridges of drier ground further out, but entire sections were flooded. At last, miserable with each other and their options, the men waded in.

At once, Footy discovered that the mud sucked the sandals off his feet. He lost one and had to bend to feel for it, face in the murk. His fingers snagged it and he was able to dredge it up. He took the other one off and held them in a hand as he continued on bare feet.

Johnny did better in his boots, but on the bank once more, they were full of water. He had to remove them, wring out the socks and dry his feet. At least he had two pairs of socks, so one dried on top of his pack while he wore the other. If he didn't, he knew from dismal experience that the wet leather would wear the skin off, not to mention the jungle rot that would invade his toes. It could eat through to the bone – he'd seen soldiers crippled that way, too many to count.

But after a few hours of going in and out of the swamp, he couldn't keep up with the socks. Soon he, too, was wading barefoot, boots hanging around his neck.

They navigated the latest shallows and came to a deep ford. Johnny felt a wave of foreboding. There were thirty yards to traverse, and crocs could be waiting anywhere – in the water, or among the mangroves. But there was no other choice. He waded in, rifle held high. Footy watched him get half way and then followed. The water rose to their knees.

Three quarters of the way through, Johnny began to sink fast. He felt the soft mud slide up his legs like there was no bottom. He shouted and Footy watched helplessly as the Yank disappeared up to his chest. Johnny was able to ease on, and at last, crawl onto drier land.

Footy stood swatting at biting flies that had joined the mosquitoes in making life miserable. Being the shorter man, he knew the water would be higher on him. He took off his pack and balanced it with his hands on his head.

He sank in the hole so fast, he thought he was going under. He sucked in a breath and held it, the stinking water almost to his lips.

Johnny stood on the far bank, covering the other man with his rifle. Footy came on gamely, crawled out and the worry spilled over his vow of silence.

"I don't like this – not a bloody bit! Now we're in the Father's country. If that bastard, or any croc, finds us in a stretch like that..."

Johnny was still angry but apprehension pushed that aside.

"I hear you," he said. "But what choice do we have? Let's go!"

The men clenched their jaws and forged on.

105

Plagued by insects and anxiety, the men toiled through the swamp. The going was difficult, and the knowledge that a crocodile could be under every watery step wore them to a frazzle. The sun fried their heads and the hours were endless.

Footy slugged along in distress and at last his irritation turned inward with a vengeance. *To let that girl seduce me — while they took my rifle and revolver! Useless chump, Footy,* a voice taunted him.

Stupid little bugger! Count on you to always do the wrong thing. You're going to pay for it now, mate — and you deserve every bit of what's coming! These were barbs that had wounded him as a child — javelins hurled by schoolmates, teachers and especially, his father. Back then, they had cut him, and now his own accusations pierced his deepest wounds. Footy's natural cheerfulness and confidence bled away.

By the end of the day both men were wrung out, as well as famished. There were no gardens now, and all they had to eat was in their packs.

How far can the ocean be? Johnny figured they had enough potatoes for one more day, and still, they'd go hungry. As for drinking-water, they had not come across a source since entering the wetlands.

The sky coalesced into a dirty haze obscuring the horizon. In the fading light, the men looked for a patch of earth to hunker down on for the night. It was dusk when they saw higher ground — but to get there, they had to make one more ford. There was no point in delaying. Johnny sloshed in.

Footy had spent an absolutely wretched day. He was at snapping point. The whine of insects even inside his ears threatened to drive him over the edge.

He stood slapping and muttering as Johnny waded through.

When the Yank was on the far side and had turned to cover him again, Footy began to cross, sandals tied to his pack. A swarm of insects dive-bombed his head. A mosquito perched on an eyelid and plunged in its needle. Footy slapped his eye and went blind for a moment. He lost his balance, staggered sideways, and stamped down hard on something sharp. He yelped.

"What is it?" Johnny called.

Footy wiggled the leg, but it was held fast. He panicked, gave a sharp tug and something snapped underwater.

"Bloody bleedin' ruddy hell!"

He limped on, edged backwards out of the water, sat, and dropped his pack.

"What'd you do?"

"Stepped on something," Footy croaked. "Cut meself." Johnny groaned.

The Aussie rinsed the foot as best he could, swishing it in the nasty water. He turned it over in his hands and inspected the sole. Johnny sank beside him and they stared anxiously. There was a gash in the ball, a jagged piece of wood sticking out of it.

Johnny rooted through his pack and pulled out his towel and the first aid kit. He used a corner of cloth to wipe most of the crud away, while Footy winced and cursed.

"I've got to get that out," Johnny told him.

"Go on, do it!" Footy said between clenched teeth. Johnny took the foot in one hand and pinched the stick. He jerked out a two-inch wedge of sodden wood while Footy gasped and gurgled.

Johnny got his thumbs on either side of the wound and pressed. Footy let fly a string of curses, some of which Johnny had not heard before. He kept the pressure on until the black flecks were gone and the blood ran pure.

Johnny opened the bottle of iodine and poured some into the wound, while Footy called down damnation on all swamps and various marsupials. When the worst of the bleeding had stopped, Johnny tipped sulfa powder into the gash.

How will I be able to go on? Footy wondered. *How can I wade through the muck like this? Hopefully, the iodine has sterilized the cut. If the ruddy foot gets infected mate, you'll not walk at all.*

I get a bit of crumpet and what – I pay with me life?

Johnny told Footy he'd bandage the cut, and they were here for the night.

He unrolled the pilot's blanket for him and helped the Aussie lie down. Johnny figured he should elevate the injured foot. He chopped a forked mangrove branch, stuck it in the mud and rested Footy's heel in it.

"How's that?" Johnny asked.

"Hurts like a bugga," Footy said.

"Do you want morphine?" Johnny asked.

"You've got morphine?" Footy sputtered. "Bloody morphine? Why didn't you say so? Yes, dose me, mate."

Johnny selected a syrette – one of three small tubes he had. He broke the seal, attached the needle, inserted it in the muscle of Footy's thigh, and squeezed. The Aussie's eyes soon glazed over and he sank back.

"Better?" Johnny asked.

"Much – ta," Footy murmured.

"I'll sew it up," Johnny said.

"Take it off for all I care," Footy said.

Johnny got a needle and thread from his pack. He crouched in front of the Aussie and said he was going to begin. He got no answer and saw Footy had nodded out.

Johnny pushed the needle through the tough skin on the sole. He looped stitch after stitch – eight of them – until the gash was closed. He swabbed on more iodine, put a square of gauze over it, cut strips of tape from the roll and stuck the edges down. He ripped more strips and covered the patch, trying to make it watertight. He fetched his spare pair of socks – none too clean, but they'd have to do – and pulled them over the Aussie's feet.

Johnny gathered firewood. The branches were spongy, and again, he had trouble getting his Zippo to flame. At last, he managed to light a pinch of moss. He fed it with twigs and got a fire going. Water sputtered from the ends of the sticks, and the smoke was thick, but with the mosquito hordes, that was just as well.

Johnny cooked the last of the yams on the coals. *One for tonight, three for the whole day tomorrow, and that's it.*

While they roasted, Johnny gathered more swamp wood for the long night ahead. He unrolled his hammock upside down on the ground so the waterproof roof would serve as a tarp. He spread his sheet on top and used a spare shirt for a pillow.

While Footy slept, Johnny took a pot to the swamp. He could still see their steps coming across like gray mushrooms in the black. He parted the wiry mangroves and palms and found a trickle of clearer water coming from higher ground. He was able to get the edge of the pot under and filled it.

He took it back to the fire and piled branches around. When it had boiled for a few minutes, he set it aside to cool. That was all the drinking water they had for the day to come. When the *kaukau* were soft, he pulled them from the coals. He ate a single one, eyeing the others hungrily.

He lay down. Clouds obscured the stars and the glow of embers was the only light. He gazed into the coals while the frogs chorused. Something rustled through the brush and plopped into the marsh.

Johnny hadn't been able to get enough sleep for days, but he was determined to remain on guard. He was staring mesmerized at the flickering coals when he heard Footy's disembodied voice.

"About that girl..."

"Let that go," Johnny told him. "Enough!"

Footy grunted. Johnny thought he'd hear more, but then realized, the Aussie was asleep. The mosquitoes were ravenous and he saw them on the man's face. He went closer, brushed them off and adjusted his hat. He pulled the square of netting from the rucksack and tented it over his face. He got Footy's spare shirt and spread it over the Aussie's hands.

Johnny lay back, rifle across his lap, and, once more, his thoughts turned to Gwyn. He wondered if she believed he was still alive. Many times on this journey, he'd pondered why she asked him to look for his heart. He still didn't know what to do about that. A soldier couldn't be mooning on about his feelings all the time! It was just the sort of thing a girl would dream up to drive a guy absolutely nuts.

For a time he thought about Dingo, reminded of the major by the things around Footy. He realized he didn't even know if Dingo was married or had children. If so, the family had no idea that their man was never coming home again.

Johnny thought about the Father. Sure, he'd seen crocodiles in New Guinea, but one that huge? He'd never imagined being hunted by something like that. How could you hope to escape that monster? If it swam up now, everything was over.

Johnny's chin hit his chest. He'd dropped off, and he shook his head and slapped his face to wake up. He peered around, but could see nothing outside the glow of the coals. He sat up and, in memory, recited the story of "Moby Dick," as much as he could remember.

"Call me Ishmael..."

The night was long. It seemed forever before there was a hint of lighter gray in the east.

And it was at that very moment Johnny's eyelids slammed shut. He knew for a second he was passing out, but he could not stop it. He tipped onto his side and was out cold.

He did not see the unfriendly eyes that stared at him. Nor was he aware when the hunter came for him out of the swamp.

106

A sound at his ear penetrated Johnny's sleep and he struggled for consciousness. He was on his back and his eyes opened in bright sunlight. Something loomed over him, and Johnny squinted, trying to make out the silhouette against the glare. He blinked and got focus.

The Jap!

The man was very much alive, and much worse, his sword was in his hands. It was a shaft of burning light over Johnny's neck. The enemy was in the act of gauging where to strike and the blade was high for the blow.

Johnny's mind reeled. The sword was at the top of its arc. His gaze went to the dark eyes. He said the first thing that came to mind.

"You owe me your life," he said. "I saved you – at least three times."

The man's face was fierce, his body committed, but the blade wavered and held.

"First – when I captured you," Johnny said, "I spared you, more than once, and you know it. In the fight with the cannibals, I saved you again. And when Mula's men asked for you, I stood up for you."

The Jap said nothing. His muscles remained taut – but he did not strike.

"You owe me your life," Johnny said again.

Within Katsu, a battle raged. His enemy was helpless beneath his *katana* and he had the one deadly act to perform. In his bones, he was Samurai. On top of that, like a suit of armor, he was a soldier of the Empire. But what the Yankee said pierced his mind and soul.

Deep in his sense of honor, he knew it was true.

In his single-minded desire to regain his *katana* and do his duty, Katsu had not considered this. But it was a fact. He owed this man his life. Now the American called for that debt to be paid.

Johnny watched the blade against the rising sun and he knew his life hung in the balance.

Then the Samurai sword flashed down and Johnny did not know if he lived or died.

The enemy's fists were locked, the blade below Johnny's line of sight.

It was an eternity of seconds before the Jap stepped back and lifted the sword away.

Johnny's hand went to his throat and he raised his fingers.

No blood. Then he knew he was not cut. He sat up, staring at the enemy. The Asian deliberately touched his thumb to the razor edge and a line of scarlet sprang up.

"When I draw the *katana*," the man said in the clearest English Johnny had heard from him, "it must taste blood." He slipped the weapon into its scabbard and stood quietly.

The man was outlined in light and Johnny saw him with hyper-clarity, as though for the first time. In the gift of his life continuing, perception flooded in. For the first time, Johnny did not see a homely foreigner. Certainly, he was of another race and tradition, but he possessed self-control, even grace.

Johnny gained this knowledge in a flash. In the hours and days to come, the epiphany would fade, but it would not be lost. Something in him had shifted.

Jap, Nip, Slant, Slope – the words chased their tails through his mind. *We call them that to make them other than us so we can kill them with barely a thought. But he is a warrior, just like me.*

"I owe you my life. I forgot that," the enemy said. He shook his head, sat down with legs crossed, and spoke again.

"It is an old thing you call on, much older than this war. But I admit it is true – I owe you my life."

Up on an elbow, Johnny stared back.

"Now I have paid my debt – or some of it. I give you your life in exchange for my own.

"Beyond that, I think this atom bomb is real. Nippon is lost – who can fight such a thing? If my country is lost, my life has no value. You say I owe you my life — I give it to you. Kill me or not — it is the same to me."

He held the *katana* in both hands, bowed his head, and placed it on the ground. Johnny noticed his Springfield had been moved out of his reach.

Johnny looked at him searchingly and saw that this time, his enemy had truly surrendered.

"What the bloody hell is going on?"

Johnny turned to see the pilot, hat and netting pushed aside. He discovered he was very glad the Jap had not hurt the man and he grinned.

"Hey, Footy. Look what the cat dragged in!"

107

Footy was unhappy. Johnny had explained what happened — *the Jap turning up like a bad penny and surrendering again.* But the pilot was suffering too much to ask a lot of questions. He did notice the socks on his feet and asked about them.

"I sewed your cut while you were out," Johnny said. "I hope you can walk, but you can't go barefoot. I got it taped, but you're going to have to wear my boots."

Footy knew he should be grateful to the Yank, but he was in a filthy mood. He asked himself why, and apart from the obvious, it was something he couldn't put his finger on.

It has to do with the sodding Jap, but what? He tried to puzzle it out, but the answer eluded him.

Johnny brought his boots and the Aussie pulled them on. They were too big and he laced them as tight as they'd go. With the Yank's help, he got up and tried his weight on the leg.

The pain was intense. Footy grimaced and forced himself to take some steps.

"It'll do," he muttered.

His head felt thick and he realized he was fuzzy from the morphine. As soon as he thought about it, he wanted more. He asked for it.

"Better not – if you can stand it, Footy. I've only got two more doses and you might need it worse later."

Footy saw the sense in that and gave a curt nod.

"Right," he said.

One more thing the bleedin' Yank's in charge of! He turned his bloodshot stare at the enemy and then back to Johnny.

It's something there.

Johnny packed his gear and poured the boiled water into the bottles. He missed the heft of the pistol on his belt and sighed.

The only food they had were the three spuds he'd cooked last night. He gave one to Footy, then looked at the prisoner and at the two *kaukau* remaining.

I could eat six myself, without taking a breath!

"Here!" Johnny said and offered one. The prisoner snatched it up and bit in, not bothering to pick off the burnt skin. Johnny ate his own almost as fast.

Footy watched the Japanese shovel it in and resented every bite.

Johnny can play the bloody saint if he likes – but not me, mate. Not bloomin' me! The Jap's eating the last of our food! He observed that the P-O-W was filthy and scraped all over. Somehow, he'd lost his shirt.

386

"Footy, we can't be far from the ocean now," Johnny said. "The Jap and I reached an understanding. He surrendered and I believe him. I'm not going to tie him anymore. He wants to run, he can go. Our mission has come down to staying alive.

"And now we've got your foot to deal with. Let's get out of this swamp!"

Footy glared at the captive.

"No bloody way he goes free," he snapped. "I don't trust him – not an inch."

Johnny stepped close to the prisoner and stared in his face.

"I want your word you will not hurt us," he said. "If you want to run, I won't stop you. But if you're with us, you come as our prisoner. You obey orders. Do we have a deal?"

The prisoner nodded.

"Say 'yes,'" Johnny told him.

"Yes."

"Okay."

"Bloody hell!" Footy exploded. "You're going to accept that?"

The Japanese stared hard at the Australian, but said nothing.

"Well then," Johnny said to Footy, "how would you do it?"

The Aussie frowned.

"Swear on your Emperor's life that you will not harm us, and that you will obey us – Johnny and me," he said.

"These people believe the Emperor is a god," Footy said to Johnny.

The prisoner spoke.

"This is an unusual thing — but I swear on the life of Emperor Hirohito I will not harm you. I am your prisoner and I will obey your orders." The man was serious, and Footy was somewhat mollified.

"Okay," Johnny said. "We've still got a lot of croc country to cover. Let's move out! You come behind me," he told the Aussie. "You come last," he said to the captive. "You carry Footy's pack, and water." The man nodded.

Footy was even more chagrined to think of his things with the Jap, but he knew what the Yank said made sense.

Johnny picked up the sheathed sword.

"What are we going to do with this?"

"Don't even think of giving that to the Jap!" Footy barked. "That's mine!"

"Fine," Johnny said. "I'm not going to hump it. You?"

Footy limped over and snatched the thing. *I'm not going to let the Jap behind me with this bloody pig sticker! The Yank forgets what the bugger did to those cannibals!* More than that, he was not going to give up his precious souvenir. He'd already imagined what a splash it would make, showing it to his mates back home.

The Jap said nothing. Johnny shrugged and got ready to go. His feet were bare, because Footy wore his boots. Johnny stared at the bog that stretched on all sides. It was not channels of water any longer, but an endless lake, dotted with mangroves and mudflats.

Johnny waded in. When he was belly deep, he saw something move and whirled with the rifle ready. It was a python, thick as his arm, undulating through the mangrove roots. It disappeared and Johnny pushed on.

He climbed the bank, turned with the Springfield at his shoulder, and called. Footy limped slowly, having difficulty when the boots mired. The prisoner followed, wearing the wood-framed pack.

They continued, wading more often than walking. Footy's pace was agonizingly slow. Johnny got an idea and studied the mangroves. He saw what he wanted – a sapling that forked at shoulder height – and chopped it down. He waited for Footy and had the man try the rough crutch under his arm. He trimmed the ends and padded it with his towel. Footy handed him the sword and tried some steps while sweat streamed down his face.

"That's better, mate," he muttered.

"Okay," Johnny said, "but what are we going to do about this?" He lifted the sword.

"You carry it," Footy puffed.

"No way," Johnny said. "I've got enough."

"Give it back then!" Footy glowered. Johnny handed it over. The prisoner's eyes flashed between the men. The Aussie gripped the crutch with his right hand and the sword in his left.

Johnny shrugged and strode away. The Japanese waited for the Australian to move and trailed him. They went like that for several hours. Footy moved better, but still went at turtle pace.

Finally, for the first time, the Japanese spoke directly to the Australian.

"I will carry the sword."

"Not a prayer in bloody hell," Footy spat.

"That has been in my family for three hundred years," the Japanese said. "It was handed from father to son. You must not get it wet. And you cannot carry it."

"I will bloody well do what I like!"

"I have surrendered," the prisoner said. "I have promised not to hurt you." He took a breath.

"The sword has a name – *'Katsumushi-maru.'* I ask you – please keep it dry. Its value is beyond price."

"I'll soak it in sheep-dip if I want," Footy shouted, shaking the sword. "It's mine!"

Now Johnny was irritated.

"What does the stupid sword matter if you don't make it, Footy? Stop being an ass!"

Johnny moved to the next ford – another deep one. He held his rifle over his head and went in. Again, black water swirled around his chest. When he got to the far side, again he covered the others and they crossed.

Footy reached midpoint, the Japanese a pace behind. Then the crutch stuck in the mud. It pulled from under his arm and Footy started to fall, the sword swinging wildly.

He would have gone face-down if the Japanese had not rushed up and grabbed him. Footy turned, still falling. They did a slow dance, the sword circling. Then the scabbard came down hard on the prisoner's head. The crack even made Johnny wince.

"Crikey!" Footy gulped.

108

The prisoner steadied Footy with a fist in his shirt while his other hand snatched the sword. Blood trickled from the gash over his eyebrow. When he had Footy steady, the Japanese turned for the crutch and shoved it at the Aussie.

"Take it!"

Footy squinted at the man's bleeding forehead.

"Well, I'll be blowed!"

"I will carry the sword across," the prisoner barked. "Then you take it!"

Without waiting for a reply, the Japanese lifted Footy's free arm and shoved his head under it. He put an arm around the injured man's waist and extended the one with the sword for balance.

Footy needed his right hand for the crutch. He was forced to wrap his other one around the enemy's shoulders. The physical reality of the fellow struck him like a blow.

They came toward Johnny, sewer water to their necks.

On the bank, the Japanese pulled away from the Australian. Johnny noticed each man brush the place where the other's hands had touched him.

"Give it back," Footy said, face red, streaming with water. The prisoner handed him the sword. The Aussie grabbed it.

"Come on!" Johnny said and led them across the mud. The day was sweltering, the insects remorseless, and the men were famished.

And as it turned out, the sword was Footy's undoing. Now he grudgingly gave it to the P-O-W every time they came to water, and then took it back on the far side. When they negotiated drier stretches, Footy had to push it through his belt so he could walk. Mangroves snagged it and made it thump across his legs.

Finally, it jammed across two branches. Footy stumbled and crashed down. All his weight landed on the throbbing foot and he did a face plant. He scrambled up and shook the sword.

"Blast it all to bloody hell!" he shouted. The other two stared at him in frustration. "Footy, this can't go on!" Johnny thundered. "Let the Jap have it!"

"Not on your life," Footy shot back. "He'll murder us in our tracks, you mark my words!" "Give it to him," Johnny bellowed, "or I'm going to leave you behind! We need food or we're going to die out here!"

"All-bloody-bleedin-blasted right!" Footy shrieked.

"Here – take the thing!" He shoved it at the captive.

"But the instant I ask for it, you give it back! Do you agree?"

For long seconds, the men glared at each other, and the Asian spoke.

"When you say – I give it to you." He took the sword. The pilot turned away and fussed with his crutch.

The prisoner took off the rucksack, slid the sword into it so it poked out the top, and hefted it again.

Stupid bloody turn of events, Footy fumed. *Bloody Jap behind me with that carving knife!* He thought of the way the man had chopped off those heads in the Valley of the Cannibals. But there was nothing he could do about it. He marched on while the crutch jammed repeatedly into the tender bruise under his arm. A realization came to him.

The bloody Yank is taking sides against me with the bloody Jap! Exactly mate, it came to him – *that's exactly what's bothering me. Johnny is siding with the friggin' Jap. What have we come to!*

Insufferable red hairy ogre, the Japanese was thinking behind Footy's back. *You are* goshu-yaro – *a rude peasant. I speak English better than you know. And you? You will never understand my language, let alone the ways of civilized people.*

I could end your useless life before you could even turn around. But I will not do it – not because of you – but because I gave my word.

I am sick of them! Johnny was thinking. *I am sick and tired of this hellhole and worrying about the crocodile. I'm so hungry I could eat a shoe. I'd give anything for a burger – a thick patty running with juice. I'll have a plate of steak fries and a vanilla shake.*

The vision was so vivid, his stomach whined like a dog. He clamped his jaw and dispelled the hallucination with another lungful of rotten air.

What am I doing here in the middle of nowhere, while my unit invades Japan? No one knows we're here. We're all going to die.

And so, three furious men toiled across the sodden landscape.

Always, they watched for crocodiles. Inevitably, they began to see them. But these were all of the freshwater variety. They were able to scare them away by shouting and splashing water.

Where is the Father? That was the question. They approached an especially perilous looking ford. It had numerous channels off it, into the mangroves.

Johnny crossed on high alert, nerves near snapping, and at last reached the far side. It had been a long one, and the others had to cross the same distance. As always, he turned to cover them with his rifle.

"Come!" he called. Again, the prisoner assisted Footy, and they waded. All Johnny could see was their heads until they turned the bend.

Here, another channel connected to a deeper part of the marsh. And then from it, Johnny saw movement. A chill shook him as he took in what he'd been expecting, but desperately hoping not to see.

109

The wide scaled snout emerged from the mangroves. The head was caked in mud, and Johnny could see a yellow eye and long line of interlocking teeth.

In the instant, Johnny knew it was a massive saltwater crocodile.

It's the Father!

With his rifle, he aimed at the thick body just behind the shoulder.

He shot. The scales quaked.

The reptile kept coming.

The explosion made the other men flinch. They swung their heads and saw the huge beast swimming at them. Their faces changed as they redoubled their efforts to run, impeded by water.

The predator slid at them through the surface.

They won't make it! Johnny inserted another shell while the scorekeeper in his head began to count.

One gone – three bullets left!

The predator turned to take the men from behind and he fired. The bullet whistled by the Jap's arm and glanced off the top of the reptile's skull. Johnny heard it whine away. The brutal head swung behind the waders and it turned at them.

Johnny shot into the body. Again, scales rippled, but the brute kept coming. Johnny chambered another shell. *Two left!*

Footy and the Japanese rushed in slow motion, features contorted. Footy dragged the crutch up from the water while the Japanese held the sword aloft.

The croc's body was half hidden behind the men and Johnny fired again, into its back.

The scorekeeper screamed – *one left!* Johnny reloaded.

The Japanese was ahead, dragging Footy, the croc right behind them. They were still ten feet from the bank.

Johnny felt the urge to run sweep over him and let it pass.

Urgently calm, he peered through the scope, but all he could see was the men.

The croc's wake unfurled on each side as it rushed to take them.

"Get aside! Dive! Dive!" Johnny yelled.

It seemed to take forever for his words to reach the runners, and even longer for them to grasp his meaning.

Footy and the prisoner let go of each other and a sliver of light opened between them. Johnny centered the crosshairs.

The Jap shoved the pilot and fell aside, lifting the *katana* as he went underwater.

Johnny's view was a close-up of the croc's head and he squeezed. *Brain shot.* There was the explosion and point-blank slap of the metal-jacketed projectile cracking heavy bone.

Footy was at the bank. He fell there, twisting around, back to the mud.

The crocodile rushed him with open jaws.

The Japanese was underwater except for the hand grasping the sword. He came up gasping, filth pouring off. He drew the blade.

Johnny had no shells left and he slung the rifle and pulled his machete.

Jaws wide, the croc surged over Footy. The pilot thrust his crutch into the open cavern of a mouth. The point hit the throat so hard, it jarred Footy's arm.

The teeth slammed together and smashed the crutch, just missing Footy's hand.

The force of the charge brought the reptile on so that its snout slammed under the pilot's chin, snapping his head back. Footy was half submerged and pinned down.

The prisoner raised his sword and brought it down with all his force on the neck behind the skull. The blade did not penetrate even an inch before the scales stopped it. He swung again, hitting the same spot. It cut only a little deeper.

But the brute was already dead. Johnny's last shot had broken through the skull and shredded the brain. The water swirled a final time as a webbed foot kicked. The putrid death sigh blasted through its nostrils into Footy's face.

The explosion echoed across the water and a thousand birds lifted off and flew in widening circles.

In its final rush, the water washed the crocodile's head clean.

There was no moon scar. Still, it was a massive predator, the tip off the tail bobbing twenty feet away.

"It's not the Father," Johnny said.

He clambered down to help the Aussie.

"It's bleedin' heavy!" Footy wheezed. "Get the bugga offa me!"

The Japanese sheathed his sword, put it down on the shore, and went to Footy's other side. The two of them grabbed the pilot under his arms and pulled. He did not move. They tried again, but it was no good.

"We'll have to pick up the head," Johnny said. "We lift – you slide out," he told Footy.

The Yank and the Jap took up a place on each side of the skull and worked their fingers under the jaw. The head was about five feet long and weighed more than the two of them put together.

"Lift!" Johnny called and they put their backs into it. The head rose a little, floated by the water, and Footy tried to tug out, but could not get free. Neither could the others hold up the weight. They let it go and it settled back on the man.

"By all the bloomin' saints," Footy whimpered. Johnny wiped sweat from his eyes and took a breath. Flies were honing in on the croc's wounds. One wandered across an open eye.

Again, Johnny and the prisoner bent and lifted, muscles straining. Footy grabbed the jaws in both hands, feeling the hard wet teeth, and pushed up. Gradually, he was able to wiggle his legs out on each side. Inch by inch, he crabbed up the bank.

Finally, Johnny and the prisoner could let go. The head settled back and they climbed out of the swamp.

"On top of everything else, we're out of ammo," Johnny told a shaken Footy. "If the Father or any croc comes now..." He trailed off. But in spite of everything, a grim smile came over his face.

"Tonight we eat steak!"

110

With predator zeal burning in its blood, the Father coursed downstream. It swam through the heat of the day, aware of the pulse in its leg. Once more, infection mounted and fever sizzled through the reptilian brain.

It swam on and night fell. With every hour, it grew leaner and harder. Now the twitching images in its mind were all of the One Prey. For some time, it undulated through stagnant water, following a watercourse it knew well.

Eventually, in a new dawn, the water turned brackish. The salt tingled around the reptile's teeth and burned the ragged limb, but this hurt was welcome. The crocodile pushed on, eager for the ocean.

The South Pacific was calling its child home.

111

On the beach near the mouth of the Raub River, Captain Cleveland Karsh of the United States Marine Corps strode among his men. They jumped to meet his orders, just the way he liked it.

This, Karsh knew, was a truly momentous day and he had a celebration planned. But first he would ensure that his marines completed their task.

This morning, the captain had brought fifteen men to the beach. The launch, skippered by Karsh himself, came from the mother ship a mile offshore. Now the powerboat bobbed at anchor. Two dinghies with outboards were pulled up on the sand.

Before he'd selected this site, Karsh had the boats run in both directions along the delta of the Raub River. They'd searched for any sign of the party he'd been sent to find – three Allied soldiers and two civilians.

Priests, of all things!

The soldiers had gone missing far up-river, in the unexplored interior of the island. It was an Army scheme gone wrong, Karsh had been briefed. Now the men were M.I.A. and presumed K.I.A. Karsh was told his assignment was a long shot. *Still, whatever I can do for our boys!*

In fact, Karsh would rather be on his way north right now. There he would observe one of the most portentous events of the entire 20ᵗʰ Century. But, as always, Cleveland Karsh did his duty expertly, and with a positive attitude.

Right now, his attention was on the cache they'd brought – goods that might keep the missing men alive, if they ever got this far. He picked the logical place to deposit it, near the widest channel of the Raub River. Up the beach there, on the edge of coconut palms, was a soaring shade tree – so tall, it could be seen for miles in any direction. On the ground beneath, the marines had spread a canvas tarp. On it, they were piling the cargo they'd brought.

The captain's aides, two second lieutenants, were with Karsh. The tropical sun was fierce in spite of the breeze off the ocean. Karsh tugged off his cap and ran a handkerchief over his egg-bald head. He stood at ease, powerful legs apart, watching the activity.

The cache was almost ready to be hoisted. Karsh checked his watch and told his aides to call a break.

It was midday and the captain had planned for lunch on the beach. He'd brought the cooks and food with him, and the meal was ready. While the gunnery sergeant and the men relaxed on the sand, Karsh and his officers strolled to the place where the tent was pitched. Beside it stood folding chairs and a table.

The cooks brought metal plates piled with pot roast made from frozen Texas beef, canned peas and mashed potatoes swimming in gravy. After that, Gunny and the men got the same fare. It was one of the captain's rules: *I eat what my men eat.*

The sun blazed in a clear sky, the palms swayed, and the South Pacific glittered as the rollers came in. Most of the men were stripped to the waist. After they wolfed their chow, they smoked and shot the breeze.

At 16-hundred hours – three hours from now – they were due back aboard ship. Karsh would be early, as always. The Marine Corp motto was *"Semper Fidelis"* – Always Faithful. But Captain Karsh added his own: *"Semper Promptus."* That could mean, "Always Ready," but he translated it as, "Always On Time."

"Bring me pen and paper and the waterproof pouch," he said to his senior aide, Alexander "Chip" Calder. Chip had served the captain for two years – a lifetime out here. The younger man was Blair Pointer, who'd been with them a month. Chip nodded to Blair, who trotted to the tent and fetched the materials. Karsh uncapped his Parker 51 fountain pen and prepared to write.

"What was the name again?" he asked. Chip had his notebook out.

"The officer in charge of 'Operation Teeth' is an Australian, Major Hawsey. Our American is Sergeant John Willman. Then there's another Aussie – the pilot, a former Corporal, Glen Carmichael."

"August 17th, 1945," the captain spoke as he wrote. He went quiet as his pen scratched across the page.

"Attention: Sergeant J. Willman and Party. These things are for you. Use the radio. The order to look for you came from

Colonel Waters in Port Moresby." He wrote a few more sentences, and signed his name.

"Here."

He handed the paper and pen back to Blair. "Put this in the pouch. Write Willman's name on the outside."

Karsh and Chip returned to the tarp. Gunny saw them coming and met them with a list. Karsh double-checked the items as they were read off.

"Should we add guns and ammunition, Sir?" Chip asked when that was done.

"No, son," Karsh responded. "We hope it's our men who find this, but the truth is, that's doubtful. We don't want to arm hostiles."

The captain told the marines to raise the corners of the tarp and they lashed them together to form a large sack. A rope was tied to it and a man shimmied up the tree. Thirty feet off the ground, he tossed the end over a branch.

Those below hauled the sack high, wrapped the rope around the trunk, and tied it off.

"The pouch," Karsh said. Blair handed it over and the captain wedged it through the coils.

"That's that," Karsh said. "Gather the men, Gunny! Pass out a beer to each one, but tell them to wait for my word to drink."

In the shade were wooden crates stamped "Anheuser-Busch, St. Louis," heaped with ice. The men had heard the bottles clink when they brought them ashore. *Budweiser from home!*

When the marines were ranged before him, each with a cold bottle in hand, the captain accepted one himself and spoke:

"Men, you've probably heard the rumors. I'm making it official.

"Japan has surrendered! This war is over! We've beaten the bastards!" A cheer erupted. Karsh held up a hand.

"I've been told that yesterday, the Jap Emperor himself went on radio to tell his subjects the news. That was a first. They'd never even heard his voice before!

"All our available ships are steaming for Tokyo. The greatest armada of the war will gather to accept the surrender. There'll be a grand ceremony where the Nips will sign the documents. And we're going to the party!" Another cheer broke out.

"Here's to the United States of America!" Karsh called, raising his Bud.

"Here's to victory!"

They lifted their bottles high, the captain took a long swallow, and everyone followed suit. There was the sound of laughter and marines slapping one another on the back. A few put thumbs over the necks of their bottles, shook, and sprayed their buddies. It might not be champagne, but it was sweet!

Smiling broadly, Karsh told Gunny to set four men with Tommy guns as sentries, and the others could relax until further notice.

The captain ducked into his tent and emerged shortly, dressed in his bathing costume. It was a conservative affair that had straps over the shoulders and covered chest to groin. It was a gift from Lois, his wife of twenty-one years. The blue color matched his dress uniform. It was not the trunks the younger fellows favored these days, but it did display the captain's physique.

At thirty-nine, Cleveland Karsh worked diligently to maintain his musculature. He had a set of weights at home, and swam three times a week at the Y – fast laps, an hour at a time. In the field, he did a hundred push-ups and two hundred sit-ups before breakfast.

The Marines watched their captain stride to the sea, march into the crashing surf and dive into a wave. He came up swimming strongly.

He paralleled the shore, arms rising and falling in a fast crawl. After fifty strokes, he reversed and swam the other way. His aides looked on and Chip shook his head in admiration.

"He's something, the Old Man," he said. "The South Pacific's loaded with sharks. You wouldn't catch me out there for a million bucks!"

"Our fearless leader!" Blair smiled. They shaded their eyes against the reflection. A breaker went over Karsh and the watchers saw the gleam of his head come up.

Chip had his instructions and he went to the commander's tent. He checked that everything was in order with the uniform on its hanger, then knelt by a small wooden trunk on the sand and fished out a set of keys.

He selected a hollow one and turned it in the lock. He opened the lid, noted the personal papers and photos of Karsh, his wife and children, but he was looking for something else.

He found a velvet sack and brought it out. He loosened the drawstring and extracted a bottle. It had a coating of fine dust that he wiped away. He read the label: *Glenmorangie – Highland Single Malt Scotch Whiskey.*

Chip was twenty-two years old and did not know single malt from bar whiskey, but this had to be something special. He locked the case and returned to the table. Blair had three glasses there and a full ice bucket.

Cleveland Karsh swam hard, eyes closed against the salt.

Unseen by him, forty-five feet below, the reef was a blaze of color. It was a wonderland of hard and soft corals, thronged with thousands of fish. When the aquatic creatures looked up, they saw a dark spot moving on the ceiling of the world.

For millions of years, any creature churning the surface was a dying fish or an animal in trouble. In either case, it was food. The vibrations made by the swimmer radiated through this atmosphere and in deep water, they attracted a colossal predator. Instantly it was speeding to the source.

The Tiger shark soared in, sunlight dappling its stripes. It moved its head from side to side, searching with its eyes for the meal, and with the electrical sensors in its skin called "Ampules of Lorenzini." The hunter flashed over the reef, scattering clouds of fish.

It perceived the target slapping the surface and honed in. But then, just ahead of it, an entire length of the reef seemed to detach and float up, casting a shadow.

Suddenly the shark comprehended what it was looking at. It saw the fierce eyes staring back, and the rows of teeth. In the face of the much greater predator, the fish turned abruptly, voided its bowels, and rocketed into the depths.

112

Unaware of the activity below him, Captain Karsh swam on. The clock in his head told him it was time to get out. He oriented himself with a glance at the beach and struck out that way. He body-surfed the last roller and burst out on his feet. He took some running steps and, aware of the watching marines, marched up, smiling broadly.

Karsh accepted a towel from Chip and glanced with approval at the scotch. As he'd instructed, a bucket of freshwater stood on the sand. The captain lifted it over his head with one muscled arm and sluiced off the salt. Toweling himself, Karsh walked to his tent.

Inside, he stepped out of his bathing suit, dried himself, and donned khaki slacks and shirt, but kept the jacket with its color bars aside. He would put it on just before they went aboard ship.

He added socks and shoes and buckled on the belt with the holstered pistol. It was an M1911 .45 automatic in nickel finish with a wooden grip. He had cleaned it the previous evening and knew the clip was full. Cap in hand, Karsh stepped back into the sun. Marines lazed on the sand. The popular topic of conversation was what they would do now the war was over. Some dozed and there was a card game going. He called over.

"Gunny, give the men another beer."

"Yes sir!" Again, a cheer. The sarg had no shortage of volunteers to fetch the bottles.

Karsh joined his aides. The lieutenants stood from their chairs as he approached. He told them to sit, walked to the ocean side of the table, put down his cap and faced the younger men. He picked up the bottle of scotch.

"Gentlemen," he said, holding the amber liquid to the sun. "A special bottle for a special day! This is twenty-one-year-old single malt scotch. It was aged by the distiller for almost the length of time you've been alive, young man," he said to Chip.

"And – well, since before you were even a twinkle in your daddy's eye," he told Blair.

"It was a gift from my own father. He told me I'd know when to open it. He was right."

He cracked the seal with a nail, twisted the cork and it came out with a musical pop. He put his nose to the neck, sniffed and smiled in appreciation.

He poured two fingers into each tumbler, pushed the glasses toward the young men, and picked up his own. His aides added ice, while the captain did not.

"Chip, Blair," he said, "as you know, the war is over, but I propose a personal toast. To the end of our war! Semper Fi!" He held up his glass.

"To the end of our war! Semper Fi!" the aides responded and clinked their glasses against the captain's. Each took a swallow. Karsh closed his eyes and savored the buttery burn.

It was a moment of bliss, suddenly broken.

Karsh heard shouts and turned sharply. Marines scrambled up, pointing at the ocean. The captain spun and could hardly credit his eyes. A gigantic crocodile was crawling out of the waves and it appeared to be looking at him!

Karsh saw the curved scar across the head, and then, as it started to run his way, he noted the malformed front leg that made the shoulder dip. It loomed larger with each step.

Cleveland Karsh got an adrenaline rush as he stared at the prehistoric-looking head studded with teeth. Without taking his eyes off the attacker, his hand set his glass on the table and drew the .45. He racked the slide.

It had been mere seconds since the brute appeared, but it was close and he fired. He saw a divot of scales fly off the head but the crocodile did not slow.

And then the beast was on him.

113

At the very last, Karsh leapt to avoid the charge, but the crocodile swung its huge head and caught his leg in its teeth. Karsh heard his bones shatter. Then it turned and ran for the ocean.

The man felt the implacable strength. As his torso fell and was dragged through the sand, he fired again, point blank into the head. The croc ran as though the man's two hundred and thirty pounds were nothing. Karsh grabbed the jaw with his left hand and raised his powerful body. Jolted as he was, he shot again into the side of the head.

Karsh felt the first wave rush over him and heard the stutter of automatic fire. He saw the croc's flank shudder. Another wave rushed around him while a second line of shot kicked sand and pounded into the scales.

The animal staggered and fell onto its misshapen foot. The foreleg bent backwards as the giant fell, half on its side, and slid into the ocean. Karsh heard something pop, and then a roller loomed overhead. He was underwater, but he kept his eyes open, blurred as his vision was, and stared into the crocodile's scarred eye.

They came to the surface ten yards out. Karsh heard yells and shots as he gasped air. He raised his soaked .45 and pulled the trigger. He got three shots off before the monster took him under again.

The crocodile dove and hit bottom. The man's arms scraped and the pistol was torn from his grip. In the sudden silence, the aquatic reptile undulated down fifty feet.

The captain held his breath and felt the pressure mount in his head. He moved his jaw and his ears popped.

The crocodile let go of his leg and Karsh had an irrational burst of hope that he might yet escape, but it was merely re-positioning him.

Karsh felt the long teeth scrape his chest and back, and then the horrific penetration as it bit down.

He knew then his war was over.

Still, he tried to hurt his attacker. He ran a hand along the jaw until his thumb found the eye. He gouged. At once, the reptile rolled. The captain was flung around and salt burned up his nose. He had a moment of terrible panic that faded into serenity.

The crocodile felt the prey go still. It came out of its roll and swam deeper.

For an eternity of heartbeats, Cleveland stared at reversed waves and the liquid sun far overhead. He had never seen anything so beautiful.

The Father had escaped the thunder, but its head and side burned. The pain in its foreleg, however, had suddenly eased.

Between its teeth was the Smooth-headed man and it knew deep satisfaction.

114

Chip was facing its way when the crocodile erupted from the waves and came at them. It ran unbelievably fast, with a rolling gait. He saw the Old Man shoot the monster and then it was on them.

Chip found himself leaping sideways. He saw a blur as the beast bit the captain and dragged him off. When he was able to look again, the enormous creature was racing back for the water, tail raised. He heard shouts and the stutter of the Tommy guns. He saw the animal get punched by the bullets along one side as it entered the waves. The men were shooting into the body, not the head where the captain hung from the jaws.

He saw the giant fall onto its weird front leg. The foot buckled back, and something squirted out. Then the croc rolled on its belly and slid into the surf.

Chip watched a wave crash over it and fall away. The tiny figure of Captain Karsh rose up in the jaws and fired into the head. It sounded like a cap gun – *bap, bap, bap*.

Another roller slammed down, and when it was gone, so were man and beast.

Gone, gone!

Chip was in a waking nightmare. Yet the ocean sparkled merrily and the sun beamed down.

Chip watched as marines ran helter-skelter to the water. He heard a sob and saw Blair sprawled out, lip bleeding, an empty glass still in his fingers. His own, he noticed, was near his feet, half filled with sand.

He staggered up, went to the table, and there was the captain's bottle. It stood beside the glass the Old Man's hand had set there only a minute ago. The liquor still trembled. Chip grabbed the bottle, tipped it up and drank. His gullet and eyes seemed to catch fire. Clutching the neck, he stumbled down the beach, gaze fixed on whatever had burst from the croc's leg.

He saw a gelatinous mass laced with yellow and red, dark at the core. It looked like a jellyfish. He prodded it with his toe. A wave swirled around his boot and when it retreated, some goo was gone. He was looking at a shaft of shiny black wood. One end came to a point, while the other was a mass of splinters.

409

Again, Chip tipped up the bottle and his Adam's apple bobbed. Heat spilled from his eyes and the world melted. His arm fell and his fingers went slack. He heard the thud of boots while the surf sizzled around him like hot grease.

Just as his knees gave out, strong hands grabbed the looey. His eyes rolled back, and marines dragged him up the beach.

Ten minutes before, it had been an idyllic scene out of some Hollywood South Pacific movie. Now it was pandemonium. Men ran waving firearms.

Some pushed the small boats into the waves and yanked the motors to life. They roared back and forth, staring into the water.

Eventually, the gunnery sergeant took charge. The young officers would be no help, he saw. Gunny saw no option but to return to the ship, and there report the bizarre death of Cleveland Karsh.

An hour later, the beach was deserted. Where the surf met smooth sand, a glittering object moved. Each time it rolled, amber spilled. Another breaker rushed over and bowled it up the beach. Single malt scotch blended with a far more ancient vintage. The bottle slowed and gravity pulled it back. Down it spun, picking up speed, until it struck something hard.

Cleveland Karsh's victory bottle and the business end of the cannibal chief's war spear clinked together in the foam.

115

Johnny was terrified, running through rancid mud that crawled with maggots. The stench of death was thick in his nostrils. His legs pumped but he only sank deeper.

The Father was coming!

It slid at him across the muck and Johnny redoubled his efforts but he could not move and the crocodile knew it. Its jaws curved in a toothy smile. Johnny stared at the crescent scar that oozed blood. The yellow eye stared with malevolent intelligence.

Johnny raised his rifle and squeezed the trigger, but it only clicked. He heard the scorekeeper scream:

"None left!"

The crocodile came on, jaws strung with saliva. The red moon scar filled the sky and the maw grew to a size that could swallow the entire swamp.

Johnny heard agonized cries and saw human heads wedged between the teeth.

The faces were stacked deep and the cries came from them.

Chief Bumay was among them. The whites of his eyes rolled in his gleaming black face, ebony teeth exposed. His death scream was endless.

Johnny heard a voice he knew far better. In dread he searched for the source and found Footy also among the teeth. The blue eyes were wide, and the lips mouthed words. He was trying desperately to tell Johnny something, but it was lost in the howl of the damned.

The Father's upper jaw came out of the sky like a redwood falling. It smashed down on Johnny and the teeth shot through him.

Johnny woke and smelled dead crocodile. He saw the Japanese in the firelight, staring at him, and realized he'd been moaning.

I put him on watch.

There was Footy, asleep on the other side of the coals.

411

Johnny took deep breaths and slapped the mosquitoes.

Trembling fingers found a cigarette. He did not try to use the Zippo. It had taken a lot of shaking, flicking and coaxing before they'd been able to light the fire. He rolled closer and held the cigarette to a coal. He smoked it halfway down, then passed it to the prisoner. The Japanese nodded and puffed.

Johnny rose and indicated that the prisoner should lie on his bedding. Johnny sat on a boulder and stared at the carcass of the crocodile. The coals gave a glimmer that lit a patch of dark water and outlined the hulking head.

As night had fallen, he and the Jap had used the bayonet and Bowie knife to saw through the tough scales along the back. Johnny asked the prisoner to use his sword – it was sharper – but was refused. Johnny asked why, and was told, the man did not want to use the *katana* for that. Johnny had not insisted.

At last, they got a flap of hide peeled back and carved out slabs of muscle.

These, they skewered on sticks and roasted over the fire. The men had a meat-fest. They ate until they were gorged, and cooked more for the trail.

Johnny pulled his boots off Footy and tended to the cut. He removed the bandage and was pleased to see the wound was relatively clean. The ball of the foot was purple, the cut's edges red between the stitches, but he did not think it was infected. Johnny used iodine and sulfa and taped it again.

Footy was suffering badly and Johnny asked if he needed the morphine. Through gritted teeth, the Aussie said yes, but not yet. Footy lay quietly until he fell into an uneasy sleep.

Johnny told the prisoner they would share sentry duty, and the other man could go first. There was no point giving him an unloaded rifle. The sword would have to do.

Johnny took over the watch. He was concerned the dead croc would draw big feeders, but so far, none had shown up. Gradually the cloud cover lifted and Johnny watched the stars until they faded into dawn.

Seagulls drifted overhead, coming from the north.

They landed on the dead giant and pecked at the eyes and exposed flesh.

The light intensified and Johnny saw a line of trees on the horizon that had been too dim to make out the previous evening. His spirits rose a little – *palm trees mean solid ground!* He woke the others and shared the news. Even the Jap managed a smile.

"Let's get out of this hellhole," Footy said.

"Things will get better out of the swamp," Johnny told him.

As they moved off, they saw numerous freshwater crocs coming for the feast.

116

The Father swam through the balmy ocean. The inflamed foreleg had burst and it stung, but this hurt was good. The crocodile had the Smooth-headed man in its jaws and it carried him to the bottom. The corpse leaked what looked underwater like green fluid and the reptile bled as well.

The tang drew a welcoming crowd up from the reef. A thousand fish rushed to feed on the ripped flesh. Even the tiniest of the newcomers had a significant advantage over the immense reptile. They could feed in the depths, while the Father could not. It could bite, but it could not unseal the flap that sealed its throat, or it would drown.

A frenzied ball formed around the crocodile's head. Reef sharks followed the blood scent as well, and a squadron of bigger Silvertips soared together from open ocean.

In its excitement, one extruded its jaws, displaying a circle of razors, and pulled them in again. But when they saw the enormous swimmer, the sharks stayed well back. The Silvertips could not compete with this monster, and they swept away. The territorial Blacktip reef sharks remained, but kept a safe distance.

The Father descended on the reef as a barracuda shoal a thousand strong swirled above. They formed a gigantic cone, each with its head to the tail of the one in front, undershot jaws lined with daggers. They stared down at the master and its kill.

The Father cruised majestically on, ignoring the lesser creatures. It wanted to store its meat and it swam to a place it knew. It swooped down a coral canyon, eyes on the overhang at the end. There, it settled on the bottom. A million coral polyps fired their poisoned stingers, but these had no effect on scaled armor.

The Father pushed its head into the cave. It had used this as a larder before, and it nosed the carcass in.

The captain's crushed left leg, still wearing a pant leg, shoe and sock, sliced off on razor coral and spiraled to the sand.

The Father lay still and contemplated its victim. It saw the Smooth-headed man with staring blue eyes, the purple tongue protruding.

But it no longer perceived the One Prey.

The Father had been down on the reef when it was startled by movement on the surface. It had stared up and there observed its enemy in the water!

At once it was consumed by the urge to kill. The predator rose to take the man. Momentarily, it had been distracted by the Tiger shark. When it looked up again, it saw the two-legged prey exit the water.

But that would not stop a crocodile! It pursued the One Prey onto the beach and there, it took him.

But now in the coral cave, the Father no longer perceived its enemy.

Restless and enraged, the crocodile backed out and surged across the reef. It came to the wall that dropped off into deep water and went over. It allowed itself to sink down. Its eyes watched waves passing a hundred feet overhead. It twisted its head to look down and saw sharks patrolling the sand two hundred feet below.

The instant the crocodile pulled out of the cave, a thousand fish rushed in. They flew at the carcass and began to tug at the ribbons of flesh.

The reef sharks approached. One ventured under the overhang, but did not like the tight quarters and withdrew. The second saw the joint of meat on the sand. It entered far enough to take it in its teeth, turned, and shot away. Its kin pursued. A tug-of-war ensued, big bodies charging in and out of the bloody haze. One chomped off the foot – shoe and all – and bolted it down.

As if with a single mind, the barracuda circled over the site. A lower one peeled off, and others followed in formation. The first swooped under the overhang. Small-fry fled as the hunter honed in. It plucked out an eye and zoomed off. The second slashed off the nose. The third took the tongue.

All the brethren followed. The smaller feeders surged aside each time, then rushed for the newly exposed flesh.

Rapidly, they entered the bones of head and chest, then the pelvis. Here they supped on tissue and organs.

In mere minutes, there was only a skeleton in the cave — arm bones dangling, the skull, a permanent grin that glinted gold on a back tooth.

The buffet over, most diners drifted away. The diehards remained, picking at gristle.

An octopus flowed across the canyon floor, emotions flickering over its skin like light. It slipped under the overhang and saw what was there. It went bright blue, then mottled green. It unfurled tentacles, grasped the ribs and pulled up. It oozed between bones and turned to stare out of the ribcage.

It flared red and then seemed to fade entirely away. All that remained were the black bars of its irises.

The crocodile hung weightless beside the wall. Shrimp, and a thousand small fish flowed out from the coral and swarmed over the body. Many nibbled at the edges of fresh wounds. Others plucked off parasites. An entire bouquet flared around its anus.

The crocodile parted its jaws. Tiny creatures flooded its mouth. They cleaned palate, tongue, and around each tooth. The giant let them work and did not harm them.

The most frantic feeding occurred at the injured foreleg. A bleeding hole gaped in the clubfoot. Cleaner wrasse wiggled inside and fed in the slick darkness.

117

It took Johnny and his companions a full day to get out of the swamp. But that night, to their relief, the travelers slept on *terra firma*.

In the morning, Johnny cut a new crutch, and Footy was able to walk in his sandals again. Johnny got his boots back. They continued on, once more following a river channel. They were on the delta, and the sandy soil was covered in grasses and minute flowers.

The men wandered between palms and coastal deciduous trees.

The first morning out of the marsh, they passed another empty village. They guessed the people had been gone a long time because the huts were broken down. To their relief, they found weed-smothered gardens.

While Footy rested, Johnny and the prisoner gathered all the *kaukau* and other vegetables they could find. Again, Johnny struggled to light his Zippo. He shook and coaxed it for a long time before he got a momentary flame and lit the tinder.

The ravenous men cooked all they could eat, and more for the journey. The remaining croc steaks were taking on a gamy smell, but they choked them down anyway. It was the last of their meat.

They continued over open land. Johnny and the Japanese toiled under packs weighted with vegetables, while Footy had enough to do just to drag himself along.

If I can only make it to the ocean, the Aussie thought as the crutch jammed under his arm for the millionth time, *everything will be jake, mate! Just keep taking the next step!*

On and on they toiled across a deserted landscape. The day passed and they made camp. That night, Johnny could not get the Zippo to fire at all, no matter how hard he and the others tried. In addition, they were out of cigarettes. The men ate the last of the cooked food, and in the morning, they were reduced to gnawing raw tubers that hurt their stomachs.

They pressed on. The skies clouded over and it rained, but at least it was a warm downpour.

At noon they came to a wide and puddled plain. Johnny led through and heard snapping under his boots. He crouched and studied the shards.

He pulled a curved shape from the mud and tossed it away. *A rib! Human bones!*

"We're on a battlefield," he said. Footy looked down.

"Mate, we're walking on dead men." They went on.

Does anyone even remember this place? Johnny wondered. *Did this battle make any difference?* It didn't look like it in this deserted place.

Poor sodding bastards, Footy thought. *Now they're part of the mud forever.*

How terrible to be lost so far from home, the prisoner reflected as he hobbled on bare feet over the protrusions. *But at least they did not live long enough to know they were defeated!*

The hikers observed shredded uniforms, skulls, rusted rifles and helmets – even broken-down artillery.

At last, they were off the killing field and that was a relief, but the ocean remained somewhere over the horizon. They slogged that day away, passing burned-out trucks, armored vehicles and downed aircraft. They detoured by one to see if there was anything usable, but it was rotted out.

That night they camped near the wreck of a Japanese Betty Bomber. Again, they had to choke down a raw dinner. The potatoes were too hard to chew unless carved in slivers. The green beans were easier to crunch, but they all slept with aching bellies.

When breakfast could only be more of the same, Johnny decided their already bleak situation had become intolerable.

"Footy," he said, "we can't even cook now! I'm sorry, but I'm going to have to leave you. Stay with the Jap – I'll go for the ocean. At least I'll try and find some help. I'll come back for you."

The pilot gave the Yank an anxious frown, but he'd arrived at the same conclusion.

"Yes," he said. "My thoughts, mate. I'll wait here," he said, making his voice as unconcerned as he could.

"But you take this one," he nodded at the prisoner. "I don't need company! I'll get some rest. It'll do this bloody foot some good. You blokes get along now – find us some food."

Their camp was a few trees near a stream. Johnny left his hammock strung and told Footy to use it. He placed the pilot's pack with raw vegetables close by, and filled their available containers with fresh water. For defense, Footy had Dingo's big knife, and Johnny handed him the rifle as well.

"It's got no ammo, but if someone comes by, they won't know that. You take care of it, you hear? I want it back."

"I'll be right, mate. Not to worry."

"We'll be back soon," Johnny assured him. "A day – two at the most. Then, no matter what, I'll come for you. Don't wander off!"

"What – on this sodding leg?" Footy snorted. "Get on with you!"

Johnny and the prisoner departed. With only his own pack on, very little food in it, and no Footy to slow them down, they made much better time. In the early afternoon, a patch of jungle blocked their path, and they began to detour around.

The prisoner stopped. "Look!" He pointed at something bright, winking deep between the trees. They stared but could not make it out. But clearly, it didn't belong here.

"Let's go see," Johnny said.

118

Johnny swung his machete while the other man used the bayonet knife, and they worked into the bush. Twenty minutes later, the shining patch was much larger, obviously metallic. They continued. At last, they cut their way into the open, and there it was.

A wide-bodied cargo plane lay pointed away in the trees. Johnny recognized it as a Douglas C-47 Skytrain, a military version of the DC3. It was clear that it had crashed into the forest. There was the path of smashed trees behind it. The jungle had made a comeback, but they could see the broken-off tail section in the foliage.

Johnny noted the U.S. Army insignia on the fuselage – this had been part of MacArthur's air force. One wing was gone. On the other one, he could see the engine with the prop blades bent back.

The men walked to the torn off end and stared into deep gloom. The ragged metal tube was above their heads and vines draped the opening. Johnny cut a way through, and he and the prisoner walked up the ramp. Their eyes adjusted and Johnny whistled.

Lashed to the metal floor were two Army jeeps. The straps held them in place, and creepers curled around these and almost covered the vehicles.

Johnny pulled a load of vines off, watching for snakes and spiders. The jeeps looked brand new. He dropped his pack in the back of the first one and led the way forward to the cockpit. He stepped through into harsh sunlight, the windshield smashed in.

The pilot was still sitting in his chair. *Or what's left of him!*

It was a skeleton, skewered through the chest by a broken off tree. The corpse wore a flier's cap and rotted bomber jacket. Johnny saw the moldy American flag on the shoulder.

In the other seat – or rather, mostly on the floor in front of it – was the co-pilot, a pile of bones and rags. The Japanese entered as well and grunted in surprise.

Johnny checked the aviators' pockets, at least the ones he could get to. He found nothing useful – mildew and rot had done their work. He did collect one each of their ID tags, and left the others with the bodies – standard procedure. Maybe he'd get an opportunity to turn them in.

"Let's see if we can get the jeeps running," he said. "I've done enough walking to last a lifetime. These vehicles are made for tough conditions – we've got a good chance."

The jeeps faced the open tail of the aircraft. The men checked their fuel. Both were full. The tires held air. Brushing away cobwebs, Johnny climbed into the forward vehicle's driver's seat. He turned the switch and stepped on the starter button in the floor. Nothing.

"Flat battery," he said. "Let's try a push-start. Get the straps off. You know how to drive?" The prisoner nodded.

"Okay," Johnny said. "If we can get 'em going, you take the other one. Give me a hand with this first."

The men dropped the tie-downs. Johnny took the seat again and pumped the accelerator to get gas flowing. He pulled the choke and put the stick in neutral.

He got back out, the Japanese ready at the back bumper, and shouted.

"Push!" They both heaved, the jeep started rolling, and Johnny jumped back in.

He put a foot on the clutch, jammed the stick into second gear, waited for enough momentum, and popped the clutch.

The engine caught, fired up and turned over, backfired smoke, and stuttered for a time while Johnny nursed the gas pedal. He had to duck as the jeep crashed through the net of creepers. In sunlight again, he took it out of gear, pushed the choke in, and revved the engine. It sputtered unevenly, blowing smoke and insects out of the pipe.

Johnny got it roaring, then let it settle back so it was chugging evenly. He drove to one side, pulled the emergency brake, and left it idling.

"Let's get yours," he told the Jap. Ten minutes later, there were two jeeps with engines humming. Johnny got into his driver's seat again and stashed his helmet on the floor.

"Let's go get Footy!"

He gunned the engine and shot through the brush, weaving between the trunks. The Japanese was right behind as they burst into open country.

Johnny spun the wheel back the way they'd come and the

Asian sped up beside him. They glanced at each other and grins split their unshaven faces. They drove fast, covering in an hour what had taken all day to walk.

Footy was dozing in the Yank's hammock when he heard the motors. He struggled out, grabbed up the rifle – and gawked in open-mouth surprise as two jeeps tore up and skidded to a stop.

"Want a ride?" Johnny drawled.

"Struth, mate," Footy crowed.

"It's the bloody Jungle Express!"

119

Johnny and the Jap piled out of the jeeps and broke camp. Footy limped to the passenger seat of the Yank's vehicle and climbed in. His mood had lightened a hundred percent. He even spoke to the prisoner.

"Brilliant, eh?" he grinned. "Maybe our luck has changed!" The man responded with a nod – almost a smile.

Johnny gunned the engine and spun the wheels, heading north. Two jeeps raced between the trees, gobbling up the miles. Footy's hat whipped back on the tie and his sweaty hair dried. Johnny shouted an explanation of how they had found the jeeps.

"There are wrecks all over New Guinea," Footy replied. "A pilot I know found another crashed cargo plane stuffed with crates of brand-new jeeps. He salvaged them – made a fortune. Good on ya Johnny!"

In fact, Footy had spent the day fretting he'd never see the Yank again.

He admitted – only to himself – that he'd never seen anything as sweet as those jeeps pulling up!

"That bleedin' great lizard can eat our dust!" he crowed. Johnny grinned.

They sped by palms, splashed through streams, and dodged gullies. They careened around a patch of jungle, and Johnny yelled that it was in there they'd found the jeeps.

They were by in a flash, and he thought how fortunate it was they'd seen the glint of metal. A slight change in light, like now, and it was invisible.

The hours blew by and the men's desire to see the Pacific grew strong.

The Japanese knew the ocean was the same one that surrounded his homeland, only a few hundred miles north.

Footy longed to see the same water that lapped his doorstep to the south in Queensland.

Johnny was flooded with memories of this ocean. His whole life, he'd lived on the Pacific. The closer he got, the more vivid were the images that washed over him.

I learned to swim off San Diego. I began surfing there, and then in Hawaii, I really learned to ride the breakers!

The scent of salt air brought his boyhood sweeping back. The excitement even caused cracks in the Hard Case's hide, toughened by years of despair and death in these jungles.

Johnny was jerked from his reverie when he drove up too fast on a flooded slough. He slammed on the brakes to keep from careening over the bank, and the Jap fishtailed behind him. He almost ran over a beefy basking crocodile. It hissed and flung itself into the water.

"That's a bloody salty like the Father," Footy said. "This is its billabong."

"Glad we're up here and not down there with it," Johnny said.

"When you're right, you're bloody right," Footy said. The jeeps drove around the place and continued. It got to be late afternoon and the light went golden. Seabirds dipped and cried on the breeze. The terrain changed again. They began to run through orderly rows of coconut palms.

"It's an old plantation, mate!" Footy shouted. "We're close!"

Thousands of nuts were strewn on the ground. When the tires struck them, some burst, while others shot away like cannon shells. After a couple of near misses, the Jap dropped back and they drove single file.

Then, ahead through the palms, Johnny got a glimpse of delicious, gorgeous, shimmering blue. He gunned up a sand dune, hit the top, and got air before thumping down. Now they drove along open beach.

He and Footy drank in the ravishing South Pacific stretched before them. They cheered and there was a shout from the other jeep.

Rich blue filled the world, an army of gigantic waves all the way to the sky.

When his front tires hit wet sand, Johnny braked and killed the engine. The other jeep pulled up.

At last, the trek down the Raub was over! They were on the South Pacific coast.

A wave ten feet tall swept toward the beach, fell on itself, and foamed towards them. The roar of the ocean and the cry of the gulls filled their ears.

Johnny and Footy shared a grin and then Johnny was running. He stumbled out of his trousers, threw aside his filthy shirt, and wearing only boxers, he raced into the surf and dove. He swam a long way underwater, then burst up and turned shoreward. The jeeps sat side-by-side on the sand, and the prisoner was already bobbing in the ocean.

Footy with his injured leg limped into the water wearing briefs and a smile. A wave knocked him over and then he was swimming strongly towards Johnny. The young men luxuriated in the warm sea as it washed away the sweat and marsh stink. They swam side by side and began to splash each other.

In the ocean at last, weight off his injured leg, Footy was in high spirits. He surged up behind the Yank and pushed him under. Johnny grabbed him and they both went down.

For a time, they played like the boys they'd once been – on opposite sides of the world.

The Japanese flipped onto his back and floated in blessed relief. The warm water caressed him and brought back potent memories of his home city on the coast of Japan.

Johnny and Footy roughhoused until they could barely breathe. Then Johnny caught sight of the Jap floating by himself. He dove under and swam. Below the prisoner, he grabbed a leg and pulled.

A little game we call 'shark attack.'

Johnny heard the man's shout cut off in bubbles. Shocked Japanese eyes underwater took in the Yankee and he kicked at him.

Johnny shot to the surface to breathe and saw outrage on the other face. He laughed and dove away as the Japanese lunged for him. He twisted out of the grasp time after time, but the man was relentless.

At last, the prisoner got an arm around the American, but Johnny found sand under his feet. He towered up with the Jap on his back, pried the arm away, and the smaller man crashed back in the surf. A wave sent them tumbling, then withdrew and left them beached.

Johnny staggered up the burning sand and flopped onto his back. Footy came out chuckling and threw himself down. The prisoner adjusted his ragged trousers, now much cleaner. An unusual feeling came over him as he trotted out of the water and a noise burst from him.

For the first time in months, he was laughing.

"You know something?" Johnny told him, "I don't even know your name. What do they call you?"

"My family name is Takano," the Japanese said. "My name is Katsu."

"Cat-soup?" Footy asked.

"Kat-su," the Japanese said firmly.

"Katsu," Johnny repeated.

The Asian lay down and turned away. The mirth passed out of him.

He felt the blaze in the sky and, like a nightmare, he saw the cloud of a great bomb boiling over Japan. In his mind's eye, a city of people was enveloped in white light. They flared and burned in the merciless heat like blades of grass. He lay with sunlight blinding him, his back to the other men, and water leaked from his eyes and ran with the seawater from his face. He drifted to a hazy place somewhere beyond pain and pleasure, and for a time, he knew no more.

Sprawled on the beach, three men slept like babies.

TEETH

Book 3

The Beach

"I, Ishmael, was one of that crew...
Ahab's quenchless feud seemed mine.
With greedy ears I learned the history
of that murderous monster
against whom I and all the others had taken
our oaths of violence and revenge."

– Herman Melville, Moby Dick

"Forgive your enemies, but never forget their names."

– John F. "Jack" Kennedy

"To do right is heavy as a mountain but
death is lighter than a feather."
"Gi wa sangaku yorimo omoku
shi wa komo yorimo karushi."

– Emperor Meiji, Imperial Edict
for Soldiers & Sailors, 1882

120

July 1945

"WORLD WAR II IN THE SOUTH PACIFIC"
- BY COLONEL HENRY CHAMBERS III

The Samurai and the Cowboy

Dear Reader, in order to illuminate the profound differ-ence between East and West, Japan and America, indulge me in a metaphor.

If Japan is the Samurai, America is the Cowboy.

The Japanese have their traditions, and so do we. Ameri-ca's mythology centers on the legendary Cowboy who tamed the Wild West. He is the frontiersman who rode the range and brought order to a hostile land. The Cowboy is self-sufficient and a man of few words, but when he does speak, you better listen! He has hard fists, rifle in hand and a six-shooter on his belt, and he knows how to use them. He is slow to anger, but when push comes to shove, he comes out blazing.

In the face of bullies, bandits, gunslingers and mercenar-ies, he is the ordinary folk's last, best hope. He is the champion of a woman's honor, even when that is a tarnished virtue, as it might well be in a frontier town. At times, he is both judge and executioner.

The Cowboy is part outlaw, part sheriff, and all man. We admire such a fellow, even when, at times, he walks on the wrong side of the law. In this, we are unique. Americans love a goodhearted rogue!

Our Cowboy knows a deep truth: crooked men bend right-eous laws to evil purpose. The upright man must stand against them.

It is the Cowboy's conscience under God that tells him what to do. He must follow that path, even when it leads to his own destruction.

So where is our hero in the mid-20th Century? Where was he when the Samurai swung his sword and our boys died by their thousands at Pearl Harbor?

For Nippon, the strike was in keeping with their warrior code. But the Cowboy knew nothing of this. He held ultimate contempt for the lowlife who would attack a man from behind. Sucker punchers and backstabbers! The worst kind of villains.

When Japanese warplanes screamed out of peacetime skies on Pearl, the Cowboy saw nothing but the despicable act of a coward.

On December 7th, 1941, Japan committed the worst error in its 2,500 years of empire.

Nippon imagined a bold blow that would cripple its enemy and win what it desired above all else – vast territory in Asia and the South Pacific.

Instead, it thrust a needle into the eye of a sleeping giant.

America felt the sting! With a shout of outrage that echoed around the world, the Cowboy leapt to his feet. Through a sheen of blood, he drew his guns and glowered across the oceans. He intoned the name of his enemy and swore righteous war upon him.

Both the Samurai and the jackbooted Nazi must have felt the icy wind of destiny turn and blow in their faces!

America rushed first to mother Britain's side to battle Hitler's hordes — but our special fury was reserved for Japan. The slaughter of the 2,300 in Hawaii; the destruction of the Pacific fleet; the invasion of our Philippines and the egregious assault on our sons there — all these would light an unquenchable fire in the mind and heart of America.

Already as I write this, the Japanese Empire has paid dearly for its sins, and we fight on. America has sworn that the entire future of Nippon has been reduced to two words — "unconditional surrender."

We bested the Nazi beast. Now we batter on the very doors of Japan. The Samurai fights on, but he is grievously wounded, and he must sense his imminent doom.

The second global war in the history of Planet Earth is in its final grim chapter.

The old world lies in ruins.

And now, towering up from the rubble is the United States of America. We look around and see only one other world power still on its feet — our ally of necessity, the Soviet Union. Of that sinister nation under Joseph Stalin, we will say little here.

But where are the other once-great nations?

Germany's star burned briefly and flared out. Hitler's dream of a thousand-year reign did not last a single decade. Other nations try to regroup, but the world has moved on. Former colonies have tasted heady freedom, and there will be no turning back.

The glory that was once the British Empire fades into sunset. Vestiges can be seen here and there in trains that run on time, a system of democracy, a body of law worked out over centuries, and the greatest legacy of all, the English language.

The heir of all that is the USA. Yes, we had to fight a war to break free of the tyrannical British king, but we kept our inheritance.

We are the last champion of the world, committed to freedom and justice for all. We are not there yet, but we know better than our critics, how far we fall short of our high ideals. We will continue the great battle for life, liberty and the pursuit of happiness. Our experiment in a democratic republic may yet fail, for even now elements in our own nation pretend to serve the common good while undermining our Great Experiment on a thousand fronts. Be forewarned: they seek to impose themselves as a new aristocracy.

Fortunately, we have that work of genius, the Constitution, to rely on. It enthrones the rights of the individual against the kind of tyrannical government our Founders fought so hard to escape.

This much is clear. America is the last great hope of the free world.

121

August 1945

Johnny's face was in the sand and he sat up and spat. He brushed the crust off his beard and squinted at the blazing sunset. He saw Footy on his back, staring up. The Jap lay further off, turned away.

"How's the foot?" Johnny asked. "Hurts like a bugga," Footy said cheerfully. "But it's better than a sharp stick up the bum."

"Maybe I'll call you 'Hopalong Cassidy.'" Johnny remembered the limping cowboy from the books his dad read to him when he was a kid. "Hopalong" had gone on to be portrayed in a series of movies, although some Hollywood dim bulb had removed the limp – a sore spot with his father.

"Aw yeah," Footy told the sky, "the Yank makes a joke. You feeling better then?"

"You bet!" Johnny said. "I'm glad to be off the river – out of that swamp – at the beach! Did I tell you I lived in Hawaii?"

"Is that home then?" the Aussie asked. "Is that where your parents are?"

"My folks are gone," Johnny said. He got up.

"It's getting late. We'd better find a place to camp."

"Sorry mate..." Footy began as the American offered a hand and pulled him up.

"Not your fault. Hey!" Johnny called. "Hey – Kato!" The man rolled over.

"Katsu,'" he corrected. "I'll call you Cat," Johnny said. "Cat! Sounds right," Footy said.

"Cat." The Japanese tried it out. Katsu meant "victory." It was a noble name, and "cat" seemed almost insulting, but he decided not to protest.

They gathered their clothes as they went. Johnny stepped into his trousers and rolled up the legs. The Yank was all lean muscle, Footy saw, not a lick of fat on him. The pilot pulled on his filthy shorts. *I'm a bit stringy meself.*

Johnny strode to the jeeps and the Aussie hopped on one leg to keep up. *Hopalong,* he thought, hoisting himself into the seat. *Could be, mate. Except not a Yank – never in a million bloody years!*

The Japanese climbed into his jeep and they started the engines. No problem this time – the batteries were charged. Johnny aimed for a line of trees in the distance that marked the river's course.

"If anyone's still looking for us," he told Footy, "I'm betting they search around the mouth of the Raub."

"Yes mate, that's the obvious place we'd end up – but a bloody big 'if.'"

Johnny tapped the gas gauge. The needle banged the "empty" post. Cat drove alongside and the jeeps ran together.

Ten minutes later, not far from the fringe of jungle, the men saw an arrow on the beach made of coconuts. The sand around it was pocked by boot-prints. The jeeps slowed and the men scanned the area.

"The arrow points at something," Johnny said. "There!" Footy called. An enormous shade tree towered over the palms, a bulging shape dangling from its branches. The vehicles pulled up below, and the men gazed up at a large canvas bag, tied by a rope around the trunk. There was something stuck in the coils. Johnny went over and tugged out a military pouch.

"What? You're not going to believe this," he called, waving it.

He was truly astounded to see his name, "WILLMAN," written in big letters.

122

The men sat smoking fresh Lucky Strikes on the edge of the tarpaulin. It was spread wide, displaying their treasure trove.

"Read it again, mate," Footy said. Johnny had a letter on his knee and he read the last part first.

"'The Japs have surrendered. The war is over. Good luck and God Speed.'" He looked up. "That's what it says."

"Japan has surrendered!" the prisoner repeated in wonder.

"And the war is over?" Footy added. "Bloody cryptic, mate. Could have given us a few details."

"It's signed 'Captain C. Karsh, US Marine Corps.'"

"What else?" Footy asked, lighting a fresh ciggy from the butt in his fingers.

"'The request to look for you comes from Colonel Waters in Port Moresby,'" Johnny read. "Waters – Colonel Chambers is gone."

"What's it dated?" Footy asked.

"August seventeenth," Johnny said.

"What is it now?" Footy asked. "I've been trying to keep track. I reckon it's August twenty-first."

"I've been doing the same," Johnny said. "But I think it's the nineteenth. 'Course I might have lost count, especially while we were sick. Any idea?" he asked the Japanese.

"What bloody good will that do?" Footy hooted. "Nine hundredth day of the year of the pig?" But the prisoner was counting on his fingers.

"Hachigatsu," he said. "I believe it is *hatsuka."* He turned a look of scorn on the Australian.

436

"You do not know that you use the same calendar as we do?" He turned back to Johnny.

"This is August twenty. But also – I may be wrong."

"Well, near enough. We missed the rescue," Johnny said, "but at least we've got food and supplies! Enough to keep us alive until we see a ship or aircraft. Too bad they didn't think to leave us guns and ammo."

Slower now, the men sorted through the cache. Footy had gone directly for the cigarettes, with a big box of matches. All three were grateful to have the means to make fire again. Not being able to cook had been a disaster.

There were boxes of canned food – beef stew, soup, potatoes, various kinds of meat, including a full cooked ham, wieners, chicken, green beans, corn, carrots, baked beans, and more. There were cans of fruit, pudding, packages of hard biscuits, and even several bars of chocolate. Packed into four shiny new buckets were a percolator coffee pot with a glass knob and metal filter, with three big cans labeled "coffee," "sugar" and "powdered milk."

Wrapped inside a half-dozen new Army blankets was a kerosene two-burner stove, cans of fuel, assorted pots and pans, metal plates, and cutlery. There were bars of soap and terry-cloth towels. They had spools of fishing line and hooks. There was a new first aid kit, complete with more morphine tubes.

The *pièce de résistance* was the radio in four wooden crates with batteries for it.

"Look at how small they're getting!" Footy exclaimed. "Two men could carry that. Imagine!"

They turned to their pressing priority, something to eat.

437

The prisoner fueled the stove and lit it. Johnny and Footy opened four cans of beef stew and sloshed them into the biggest pot. They put it on the heat, but as soon as the steam started to rise, the aroma was too much.

Johnny dumped the contents onto plates. As fast as he could pour, the others shoveled it in.

Johnny opened three cans of cling peaches. Each man slurped one down. Cat offered to make coffee with the water from their bottles. When it was ready, he poured the brew into new enamel mugs and dosed them with powdered milk and sugar. The men dunked sticks of chocolate in the steaming liquid.

Sated at last, they lay on the sand and smoked. The sun had set and the sky blazed with stars.

"I still can't believe we're here!" Johnny sighed. "I'm beat. I vote no watch tonight. We haven't seen any sign of life for a long time, and we left the crocodile way back."

He did not even bother to rope up his hammock. The three of them spread new blankets on the sand and turned in.

The waves hissed along the beach and the moon rose against the tropical night.

123

It was during Gwyn's second month in London that she fell for the English pilot. Reginald flew fighters and had come out on the losing end of a clash with the Luftwaffe. She'd assisted in the surgery where most of the shrapnel was removed from his side. A few shards were too tangled in nerves and blood vessels, and these he would have to live with.

The pilot's friend and squadron leader, a man not much older than the patient, came by when he could. He told Gwyn the aviator was from northern England, near the border with Scotland, and had only his old mother left. The pilot had no family in London, so Gwyn came by to visit on her own time. The flier was grateful. He asked her to call him Reggie.

Professionally, Gwyn nursed Reggie back to health. Privately, she fell for him. With his tousled auburn hair and kind eyes, he reminded her of her father's English wit and quiet strength. Behind the humor, she saw depth – he was thoughtful, mature beyond his nineteen years.

It developed that many nights, her shift done, Gwyn sat with him for hours. On one occasion, while the rest of the ward slept, Reggie reached for her hand. At first ironically, and then more seriously when she did not laugh, he began to talk about a possible future. Could he dare hope it would be with her? He drew word pictures of a life they might share after the war.

They would find a cottage in the countryside in Bowness-on-Solway, where he was from. He would raise a flock of sheep, he said, which was how most men in his family made money – that is, when they weren't raising hell, he added with a chuckle.

He was interested in her home in the former colonies. Gwyn described the orchard and farming country of British Columbia where she'd grown up.

A few nights later, he put a hand behind her head, drew her to him and kissed her lips. Gwyn's heart beat fast.

Another week passed and Reggie dared to slip his hand under her blouse, and after holding her waist for some time, he moved up to her bra. Aroused and alarmed, Gwyn permitted a few minutes of exploration, then pulled away. By training, she was a modern woman, by her morals, an old-fashion one.

Both aspects of her nature warned against rushing into a sexual encounter. Getting pregnant in a foolish wartime tryst was not acceptable.

Then there was the sobering reality of the men in the other beds who were sleeping – or worse, pretending to.

Gwyn was determined that, as far as sexual intimacy went, she would wait for marriage. She intended to find the love of her life. During high school, a teenage friend had gotten "in the family way," as it was said. She vanished for a year. Her parents put it around that she had a pulmonary disease and was recuperating with grandparents. But as some joker said at the pub, presumably the infection had entered somewhat lower than the lungs.

In fact, as in all small towns, the truth was known to all.

Then, at the nursing school in the city, over time, three of Gwyn's fellow students were forced to drop out because of unplanned pregnancies. She made herself a solemn promise that such ruinous behavior was not for her.

Her weeks with Reggie became two months, and the doctors told him he could return to duty. His squadron leader remained his only regular visitor, but Gwyn grew weary of the way he always went on about the desperate need for pilots. That was when she first learned to despise (or perhaps it was to fear) men who spoke so ardently about the need to be in the fight.

The night before he was to be released, Gwyn stayed with Reggie on the ward. He was mobile by then. Sometime after midnight, he took her hand and led her down the stairs. They skirted the bombed-out wing that was boarded off and entered a courtyard. Most hours, it was crammed with doctors and patients smoking, but at this hour, it was deserted.

Reggie went on a knee and proposed marriage.

Her emotions awhirl, she barely heard him say he had no proper ring to give her. He swore there would be a diamond coming, but in the meantime, he begged her to accept his signet ring. He also, somewhat shyly, offered a photograph of himself. Gwyn told him she needed time, but she accepted his gifts. He took her in a passionate embrace and truly kissed her.

She made herself be prudent, but in her heart, she had already said yes.

Early next morning, Reggie departed for his base. He promised to see Gwyn the following weekend. She was there to wave as the car drove off. It struck her then that she'd never even been with him outside the hospital.

But Sunday morning, it was not Reggie, but the young squadron leader, who appeared. Gwyn was on the ward when he entered, face grim, looking for her. He took her arm and led her into the hall.

In blunt words he told her that Reggie's Spitfire had been shot down. They were returning across the Channel from a mission, almost to safety, when a Messerschmidt dove on them. The attack was over in seconds, the leader said. He'd followed Reggie in his own fighter, all the way down. He'd even broken radio silence to order Reggie to bail out, but there had been no response.

Gwyn's heart was hammering so fast she put a hand to her chest.

"Was there any chance...?" she rushed to ask, but she saw the tears that formed in the man's eyes and all her hopes crashed and burned. Unable to speak, he gave her arm a squeeze and hurried away. She never saw him again.

In the crucible of her suffering, Gwyn vowed never to get involved with a military man again. Even though it was no fault of their own, they were not to be trusted.

All she had left of Reggie were the pitiful gifts from that last night. Eventually, she mailed the ring and photo back to his squadron, with a note to please forward them on to his mother.

Since meeting Reggie, she had written page after page in her diary. Now she found it unbearable – the pathetic gushing of a schoolgirl. She locked the book, pushed it to the bottom of her trunk, and left it there.

Her anguish, Gwyn discovered, made her work far more difficult than it needed to be. It was hard to muster a kind word for a suffering man when she, herself, was in agony. Yet her patients deserved nothing less than her best.

From then on, Gwyn put her calling first. She hid herself behind her uniform and professional face. She made a point of treating those in her care with compassion and consideration, while keeping her heart firmly out of reach.

But after Reggie, Gwyn found it difficult to remain at the hospital. The halls were haunted by more than the usual ghosts. It dawned on her that she must move on.

She saw a newspaper story that they were desperately looking for nurses for the South Pacific theater, and that seemed suitably far away. She announced her decision to her flat mate. To her surprise, Ruthie said she'd love to come along. She hadn't left Ireland, had she, only to meet Englishmen? Could they please go together?

And so it was that the two volunteered for reassignment.

A month later, they were on a ship for Sydney, New South Wales. From there, the Australian Army sent them north to the Territory of Papua in New Guinea. It was the first time Gwyn had really heard of the place, somewhere over the edge of the world.

And there, at the military hospital in Port Moresby on the southern coast of New Guinea, Gwyn had more than enough to do to distract her from her broken romance. She and Ruthie rented a flat owned by a Kiwi husband and wife. It was two rooms with a kitchenette, while the elderly couple resided upstairs.

When the young women did get a day off together, they ventured to the beach. Under a layer of coconut oil, Gwyn browned like a hazelnut. Ruthie, with her red hair and peaches-and-cream complexion, had to remain under her parasol, or she burned like a lobster. The young women enjoyed these outings, but would not swim. They heeded the local's warnings of sharks in the swells, and the fearsome crocodiles that could even come out and attack over land. The nurses shuddered and stayed well back from the waves.

As for nightlife, there were some notorious taverns they would not even walk by after dark, but they did attend the dances at the better hotels.

The entrances to the public rooms were segregated between the rough men's bar, and those reserved for "ladies and escorts."

There was no escaping the fact that Port Moresby was a military town. The ratio of men to women was daunting. A girl could be danced off her feet all night and still have a string of suitors, some willing to compete with their fists.

The women came to prefer the invitation-only soirees at various plantations circling the town. Many of these places were grand homes where the Australian owners lived like the rough royalty of the bush. They had gardens, native servants, even swimming pools. Two beautiful young women on their own were much desired as guests, and the nurses had a roster of social outings on their calendar.

Sunday mornings, if they were off shift, they went to church. Only the most hardened reprobates in the colony did not attend services. Ruthie went to mass at 8:00, while Gwyn chose the Methodist service at 10:00. She enjoyed the old hymns, played enthusiastically by the minister's wife on her prized pump organ.

Sunday afternoons, Gwyn was busy with her orphans. In fact, it was because of this project that the young women found themselves spending more time apart. Ruthie was happy to lend a hand now and then, but she did not share Gwyn's passion for the lost children.

As well, Ruthie now had a steady boyfriend. The fellow was nice enough, Gwyn thought, but she had her suspicions. He was an older man – all of thirty-two, to Ruthie's twenty-three. Gwyn suspected that he might even have a wife and family back in Aus.

"Never trust a man who calls himself 'Dick,'" she teased. But Ruthie was infatuated with the handsome military clerk. Gwyn had a feeling she was about to get hurt again. But whatever this beau's intentions, it was coming to a head. He was due back in Aus in a few weeks, and then Ruthie would discover if she was part of his future, or once more, left in the dust.

When Gwyn had volunteered for overseas service, she thought she'd be gone from home for two years. Her plan was to pursue her nursing career in Vancouver. But now, she'd already been away from Canada for longer than that. In the meantime, her commitment to the children of the Good Shepherd Orphanage grew deeper each day.

She did wonder what life here had to offer. In this far outpost of the civilized world, would she ever find a good man of her own? Would she have children?

She knew that when she gave her heart to the right one, there would be no half-measures. Therefore, she would not do it lightly.

But her single state was not for lack of suitors. One was a former soldier. Gwyn encountered the corporal at one of the plantation parties. He was a good-looking man, about her own age. In the first minute he met her, he told her she had "smashing green eyes." He took her hand in his own and made a production of kissing it. He was funny and quick-witted, and that night, he monopolized her dances. She liked him at once, but he was military, of course, and so, out of bounds.

It turned out they knew many of the same people. After a couple of weeks, he begged her to at least let him escort her to various get-togethers. She agreed, at least to some of the parties. Not long after, he let her know he was keen on her, but Gwyn was direct in telling him that she had no romantic interest in soldiers. He was crestfallen, but she did offer her friendship. Reluctantly, he settled for that.

Then a few months ago, he announced that his military service was up. He would stay on in Port Moresby, but he was a pilot, and he intended to go into private business. Gwyn had heard him say more than once that there was nothing made with wings that he could not fly. His plan was to found an air cargo business between Australia and the New Guinea Territories.

He had many contacts and already had promised contracts. And after the war, he enthused, with the resumption of trade, it would get even better.

His name was Glen, but everyone knew him as "Footy." He let the nurse know frequently, he had never given up on his chances with her. All he wanted was to prove himself!

Gwyn was fond of Footy. So how terrible that he was now lost somewhere in the wilds of this massive island! It was even more bizarre that he was with Johnny, the soldier she had nursed back to health.

As for Johnny Willman himself, he touched her somewhere beyond her intellect. Under other circumstances, she would have liked to get to know him better. She observed that Johnny was smart, determined and persistent, and those qualities were essential to success. She'd watched how hard he worked to get well again. She saw how enthusiastically he lobbied for his goals, no matter how misbegotten she thought they were. Gwyn wished she'd met him before the war – before the years of turmoil had changed him. If they'd met, say, in Honolulu where he'd gone to high school, would they have been smitten?

But this is foolish, she told herself. There was no getting around the fact that he was a hardened killer who loved his work. You might even say he lived for it, and that was extremely disappointing.

When Gwyn imagined her ideal man, she saw someone brimming with life and joy. He'd face life's challenges with resilience. He would respect her and celebrate her strength and passion. He would help with the orphan children and give her space to have her own friends and interests. But at the same time, she must be able to lean on him when the going got rough.

In her heart-of-hearts, she dreamed of a lover to whom she would reveal her deepest self. She longed for someone who could see her faults and yet forgive them – who would adore her as she was. And she would give all of herself to him.

She was a critic of her own character, and she judged herself to be overly idealistic, even naive, compared with modern girls like Ruthie.

That was why, even though Gwyn shared most things with

her friend, she kept the deep secrets of her heart to herself. It all boiled down to this: could Johnny Willman be the one? The fact was, she did not know. Yet, when Ruthie told her Doc had turned the soldier loose, she had gone looking for him. In that last conversation with Johnny, in spite of her rules, she'd promised him a date!

Night after night now, she lay alone in her bed, turning these things in her mind. But what was the point? Johnny and Footy were lost in the uncharted New Guinea wilderness.

The next day, her mooning over a lost soldier paled in the face of astounding world news. All of Port Moresby was in an uproar. The Americans had dropped some sort of devastating new bomb on Japan. The word was, it was going to end the war. The nurse was caught up in the general euphoria. The hospital had never been livelier, and even the injured were dreaming about peace.

But Gwyn did worry that, in all the commotion, the men of Operation Teeth had been forgotten.

124

Johnny was on his favorite surfing beach. Hawaiian music played, ukuleles plinking over steel guitars. And there was his father! Dad wore swimming trunks and he came dancing, a hibiscus flower behind his ear – which was not like Dad at all.

From behind his back, his father produced a platter that bore a roast piglet. It had baked pineapple rounds all over. Johnny's mouth watered.

And here came Mom! She was doing the hula moves she'd learned in class, wearing a grass skirt, bikini top, a lei and sequined sunglasses.

"Here's our gal!" Dad grinned. Mom held out a steaming mug.

"Coffee, Jo-Jo?" she asked, using her private nickname for him.

"Mmmumph?" Johnny mumbled.

"Coffee?" Mom asked, and her voice dropped an octave.

"What?" Johnny protested.

"Coffee?" Mom asked and she had an accent. Her skin turned yellow and black hairs sprouted on her lip. Johnny grunted and there was Cat, offering a mug.

Johnny sighed and accepted the cup. He sipped while the Japanese returned to the stove and brought back a plate. It was piled with corned beef, fried with canned potatoes. And there were fresh clams, open and steaming, and fruit cocktail with wedges of coconut. Johnny shot the man a look of astonishment.

"What in the world...?"

"Breakfast," the man shrugged. Footy sat up groggily, accepted his plate, and blinked at the spread.

"It's the bloody Cairns Hotel!" he crowed.

Katsu brought a plate for himself and ate on the sand. After the men had cleaned their plates, there were second helpings and another round of coffee. They smoked. The sun was already hot and all three were shirtless.

"Where did you learn to cook like this?" Footy asked.

"Cook?" the Japanese said.

"No, this is not cooking. This is opening can, and..." he made a noise and mimicked pouring.

"And the shellfish? My boy Tojo!" Footy said.

"Not Tojo!"

"Cat," Johnny said. The prisoner nodded.

"My boy, Cat!" Footy said.

Johnny got out the impressive new medical kit and set it by Footy.

"You should change the bandage," he said. "Meantime, me and – Cat – we'll go find drinking water."

"I know where," the prisoner said. "I found it."

He led the way into the coconut palms and Footy got to work. He turned the sole of his foot over and peeled the bandage off. The gash had knitted. He used the tip of the Bowie to cut Johnny's stitches, pulled out the bits of thread, and wiped the area with iodine.

Johnny and Cat carried their new buckets through the trees. The prisoner led to a place thirty yards inland. There, a trickle of freshwater ran out of a clump of shrubs. Taking turns with a machete, the men chopped the brush away. They exposed a bank down which water dripped onto a bed of stones. There was a puddle, and Johnny tried a handful and found it sweet. He drank his fill and Cat took a turn.

A bamboo grove grew nearby and Johnny cut down a thick column, and trimmed it to about four feet. He split it lengthwise and knocked out the internal walls. He cut forked sticks and he and the prisoner wedged these between stones. On them, Johnny laid the bamboo trough and shoved an end into the sodden moss where the spring emerged. Now water flowed along the tube and splashed into the pool.

Beneath this, they filled the buckets.

When they got back to camp, Footy was operating the radio. Wires ran between the boxes. Dials and tubes glowed.

The pilot had headphones on, and the microphone and Morse key plugged in.

"S-O-S," Footy spoke into the mike. "S-O-S. This is Footy Carmichael with Sergeant Johnny Willman of the Allied mission, 'Operation Teeth.' We are located at the ocean at the mouth of the Raub River. Come in, over. Come in, over." He changed the frequency and repeated his message. Then he tapped away in Morse code. He left the radio on for a response, but there was only static.

"I reckon I'll call each morning and night," he said.

"I'll leave it on a half hour each time, but we must make the batteries last as long as possible." It was broiling hot. Johnny thought that the only way he would leave this beach was a rescue. After what they'd been through, this was pretty close to paradise.

He took his knife and sliced his trousers off at the knees. Now he had a rough version of the longer shorts called "Bermudas" back home. He picked up his shirts, sliced the arms off at the shoulders, and put one on. He fetched his boots and cut the leg tops away, then carved off the toes, sides and backs, leaving straps. He stood to try his new sandals on.

"Hey, I'm a beachboy again!"

"You look like a bloody great poofter," Footy observed. "You're a real fashion plate, mate."

Cat asked to use the knife. He sliced the legs off his own trousers and now had shorts as well. The prisoner no longer had a shirt and Johnny tossed him his spare.

"Try that," he said. Cat put it on. It was too big, but now he could have passed for one of Johnny's friends from Waikiki.

"You both look utterly ridiculous, of course," Footy said.

"Sure, Footy," Johnny said. "Now, with that foot, you'll have to stay here. Cat and I will take a look-see around the neighborhood."

"This is an old plantation, mate," Footy said. "There must be a house somewhere."

"We'll make the rounds," Johnny said. He stuck his machete through his belt, but left his empty rifle behind.

"Bring the sword," he told Cat. The prisoner nodded and got it, glancing at the Australian.

"Yes, go on then," Footy muttered. "I lend it to you. Bloody hell."

The two walked along the beach toward the river. The line of jungle ended in another enormous shade tree dominating the point. The men wandered below its wide branches. Under the fallen leaves, Johnny saw, was an old road, two lines of ruts with a mound in between. The jungle was taking over and he hacked through hanging vines and chest-high weeds. After a few yards, they broke out onto the clear riverbank.

There was the Raub once more.

The men were standing at the mouth where the brown water surged into the blue ocean. Thousands of birds hovered over it or splashed down to feed along the swirling edge. The track paralleled the shore.

They peered upstream, looking for crocodiles. Johnny spotted a big one basking a couple of hundred feet up. It saw them and slid into the murky water.

The ruts continued thirty feet, then turned inland.

They walked that way and came to the place where the path disappeared under fallen leaves and palm fronds. Beyond, they could see the regular rows of planted palms.

The tops were heavy with nuts and the ground was littered with them.

"No one's harvested these for years," Johnny said.

Cat pointed. Back in the trees, the ruin of a building loomed in the shadows. It was a fallen-in house, palm trunks stacked log-cabin style.

Johnny took a step towards it, glancing down at the place where the old ruts ended. Curiously, a dozen feet inland, they appeared again.

He took another step and his foot sank through old leaves and kept sliding down. Johnny tilted forward and would have gone over if Cat hadn't grabbed his belt from behind. For long seconds they teetered there – Johnny off balance, arms flailing, the prisoner at his heels, holding him back. But Johnny out-weighed the Jap and he continued his slow-motion fall, drag-ging the other man with him.

Then Cat crouched, jerked hard, and both men tumbled back, landing in the dirt.

"What the...?"

Johnny scrambled forward and shoved his hand in the hole his foot had made. Instead of earth, his fingers snarled in some-thing that had bounce. He shook it and leaves fell aside.

He realized what he was looking at – a camouflage net, clev-erly placed. Branches and fronds obscured the edges, and scat-tered with fallen leaves, it was virtually invisible.

But now the men knew it was there, they could make out the shape – a rectangle about twelve feet long by eight wide. To-gether they tugged up the rope edge and gazed into the gloom below.

Johnny gave a whistle and Cat's breath hissed.

452

"Now you owe me a life," Cat said.

"Yeah," Johnny said.

"Yes, I do."

125

Johnny and Katsu were staring down into a pit of death – six feet deep and bristling with sharpened bamboo stakes. The spears, dozens of them, were hollow shafts three or four inches wide, their angled tips cut to razor points just below the net.

Johnny felt sick. "Yeah," he said again. "I owe you my life."

"But I owe you three," Cat replied, holding up fingers. "Now you owe me two."

"Forget that! And thanks."

They stood a moment and Cat asked, "Who made this?"

"Maybe natives," Johnny said. "But that net – probably soldiers."

"Yours or mine?"

"Who knows?" Johnny muttered, shaking his head.

They circled the pit and rejoined the road. Now the shack was close, surrounded by collapsed trenches and a fence of saplings, mostly knocked down. The door lay off its hinges and the roof was caved in.

The place looked long-deserted, but Johnny was not going to take chances. He raised a finger for silence and gestured for Cat to go one way, while he went the other. But then the silence shattered.

There was an explosion of squawking, and a bird launched skyward. At once, the sword flashed. A wattled head fell one way, the body the other.

"Sheesh," Johnny said. "No need for quiet now!"

"Sorry," Cat shrugged. "It jumped."

He wiped the blade on some leaves, sheathed it, and picked up the skinny bird. "I will cook."

"All right. Let's move."

The men went opposite ways around the ruin. Johnny passed a woven reed wall riddled with bullet holes. One end was torn off and he looked into a simple room. The pole rafters appeared intact and he stepped in. Light streamed through gaps in the thatching. The dirt floor was littered with half buried shell casings and dark stains.

There was an adjoining room at the back of the house and he stepped into it. Another empty doorway showed the overgrown backyard. There were more bullet scars in the log walls. Cat's head appeared outside in a window frame.

"No one here," Johnny told him. "Not for a long time. This must have been where the plantation family lived."

"Then the soldiers came," Cat said.

"Men died," Johnny said. "Many."

There was a fire pit in the center of the room with some ends of charred furniture in it. Against one wall was a makeshift bed with a rag of a blanket on it.

Johnny walked over and saw more black stains. He pulled the fabric away and found himself looking at the remnants of a large office desk. It sat on splintered drawer columns, buried in the sand.

The planter's pride and joy, Johnny realized, *brought a long way from home.* He studied the surface, carved with both English and Japanese characters.

"Davey 43," he read.

"They got their supplies via the river, I guess," Johnny said, "but there must be paths through the plantation. We can probably get back to our camp that way."

"We go see."

Johnny met Cat outside and they walked through the coconut palms. They stayed on the faint but clear footpath. They came to a banana orchard. The trees were heavy with several types – long and short, red, green and yellow. They cut bunches and slung them over their shoulders.

Their trail intersected with another going towards the sound of the surf. They followed it and arrived at their freshwater source. A few steps later, they emerged at their camp.

"Look at Cat's surprise!" Johnny told Footy while they hung the bananas. The man held up the decapitated fowl.

"It's a proper bloody chook!" Footy exclaimed.

"Wakadori," Cat said. "I will cook."

"What's back there, mate?"

"There's the old plantation house, like you guessed," Johnny said. "It's a wreck. It looks like both sides used it as a fort. There are old trenches, and a wicked ambush pit on the road from the river.

"Anything we can use?" the Aussie asked.

"I don't think so. The place is all shot up," Johnny said. "The good news is, we're alone. No sign of natives. We did find bananas – and well, there are more coconuts."

455

"Oh goody, more ruddy coconuts!"

"Let's have a powwow," Johnny said.

The three hunkered down. Johnny said they needed to talk about the best place for their camp. Footy wondered if the house could give them shelter.

"No, it's all broken up. Also, I think it's too far back," Johnny said.

"Many men died there," Cat said. "Too many insects. Better here."

Footy frowned. *We give him a name, and now he thinks he gets a say?*

"Fair enough," the pilot said. "This is a good spot anyway — much easier to see a passing ship or aeroplane."

They talked about food. Johnny figured they had enough for two weeks, and much longer, if they augmented it with what they could gather and catch. Cat spoke again. He would like to do the cooking. The other two were only too happy to let him have the job.

Footy said they should prepare a bonfire on the beach, ready to light the moment they saw the chance of a rescue. Johnny agreed. They'd get on it the following day.

"Next order of business. We need to wash all our stuff."

"Bloody right!" Footy agreed. "I'm about to pass away from the stink. I believe I can get as far as the spring."

The three gathered their clothes, old blankets and towels, brought bars of soap from their cache, and took to the trail. Footy hobbled on the toes of his injured foot. They scrubbed the laundry and then, themselves. They hauled everything back to camp and spread the items on bushes to dry.

As another tropical sunset fired the sky, Johnny said he'd take a look at Footy's cut. He removed the bandage and saw the wound had healed over, but the site remained livid. He pressed it, and Footy exercised his vocabulary.

"It might be abscessed," Johnny said. "You need a doc with sterile equipment to open it up."

"Aw yeah?" Footy said. "And while you're at it, how about dancing girls and a lorry full of beer? But at least I can walk."

Cat went into the forest. During the hungry years in New Guinea he had discovered a number of edible plants. He pulled up one he recognized. The ribbed rhizome made a peppery ginger. He discovered a patch of spiky grass and plucked a handful. It smelled like lemon. He returned to camp with that and an armload of green coconuts. The milky liquid was a refreshing drink and he would use some of it in his cooking.

He went back for brown coconuts. These he husked with the machete and hacked in two. They were almost solid with white flesh. He chopped it fine. He searched the beach and found a flat stone he carried to camp. He piled shredded coconut on it, took a fist-size rock, and ground the nutmeat. Oily liquid emerged, which he dripped into a can.

Cat plucked and cleaned the chicken. He made a fire, split the carcass, and roasted it on sticks over the coals. He boiled the organs and made soup by adding canned tomatoes and mixed vegetables. He fried yam slices, spiced with wild ginger.

As the men ate, the sun hit the horizon like a ball, squashed flat and disappeared. The clouds turned mango and tangerine, and the sky went purple, then black. Points of light began to gleam, and the heavens became infinitely deep.

Cat made coffee and Johnny and Footy stretched out on the sand and stared up. One brilliant constellation stood out.

"That's the Southern Cross!" Footy pointed. "That's Australia, mate – that's our flag."

"In the northern hemisphere, sailors navigate by the North Star," Johnny said. "South of the equator, it's that cross."

"See the bright cluster inside?" Footy asked. "That's the Jewel Box."

The prisoner passed around mugs of coffee and sat. He gazed at *minami-juji-sei* as well. It had become a companion during his hundreds of nights in New Guinea.

A white streak shot across the sky. Another followed, leaving a trail. The men watched without speaking. It occurred to Johnny that "meteor shower" did not do justice to what followed. It was more like a cosmic fireworks show – soundtrack courtesy of the South Pacific.

Eventually it tapered off. Johnny murmured goodnight and went to his hammock. The others wrapped themselves in blankets and put their backs to the coals.

They slept under the faint light of a billion suns.

126

Johnny woke again to coffee and a hot breakfast. Once more, Cat was up first. Johnny and Footy agreed that this morning, they'd work on their camp. After eating, Footy tried the radio again, without response.

While he was busy, Johnny and Cat climbed the trees. They carried up the tarp that had wrapped their cache. They roped it from four corners between the shade tree and surrounding palms. Now they had a roof, slanted to let water run off the back.

Beneath it, Footy and the prisoner arranged mattresses of layered blankets. Each placed a crate for a bedside table. Johnny was happy to stick with his hammock, enormously improved by a washed and sun-dried sheet.

Under one end of the tarp, they set up their kitchen. Cat had found an old harvesting table among the palms, and he and Johnny cleaned out the spiders, carried it to camp, and set it up as a worktable.

Cat said he would organize the rest. He made a shelving unit from stacked supply boxes and filled these with food cans. He put everything perishable into a box he could raise on a rope.

Johnny and Footy made a fire pit on the beach a few steps away. They scooped out a hollow and rolled over boulders for seats.

By noon, the camp was shipshape.

After lunch, Johnny said he and Cat would build the signal fire. He suggested that Footy, hampered by his leg, do another job. He could spell a giant "S-O-S" with coconuts on the sand. Someone might see it from the air. They used the nuts from the arrow that had pointed to the cache, and Johnny and Cat collected more armloads. Footy drew huge letters in the sand with a stick and then crabbed along, placing coconuts.

Johnny and Cat scoured in the nearby area for driftwood and deadfalls. They started with moss and twigs stacked with kindling. Over this, they leaned larger logs and branches.

While they worked, Johnny thought about his future.

If the war is over, what will I do?

Once, it had all seemed so clear. He would become a career Navy officer, like his father and grandfather before him. But now Johnny felt in his bones this would not happen.

As for the Army, Johnny had sworn he was in the fight against Japan to the finish. The truth was, he hadn't expected to survive, so he had no plans beyond that. Now he had to grapple with the possibility that life went on in this strange new world. A quotation his father liked came to mind: "peace shall destroy many." Would that be his story?

Johnny's hometown was San Diego, but his family had moved on from there. His grandparents were gone, their house sold. That was a closed chapter. He remembered his mom's family from Colorado. They'd visited there when he was a boy and he liked the mountains – but now he felt no special pull.

What about Hawaii?

Johnny's family moved to Oahu when he was sixteen. He'd loved the island. But after what had happened there, that was another dead end. *I'll never go back!*

So what about the mainland? Once he'd dreamed of life in the big northern cities he saw in the magazines. *New York – maybe Chicago.*

But no, he decided. That was a daydream from a much younger life. People stacked in boxes on top of one another, up twenty or thirty stories – that sounded like a nightmare.

Truth was, now he only felt at home in the outdoors.

Johnny and Cat made trip after trip into the plantation and hauled out dried palms for the fire.

I like hot climates. Everything is bolder in the tropics. So – what if I do something totally different?

Johnny spoke some street Spanish he'd picked up from his amigos in Southern Cal. He got an image of himself journeying through South America. Maybe he'd trek up the Amazon – or hunt big game in Africa like Hemingway.

Johnny and Cat propped the poles over the other wood in a tepee shape.

Get serious! Johnny told himself. *Really – what can I do? Maybe sell life insurance.* He'd met a soldier who bragged on how much money he'd made. But the idea of selling door-to-door struck Johnny as about as much fun as digging latrines. *Maybe I can sell cars.* He warmed to that, because he liked automobiles. With the war over, the government's ban on manufacturing was bound to be lifted.

Like most men, he knew them by heart: *Buick, Cadillac, Chevrolet, Chrysler, Dodge, Ford, Hudson, Lincoln, LaSalle, Mercury, Nash, Oldsmobile, Plymouth, Pontiac, Studebaker and Willys. And Dad's favorite – Packard.*

Thinking it over, he couldn't get enthused. Once you'd spent your days fighting for your life, everything else seemed boring.

Strange! During the war, he wished for it to be over. But now he saw a long road stretching ahead and he had no idea what to do with himself.

The signal fire was done and so was Footy's S-O-S.

That night, Cat's offering was the canned ham, with potatoes and fresh beans. Dessert was custard folded with sliced bananas and coconut. The men slept with full bellies.

127

Over breakfast, Footy had an idea.

"I'm dying for fresh meat, mate. Let's go fishing!"

"Sure!"

Even Cat nodded agreement.

They dug out the spools of fishing line with ten hooks on a card.

"We'll make lures," Footy said. They cut bits of tin and tore strips of bright paper from their growing garbage hole in the sand.

Johnny had done a lot of fishing, both fresh- and salt-water, but not without a rod. At the surf, Footy showed him another way. He tied a piece of broken coral to the woven linen string for a weight, knotted a hook a yard up, and wove a strip of paper over it.

Footy stripped line off his spool in loops at his feet. He spun the weight over his head and let fly. It soared over the waves and splashed down. Cat moved further along the beach and cast the same way. Johnny watched them retrieve, tugging rhythmically. When the lures were close, they flashed and danced in the shallows.

Johnny rigged up and made his first attempt. He got the line spinning, but when he let loose, it tangled a few feet away. He spent some time unraveling.

Cat jerked a little fish from the brine. It flipped on the sand and he pinched its head. He came to Johnny and borrowed his clasp knife. He cut the fish in strips, leaving a little tail on each one.

"Now we catch big fish!" he grinned. He gave Johnny a couple of slices, and did the same for Footy. Johnny worked a fish wedge over the hook. He got the weight whirling and let go. This time it went about twenty feet before it plopped down – not as good as the other men, but a start. Johnny retrieved and cast again. Each time, his technique improved.

Fifteen minutes later, Footy whooped. His line cut across the waves. He brought it in hand over hand, getting a good fight. Johnny and Cat hauled in their gear so it wouldn't tangle

462

and went to watch. There was a flash in the shallows. Cat ran in and scooped up a fish as long as his forearm.

"Trevally," Footy announced.

"That's a Jack," Johnny called. He'd caught them in Hawaii.

"Trevally!" Footy said. "Don't try and tell me about fish!"

"Oh, I wouldn't try and tell you about anything," Johnny called back. "But that's a Jack."

Footy took up a stick of driftwood and cracked it over the head.

"Now it's supper," he smirked.

An hour later, they were all casting well. Johnny let line burn out and plop into the swells. At once there was a strong hit and he got the heart-leap that is the fisherman's addiction. The string pulled taut and he could feel every tremor between himself and the living thing on the other end.

He hollered, and the others got out of the way. Johnny was hauling steadily when the fish burst through the surface. It looked like something from another planet – white, covered in polka dots.

It splashed down and flipped away, but Johnny fought it in, hand over hand. Footy waded out and grabbed it by the gills.

"Barramundi, mate!"

"I'll take your word for that," Johnny said.

"Nice fish!" Cat called.

After that, Johnny took a break. He went and got banana leaves, wrapped the fish and soaked the bundle. He stretched out and smoked while the others kept casting.

Then it was the prisoner who yelled.

"You're on!" Footy pulled in his line. Cat retrieved, but suddenly his arms jerked and the filament went slack. He muttered and kept pulling in.

There was something silver in the shallows and then on the sand, but it was merely a fish head, mouth gasping, a stump of spine behind.

"It was hit!" Johnny called.

"Shark?" Footy asked.

"Goni-kamasu!" Cat pointed.

The men saw the long shape flick into deeper water.

"Barracuda," Johnny said.

And that was the beginning of the end of fishing that day. Everything they caught after that came in chopped up. Then Footy's line was cut and he lost his hook as well.

"Better give it up for now," the Aussie said. The men agreed – next time a 'cuda found them, they'd quit right away.

Cat said he'd clean the catch. He stood in the surf, sliced open the bellies, scooped out the guts and flung them into the sea. Where they dropped, water rippled with feeders. He scraped scales off and was silver to the elbows.

He rinsed off and carried the catch to his kitchen.

On the table, he sliced off the fillets in deft strokes. He lit the stove and poured coconut oil in a pan with a spoonful of white fat he'd saved from the stew. When it was sputtering, he slipped in the fish. He drilled the eyes of a green coconut with a knife and splashed in some liquid. He sprinkled ginger root and lemon grass.

The smell was bewitching and the men's mouths watered. In less than five minutes, Cat handed around the plates – white flesh in a savory marinade. Johnny took a bite that fell apart in his mouth.

"I've been to some good restaurants, but that's the best I've ever tasted," he said with his mouth full.

"Cor mate, fair dinkum, on me bloody oath!"

The men dug in while the prisoner's eyes flashed between them. Then Cat ate as well.

Life is not half bad, Johnny thought, *now we've left the Father behind*.

128

The following morning, Footy worked the radio while Johnny rinsed the breakfast dishes in the ocean. Cat came with him and said they would make some salt. They carried pans with a little seawater in them and set them in the sun to dry.

Footy worked the radio and wanted to fish again.

"With no sheilas to talk to," he said, "we might as well enjoy the next best thing."

Cat got his gear as well, but Johnny said he'd had enough of the twirl-and-throw method. The others could go ahead.

The thick beard Johnny had grown on their journey was salty and beginning to itch. He sharpened his clasp knife against a stone until the blade shaved the hair off his arm. He warmed water on the stove, made suds with soap, and spread it over cheeks and chin.

He stuck Footy's giant Bowie sideways in a tree for a mirror and went to work with the blade. It pulled, but he got the hair off with only a few nicks. That felt better.

Johnny went to the bamboo thicket and cut a thin pole about seven feet long. He flexed it like a whip. He scoured the garbage dump and chose a large tin can. This he tied sideways on the thick end of the pole – a makeshift reel. He pulled out a strand of wire from their cache and wrapped a circle around a finger, left a couple of inches on each end, and bent the wire back and forth until it broke. A couple of feet up from the can, he wrapped these ends tightly around his rod – a line guide. He repeated the process every couple of feet, last one at the tip. He wrapped fishing line around the can, then threaded the end through his wire guides. He tied a hook with another home-made lure on it and headed for the beach.

Johnny hiked by the other men to the place where the dark water came close to shore. This was a drop off, he figured, and the big fish would be down in deep water. He spooled line off the can onto the sand, pinched it with one hand while he cocked the pole back with the other. He whipped his right arm forward while he released the line with the other. The weight carried his lure way out – the longest cast any of them had made. Footy and Cat watched and the Aussie crowed. Johnny retrieved, wrapping the linen around the can as he went.

After a dozen casts, he was rewarded with a heavy strike. Johnny fought the fish shoreward. Again, the other two withdrew their tackle and came to watch. Johnny's rod quivered and dipped like a living thing. At last he muscled the fish into shallow water and Cat splashed in to seize it. It was two feet long, shaped like a mackerel, with blue bars down its side, and an undershot jaw like a barracuda.

"It's an 'Ono,'" Johnny said, the Hawaiian name.

"Oh – no!" Footy joked. "That's a bloody Wahoo, mate! It must weigh eight pounds!" At least they could agree on that.

466

Once more they enjoyed a superb dinner. The men were starting to put flesh back on their bones. Katsu must have been nearly starved, because the change was most obvious in him.

129

The next day, Johnny helped the others make their own bamboo rods. By noon, they'd brought in as many fish as they could eat and they quit.

Johnny was restless hanging around camp. There'd been no ship or plane since they got here. It struck him that he'd been in the fight so long, he didn't know what to do with leisure time.

I want a project, he thought, *but what?* He cleaned his rifle and reorganized his pack. He couldn't come up with anything else and took a long walk down the beach.

Again, Cat made dinner. First, he scraped up the residue of the evaporated seawater. Now they had salt. He saved it in a twist of paper. Tonight's meal was fish with stew. The men ate in silence. Again they smoked and turned in shortly after darkness.

Katsu lay on his blankets and the breeze smelled like home.

This air was over my city only hours ago, he thought. He caught a fragrance that tugged him back in time. He saw his wife and children and was flooded with regret and longing. Eventually he drifted to sleep.

Before him was an elaborate garden. Trimmed trees and shrubs ranged around a grand mansion.

This estate had been in his family for generations. The dreamer saw the pond with the stately white swans, swimming with their wings back.

He saw a man in the garden, a younger Katsu. This man held a glass of golden liquor. His glossy hair was brushed back from an unlined face.

His body was rounded and muscular. He wore the crisp uniform with the insignia of a captain in the Imperial Army.

Around him were other men in uniform, each one with a drink. Senior officers stood nearby: the dreamer searched for a particular face. Ahh! There were the stern features and full head of hair, white at the temples. His father was in uniform, chest ablaze with medals – the Rising Sun, Golden Kite, and the Order of the Sacred Treasure.

Katsu saw the group of women in their dress kimonos – his mother with her heavy hair and sweet smile. But his eyes searched for Koto. His wife was so lovely! He drank in her pale, flawless skin and long neck. Her shining hair was coiled up, adorned with the mother-of-pearl combs he had given her on their wedding night. The dreamer's heart swelled as he saw their children beside her – Ryo, his nine-year old son and Yuriko, his five-year old daughter, as they had been when he last saw them.

The father spoke in his hard, grating voice.

"The war has come! The Takano family is Samurai and we live to serve the Empire. A toast to the Emperor and his family! A toast to Nippon and our sure victory!"

With the others, Katsu raised his glass and drank. The liquor was his father's favorite – Talisker Whiskey from the United Kingdom. It was expensive and impossible to come by now, but his father had visited London before the war, and brought several cases home.

The scene changed. He was with his father inside the house, in the alcove where the sword rested on its stand, the scabbard on the rung below. It was the most precious of the family heirlooms. The senior Takano picked it up and his eyes glistened with pride.

"My son," his father said, "tomorrow you leave for war. Take Katsumushi-maru from my hand. It is the warrior spirit of our ancestors. It is yours."

Katsu, overcome by the honor, accepted the katana in both hands and bowed.

"Use it well!" his father said. "Protect Katsumushi-maru and it will protect you. You are a captain in the army. But more than that, you are Samurai in service to the Emperor. Honor your heritage!

"Many families would not send this katana into war – it is priceless! But to think that way is to invite defeat. Victory is the only possible outcome. You must teach the enemy the tune Katsumushi-maru sings!"

Now Katsu was in his own quarters. He saw Koto waiting on the bed, her hair loose, spilling down over shoulders and breasts. Katsu took her in his arms and breathed in the scent of her. He crushed her to him, as he had that last night before he sailed to war.

The dream was so heartbreaking, Katsu awoke, his hands clutching sand. Koto was gone. He yearned for her so strongly that if he could not have her, he desired death.

He rolled onto his back and stared up. The cold face of the moon gazed back. Koto filled his heart, as did Ryo and Yuriko. He wondered if any of the people he loved were looking, right now, at this same moon. If so, did they wonder if he was also under it, or did they believe he had died years ago? There had been no communication for so long now.

His hand went to the *katana* at his side and he clutched the hard comfort. It was his last shred of pride, the one possession that still connected him to his people.

It occurred to him then, even though he had made a solemn promise, it was unthinkable for him to return to Japan without *Katsumushi-maru*. Yet he had promised the Australian that, when the time came, he would surrender it to him.

The cosmic light allowed no lies. Katsu admitted he no longer hated the Australian, but at the same time, he was *gaijin* and unworthy of this prize.

It was something he could never begin to understand. Katsu pictured the fellow drunk among his rough friends, handing around the blade while he spun his threadbare story.

Katsu turned his head and stared at the man himself, a dark form in moonlight. How easily he could slice the life from him! But even as that thought came, Katsu knew he would not do it. His war with these two men was finished.

Unbearable as it was, he must humble himself and give up his heirloom. *But not before the time – not until the very last second. After that, my body may live, but my warrior heart will be dead.*

Katsu sat up, his breath hissing like the waves. This night, the South Pacific was gentle. He saw the tender way it kissed the sand. The moonlight made a path across the ocean and the fantasy struck him that he would run across it until he was home!

But even as his eyes followed that light, a hundred meters out, the path was shredded by darkness. Something big disturbed it, shattered it in fragments. Perhaps it was only the ocean tossing, Katsu told himself. Otherwise, something enormous moved on the deep. He rubbed his eyes and looked again, but saw no more. Again, the moon path was serene.

What was it? Could it be the crocodile? More likely a whale or shark, even a school of fish.

Sharply now, he recalled the first confrontation with the Father. It had knocked the rifle from his hands and batted him aside as a man slaps a fly. That was why he had been captured without a fight!

But how could even an expert warrior battle that dragon of the deep?

Whatever you fear, you must face it – the familiar voice. Katsu sighed. His father always had an answer.

Moon gone, alone with the infinite stars, Katsu yawned and closed his eyes.

"To do right is heavy as a mountain but death is lighter than a feather," he thought in Japanese.

It was something his father liked to say.

130

Katsu woke when light from the east played across his eyelids. He knew he had been dreaming but the details were gone. Koto was an aching void. He sighed, rose, and moved to the kitchen.

In Katsu's home, there had been servants to prepare the food, but ever since he was a boy, his secret passion had been to cook. He had haunted the kitchens and the chefs had indulged the master's son. Katsu liked knives, and this was blade work. Now, here with his former enemies, the humble task gave him something to do in a world that had become nearly too much to bear.

As Katsu brewed the coffee, he had a sudden image of the moon path shattered by darkness. His gaze flashed to the ocean, but all he saw now were the waves, rising in the dawn to mount their eternal battle against the land.

It was the magical twilight between night and day. Gulls rose hovering in the breeze, while others huddled in groups on the sand. Katsu saw the other men sleeping.

They are my captors and yet I am free!

He pulled the food off the heat, took Johnny's clasp knife, soap, a towel, and the largest pot. He went among the palms to the pool of water. He filled the container, then sat under the spout and scrubbed himself from head to toe. He had seen that Johnny had shaved, and he did the same. He lathered his chin and used the knife. During the war, he had shaved his head frequently to keep down lice, but it had grown during the time on the river. He left it as it was. His beard grew sparsely and he drew the blade. His fingers told him when the stubble was gone. He brushed his teeth with a twig and returned to camp.

He put the food on the plates and woke the men. This morning's new offering was fried bananas. Johnny climbed out of his hammock and saw Footy hunched by the fire pit. Johnny joined him.

Cat brought coffee and plates and the men ate and watched the awakening day.

"Hey Cat – thanks for breakfast."

"Yes, ta very much."

Cat nodded and gathered the dishes. Johnny and Footy busied themselves at the radio where the Aussie broadcast their S-O-S.

After that, the men went fishing. It was not for sport. They needed the meat. They cast for a couple of hours, but the surf was up, nothing was biting, and they quit. They took a nap. In mid-afternoon clouds drifted over the sun. Johnny took his pole and went to fish the wall. He prepared his lure and let fly. The other men awoke and came to watch. They sat some distance apart, their shadows stretched down the beach.

It was an hour before Johnny got the huge strike. His rod bent nearly double and he whooped and spilled line as his adversary hauled out to sea. It felt like he'd hooked a tow truck, and he knew he had to slow it or he'd run out of line. Footy and Cat pointed as the taut cord zigzagged across the waves.

Finally Johnny managed to slow the monster. Good thing — he was almost out of line. Using the rod for leverage, he dragged it in little by little, winding in the slack as he went.

He'd muscled the fish twenty yards when it launched another rush and he lost everything he'd gained. Over and over, he and the fish matched force and will.

Finally, Johnny dragged it over the lip of the drop off and caught his first glimpse of the dark shape. Worn out as he was, the sight gave him strength. But the fish grew desperate. Again, the pole slammed over, and Johnny rushed to spill off line. It hummed and could snap at any second.

He ran into the ocean up to his waist. For long moments he battled the swimmer, muscles straining, locked in a standoff. Then again, dip by dip, wrap by wrap, he muscled it in. Gradually, he backed onto the beach.

Then the giant jumped. It came out of the water glorious and glittering green, flashing droplets. It tossed its massive head with the prominent hump and tried to shake the hook from its jaw. The men shouted as the fish splashed down and pulled away. Again, Johnny was forced to go in after it.

"Did you see?" Johnny called. "Napoleon wrasse!"

"Maori! Maori, mate!" Footy yelled. But Johnny knew this fish. When a Hawaiian caught one, he could trade it for a stack of dollars at the best restaurants in Honolulu.

"Napoleon!" Johnny called back. "See the hat on its head?"

"Maori, mate!" Footy insisted. "See the tattoos on its face?"

Another half hour, and Johnny was played out, but so was the fish. Finally it finned on its side in four feet of ocean. Johnny's arms were quivering.

Footy and Cat went into the water, coming at the big fish from each side. Together, they rammed hands through the gills. Shouting, they half carried, half dragged it out. A wave broke over its back and left it stranded on the sand.

"Bloody great fish, mate!" Footy cried. Cat grabbed driftwood, cracked it over the hump and it quivered and died.

Johnny sat down panting. Footy rolled the fish on its side. Cat slit it anus to jaw, and began to haul out the substantial guts, arms in to the elbows.

"Jolly good show!" a British voice called behind them. "Now, kindly turn around – and be so good as to raise your hands."

131

Johnny looked over his shoulder and saw a man in khaki shorts and a loose cotton shirt. He wore a bowler hat and had a patchy black beard. A kerchief was knotted around his neck and he wore sandals on his feet. His features were broad and deeply tanned, but there was that plum British accent.

The newcomer's most conspicuous feature was the revolver he pointed at the men.

"Hands up, please!"

Johnny raised his. Footy and the Jap put theirs up as well, Cat's dripping fish guts.

"Splendid," the newcomer said. "Who's in charge?"

"I guess that's me," Johnny said.

"Let's have the introductions, shall we? You first."

"I'm Sergeant John Willman, U.S. Army. That one is Glen Carmichael, our pilot."

"And the Nip?" the Englishman asked.

"He's our prisoner, an enemy officer we captured up the Raub. His name – say the whole thing again, Cat?"

"I am Takano, Katsu," the Japanese said.

"We call him Cat," Johnny said.

"Cat – very well," the Brit said. "And your reason for being here?"

"We're part of an Allied mission," Johnny said. "We were sent on a rescue to Kissim. Cat's our prisoner, the only survivor of his party."

"Name of your assignment?" the man asked.

"You need to know that?"

"Indeed."

Johnny shrugged.

"Operation Teeth."

"Jolly good," the interrogator nodded. He lowered the gun. "Who I hoped you were – the chaps on the wireless." He turned to the Australian. "That would be you, ah, Footy."

"Right you are," Footy said.

"And who are you?" Johnny asked.

"Yes of course. Charles Rutherford, Captain in the Royal Marines, at your service." He gave a bow, with a flourish of his hand.

"Or rather, formerly with the British Forces. Demobbed – all that. Call me Chas.

"I came by way of Asia, and I reside these days at my plantation, a day's walk inland. I served his Majesty, King George, most recently in Burma. For the last few months, I've been a Coast Watcher. I report the various movements of his crowd," he nodded at the Japanese. "We've been quite busy. You do know the war is over?"

"We heard," Johnny said. "We dropped some new bomb on Japan and they surrendered. But that's all we know."

"Quite right," Chas said. "The atomic bomb! At this very moment, gentlemen, the greatest Allied armada of the Pacific War is steaming for Tokyo Harbor. There they will accept the formal surrender of the Japs. The new American Emperor is on his way to Japan," he said ironically. "I mean your Douglas MacArthur," he winked at Johnny. "His High and Mighty Supremacy Himself, long may he live."

"The war is over?" Katsu asked. "This is true?"

The Brit looked at the prisoner. He had not realized the man was fluent in the King's English.

"And General MacArthur is in Japan?" Johnny asked.

"Yes to both. Today is August twenty-fifth. On the fifteenth of this month, Emperor Hirohito himself went on the wireless and told his subjects that Japan had no choice but to surrender. I heard the translation on my radio some days ago – words to the effect that should Japan fight on, the new bomb would result in the total extinction of the nation.

476

"There are tens of thousands of your countrymen still remaining here in New Guinea," he told Cat. "Mobs of you in the Wewak area alone. But now, no doubt the unpleasantries will draw to a close. I imagine you'll be joining your countrymen on the ships home.

"I've just returned from a walkabout with my *wantoks*, spying out enemy activity. It's clear some of the them refuse to believe Japan has lost. I returned to my village to report, and there I heard your cries for help on the radio. Voilà – here I am. Rutherford to the rescue."

"Lots to talk about," Johnny said. "How about you stay for dinner?" He indicated his catch. "We're having wrasse."

"Very kind. Yes, let's have a chinwag. First thing." He looked at the jeeps parked nearby as he holstered his pistol.

"These are yours?"

Johnny scratched his chin.

"Not ours. But we found them in a wrecked cargo plane in the jungle and drove them here. I guess they belong to the US government."

"Mmmm," Chas said. Johnny gathered his tackle while the other men finished cleaning the fish. Cat sliced off the wide head and the men piled the guts on it. They carried it to the waves, heaved the mess out and there was a furious swirl.

"Don't mean to tell you your business," Chas called, "but I wouldn't do that."

"Not do what, mate?"

"Throw offal in the ocean," Chas said. "This is crocodile country, gentlemen. But if your intention is to encourage large visitors, by all means, carry on."

"Bloody good point," Footy said, glancing out to sea.

He and Cat shared a look. Johnny and Chas sat at the fire pit.

"Hey," Johnny said, "do you have any thirty-aught-six ammo? I'm out."

"Sorry, Johnny," Chas said. "I've got my revolver. I have a rifle in the village, but wrong caliber. What other firearms do you have?"

"Only my rifle," Johnny said. "But no bullets. We used up the rest on the river."

"That's poorly prepared for the New Guinea bush!"

"We'll, this was supposed to be a three-day op," Johnny said, "and we ran into trouble."

"I see." Chas nodded.

Cat and Footy approached with heavy fillets draped over their arms. Cat went to the kitchen while Footy washed himself, then he came and sat as well. Johnny recounted the beginning of Operation Teeth – the rescue mission, how they came to Kissim and learned of the deaths of the priests. He sketched in the battle with the enemy squad, the confrontation with the enormous crocodile, and the death of Dingo. Footy chimed in from time to time. Rutherford proved to be a good listener.

Cat heated the frying pan and slid in the wrasse. He opened cans of potatoes, distributed these around the fish, and sprinkled on his spices. The delicious scent permeated the campsite. Cat passed around the food and they tucked in. The wrasse came apart in flakes so tender it made their eyes water.

When the plates were scraped clean, the men paid their compliments to the chef. Cat brewed coffee.

"You were here before the war?" Johnny asked their guest.

"Correct," Rutherford said. "I was born in New Guinea –

grew up here. My father founded the large plantation where I live. He was a British subject. This place...", he held up his palms, "...belonged to friends of the family, although I only met them once or twice. Then I was sent by my father to boarding school in England.

"When the war came, dear old Dad abandoned our home. 'Not worth dying for,' he wrote in a letter I received many months later. He left my mother in the village."

"She's indigenous, you see. Now she lives with me. The people that had this place thought they'd stay on. Terminal error. They were slaughtered. There was a lot of fighting here.

"As for me, this place may look like one of your Hollywood pictures, but I would not have it for all the tea in China. Too many of the very large saltwater crocodiles, I'm afraid."

There was a pause while the men took this in.

"Well, I hear that," Johnny said.

"We're bloody ready to bugger off at our earliest convenience," Footy said, passing around cigarettes. The men lit up.

"If you don't mind me asking, why'd you come back?" Johnny said. "The men I fought with here – no one ever wanted to see New Guinea again."

"In England I managed to get along, but barely," Chas said, leaning back on an arm. "My schoolmates referred to me as 'that mongrel from Cannibal Island.' Never could get any sense through their thick English heads.

"On the other hand, here I'm a 'Big Man' – important rank in New Guinea. I'm the son and heir of Master Charles Rutherford, Senior. My father, by the way, never made it back to Olde England. His ship was sunk by the Germans. So I own the plantation.

"I have three wives and seven children, with two more on the way – wives that is. They are from surrounding tribes. Marriages make good allies."

"Bloody hell!" Footy exclaimed. "You've gone native, mate!"

"Well Footy," Chas said as he pulled off his hat to reveal a mass of black curls, "I am native, you see. And English. Got the passport to prove it. But not to worry. I live in 'oriental splendor,' as Mr. Kipling would say.

"I've got a large house with electric lights and fans, run off a diesel generator. I've got a kerosene refrigerator. I have a thousand acres and will soon have copra and coffee going again – and I'm planning to expand into peanuts. There is a world market."

Footy passed cigarettes again and Chas lit one.

"I'll try growing tobacco as well. When the war came along, I joined the Royal Marines. I saw action in Asia – Burma in the last year. Got a few stories to tell."

"We've got the time," Johnny said dryly.

"Please do, mate," Footy chimed in.

"Hmmm. Well, one in particular might interest you – involves crocodiles."

"In Burma?" Footy asked.

"Just so," Chas said. "The place was ours. Japs grabbed it. We took it back.

"Any rate, I was assigned to the engineers. With our British India troops, my last job was to help clear a God-forsaken island by the name of Ramree."

"Never heard of it," Footy said.

"Not a surprise. Middle of nowhere, all bog and pestilence. There were perhaps a thousand of your countrymen there," he nodded at Cat. "We had 'em surrounded. As we saw it, they had two options. Surrender, or die."

Cat sipped his coffee while Chas studied him.

"Your side was in a pickle. Through our Burmese translators, we gave 'em the opportunity to surrender. Yelled into the marsh — 'throw down your arms and come out, and you'll live.' That sort of thing. But the Japs made a third choice. They decided to escape through ten miles of swamp.

"Of course, they knew the crocodiles were there — big ones, the largest living reptile on Earth. That swamp was home to an entire colony of salties. A thousand Japs went through filthy water up to their necks. Then, like now, the night came on."

The sky had gone dark while they talked. A wave sighed up the beach.

"And then we heard the screams."

132

Rutherford went on.

"We could no longer see 'em, but we could hear the Japs moving in the water. Voices calling to one another."

He paused to light a cigarette and the flare outlined his features.

"We heard the crocs on the move, heavy bodies in the water.

"What would curdle your blood were the screams when one of those bastards found a soldier! On my soul — I can still hear the sound!

"In extremis, you know, all men are the same," Rutherford said.

Johnny grunted. He knew exactly what the man was talking about. Footy did too. He poked the fire and orange light flickered.

"The following morning, we had very little trouble rounding up the Japs that remained! The fight had gone out of them. But we captured only seventeen men. Where were the thousand?"

"Did the crocs get 'em all?" Footy asked.

"No way to know," the Brit shrugged. "What we did see was the crocs feasting on corpses. Fast as we could, we departed that God-forsaken place." There was a pause.

"When was this?" Johnny asked.

"Back in February of this year," the visitor said. "That was the last action I saw. A month later, I was released and came here."

It was Johnny's turn to talk. He continued with their trek down the Big River. He got to the fight in the Valley of the Cannibals and the carnage they'd seen a single crocodile inflict. Rutherford listened keenly.

"You men survived the Valley of the Cannibals? By Jove! Never heard of anyone doing that! Last place I'd want to be! And this Father of the Crocodiles killed the *Mambu-Ato?*"

Johnny and Footy assured him it was so, and even Katsu nodded. Johnny sketched in their visit with Mula, but skipped the getting sick part and Cat's escape and return. He also deliberately left out the women in the jungle and how they'd lost most of their guns. There was a pause.

"Can a croc track a bloke over a long distance?" Footy asked, pinching tobacco off his lip.

"Certainly," Rutherford said. "I'm something of an expert on crocs, freshwater and the big salties. You don't live long around here without knowing the top predator – the Father in particular. My own father spoke of him in the old days.

"My people have a saying. Once a *pukpuk* chooses you, you are already dead. Your croc selects its prey. It watches him. Then it sets its ambush, and when the time is right..." He clapped his hands and the men jumped.

"Right here – delta of the Raub – this is prime salty country. And your infamous Father, he's been the dominant bull in this region since before I was born.

"Gentlemen," he spread his arms, "you are camped in the heart of the Father's territory."

"You're sure we're talking about the same croc?" Johnny asked. "This one – he's got the scar on his head?"

"Ahh, the very one, Johnny – the Father himself! Infamous on the Raub! My people tell me he disappeared during the war, but now he's back."

"That's the bugga that killed Chief Bumay in the Mambu valley!" Footy said.

"Indeed!" Rutherford said. "I thought my croc story was good, but yours is a corker!" He paused.

"Have you seen the Father since you got here? You'll be interested to know, he's been observed in these parts quite recently."

"No, we haven't," Johnny said.

"It's been seen?" Footy asked.

"On my way here, I came through a village – all the people in mourning. One of their men had been fishing.

"They say the croc swam up, swamped the canoe, savaged him in the water, then went on its way. Didn't eat him. Killed from sheer spite. Strange, that."

"Did the natives notice anything unusual about it?" Johnny asked.

"Apart from its enormous size and scarred head?"

"Its right foreleg," Johnny said. "I shot its foot off."

"Did you now? No one said anything about the leg," Chas said thoughtfully. "But then, it was in the river."

"I believe the Father is stalking Johnny," Footy put in. "He's been after this Yank ever since Johnny shot it back at Kissim."

"Is that so?"

"I don't know," Johnny shrugged. "It was on our trail for quite a while. But we lost it way back."

"Well, my friend, the Father is not lost! It knows this part of the coast better than any of us ever will. My advice is to leave," Chas said.

"Suits me," Johnny said. "And that's where you come in. We need a rescue."

"Right you are," the Brit said. "Soon as I get home, I'll put the word out. I have a top-notch wireless – need it for my Coast Watcher work.

"Now, if you don't mind, I'm knackered. I have some *wan-toks* with me, back along the trail. I thought I'd come on ahead and get the lay of the land. You fellows are good company, but I'm out on my feet. We walked all day, and I will leave first thing for home.

"I strongly recommend that you fellows come along – leave the Father's territory."

"My vote?" Johnny said. "Thanks but no thanks. We were left a cache of supplies on this beach with my name on it. Somebody is looking for us and the brass will know the place. And then there's Footy's bum leg."

"Another trek is not on for me, mate," Footy said. "Also, from a pilot's point of view, it's best to stay here. The mouth of the Raub is where they'll look."

"There is merit in what you say," Rutherford acknowledged. "As you wish."

Johnny got him a blanket and Chas spread it on the sand and promptly fell asleep. Cat and Footy stretched out as well, the Aussie with his injured foot propped on a log, and they drifted off.

Johnny sat up a little longer and watched the moon rise. It was almost full, and its light cast shadows.

He watched the wine-dark waves glitter silver and thought about the story Rutherford had told. Thousands of Japanese soldiers, slaughtered by a colony of giant crocodiles!

At last he made his way to his hammock and zipped himself in. So far, they'd seen no sign of the Father, and he hoped it would stay that way.

133

Johnny woke to the sound of voices. It was early morning, and he peered through the netting of his hammock. There was Chas Rutherford with a group of natives. He counted five men, three women and some lighter-skinned children. Chas had a boy and a girl in his arms, while another little one clung to his leg.

Johnny got up and went to the kitchen. Cat poured him coffee. Footy lay near the fire pit, sipping a mug. Johnny sat beside him.

"Our Pommy friend has the wives and *pikininis* here," the Aussie observed.

Chas and his entourage approached. The men carried bows and arrows, and had white beads woven in their hair, with plate-like shells hanging on their chests, and bound pairs of crocodile teeth through their noses.

Rutherford made the introductions. These were his *wantoks,* some wives and progeny. Chas explained that he had expected to rejoin his people on the trail – but, well, they had come to collect him.

Cat filled every available mug and some empty cans with coffee, lots of sugar and condensed milk. The people passed these around, slurping appreciatively. After that, Johnny led the group into the plantation where they cut bunches of bananas for their journey home. He brought back a stack of banana leaves and Cat wrapped cooked wrasse. The warriors accepted the food, but frowned at the Japanese with obvious dislike. Cat noticed that, and kept to the kitchen.

Rutherford announced it was time to leave.

"Now, about your jeeps," he said to Johnny. "Once you're gone, mind if I collect them?"

"Like I said," Johnny replied, "they're not ours."

"Here, more than most places, possession is nine-tenths of the law."

"Help yourself," Johnny said, "but they're almost out of gas."

"Petrol, I have," Chas said. "Thanks for your hospitality.

"I'm delighted to have met the men who helped end the reign of terror from the Valley of the Cannibals. Over the years, the Mambu war parties have come on the hunt and murdered many of my people."

He reaffirmed that he would radio for a rescue as soon as he got home. If he was lucky, he'd talk directly to Port Moresby. Otherwise, the message would go from radio to radio through Wewak, Madang, Mount Hagen or Goroka.

"I'll ensure it goes through."

"I'd like a word, mate," Footy said. "I'm setting up an air cargo business. I lost my aircraft at Kissim – pranged beyond all hope – but I'll get another. Your plantation will need my services, am I right?"

"Right you are, Footy," Rutherford said. "When you're ready, reach me by wireless. We might earn a few pounds together."

At last the farewells and handshaking were done. As always in New Guinea, that took time. Rutherford noticed Cat hanging back in the kitchen, and made a point of going to him and offering his hand. They shook.

"This terrible war is over," Chas said. "Difficult as it is, we must let bygones be bygones. Time to get on. Cat, I wish you best of luck on your return to Japan."

"Thank you," Katsu said, and bowed.

"I visited Japan with my father, before the war," Chas said. "What city are you from?"

"It is a beautiful city by the ocean," Cat said. "Nagasaki."

"Nagasaki?" Chas repeated, eyes going wide.

"Yes – Nagasaki," Cat said. "It is not famous. You probably do not know it."

Johnny and Footy were listening.

"Oh, I've certainly heard of Nagasaki," Rutherford said, voice somber. "The whole world knows Nagasaki. Do you know your city was bombed?"

"Bombed?" Cat repeated. "I think many Japanese cities have been bombed."

Rutherford's strange silence made Katsu anxious. There was something wrong with the way the Englishman was looking at him.

"So you have not heard," Chas said slowly.

"Spit it out, would you?" Johnny barked. Rutherford nodded.

"Yes, right. As you say, many Japanese cities were bombed, including Tokyo. They say the fire storms were terrible, but that was from conventional bombs.

"Cat, I am very sorry to be the one to tell you this, but there were *two* atom bombs dropped on Japan."

"We heard about the one," Footy said. "On – what was the place?"

"Hiroshima!" Cat spat, his eyes locked on Chas.

"Yes, Hiroshima. That was on August seventh.

"Then – on August tenth, the Americans dropped another atom bomb. On Nagasaki."

"Nagasaki!" Cat said, thunderstruck. "This is true?" He looked at Rutherford's face and read the reality there.

"This bomb, what does it do?" he asked urgently.

"Afraid I can't tell you precisely," Chas said.

"But the news reports say those cities are destroyed. Knocked flat. The people? Well, most are gone. Simply – atomized."

"My family," Cat said in horror, "my wife, my children, my parents..."

"I'm dreadfully sorry old chap," Chas said. Cat's face showed such naked anguish the others looked away.

"Thought you knew," Chas said lamely. "Thought you'd heard."

"We heard about the one – not the other," Footy repeated. There was an awkward silence. Down the beach, a child called for his father.

"Listen, Chas," Johnny said. "There's nothing you can do about it." He took Rutherford's arm and guided him toward his group. Chas shot Cat a final look, nodded, and rejoined his people. With a last wave, they disappeared into the trees. Katsu sat down hard and put his hands over his eyes.

"Listen," Johnny said, crouching beside him and putting a hand on his shoulder. "You don't know what happened. The war is over and you'll go home. You'll find out. Maybe your family survived. No bomb can kill everyone!"

"Johnny's right," Footy chimed in. Cat looked at them with shock and grief on his face.

"Please," he said, shrugging the Yankee's hand off, "do not talk to me!"

He lurched up and stumbled away, head down.

Things might have been bad for him, but now they were infinitely worse.

134

Cat disappeared far down the beach. Footy said he might as well go fishing and Johnny joined him. Footy fished his way along the shore until they were separated by a hundred yards. Johnny was not having any luck this morning and he packed it in. He tidied their camp and sharpened the knives.

Eventually Cat returned. Johnny thought he looked about as down as a fellow could get. The man slumped at the fire pit, staring at the dead coals.

Johnny felt he knew something of the anguish the prisoner must be feeling. Like a cable through memory, he was pulled back to that morning when he was sixteen. In some ways, it seemed like another lifetime. In others, it was as fresh as a knife cut.

That event had been buried within him all during the war. It was a wound he could not deal with, so his mind pushed it down. That wasn't a plan, simply a way to cope. While that had let him get on with the war, it had not dealt at all with the root of his torment.

That was one reason why Gwyn's request had eaten at him. *Find your heart.* But his deepest emotions were sealed off. Now, in this strange new peace, the old agony was festering, working its way to the surface.

Johnny sat beside Cat and was moved by the man's suffering. He lit two cigarettes and passed one over. The prisoner took it without looking up.

Johnny started talking, and once he got going, he couldn't stop.

"Maybe you've heard me say I lived in Hawaii." The Japanese did not respond and Johnny went on.

"My family moved there when I was a teenager. I grew up in San Diego, a Navy port on the border with Mexico. My Grandfather was a Rear Admiral who retired before the war. He died last year. My father was a Lieutenant Commander of a battleship. In early 1941, Dad was assigned to a new ship.

"We moved – me and my parents – to Oahu. You know where that is?" Cat shrugged, and after a moment, Johnny went on.

"I didn't like it much. My friends were all back in the States. But I learned to surf in California – and now I was in 'surfer-central.' You know what surfing is?" Cat nodded and Johnny continued.

"There were lots of surfers around Honolulu and Diamond Head – the 'beach boys.' The girls liked them. That looked good to me. I talked my folks into buying me a board. It was a beautiful thing – used, but in good shape. All polished wood, twelve feet long.

"Soon every chance I got, I was on the waves. I made new friends. Turned out, Hawaii was a pretty great place to be.

"At last I was good enough for the big waves up on the north shore – Waimea, and Sunset Beach."

Johnny might as well have been talking to himself.

"December rolled around. Christmas was a few weeks off, and my parents promised me a new board if I kept my grades up.

"Dad was on his ship, out at sea. Saturday, they were back in port. Dad got home that night, but he was ordered back aboard first thing Sunday. That was unusual. When he got shore leave, it was usually the whole weekend.

"My folks went to a barbecue at a friend's house. But they came home early because Dad had to be up at 6-hundred hours. My mother planned to go with him to the harbor at 7:00. At 10:30, she wanted me to drive her to church.

"Usually, I went along to see Dad go aboard. I liked to look at the battleships. But I wanted to go surfing. I figured I'd get in two or three hours before church.

"I was up at first light. Night before, I'd tied my board on the 'Woody,' Dad's old car.

"Mom was cooking breakfast. I remember she said, 'wait, have breakfast with us.'" Johnny's voice slowed and at last, Cat looked up. Johnny was lost in that other time.

"She was wearing a blue dress with yellow sunflowers on it. I'll never forget. My dad was getting ready at the back of the house.

"I told Mom, I can't stay! My friends are waiting. But she made me sit long enough to make me a sandwich. I grabbed it and ran."

Johnny paused and Katsu was watching.

"I never even said goodbye to my dad! What did I know?

"I was at Diamond Head. I was surfing when I heard the hum of engines – a lot of engines – but where?

"And then the sky was full of planes. But Dad had said our aircraft carriers were out of port. Even after I saw the red circles on the wings, I didn't get it. Then one dove down at us and zoomed over our heads. I remember, it was so close, I fell off my board.

"It was a fighter. We had a book of aircraft silhouettes. My dad drilled me on them. I knew all of ours and most of the German and Russian ones. I knew yours too," he nodded at Cat.

"It was a Mitsubishi Zero. And that circle was your rising sun."

"I saw the pilot for a split-second. Then I knew he was a Jap. He even waved. He waved!

"I paddled my board to shore. Your planes had passed over. Then I knew where they were going. I thought, 'it can't be real!' – even when I saw the black smoke shoot up behind the hills. But it was."

Johnny's voice had slowed.

"I heard a radio, some corny Hawaiian song. I was crazy-worried about my father! I ran for the car. I never saw my surf-board again. Diamond Head to Pearl is about twelve miles. Normally, that'd take half an hour. I got there in fifteen minutes.

"There was billowing smoke – hundreds of planes overhead. They were all diving on Pearl. There were bombs exploding. Every plane I saw was yours, none of ours.

"I blew past the guard house and pulled up at the edge of the harbor."

Cat was staring at the Yankee.

"It was crazy, sailors and soldiers running everywhere. The sky was black and the harbor was burning." Johnny took a breath.

"All the ships – Battleship Row – they were all on fire. I saw a huge hull rolled over. There must be men inside! My father could be in there.

"Then, like that, your planes were gone. Men were screaming. The water was on fire. I saw dead men floating. The first ones I ever saw.

493

"I looked for my dad's ship but I couldn't see it. It was all just smoke and flames and men shouting.

"I saw a sailor shooting at nothing, at the sky. I asked about my father's ship. 'Where's the Arizona?' 'There!' he pointed. I saw nothing but burned metal towers sticking out of the water.

"That couldn't be my father's ship! But it was.

"I saw men swimming and boats picking them up. When they got to shore, I saw burned bodies – sailors covered in oil, some with their skin coming off."

Again, Johnny paused.

"I never saw my father again."

Cat lit two cigarettes and passed one over. Johnny took it, but it dangled from his fingers, forgotten.

"I looked for his car, 'Big Blue.' I found in its usual spot. That's when I knew my mother still had to be there.

"I ran to the lookout where she always watched the launch take Dad to the ship." Johnny's voice cracked and he took a long drag. He spoke through the smoke.

"I should have been with her! But no – I was surfing." His voice was bitter.

"There on the lookout was a crashed fighter. I saw my first dead Jap, hanging out of the cockpit.

"Then I saw it – the blue cloth under the wing. I didn't want to go closer, but I had to.

"It was my mother's dress, soaked in blood."

135

Johnny stopped because his throat had seized up. He threw the cigarette butt into the fire and wiped his eyes with the back of a hand.

He turned raw eyes on the Jap.

"My parents died a little after eight in the morning, December seventh, 1941. The day you murdered two thousand three hundred people – my mom and dad included.

"We weren't at war! You attacked us in peacetime!"

Cat cleared his throat. Johnny locked eyes with him until the other man looked down. Then he went on.

"But it wasn't over. Not by a long shot. There was a second wave of your dive-bombers. I could shoot a rifle better that most of those sailors. I asked for one and they gave me it to me, no questions. I took my first shots of the war at your aircraft. Men were shouting that the Japs were coming ashore! This was an invasion! We had to defend Hawaii. That didn't happen, but what did I know?

"Hours later, I was back at our house. I watched with a rifle for a long time. Next day, the Navy sent someone around. The officer confirmed what I already knew. My father was missing, presumed dead. They'd found my mother's body.

"I was shipped to my grandparents in San Diego. That was a bad Christmas, the worst. By New Year's, I had a plan.

"I was going to kill you people! I was going to fight for my parents and every other American you murdered. I was going to kill as many Japs as I could. And I swore on my parents' memory – I wouldn't quit fighting until Japan was finished.

"My granddad approved of my desire to fight, but he said the war was going be a Navy show.

"He said we'd re-float most of the ships sunk at Pearl. And we'd build the finest warships the world had ever seen and send them on the hunt for you.

"My grandfather knew Admiral Nimitz – he'd put in a word for me. His thought was, I'd finish high school, take officer's training, and get assigned to a good ship.

"That was not going to happen! No way I was going to wait!

"I left a note and joined the Army. I was seventeen but I lied, and tell the truth, no one cared." He paused.

"I've been killing you ever since."

Minutes dragged away and at last Cat spoke.

"I see why you hate us," he nodded. "I would hate you too. Do you wonder how I speak English?"

"Well, I figured you learned it at school," Johnny shrugged.

"I learned at church," Cat said.

"Your temple?"

"My *church*," Katsu said. "I learned from a priest. I am Christian."

"You – Christian?"

"Yes, me," the Japanese nodded. "How long has there been an America?"

"Well, I learned that at school. The Declaration of Independence was written in 1776."

"Oh – less than a hundred and seventy years?"

"I guess," Johnny said.

"My family has been Samurai for five centuries. And we have been Christian for four hundred years.

"Yes, *Christian*," he repeated, seeing the surprise on Johnny's face.

"Ships came from Europe to Japan hundreds of years ago. Many important families in my area became Christian. But the Shogun – the leader, like your President – outlawed this new religion. In my city alone, he crucified twenty-six people.

"To survive, we became *'kakure Kirishitan'* – the hidden ones. But finally the ban on our religion was lifted, before I was born. In my neighborhood of Nagasaki, 'Urakami,' there is the biggest, most beautiful cathedral in all Asia – if it is still there!

"If your atom bomb demolished Nagasaki, America has destroyed the center of Christianity in Japan! You have killed who knows how many hundreds of thousands of my countrymen, and tens of thousands of Christians. You have slaughtered all the people I know – my family – my wife, my children!"

The prisoner looked away so the Yankee could not see the moisture that welled in his eyes. It was Johnny's turn to find nothing to say. Eventually, Cat went on.

"Of course I was not at Pearl Harbor. But my father and – well, we supported the war. I am sorry for what happened to your parents. I accept responsibility." He took a deep breath.

"But now, Japan has paid the price. I, myself – I have paid the price!" Johnny saw Footy returning along the beach.

"You and me, what do we do now?" Johnny wondered. "I've hated your people so long I don't know if I can quit."

"I do not know," Cat said. "My problem is, I cannot see how to go on."

"I know this," Johnny said slowly. "I have killed and killed, and my parents are still dead. Revenge felt good at first. Justified. But then it turned into just another job."

The prisoner nodded. He, too, saw the Australian coming.

"I don't talk about this," Johnny said. "Never! Keep it between us, will you?"

"Yes," Katsu said. "And I ask the same."

Cat took towel and soap and retreated into the forest. When he returned, he cooked the fish Footy brought back, and handed around the plates.

It was a quiet dinner, each man lost in his thoughts.

136

In the morning, Johnny and Footy talked things through. They figured it would have taken Rutherford a day to get home before he could send his radio message. And then? With all the monumental events the end of the war must have put in play, how long would it be before three men in the wilderness got any attention?

Again, they took stock of their supplies. They were doing well at augmenting the canned goods with what they could catch and gather. Of coffee and cigarettes, they had enough for two more weeks, if they were each restricted to two cups and four cigarettes a day.

Fishing was a daily necessity, and a subdued Cat joined in the effort. They went barefoot into the surf, casting over the drop-off. Within hours, they had enough. They napped through the midday heat. Later, when a cooler breeze drifted off the ocean, Johnny walked for miles along the beach. Footy limped into the forest to get bananas.

Cat cleaned the fish. After what the *Engli* had said about crocodiles, he scraped a hole in the sand back in the trees and buried the guts. He poured himself the dregs of the coffee.

He would have preferred green tea, but that was a long-ago memory. He smoked the second of his ration of cigarettes and stared at the ocean.

His attention was drawn to a flock of screaming gulls over agitated water. The birds dove repeatedly and rose with small fish flipping in their beaks. There was a ball of bait fish just under the surface. They glittered like tossed coins as they leapt. *They try to escape!*

He saw the torpedoes come – sharks, distorted through water. They rushed into the fray. The activity grew even more frenzied. It was not only the small fry that got airborne now, but big ones with yellow fins arced up as well. The gulls shrieked and fanned up as the heads of the lunging sharks broke surface.

Suddenly the whole thing melted away. The seabirds rose complaining. The sharks vanished and the sea was placid once more.

We live in paradise, Katsu thought. *But it is Eden that becomes a bloodbath in an instant! Death lurks just beneath the skin of beauty, and this is also the truth.*

The whole world is at war! It is not just men. Always, something kills something else. The difference with men is that we do not slaughter one another from hunger – unless you include the cannibals. But we civilized people do it out of tribal hatred as well. We do it for pride. We kill for an idea! And we are so clever, we have learned to slaughter even women and children with our machines, from far away.

This is what makes us "civilized," he thought sourly. *Our aircraft rain death on the people from the sky! My nation is not innocent. We dropped many bombs on China before we made the fatal mistake of attacking Hawaii.*

But now, with this atom bomb, the Americans can destroy the world! And so, have they become gods?

499

No! The answer came in a flash. *God creates life. Man only takes it! And that is the absence of God. And that is evil.*

He gazed at the scene. *Even so – the world is so beautiful!* His eyes drank in the scene of beach and the verdant trees, the swell of the ocean's breast under the blue dome.

Then, in his mind's eye, he saw his parents, and Koto, Ryo, Yuriko, Yuji, his older brother and many more friends and family. He pictured Father Valenti, the priest who had been so patient as he wrestled with the impossible foreign tongue called 'English.'

Each cherished face was like a living photograph. But even as it appeared, it was consumed by fire. Katsu closed his eyes and wished he would sleep and never awake.

If I were truly a man, I would commit seppuku – the honorable suicide of the warrior – by slicing my belly. But I am Christian, and I am forbidden to kill myself. So my Samurai spirit is at war with my eternal soul.

My war cannot end!

At last he drifted into a ragged and unsatisfying sleep.

Footy returned under a load of banana bunches to find Johnny at the stove.

"Where's the Jap then?" he asked.

"Shhh!" Johnny pointed to the prisoner, sleeping near the cold fire pit.

"What's the story?" Footy said low.

"Think about it," Johnny said, turning the fillets. "He just found out his wife and kids and whole family are probably dead – most likely dead. What would you do?"

"Fair dinkum," Footy said.

"I actually feel sorry for the blighter."

"Open that, will you?" Johnny asked. Footy picked up the baked beans and worked the opener. Johnny dumped the contents into a pot on the heat. He poured mugs of coffee and dished the food, leaving a plate for Cat. The two of them walked down the beach and sat near the ocean.

"What are you going to do when we get out of here?" Johnny asked between bites. The future was on his mind these days.

"*If* we get out of here," Footy said, "the air cargo business, like I told the Pommy. And you?"

"No clue," Johnny said. "I was seventeen when I joined up. I can surf and I can shoot. Don't see how I can make a living with those."

"Don't be too shore," the pilot said. "I'd say it's likely there will be another war – with the Russians. If the Krauts couldn't beat the buggers, maybe you Yanks can. There's work there, right up your alley."

"Maybe," Johnny said, "but with this new bomb, it'll be over fast."

"Ah," Footy said. "Yes, of course. Boom – there goes bloody Moscow. Bye-bye Joe Stalin. Well, first things first, then. When we get back, I'll have an ice-cold beer – or a truck load. I'm ready to go on a real stinker. I've got a girl to see in Moresby," he winked. "Then I'll hop a plane to Cairns. Me parents are gone. I need to take care of things. I've got to find another aircraft. I expect there'll be lots to choose from, with the war over."

"We'll deliver Cat to the authorities," Johnny said. "They'll be shipping the P-O-W's home. And I've got a girl to see myself. I can't wait to leave the croc behind – and the mud..."

"...and the bloody jungle..." Footy said.

"...and the mosquitoes..."

"...and the cannibals."

"Right," Johnny said. "And the mud. Did I say the mud? I'd like a platter of barbecued ribs and..."

"Awww, put a bung in it, mate," Footy protested. "Fresh red meat! Cor! I may drown in me own spit."

Johnny went to Cat, shook his shoulder and put a plate beside him.

"You need to eat." The man forked the food in, then rolled in his blanket and slept again. Johnny and Footy washed the dishes, smoked their last cigarette of the day and bedded down.

137

They were in the habit of rising with the dawn. Again, Cat had food ready. He handed the men their breakfast, took his own, and sat by himself.

The three fished and caught enough for dinner before the barracuda raided their lines. After a lunch of pan-sized perch, Johnny spoke up.

"I need a project," he said. "I'm going stir-crazy. I'd like both of you to help with something – but no questions 'til I'm done."

"What is it?" Footy asked at once.

"You'll see," Johnny said. "Come to the old house, okay?"

He led the way through the plantation. Footy's leg had kept him from exploring when they first arrived and he was intrigued. The trail was thick with ferns and littered with deadfalls. Eventually they emerged at the broken-down house.

Johnny led Footy through the ruin, Cat trailing. After the

quick tour, Johnny returned to the back, to the bed that had once been a desk. The top was a rectangle of thick wood, eight feet long and four feet across, attached to the broken-down drawers.

"This is what I'm after," Johnny said. "Help me carry it to camp." He faced away and hoisted one end. Footy and Cat each took a back corner.

They pried it from the earth, got it outside, and began to walk. It was heavy and the men were sweating. Footy grumbled it was too much work not to know what it was for, but Johnny bulled ahead.

Cat plodded doggedly with his head down. They stopped to rest several times, but at last they were back in camp. Under Johnny's direction, they set the desk upside down near the fire pit.

"I'll take it from here," he said. The other two watched while, using a kitchen knife, he removed the screws holding on the drawers. He put the shattered wood aside and fetched his machete. He leaned the desktop against his knees, grasped the blade with both hands and drew the edge towards him, spilling a curl. Beneath the ruined surface, he was pleased to see, the wood was sound. A pile of shavings grew around his feet.

Footy went to fish. Cat wandered aimlessly down the beach and Johnny saw him sit and stare over the ocean. *In the direction of Japan.*

The sun was in his eyes. Johnny got his helmet and fashioned a brim from a big leaf he poked through the netting. He continued to carve, finding a rhythm.

Maybe because of the long pent-up story he'd told Cat, this afternoon, his mind was flooded with memories of his parents. During the war, he'd done everything he could to keep these at bay.

They hurt too much, and the Hard Case told him that mooning about the past would get him killed.

But now the floodgates were open. Johnny's hands moved while his mind filled with memories, especially of the man who had loomed so large in his life.

It was his father who taught Johnny to love stories and books.

During the long weeks Johnny's dad was at sea, he told the boy he spent his free time reading. He avoided the card games some of his peers used to pass time. Instead, he ventured alone into the worlds contained between board covers.

Before he left home, the man selected the volumes for the voyage. His all-time favorites were the seafaring yarns – "Moby Dick," "Robinson Crusoe," and anything by Conrad. He also had a selection of Robert Louis Stevenson, Rudyard Kipling, Jack London, and, more recently, Ernest Hemingway. Apart from that, he had a full set of Dickens.

When Johnny was young and his dad was in port, bedtime meant passages read aloud from whatever novel the man was reading. When Johnny was about seven, his dad changed the process. First, he'd read a chapter, and then Johnny had to try and do the same. At first, the boy could only stammer through a paragraph or two. His father told him the practice would set him up for school, give him the literal taste of fine prose, and prepare him for public life.

By the time Johnny was nine, his father was lending him books from his library. As with all things with his father, there were rules. Books, except gifts, were a loan. His parent expected them back in the same condition he lent them in. Dog-earing corners to mark place was forbidden.

When Johnny was through, he was expected to discuss the story in an intelligent manner. The boy learned that what his father wanted was not like a book report for school – all about getting the characters' names right, and outlining the plot.

Dad liked to chew over a story – was a book worth its salt? Could the author conjure a credible world, and did the yarn take you with it?

There were two other tomes his father always carried. One was his Bible, and the other was a collected works of Shakespeare. The man told his son the scriptures were packed with nefarious characters and intrigues most preachers didn't have the courage to repeat.

"You want to understand literature – especially anything before the last few years – you've got to know your Bible," his father told Johnny.

"If you don't know the source, you can't get the reference."

Most great quotations were either scripture or Shakespeare, his dad said. One of his games was to quote something and Johnny had to name the source.

"How sharper than a serpent's tooth it is to have a thankless child."

"Proverbs?" Johnny guessed.

"Nope," the man smiled. "It's the other one – but you'll have to find the play yourself."

Now, as Johnny's blade shaped the wood, he heard his father's voice:

"They sow the wind and reap the whirlwind."

Hosea, his mind shot back. *Well – at Pearl, Japan sowed the wind. And with the atom bomb, they reaped the whirlwind!*

But thinking about his father brought the bitter loss of both his parents to the forefront. Once more, the rage washed over him like a tidal wave. The familiar hatred rose, and he found himself gasping through clenched teeth. His blade dug too deep in the wood and jammed, and Johnny had to pause and tell himself to ease up.

Justice is done, he assured himself. *We've taken back everything the Japanese took, and then clubbed them to their knees. Now, with these atom bombs, we've kicked them hard onto their backs.*

But knowing that intellectually didn't get rid of the inner torment.

Maybe that's what Gwyn wanted – at least, part of it. I can't enjoy the things she asked – kindness and laughter and whatever – until I figure out how to let go of the hatred.

Johnny pulled the machete again, working with focus. Sometime later, he saw he'd cleaned an entire section of wood.

Footy returned with his pole over his shoulder and hung a string of fish in the kitchen. Cat appeared, soaking wet, with an armload of shellfish.

"Where'd you get those?" Johnny asked.

"I dive," Cat shrugged.

"Not afraid of sharks?" Footy asked.

"No," Cat said. He spilled the shells into a pot of water and fired up the stove.

"What kind are they?" Johnny asked.

"I do not know in English. *Hokkigai.*"

"Okay then. Hokey guy it is," Johnny replied.

By early afternoon, Johnny had smoothed one entire side of the desktop. He turned it over and started on the other. This was the top of the desk, where the names were carved. He felt the rough texture under his hand and decided to keep some of it down the middle, and went to work on the sides. By late afternoon, it was beginning to take shape.

When the western sky blazed scarlet again, he stood and stretched.

"Let's go for a run."

"What mate?" Footy asked. Cat looked over.

"You know – a run," Johnny said. "Something you do with your feet."

"Yes – and what about my ruddy foot?"

"What about it?" Johnny asked. "Come on, I'll take it easy on you. I played football in high school. A little workout is just what the coach ordered."

"Football?" Footy said. "You're going to teach me, mate? Why do you think they call me 'Footy'? But now..." he frowned.

"Come on – have a little backbone," Johnny said.

"You too, Cat."

"Do what?" the Jap asked.

"I'm talking about a run," Johnny said. "Sheesh. Do I have to spell it out? Come on!"

He headed off and, after a minute, the others followed.

138

Barefoot and in shorts, the men jogged down the beach. Johnny began to run along the firm sand near the water and Footy and Cat followed. After a dozen steps, he turned and ran on the spot.

"Move it!" Johnny shouted. Cat went by, arms pumping. The Aussie came gamely enough, favoring his sore leg.

"Come on, Hopalong!" Johnny said and ran off.

"I'd show you bleedin' Hopalong," Footy fumed.

When Johnny and Cat got too far ahead, the American led them back and they ran circles around the Aussie. Then off they'd sprint again, while Footy lurched after them. Johnny got a burst of high spirits. He went into the surf and ran with knees up.

"Like this!" he called. Cat chugged behind, getting soaked.

"Way to go Cat!" Johnny said. "Footy, get with the program!" But the Aussie leaned over, hands on knees, face scarlet.

"Bloody bleedin' blasted foot, mate," he puffed.

He collapsed on the sand. The other two continued to splash back and forth as waves surged around them. Johnny pointed back the other way, not far from camp. On the point stood another shade tree towering above the others.

"There!" he exclaimed. "That's the Finish Tree. Come on Footy – you can make it!"

The Aussie groaned and pushed himself up. The other men were off, running in their different styles. Johnny leapt along, his dark hair blowing back. The shorter Japanese ran with his lower center of gravity, legs pumping. Footy came gamely after them.

The leaders sprinted the last few yards and Johnny got there first. He slapped the trunk and then fell back on the carpet of leaves beneath the widespread branches. A few seconds later, Cat touched bark and toppled as well.

It took a few minutes for Footy to limp in. He put a hand on the tree and then pitched out full length. The men lay panting until they recovered. Then they sauntered back to camp, letting Footy set the pace.

That night, as the stars came out, Cat poached fresh clams in ginger and coconut milk.

139

Johnny and Footy awoke to Cat's shouts. He waved to them from the line of coconut trees and they scrambled up. In the early light, they saw a column of invaders.

Gigantic crabs followed one another between the palms. Johnny thought they looked like lobster musclemen. Their backs were up to three feet long, and they stood at least a foot tall.

The men watched one hoist a coconut in a massive claw and squeeze. The orb, husk and all, exploded like a Christmas nut. The crab picked up white shreds and began to feed. The others spread out and did the same.

The prisoner snatched up a stick and ran at the big crustacean.

"Kani!" he shouted. As he came close, it dropped its meal, stood on its hind legs and raised its claws. Then it actually rushed the man.

For only the second time since they'd met him, they heard Cat laugh.

"Ohhh!" he crowed.

He jumped forward and swung his cudgel between the pincers. The carapace cracked and the crab fell on its back. Cat grabbed it from behind and held it up, massive claws swinging.

"Good eatin' there!" Footy observed, searching for a club of his own. Soon he and Johnny were crab-bashing as well. They needed to take care: their opponents might be smaller, but they were feisty and well-armed. Pincers like that could take off a hand.

Johnny had never tried crab for breakfast, but it was excellent. The men gorged themselves on tender meat dredged in coconut oil, seasoned with salt and lemon grass.

After that, Footy and Cat went fishing. Johnny nursed a coffee and returned to his project. Soon he was in shavings up to the knees. He carved one corner into an arc, turned the board over, and started on the opposite edge.

By midafternoon, hands cramped, he took a break. He saw Footy casting a long way off. Cat was nearer, drawing in the sand with a stick. Johnny went down to him. Cat was on the smooth wet band, scratching Japanese characters.

"What's that?"

"Nothing. A poem."

"You're a poet?" Johnny asked.

"No," the man said. "I try."

"What's it say?"

"You will not understand."

"Try me," Johnny said. Cat shrugged.

"Meigetu ya," he read,

"kuni moetukite,

kagayakinu."

Johnny stared at him.

"In English?"

"I will try," Cat said. "Forgive my poor translation." He thought it through, nodded and spoke:

"Since my country burned down,

how clearly

I see the moon."

He looked at the Yankee.

Johnny repeated the words.

"Hmmm," he said. "It's got something, I'll give you that. It's mournful. I'll think on it."

"As I said," Cat shrugged, "it is Japanese – we call it *haiku*." Johnny nodded and went back to his project. Footy returned near sunset and looked at Johnny's handiwork.

"It's a wee boat. Give it up, mate. You'll never get to Bora Bora on that!" Johnny ran fingers through his hair and pinched his tired eyes.

"You're a scream. Ready for another run?"

Cat nodded. Footy griped but went along. This occasion, although the Aussie still reached the Finish Tree after the others, his time had improved.

That night, Cat's entree was seafood stew, featuring crab claws, with canned corn, tomatoes and coconut milk. Afterwards, they relaxed around the fire and smoked.

They felt alone, forgotten, as if the world had passed them by. In fact, a thousand creatures of forest and ocean watched them.

And on this particular night – as on several before – they had an exceptionally large observer. Just after nightfall, it had emerged from the river and drifted into the ocean. It had rounded the point and now floated fifty yards offshore, hidden in the night.

This witness had sharp senses. It still felt a dull ache in its foreleg, but was no longer driven mad by infection. It floated beneath the surface, eyes raised, and watched its enemy in the glow of the fire.

The Father had not eaten for weeks and it was cranky with hunger, but only for the One Prey. It followed its deepest instinct to set an ambush. Now, under cover of night, it fixated on the three men.

The crocodile knew it could not remain where it was when the bright light came, because it would be seen. That was not the way of the predator.

Eventually the glow flickered out and the reptile returned to the river. When the sky grew bright, it crawled over land, sheltered by the jungle. It moved its massive weight carefully, in silence, until it was separated from the beach only by a veil of leaves.

Again, it watched the two-legged ones and the Father was troubled. It saw three animals, but could not decide which was the One Prey. Sometimes it saw the Smooth-headed man with two furry companions. Other times, there were three hairy ones, and it could not distinguish one from the other.

The cunning reptile waited, watched and learned.

It observed that each day now, as the light was growing dim, the three ran along the beach and then lay down to bask. It absorbed this behavior for two days. On the third, once the animals had departed, the crocodile stole to the place they rested.

The great head slid from the undergrowth and hovered over the forest floor. It snuffled up the unique spoor of each creature. One of the three beds inflamed its senses. Several times, it inhaled deeply and knew the unmistakable odor.

The One Prey had lain here only moments ago.

In the fading day, the crocodile slunk to the river and submerged.

It had a plan and the time was near.

140

As the sun floated up from the ocean's horizon, the men rose to hunt coconut crabs. There were not as many as yesterday, but enough for a decent whacking. After another feast of claws, Footy and Cat went fishing.

They were not natural companions, and unless Johnny was with them, they kept their distance. The Aussie had taken to wandering further down the beach, while Cat preferred the drop off.

Johnny put on his helmet with the leaf visor and continued his project. At one end, each of the sides came to a sharp point. The other end was rounded, but blunt.

Johnny shaved more off an edge, flipped the wood and matched the other side to it.

He made himself a lunch of cold crab and bananas and carried a plate to Cat. The prisoner had a pile of fish wrapped in wet banana leaves. Cat wound in his line and ate.

"Where do you get the clams?" Johnny asked.

"You want to try?"

"Yes."

Cat led along the beach to the place where the coral bed came close to shore. Shaped like giant cauliflower, the heads reached so near the surface, they damped the waves.

"We must swim," the Japanese warned.

"Good. We'll cool off," Johnny said.

Cat waded in and Johnny followed. They swam out about thirty yards.

Looking down, Johnny could see the coral columns, and the sandy bottom a dozen feet below.

Cat upended and breast stroked down, pinching his nose to clear his ears as he went. Johnny took a deep breath and swam after him.

Footy saw them from further along the beach. In the last few days, he'd found a hole the barracuda didn't seem to know about. He saw the other men come his way, but then turn into the ocean, swim – and disappear. He shaded his eyes and stared.

Are they daft – that far out with sharks about, let alone the Father and his mates?

In the euphoria of finally arriving at the beach, Footy, too, had raced into the water without a care. But he'd come to his senses. He'd seen the shark fins cut the waves. And, while he hadn't spotted any crocs on the beach yet, that did not mean they weren't nearby!

Remember what Rutherford said about the Father! And what's that shadow in the water?

Footy's heart tripped and he squinted into the blinding light. Muttering anxiously, he started to wind in his line, even as he began to stride that way.

Submerged by a coral head, Cat picked up a stone. Johnny held himself to the column, eyes open. Without goggles, he saw only a blur. Cat pulled himself to a clam colony on the coral and struck. Quickly, he tugged loosened shells off and Johnny held them with an arm against his chest.

Then Johnny got the spooky sense of being watched.

He stared out into the deep blue and his heart jumped. Something big slid by, but he couldn't make it out.

Cat clunked with his stone and grabbed clams for himself. Johnny's lungs were burning and he pointed to the surface and pushed off. Cat came right behind.

Then, from the corner of his eye, Johnny saw a large shape arrowing at them. He kicked hard.

Footy saw the dark shape in the water, dropped his rod and ran.

The men broke surface and side-stroked hard for shore.

"Look out!" The Aussie shouted, hands around his mouth. Johnny peered down and found himself staring at a long-pointed snout and rows of razor teeth, the eyes looking right at him.

"Move your arses!" Footy bellowed.

Johnny kicked like a madman and his feet touched sand. He burst from the waves, Cat beside him, just as Footy got there.

"'Cuda!" Johnny gasped. "Big one!"

"You bloody dunderheads!" Footy stormed. "You about gave me a stroke!"

Johnny laughed helplessly and looked at Cat. They had been spooked well and truly, but each still had clams clutched to his chest. Cat snorted and they both exploded with laughter.

"Aww, yeah!" Footy said, arms akimbo. "Right – it's all a big bloody joke! Go on then, keep playing silly buggers!" He shook his head and went back to fishing.

Johnny and Cat carried the clams to the kitchen and put them in fresh water. Johnny returned to his carving, and Cat went to the forest to wash and haul drinking water.

Footy returned in the heat of the afternoon. He had a brace of cod he set in the kitchen, then lay down in the shade for a nap.

"I'm sorry," Johnny called. "You were right! When I saw the size of that 'cuda, I about walked on water."

"Come on mate," Footy said. "This is no joke! Tell you what Johnny – I'm not going in again. You want to, it's your funeral."

"Maybe you're right," Johnny said, "but the Pacific feels like home to me."

"Not here, mate!" Footy said, "This is bloody New Guinea! Stupid to survive the bleedin' war, only to end up in a croc's belly! Remember what Chas told us – the Father is here some-where!"

"I hear you," Johnny said, carving another spiral of wood. He kept at it until the sky turned gold and the shadows grew long, then called for another run. He noticed that his compan-ions were getting beefier by the day. He could feel his own body filling out.

This time out, Footy changed his running style. It was more like a skip, followed by a long hop off the strong leg. And while Johnny still hit the Finish Tree first, both Cat and Footy crowded him.

Again they lay on the leaves until they caught their breath.

Johnny was on his back, looking up into the branches when

he got a prickling sense again – something watching. It was becoming a pattern, and it annoyed him. He sat up and stared around, but nothing moved in the quiet clearing.

"What is wrong?" Cat asked.

"Yes – what, mate?"

"Nothing," Johnny muttered.

He was interrupted by an unearthly scream. Something large lifted in the branches and the men's hearts hammered. They saw the silhouette move across the tree as a huge fish eagle flapped away.

Eventually, the men went back to camp. Tonight, Cat's entrée was steamed clams.

"Changed me mind," Footy said, popping another succulent tidbit into his mouth. "If you blokes want to die getting these, bloody well carry on."

"I hope Chas made it safely home," Johnny said later as they sat by the fire.

"And we see an aeroplane any day now," Footy added. He turned to Cat. "Not long and you'll be back in Jap-land."

"What'll you do when you get home?" Johnny asked. Katsu was silent a long minute.

"I do not know," he said.

"What do you do? What's your job?" Johnny asked.

"I am an army officer," Cat replied. "This is my career. But everything has changed."

"Well, there'll be money to be made," Footy observed. "You've got a country to rebuild."

The Japanese turned on him.

"With my family dead? Burned to nothing? My city gone? And you think I care about money?" There was an awkward pause filled by the crashing surf.

"Sorry, I meant no harm," Footy said stiffly.

"He was trying to help," Johnny said. "There'll be millions of your people in the same situation." This time the silence stretched out until there was nothing left to say.

During the afternoon, the waves had climbed higher. Now they were giants that slammed onto the beach. The wind picked up and made the tarp crack like a whip.

Finally the Japanese spoke.

"I am sorry," he said. "This is not your fault. But I do not know if I can face this new Japan.

"Defeat is harder than war."

141

The following day, the palms shed fronds as the ocean stormed ever higher. Johnny kept carving and the shavings tumbled down the beach. Footy and Cat attempted to fish the booming breakers, but caught nothing. The men had a canned lunch.

In the afternoon, Footy tried again to fish. Cat fetched the sword and sat beside Johnny. He drew the blade from the scabbard and set it across his knees. There were patches of rust beginning to form. With a chunk of coconut husk, a rag, and some nut oil, he scrubbed for an hour until the metal gleamed.

He stood, took the long grip in two fists, and made a sweep through the air. He paused and then slashed again, this way and that, time after time.

Johnny watched while he worked. He took in Cat's stance – widespread legs, the severe face and sure strokes. Johnny admired the long curve of steel, the point an angle across the end. Behind the cutting edge, a wavy line ran the length of the blade.

"That is one fine sword," he said. Cat made another pass.

"When I was home, six days a week I must practice! At first the sword was bamboo, later wood – never *Katsumushi-maru!*

"My father was a master. He taught me himself, although I had other *sensei* – other teachers – as well.

Footy returned without any catch – the weather was too rough. He sat beside the other men.

"Mostly we drill. Practice, practice, practice! But at last – when I was good enough – my father and I cut *makiwara* together."

"Maki...what?"

"*Makiwara.* Straw tied in bundles – about as thick as your neck." He looked at Footy with a thin-lipped smile.

"It was a long time before I could cut one with a single stroke! My father did it every time."

Katsu paused.

"My father and I did not agree on some things. He had many rules – very strict! But our best time was when we cut the bundles together.

"We believe a warrior's sword is alive," he continued. He spun on his heel and cut air.

"We call this a *katana* and it has a name, given by one of my ancestors after a famous battle. It is *'Katsumushi-maru.'* *Katsumushi* means dragonfly."

"Dragonfly?" Footy said. "Sounds girly."

Cat shot him a look, sighed, took a seat and placed the blade across his knees.

"To my people, the dragonfly is the invincible one," he said. "It means war – and victory. *Katsumushi-maru* is three hundred years old. It has been in my family all this time. We know the stories – each one of them.

"It has killed more than five hundred men. You should remember its name," he said to the Australian.

"It took three masters at Bizen to make this *katana*. Each one had his apprentices. One group made the steel. The second forged the sword. The third polished and finished it.

"You see where the metal joins?" Cat held the *katana* so the light caught the wavy line. Johnny nodded.

"The edge is very hard – very sharp! This is necessary! But also, the sword must be flexible, or it will shatter. The gift of the masters is to marry the two steels."

Cat turned slowly to stare at Footy.

"When you take *Katsumushi* to your home, you must treat it with respect."

Footy felt a retort boil up but thought better of it. He wanted the blade, but he could see how much it mattered to Cat.

"Yes. I will," he said.

Katsu nodded and returned the sword to its scabbard.

142

They ended the day with another run. On the return leg, as they approached the point, Johnny was once more in the lead, but he stumbled on seaweed. The Japanese pounded by and was first to the Finish Tree, Johnny next, Footy close behind.

As the men walked back to camp, the clouds turned to pink cotton candy against a lemon sky. Within minutes, the color bled away and the rising wind blew a dark blanket across the heavens.

The men ate, then lit their fire, but the wind sucked the glowing embers toward the trees. They kicked sand to smother it and turned in. Johnny lay in his swaying hammock, while the others wrapped themselves in their bedding and put their backs to the grit.

Katsu heard the wind in his ears, but that was not why sleep evaded him. He was troubled by an inner storm. It had begun with the sword practice, but again he was drawn into the conflict between his lethal warrior self and his peaceful religious one.

Samurai tradition required that he be ready to kill himself for honor at a moment's notice. The priests forbade it, though, and taught that one who committed suicide could not enter Heaven. How could he resolve this? How had his ancestors done it?

He turned it over in his mind like a Buddhist koan – a riddle with a nugget of truth that must be coaxed out. His father had taught that the essence of a Samurai was to be of service, to give absolute loyalty to his lord. But it was a Christian family that attended the cathedral and served a different Lord. As a baby, he had been baptized, and confirmed in the cathedral as a teenager.

In a way, he'd had no choice. It was family tradition, and Katsu had not questioned it.

But in the kiln of war, and now in defeat, his once-sure beliefs were a jumble. If this atom bomb on Nagasaki had destroyed the *Urakami Tenshudo*, the cathedral, then it was all gone – the mass, the incense, statues of the saints – and, of course, the politics of the priesthood. Oh yes, Katsu had observed that the church was also a community of men jockeying for position.

Now, with all that stripped away, he was left with the image of the Christ at the center. Katsu pieced the remnants of his once-clear beliefs together, and found there was an essential core after all.

He lay in the growing storm and perceived one common element.

Service.

Jesus fed the people. He healed the sick. He comforted the suffering. Two thousand years of humanity had turned him into something else – a golden icon on a cross, hanging high in the cathedral. But there was another reality.

The God of the universe as a modest working man, on his knees, washing the feet of peasants.

Katsu had an epiphany.

That is it! Humble service. I have been blind! Only here can my warrior heart and Christian soul come together.

I must serve.

Nippon was overwhelmingly Buddhist, he knew – and did not both the Buddha and the Christ teach peace? And were they not the spiritual leaders of both Nippon and America? But the nations themselves had forgotten that. They had spoiled for the fight, put their sons in uniform, and marched them out to kill each other.

How much blood have we spilled? How many millions have been slaughtered? Can we ever learn the way of peace?

And then, through his torment, Katsu felt the tiniest flicker of hope.

My family is dead, my world is in ruins, but I can still find purpose. I can serve. This will be my peace.

His hand, again, touched the hard reality of *Katsumushi-maru* and he sent a thought to it.

It is best that I give you up, spirit of my fathers, my warrior heart. Our prideful nature has destroyed us. So, when I must, I will surrender you.

But not yet, his mind protested.

No, not yet!

143

Three men woke to tumultuous seas and clouds scudding across an iron sky. The crab migration had ended. The men spent the morning huddled in camp, watching the ocean turn to white-capped fury.

Johnny counted on his fingers and figured it was the seventh day since Chas had departed. He inspected his project. He'd carved a third away from the original desktop. What remained was all curves and golden surfaces, except for the band of carved names he'd left along the top.

This morning with the weather so rough, Footy and Cat were huddled over their coffee, smoking and watching Johnny work. Cat warmed another canned lunch.

At last, Johnny stood up with a wide smile and announced he was done. He picked up his creation and held it standing on the blunt end. It came to a point above his head, flared at his shoulders, and then narrowed again.

"It is a boat," Cat said.

"No mate," Footy said. "I know what it is."

"What's that?" Johnny said.

"I've seen a few," the Aussie said. "It's a surfboard!"

"Head of the class!" Johnny told him. "It's the first I've ever made." His finger traced the grain.

"I only had eight feet to work with. It's not as big as the Hawaii ones, but it's all I've got."

"Why'd you leave some of the names, mate?"

"So I can grip with my feet," Johnny said.

"I've known what you were up to for some time, but didn't want to spoil your fun," Footy said.

"Still, mate – you're going to surf this bloody ocean? You're as *longlong* as that crazy woman!"

"I don't know," Johnny said. "It was something to do."

"It is ready?" Cat asked. "I would like to see surf-board-ing."

"Surfing," Johnny corrected, "and it's not quite ready yet. I have to waterproof the wood. I want coconut oil, lots of it."

The three of them collected seasoned nuts, split them and chopped the meat. They took turns crushing the nutmeat, squeezing out enough oil to fill a tin can. Johnny took it and a half coconut husk to the board and scrubbed layer after layer into the wood. After each coat, he let it soak in.

Half an hour later, the surface would be all matte patches and he'd do it again.

By late in the day, the wood was saturated. The men studied the shining flanks. Even Footy had to admit that the Yank had made a handsome thing.

Johnny finally put it down. He announced that, storm or not, it was time for their run.

"Ready?" Johnny asked. They crouched. "Set – go!"

Footy and Cat exploded away, and Johnny leapt after them. For the first stretch, he was on Cat's heels. Footy ran hard beside them with barely a limp.

When they'd gone one way for fifty yards, they turned back towards the point. Johnny rushed into the lead, but, straining furiously, Cat caught up and they pounded neck-and-neck.

Then Footy seemed to fly by, going faster than Johnny had seen him run since their escape from the Valley of the Cannibals.

This time, it was Footy who slapped the Finish Tree first. He jogged in a circle, face tomato red, showing his familiar grin. Johnny and Cat grabbed bark at the same time and dropped to the forest floor. Footy threw himself down near the edge of the clearing, leaning back.

"I won!" he crowed. "I bloody won!"

Their chests heaved and for a time, there was only the sound of men gasping for air.

Johnny rolled on his side, looked at Footy and had to smile. The Aussie had a blissful look as he leaned back, eyes closed.

Johnny stretched out again, breathing hard. But then, somewhere in his mind, a warning bell jangled. He couldn't figure it out, but it wouldn't quit.

On the contrary, the alarm rose in pitch. Johnny's eyes snapped open and he stared all around.

It was absolutely serene under the widespread arms of the Finish Tree.

But his senses shouted that there was something terribly wrong! Still, he could not see it. His gaze went to Footy and he saw the man relaxed near a puddle of water.

And then it struck Johnny. Sure, there was a storm but it had not rained.

He stared around, trying to put it together. Footy sat with his legs straight out, leaning against a log in the foliage.

What log?

And suddenly Johnny knew. He jerked bolt upright.

"Footy!" he growled urgently. "Get up!"

"Why mate?" Footy said dreamily.

"Footy!" Johnny shouted and jumped up. "Get away from there!"

The pilot glanced to his right and then to his left, peering through the leaves. A change came over his face. Through caked mud, Footy saw the rows of scales.

Then the bank *breathed* – and dry mud burst from a thousand scales.

Cat jerked to his feet as though pulled by a string. Johnny took a step forward as Footy flung himself up, trying to get away from the horror that waited in the woods.

Chunks went flying. Then the massive, blunt-arrow head of the Father swung into the clearing. Murderous yellow eyes looked at the puny prey.

The men absorbed the ridged skull and the moon-scar. Their breath hissed in as they took in the rows of teeth along the jaws.

"Run!" Johnny's mind screamed, but like one of his nightmares, his mouth did not work and his feet would not move.

The Father abruptly stood off its belly and stepped fully into the clearing. Its shoulder struck a thick branch that broke like a gun going off. Another shower of clay, and its massive body was fully exposed.

The crocodile opened its jaws and let out a rumbling growl that shook their bones. They gasped in pure animal terror.

Footy leapt away from it, the impression of scales still on his hands. But the predator was swift.

It bit him.

Cat and Johnny saw the teeth go into Footy's leg. There was a crack of bone and the man screamed. The Father lifted the pilot and whipped him like a rat.

Katsu was finally able to move. He turned and ran.

Johnny was frozen by warring impulses – run for his life, or fight for his friend.

He saw the crocodile lash its head and Footy's leg tear off at the calf.

Footy's body flew through the air and slammed upside down against the Finish Tree. His good leg wedged between branches. His body hung down, arterial blood spraying in arcs from the ruined limb.

Footy's blue eyes were wide open, but Johnny could tell, they saw nothing. It came to him in a flash that his friend had died from shock alone.

Johnny's gaze fixed on the Father. The giant was so close, he could have touched its snout.

In ecstatic rage, the predator glowered back at the One Prey.

Johnny watched the thick throat contract and realized that the brute had just swallowed Footy's leg. Something twisted in him. He bared his teeth.

The fighting rage exploded and he no longer wanted to escape.

He glanced around for a stick or a rock — something to attack the beast that had just murdered his friend.

144

The Father bit the first man because it tried to run. That was all instinct. But now the reptile faced the One Prey and the urge to kill was immense. The creature before it had fur on its head, but the crocodile sniffed and knew it was in the very presence of its enemy.

The crocodile stepped to Johnny, head at the man's waist, so close its snout brushed him. Again, it rumbled so its throat and belly vibrated, and saw the creature tremble in its breath.

Johnny glanced around for a weapon and spied the thick broken branch. It was long and heavy and would normally have been too much to handle, but the man snatched it up like a sapling.

The scarred eye was right there. With every ounce of his strength, Johnny lifted the club and slammed it down. He struck the reptile square on that eye knob, so hard his own feet left the ground.

The scar had always been sensitive. Now it felt on fire.

The Father flinched and was flooded with killing rage. It blew a putrid breath in the prey's face.

The prey jumped back and raised his puny stick again.

The predator spread its jaws and rushed him.

Again, Johnny swung his club. This time, he struck the crocodile between the eyes, forehead to nostrils. The Father jerked back and sucked air through its teeth. Being hit was a new and nasty experience. Its wrath expanded beyond anything it had ever known.

Johnny saw the massive head go sideways as the teeth parted – the way the Father had taken Dingo. He jumped back. An edge of jaw struck him and he was bowled back.

The Father bit air and its teeth clashed like knives.

Johnny cocked his branch over his shoulder like an overgrown baseball bat.

The gigantic hunter saw the small creature before it, at bay. He knew it was making its last stand. During its long life, the Father had seen countless animals in this predicament. Sometimes, in the face of their imminent death, they bared their pitiful claws and teeth.

The Father opened its jaws and trumpeted its full roar. It shoved its head forward from the hulking shoulders and fixed the man in its stare.

Johnny was almost mesmerized, but not quite. He was a killer himself and a veteran of many mortal moments. And his own fighting rage peaked.

Johnny swung the club sideways, straight at an eye, the only vulnerable spot he could see on the armored creature.

The reptile saw it come, caught the stick between its teeth and jerked.

The bark ripped through Johnny's fingers, stripping skin. The crocodile crunched the branch and spit splinters.

It stepped so close its snout pressed Johnny's belt.

Gwyn flashed into his mind and he felt a stab of regret, and there was no more time.

The Father spread those vast jaws and the man stared into the dark tunnel where he soon must go.

There was a sudden blur of motion from one side. Johnny saw Cat run up, sword in hand.

On bare feet, he nimbly climbed the malformed leg and leapt astride the thick neck.

Again, the Father experienced a new sensation. It had never been ridden before. It swung its head from side to side, trying to bite what sat there, but could not turn far enough. Again, Johnny had to jump as the jaws whipped by.

Katsu had run to get his sword. As he raced to camp and back, he tried to form a plan. The *katana* was made to slash, but that had done little damage to the brute back at the swamp.

His only hope was to pierce the brain.

Katsu sat on the monster's neck, feeling its great muscles bunch under his legs. He raised *Katsumushi-maru* in both hands, point down.

The crocodile launched itself up, trying to toss its tormentor off. It rose on its tail and Johnny saw Cat on the enormous head shoot toward the branches, so high, the forelegs came off the ground.

Katsu kept his seat by laying against the skull. Then the crocodile began to fall. It slammed down so hard, Johnny felt the ground shudder.

Cat's knees gripped the neck. Johnny saw the intensity on the warrior's face as he held the blade in both hands, aimed at one eye.

"Banzai!" Cat shouted.

With all his strength, he plunged the *katana* down into the Father's moon-eye. Razor steel sliced through the eyeball, pierced the bone, then shot into the cave-like mouth. It went on until it struck the lower jaw bone and jammed.

The crocodile's jaws flew open and it bawled pure agony. Johnny gaped into the massive mouth and saw bloody steel at the back.

The crocodile's instinct for escape took over. It spun and charged for the ocean. Johnny threw himself flat as the tail swung over him. Saplings cracked as the colossus broke through the jungle. Johnny ran behind and was in time to see Cat ride the brute down the beach and into the surf. He saw that the man was still committed to his task – weight raised, hands twisting the sword in the skull.

The Father rushed into the water and rolled. Cat was thrown off and a wave crashed down and then withdrew, leaving him beached. Johnny gaped as the Father, sword standing in its eye socket, spun and snatched the man up in its jaws.

Cat struggled, but the brute gnashed its teeth together. Johnny heard the bones snap.

Another wave crashed up and over. When it foamed away, the Father stood with Cat dangling from its jaws. Reptile blood squirted up around the blade in the eye and dripped into the sea.

The next wave broke over and washed away.

The crocodile spread its jaws and the body dropped.

The Father stood awash in the South Pacific and gave a moan of abject suffering.

Johnny stood transfixed. The croc turned his way and stared at the man with its one good eye. Then it swung its head seaward in a shower of scarlet drops.

The injured beast lumbered into deeper water and gave a shudder that rippled down the length of its body. Then it wobbled and crashed over on its side. A breaker surged along it like swamping a shipwreck.

Keeping an eye on the croc, Johnny ran to Cat. He lay in the shallows, his body cratered by the cruel teeth.

Johnny crouched and took Cat up. He was amazed to find the man still alive. His chest was crushed and he bled from a dozen wounds, but his eyes were open. He put a hand on Johnny's arm.

"We – are – even," Cat breathed, and went still. Blood spilled from the corners of his mouth. Johnny had seen thousands of dead men, and he knew beyond doubt that this was one more.

He snarled in distress. Johnny carried Cat out of the water and placed him on the beach. Again, he looked at the Father. The hulk lay in the waves. Johnny left Cat and ran back to Footy. He found him where he'd left him, upside down in the tree, eyes open but unseeing. Blood still pumped from the leg stump, but the intensity had lessened.

Johnny was stricken and overwhelmed.

Snap out of it! Do something!

He stepped to Footy, grabbed his torso and lifted, and the leg came out of the branches. The torn-off calf and exposed bone were hard to take, but Johnny did not let that stop him. He laid Footy between the tree roots. With sinking heart, he saw the pool of blood and realized how much his friend had lost. Johnny figured he was looking at another corpse, and his eyes misted.

Then, beyond all hope, Footy moved. His chest heaved and he gasped air. He groaned and blinked, and then, mercifully, his eyelids closed again, but he was breathing.

Johnny knew that if Footy had any chance, it came down to what he did in the next few seconds. He undid the man's belt and yanked it through the loops. He wrapped it tightly around the thigh of the ripped leg and buckled it.

Johnny picked up Footy and ran to camp, glancing to see that the corpses of Cat and the crocodile were as he'd left them.

Johnny carried Footy up and laid him on his blanket. He lit the stove and thrust the machete into the ring. When it glowed orange, he ran back. Footy was tossing, his eyes wild. He looked down, saw the mangled stump, and screamed.

Johnny knelt, shoved him flat, and pressed the smoking blade to the wound. The flesh hissed and smoked. Footy shrieked and arched – then collapsed. Johnny worked quickly, reheating the blade and searing the stump again. There was smoke and the stench of blackened skin and scorched blood, but the bleeding slowed.

A shard of bone jutted through the stump. Johnny propped the leg on a log, raised the machete, and brought it down hard. The bone snapped clean off.

Footy stirred, moaning. Johnny grabbed the morphine from the first aid kit, jabbed the needle into the pilot's leg, and squeezed the tube. The man went limp.

Johnny wiped sweat from his eyes and inspected the leg. Bleeding looked under control, but the wound was raw.

He had only a few tricks: he poured iodine over it, dusted it with sulfa, and loosened the tourniquet. Blood oozed but didn't spurt. He waited, then cinched it again. Finally, he wrapped the injury with gauze and tape. When he was done, the stump didn't look quite so terrible. Johnny stared into the bloodless face.

He's a hair from death – what more can I do? Footy desperately needed a doctor and all he had was Johnny. For ten minutes, he watched the pilot's waxen face. Each breath could be his last.

Every few minutes, he loosened the tourniquet, waited to let the blood blow, then cinched it once more.

For the first time since the attack, Johnny found a moment to reflect. Another brilliant tropical sunset lit the western sky and it hit him hard.

This time yesterday, I was here with Footy and Cat. Now Cat is dead and Footy is close behind.

The Father found us at last.

Johnny's gaze flashed out to the crocodile, but it was gone. He jumped up and spun all around – no croc. In growing consternation, he stared further out on the ocean. Night was falling fast, and the breakers were high.

Then he saw the birds. Seventy yards out, gulls were gathering. Beneath them, the swells broke strangely. Something huge wallowed there.

It's the corpse! Johnny felt relief course through him. He watched birds land on the long dark shape and begin to peck. It was time to adjust the tourniquet again and Johnny bent to his task.

The Father is dead, he thought.

Cat gave his life to save mine.

534

145

Darkness came on. Johnny stayed by Footy and made a fire. He was too distraught to be hungry, and he lit a cigarette that he sucked down in a few drags.

Footy began to mutter and toss. Johnny brought water, raised him up, and dribbled some between his lips. Footy choked but swallowed, then sagged again and Johnny felt for his pulse. It beat, faint and ragged.

Johnny wondered when to give him more morphine. He counted how many doses were left. With the new syrettes in the cache, added to the ones he'd conserved in the swamp, there were nine tubes. He did not know how often to administer the powerful opiate. Usually, in battle, you'd give an injured man a single dose and the medics would take him away.

Too much would kill his friend. He decided to wait until he knew Footy had to have it.

If he lives.

A waning moon sailed into the storm-tossed sky. Johnny stared out at darkness, but could no longer see anything, let alone the crocodile.

There was no way he could sleep. He kept vigil all night. At regular intervals, he loosened the tourniquet. Every hour, he trickled water into Footy's mouth and was grateful that at least a little went down.

Now I'm a nurse, he thought. *This is what Gwyn did for me.*

It came to him that caring for another in this way was both intimate and impersonal – both powerful and humbling. In those hours, Johnny gained a new level of appreciation for Gwyn and all the others who had nursed him over the years.

He remembered how badly he'd treated some of them – and felt ashamed.

In the middle of the night, he realized Footy had wet his bedding. Johnny made a new bed: one blanket beneath Footy's upper body, another for his legs, with space in between. Gently as he could, he stripped Footy's shorts off, easing the cloth over the terrible injury. His patient whimpered but did not come to.

Johnny placed him on the fresh bed. At least when Footy must void he would do so on the sand. Johnny hung the damp blanket on a branch to wash another time. The night was warm, but Footy was cold to the touch, and Johnny got a blanket and covered him.

Time passed and Footy's breathing grew more labored.

He needs so much more than I can do! Johnny thought despairingly. *Where's our rescue?*

Did Chas get the message through?

The night wore on, and Johnny felt supremely alone under the cold stars. *This is why you don't coddle your feelings,* the Hard Case spoke up.

Another thought arose: *I'd give anything to have Gwyn here. She'd know what to do.*

Johnny's spirits sank lower. He thought Footy would die at any minute. In the darkest hours, the pilot let go a rattling breath and Johnny thought it was over. He grabbed the man's wrist and found no pulse. He threw handfuls of twigs on the coals for light, and held the blade of his knife over Footy's lips. When a faint mist formed, he got a lump in his throat.

The sky over the eastern sea turned from coal to ash. A sorry morning dragged in. Foam-flecked waves beat the sand. Footy began to shout and thrash in the gray light. Johnny shot him with the narcotic and held him down until he passed out.

536

Gradually, Footy's breathing grew regular. Johnny stared at the haggard face. The Australian seemed to have shrunk and aged ten years overnight. Johnny removed the tourniquet and saw that no more blood came through the bandage. He put the belt aside.

Finally, Johnny could think about his own needs. He forced himself to eat bananas and he brewed coffee.

I have to keep strong. He felt a little less hopeless in daylight, but still desperately sad. It came to him that he was mourning. *For Cat,* Johnny realized. *He should be here, busy in the kitchen.*

Dumb! his killer mind shot. *He was just another enemy, one more Jap! Not long ago you would have shot him as soon as look at him.*

At least Footy rested and Johnny began to think about the task he did not want. He drank more coffee, smoked and put it off, but at last he stood. He walked by the jeeps, down the beach, past the signal firewood he and Cat had built together. There was Footy's coconut S-O-S, for all the good it had done them.

Johnny went along the surf and saw Cat's body on the wet sand. He half-wished something had taken him in the night. Gulls stood by him and Johnny raised his arms and ran at them. They scattered and he knelt by the corpse. With revulsion, he saw crabs feeding on the ripped flesh and he drove them off.

Johnny picked Cat up and walked the route they had run together so many times. He carried him to the point near the Finish Tree and laid him on open ground. Here, Johnny would bury the dead, but first he must tend to the living. He jogged back to camp, gave Footy more water, and held his head up until he quit sputtering and slept.

Johnny selected a wedge of board from the discarded desk drawers and went back to Cat. He felt wrung out beyond endurance, but the thing must be done. He began to dig with the wood. His hands became raw and he persevered. He grew blisters and went on.

The job was especially slow because every twenty minutes, he must check on Footy. Usually he found his patient passed out, but sometimes he was semi-conscious, eyes flickering beneath the lids. Johnny did what he could for him and went back to the burial.

His arms ached and still he labored. The blisters burst and he dug deeper. In early afternoon, he stood in a pit up to his neck and considered his labor. The hole was about five feet deep and had started out wide enough, but the sides kept caving in. He sighed and shoveled some more.

At last it was ready. Johnny looked from Cat's body to the grave. He steeled himself for the task of putting him in and balked.

He was appalled by his weakness.

During the war, he'd walked away from his own dead countless times. He'd passed enemy corpses without a thought. But now he must put Cat in the hole and throw dirt on him, and he could not do it.

What is wrong with me? And then it came to him.

He was my friend!

He was absolutely shocked. When had the prisoner crossed that line?

Johnny postponed what he had to do and went back to camp. He found Footy had soiled his bed site. Johnny made up another one, washed his patient with soap and a pot of water, and moved him again. Footy tossed and moaned and Johnny injected him with painkiller and waited until it knocked him out.

Johnny took down his hammock and carried it to the grave. He spread it beside the corpse, opened it up and slid the body in. He rolled Cat in the makeshift shroud. He untied the rope from one end and put that aside.

Quickly, before he could think too much, he pushed the bundle into the pit. He turned his back and scraped the sand in. When it was full, he packed the mound down with his bare feet. He cut two saplings and used the rope to tie a cross. He stuck this in the soil at the head of the grave.

It was done, but Johnny felt the thing was unfinished. There was a need for words.

My father would have had a quotation!

Johnny wracked his mind. At last he recalled a phrase from the years back in San Diego. His parents had learned it from their Latino neighbors and it had become a tradition. It was the last thing they said to each other before his father went to sea.

"*Vaya con Dios,* Cat," Johnny said gruffly.

He nodded once and walked away.

146

Footy was out cold and Johnny took pots and soap and went to the stream. He washed in the pool, then sat, head under the bamboo spout while the water splashed over him. He filled the containers and returned.

Johnny opened a can of potatoes and ate the chunks with his fingers. He poured the broth into another pot, added water, and heated it. When it was lukewarm, he took it to Footy.

The man was white as a ghost, muttering nonsense. Johnny sat beside him and raised Footy's head on his leg. He put a spoonful of soup to the man's mouth and tipped in a little. Footy coughed and shook his head. But then, Johnny was encouraged to see, he swallowed and licked his lips. Johnny got about half of it into him, while the rest went down his chin. Johnny cleaned him up and his patient slept again.

The day drew on, and at last it came to Johnny that this was when the three of them would have gone for their run. Again, he was drenched in sadness and sat listlessly as night fell. He roused himself, lit a fire, and kept watch. He was bereft, with only the unconscious and the dead for company.

In the middle of the night, the Australian began an unintelligible conversation with unseen companions. The hours dragged on and Footy progressed through a number of states. Sometimes he lay like death. Other times, he tossed and raved.

Johnny heard a scream and sat bolt upright. He'd nodded off and in the glow of the coals, he saw Footy face-down in the sand. The Aussie had rolled off his blankets and banged his poor leg. Johnny rushed for another tube of morphine and stuck it in him. At last Footy stopped writhing and went limp, and Johnny placed him back on his bedding.

Johnny lay awake, staring at clouds, dark patches drifting across the stars.

What does it all mean?

He'd been raised in church, like he'd told Doc Mac, and he'd once believed in a loving God. That's what he'd been taught as a kid. But three years of brutal war had wrung the faith out of him.

On his very first day of fighting – the day Walt died – he'd realized bone-deep that no supernatural force was going to step in and save him.

Nothing would deflect the bullets – not the ones coming at him, or those fired by himself and his brothers-in-arms. War was all projectiles and trajectories, the physics of death.

Somewhere along that journey, Johnny stopped believing in a loving presence behind it all. But now as he stared into space, he remembered Doc Mac's words.

"God does not require your belief in order to exist."

The Hard Case protested: this was nonsense. The real world was chaos, violence and blind chance.

At school, his science teacher had taught that everything was a mindless explosion of matter. No one knew how it got started or where it was going. Ultimately, it was meaningless. Evolution boiled down to brute strength: eat or be eaten, and only the strong would survive.

Johnny pondered all this as he listened to the ragged breaths of his friend, the thin cord that connected Footy to the living world. He sat beside the fire, body drained, mind stretched to breaking point.

And then, in the darkest moment, his awareness flew into the night – as if borne upward on the palm of a vast, invisible hand.

The wind, the surf, even the crackle of the fire faded. For a moment he was sick with vertigo – and then, stillness. He was suspended in limbo, but this space was not empty. He could feel it all around him, deep and alive.

He was in blackness that burned with stars. Their light was clear and steady, as if he were high among them. Fear did not exist here. He was in a presence that felt velvet-soft and immense. It was wild and calm, and it knew him utterly. Far above the war, there was infinite peace, and he was immersed in love.

How long the feeling lasted, he could not say, but he never forgot. From that moment, he was never again afraid of dying.

But of course, he was sitting on sand. Beside him, the fire snapped. Nearby, Footy moaned in his sleep. Wind whipped the night.

What was that?

He heard from the Hard Case.

Hallucination. You've been through too much. It means nothing.

Johnny lit a smoke.

How do I go on from here?

"You live by the code." Now, that was his father's voice.

"Do unto others as you would have them do unto you."

Sure – Johnny had been taught that growing up. But all the good things in life had been kicked brutally to the ditch by war. Johnny wished that he could ask his father how the Golden Rule marched into battle – he would know – but the man was years gone now. Johnny had learned his own hard lessons in the mud of New Guinea. There, the inexperienced teenager had been forged into the fighting man he'd become.

In those jungle battles, the Hard Case emerged and he had a new rule.

"Kill or be killed."

It was not a belief, not an article of faith. It was a statement of fact.

"Fight to live! Live to fight!"

The only reason he was even alive to think these things was

because he had followed the warrior path. But now, he felt vulnerable, unraveling from within. It felt like betrayal.

Johnny put wood on the fire and lit another cigarette. He was no longer rationing.

What if we were given paradise? What if everything we could ever really need or want is right in front of us?

But wait – there's a catch. We were also given personal choice. Was that a blessing or curse? Either way, it was a heavy burden.

The Uhuli and the Mambu – America and Japan – it all comes down to tribal wars. But now we murder by the millions and our wars threaten the entire Earth.

Where is God in this war?

Again, the Hard Case spoke.

This is a fact and you know it. God does not step in to stop men from killing each other.

Johnny flicked the cigarette into the embers and watched it flare away. He seemed to hear the barest whisper, or was it the wind?

Here is the world. Live like angels or devils. It's up to you.

Footy cried out and Johnny went to him. The man's naked suffering had become Johnny's own and he hurt deep inside.

If this is what it means to find your heart, it's too much!

He could not sleep and gradually, the sky lightened in the east. The wind died and through red-rimmed eyes, he watched the beach come to life.

Later, as the sun rose, he had another thought.

Maybe we break God's heart.

147

Day dawned and Footy still lived.

Johnny mashed bananas and stirred in coconut milk. He lifted his friend's head and spooned the sweet concoction into his mouth. Footy's eyes stayed closed but he was able get some down.

"Ta," he croaked.

It was the first intelligible thing he'd said since the Father's attack and Johnny got a lump in his throat.

What is happening to me? Don't you dare go soft!

Footy's teeth chattered and Johnny brought a blanket and tucked it up to his chin. As for himself, he felt overly emotional, even tearful and again, he felt shame.

Take it easy. I've been through a lot, he reasoned. *I'm exhausted. I need sleep, and soon – but who will look after Footy?*

He wished he had a book – "The Man Who Would Be King," or "White Fang." But there were no books, and he sat by Footy and told himself what he could remember of those stories, while clouds shredded the sky.

In the afternoon, Johnny removed Footy's bandage and inspected the stump. A scab covered the seared flesh. Johnny treated it again, and wrapped it up.

"You are doing great pal," he told Footy in a hearty voice he did not feel, even though the Aussie was out cold. "A few more days of R-and-R and you'll be fine!" Footy mumbled and raised a hand. Johnny gently pressed it down.

You desperately need a doc, but at least you're eating.

That day and another night dragged by. In a new morning,

Footy was suffering, and Johnny drugged him again. He changed the bandage some hours later. He boiled a towel, wrung it out, and washed his patient.

The sun was a faint patch behind roiling clouds. The seas whipped and wind tossed the foam. Johnny watched the breakers on their endless march to shore. A sense of longing rose within him. The water monsters called him to play, and his eyes flashed to the sleek thing he had made.

He had the urge to escape into the tumult, mount his wooden wing and never come back.

Footy groaned, and Johnny abandoned the pipe-dream. The day went by, and the weather grew worse.

That night, Footy's babbling swelled to hysteria. Johnny put a hand on his forehead and found him burning. He dosed him with morphine and that quieted the man, but the heat still came off him like a furnace. Johnny decided to soak him down but found he was out of water. He pulled a burning branch from the fire and took a pot into the jungle.

He was walking fast on bare feet when he almost stepped on the snake. It coiled up and struck and it was all instinct that made Johnny jump back. He shoved the torch at the viper's head and it recoiled and slithered off the path.

Back in school, Johnny's track and field events had been sprints, hurdles and the long jump. Now he backed up a few paces, pot in one hand and stick in the other, took some running steps and leaped over the place where the snake might lurk. He jogged to the pool and returned with the water, waving the smoldering branch in front of him.

Johnny soaked Footy down, and while the evaporation cooled him, his skin was soon radiating heat again. Johnny kept at it for hours. His arms ached and his body begged for sleep, but he persisted. Day came again and on he went.

At last Footy's fever crested in a flood of sweat. After that, the pilot began to cool. His breathing grew deep and regular. Johnny saw that his skin tone was returning to normal.

Then Footy began to snore – really going at it – and for once, Johnny welcomed the sound. He no longer had a hammock, so he laid a blanket on the sand and surrendered to fatigue.

Johnny awoke in the full glare of the noon sun. He sat up, blinking. Footy's blue eyes were wide open, staring at him.

"Johnny," he rasped.

"Where's me bloody leg?"

148

"Footy," Johnny began, "I've got a lot to tell you..."

But the patient's eyes rolled, the lids came down, and he was gone again.

Johnny got up, washed his face and made coffee. He felt better for the sleep. He opened a can of spaghetti and ate it cold. He sat by Footy and studied the raging seas. There must be a massive storm out on the South Pacific, he figured. Jumbo waves curled in that reminded him of "Pipeline," his favorite run on Oahu's north shore.

Eventually Footy had a coughing fit and raised himself on his elbows. His eyes came open and stayed that way. Johnny brought him water and he drank the whole cup.

"Hungry?" Johnny asked and Footy nodded. Johnny opened a can of fruit cocktail and brought it to him.

"What the bloody hell happened?" Footy croaked.

"Not yet," Johnny said. "Eat."

He sat, raised the Aussie's head in the crook of his arm, and fed him the fruit and syrup.

"Now," Footy said when that was done, "I can see me bloody leg is gone. Talk."

"Do you remember the crocodile?" Johnny asked. Footy closed his eyes.

"No..."

"The run," Johnny said, "the Finish Tree..."

"Ah yes," Footy said, cracking an eye.

"It was there," Johnny said. "The Father. It attacked you. But you're going to make it."

"Ahh?" Footy raised his head and looked at the shortened leg.

"No more bleeding," Johnny said. "No infection."

"Ahh," Footy said in a lost voice. Johnny took a breath.

"Cat is dead."

"Dead? How...?" Footy's startled gaze fixed on Johnny.

"The Father killed him."

"And where's the sodding lizard now?"

"Dead as well. Cat killed it," Johnny said, "with his sword."

"Ahhhh," Footy breathed. He lay back and passed out.

Johnny drew the surfboard against his legs. He stroked the warm wood, fingers tracing the remnants of the names carved there, while he watched the tempest. The gulls rode the wind and he marveled at the way they dipped and soared. The rollers were incredible, and the surf hammered the beach.

Every so often, Johnny woke Footy enough to sip water. He fed him some lunch and the Aussie slept again.

Late in the afternoon, Johnny was wandering back and forth in front of the campsite when Footy called.

"I need help, sorry to say. Toilet," he explained. "Help me sit up. There," he pointed at a log. "Get me on it."

Johnny lifted the man from behind. Footy held the stump out so it wouldn't get bumped, while his heel dragged in the sand. Johnny put him on the log and walked away to give him privacy. He went to the garbage pile in the trees and chose a big can. He filled it with water and set it beside Footy so he could wash himself. When the Aussie was ready, Johnny helped him back to bed.

"Give us a ciggy," Footy said, "there's a mate." Johnny lit it for him.

"Now," Footy breathed through the smoke, "that's better. Dig me a latrine right there by the log, would you Johnny? I'd like to take care of meself from here on."

"Okay," Johnny said.

"And bring me clothes." Johnny helped him get into a roomy pair of Dingo's shorts. Then he scooped a trench in the sand behind a smooth log. He placed a few cans of water nearby.

That evening the Aussie insisted on feeding himself. Johnny propped him up and gave him a plate of mixed vegetables and baked beans. Footy ate most of it, but he was in pain. Finally he pushed it aside and clutched his thigh, sweat popping on his forehead.

"Hell's bloody bells! Morphine!" he gasped.

"Okay," Johnny said. "We've got three tubes left. That's all.

548

Three – you want one?"

"Give me half a dose, mate," Footy managed. "Right now!"

Johnny injected him with a portion of the tube. The pilot gasped hard, but after a few minutes he calmed down. He grabbed the cigarettes and smoked four in a row, lighting one from the end of the other.

"Struth mate," he said, "in the war I worried about getting killed – but this is worse."

Johnny put cigarettes, matches, and a bottle of water beside Footy. He also set the half-dose of morphine at hand.

"Anything else I can do for you?" Johnny asked.

"A pistol and one bullet," Footy muttered.

"Besides that," Johnny said. "I need sleep too. I've been up most of the time since this happened. You want something, you yell until I wake up."

He rolled out a blanket, and for the first time since the Father's attack, Johnny slept the entire night.

149

Johnny awoke to a full gale blowing and saw Footy sitting against a log, cigarette butts stuck all around.

"'Mornin', mate," Footy said, "but I can't say it's good."

"Bad night?" Johnny asked.

"The worst," Footy said, "I gave meself the morphine. I'm ready for more."

"Okay," Johnny said. "There are two tubes left."

"Bloody hell," Footy gasped. "Give me another half."

"Right away," Johnny said and got up. "From here on, you tell me when." He gave Footy the shot. "I'll put on coffee."

"Make it easy and just chop me friggin' head off," Footy wheezed.

Johnny brought him a mug of brew, then heated beef hash and cooked the last of the bananas. He told the pilot he had to provision the camp. This morning he'd haul water, get more fruit and go fishing.

"Get on with it, mate," Footy told him. While the Yank was gone, Footy dragged himself to the latrine. It took ten minutes crabbing on hands and one foot to get there and sit on the log, but he managed. Afterwards, he groaned his way back to his blankets.

By late morning, Johnny had bunches of bananas and a pile of green coconuts, one cut open for the pilot to drink. All the pots were full of water.

Johnny put on his leaf-visored helmet, took his pole and went to the ocean. It was tough casting into the booming surf, and he caught nothing for an hour. Then he hooked six pan-size snappers in rapid succession.

When Johnny got back, he found Footy asleep and was glad to see it. To be awake was to suffer. Johnny fried the fish. He ate three, covered another for Footy's lunch, and saved two for dinner.

That night, he was forced to give the Aussie another half dose of narcotic.

"One more squeeze and we're out," Johnny warned.

"Alright mate," Footy said. "Don't leave it near me or I'll use it for shore. But the pain's lessening a bit."

"That's good news."

Johnny was aware sometime in the night that there was rain drumming on the canvas over their heads. He listened to water run and the endless tumble of the breakers.

When next he awoke, clouds were blowing off a clear sky. The sun had made a comeback and blue rollers fifteen feet high washed in from the far horizon.

Footy was awake and Johnny got up and cooked. The morning passed with the patient drifting in and out of awareness. Johnny fetched the oil and rubbed another coat into his board, then sat staring at the South Pacific.

"Why don't you go on then?" Footy's voice came. "I take back what I said before – before everything." Johnny looked at him.

"To tell the truth, mate," Footy said, "I'm overly cautious around the water. Always have been. We had crocs and sharks where I grew up. I've been hearing about this and that person being taken, long as I can remember. Don't let me stop you. With the Father dead, you might as well give it a go."

"I'd like to," Johnny told him, "but there's no way."

"Why not?"

"You," Johnny said.

Footy thought about it and nodded.

"Right," he said. "I see."

"Come on," Johnny said. "That's just the way it is. You'd do the same for me."

"Don't be so shore."

"Sure you would," Johnny nodded. "That's what friends are for."

"We're friends?" Footy asked, watching the Yank.

"Yes," Johnny said.

"Good mates?" Footy pushed.

"Best buddies," Johnny affirmed. "Now shut that pie hole, okay?"

Footy lay back with what might have been a smile.

Johnny put his board aside and got him fresh water. Then he went fishing and landed a single cod. He fried it for lunch.

During the afternoon, Footy had a nasty pain attack and begged for another shot. Johnny warned him it was the end of the last tube. Footy sweated bullets and said he must have it.

Johnny injected him and waited. When Footy was able to lie back, he went and fished the giant seas some more, but nothing was biting. They had a canned dinner.

As daylight was fading, Johnny fetched his Springfield. He didn't have any ammo, but caring for his rifle was second nature. Already, there were rust patches on the barrel. He kicked himself once more for not bringing a cleaning kit. *Of course, it was a three-day mission!* But at least he had Cat's coconut oil. He polished each spot until it was smooth.

He brought the scope to his eye and panned the beach, and another realization came over him.

I will never hunt another man again.

He hadn't expected that, and he was surprised by the intensity of the feeling. It was more than the war being over. It was a key turning in a rusty lock.

I am done killing men!

At that, something suddenly released inside him – a knot he had not known was there.

How many times did I hear General MacArthur say it?

"Duty, honor, country." I have served all three. I have done my part.

An incredible realization struck Johnny. It was so big he could hardly hold it in his mind.

The atom bomb has put an end to war!

It had not hit him until just now.

How can nations fight such a thing? They can't. The mere threat of the atom bomb will make a new Hitler or Tojo throw up his hands and quit.

That's it then! he thought with wonder. This strange new world, recreated in peace, would be a better one after all. A ray of hope lit Johnny's heart.

This new bomb means war is finished!

150

Five days passed. Footy's leg continued to heal. The skies stayed blue, the breeze was stiff, and the waves were immense.

On the morning of the twelfth day since the crocodile's attack, Johnny peeled off the bandages on Footy's leg while the patient watched, both fascinated and repelled.

"Give us a good gander."

"You sure?"

"Shore I'm shore."

Johnny turned the stump this way and that while the pilot stared. The scabs were peeling off and the skin looked raw, but whole.

"Ugly as a wombat's arse," Footy observed.

"Hell of a thing to have to show the sheilas. But at least the bloody croc got the right leg – the same one I hurt in the swamp. Always look at the bright side, that's what me old Pa said!"

He pulled his lips back in a ghastly smile.

"Good job, Johnny. Thanks mate."

"Forget about it," Johnny said.

Again, he bandaged the stump. He boiled a pair of his socks, wrung them out and spread them on a log. When they were dry, he took one and rolled it over Footy's rounded calf. It made a neat cover.

"Help me up," Footy asked. "I need to start walking – or as near as a crip like me can manage."

"Sure you're ready?"

"Shore I'm ready. Give us a hand."

Johnny got Footy balanced on his sound leg. Then, as Cat had done in the swamp, he put his head under the Aussie's arm and helped him take a few steps. Footy tried gamely, but soon was gasping. His face sagged and Johnny carried him to his blanket.

"That's a good start," Johnny encouraged him as he helped the man lie down again. Footy turned away.

"I'll try again later," he muttered.

And the following morning, he did. With Johnny half carry-ing him, he managed a dozen steps before he needed to rest.

Johnny thought he'd make him another crutch. He searched the forest for the ideal forked sapling and cut it. He tore strips off an old blanket, wound a thick pad over the crotch, and tied it tight.

The next time Footy wanted to walk, Johnny got him up and tried it under his arm.

"This feels too bloody familiar," the Aussie griped, but now he was able to take some steps on his own. Then he lost his balance and started to fall. Johnny jumped to him and propped him up.

"Crikey!" Footy gasped. "I'm seeing firecrackers!" Again, Johnny had to help him onto his bed.

"Bloody hell," the Aussie mumbled, staring at what was left of the leg that had once kicked goals. "I'll never be 'Footy' again."

"But that's not right," Johnny told him. "Now it fits better than ever.

"Now you really are Footy."

151

Three more days, and the pilot could get around camp on his own. He went back to broadcasting their S-O-S and hailed Rutherford repeatedly, but got no reply.

By Johnny's count, it was seventeen days since the Father's attack, and twenty-two since the Brit had left. The skies were blue, but the wind blew all the time and the monstrous waves continued. It seemed to be a change of seasons, one that had a negative effect on the fishing. Johnny was forced to devote long hours to the attempt, and just managed to land enough to keep them going. He lost three more hooks to barracuda.

There came a morning when Johnny woke to find Footy on his crutch behind the stove. He'd made coffee and was cooking "brecky," chunks of fish fried with crumbled hardtack.

After they ate, they smoked and watched the day. Again, Johnny found himself holding his surfboard.

The breakers frothed shore-ward in dangerous mountains whose tops curled over on themselves.

The barrel!

Johnny dropped the board on the sand and stepped onto it barefoot, testing his stance. His knees were bent, arms wide, and the rhythm came back in a rush. The wood was slippery with oil, but the center carved with names gave him grip.

Footy watched and spoke again.

"Look Johnny, give it a go, mate," he said. "I can see how much you want to. I insist. The truth is, I'd like to see you surf."

"Are you sure?" Johnny asked. Footy smiled broadly.

"Shore I'm bloody shore! If a big shark, or even the Father's brother, gobbles you up, I'm right now. No worries! I don't need you."

"Thanks," Johnny said dryly.

"No mate, I'm serious," Footy insisted. "Have a go!" At last, Johnny gave in.

"Okay!"

Footy grinned as he studied the Yank. Johnny was barefoot, wearing his well-worn shorts. The Yank smiled broadly, show-ing white teeth in a deeply tanned face, wavy black hair streaked by the sun. He'd filled out since they got to the beach.

Johnny whooped, grabbed his surfboard, and sprinted for the ocean. He ran into the surf, got on his board laying down, and paddled seaward. The first big wave broke over him. It felt like coming home.

He paddled on and shot up the next swell. It broke over his head and he was underwater, suddenly assailed by doubt.

Will it float? Will it carry my weight? And then – *do I even remember how?*

It had been four years since he'd been a rider of oceans. He hadn't been on a board since December 7, 1941. That morning, he'd run for Pearl, directly into hell.

Now he exploded up into sunlight and knew with a thrill that the wood floated high. In fact, it was lighter and more buoyant than his old board.

Footy sat on his log. He cheered while his mate disappeared into the windswept South Pacific.

152

The water rose and Johnny rode it like an elevator. The nose of his board cut the top of the wave and he spilled down the far side. Every nerve tingled and he felt fully alive. He raised his head, body resting on the board, and paddled.

Footy watched the Yank go out of sight, and there was the lad again, zooming up the face of an incoming roller. The swimmer paddled on and was out of view much of the time.

Johnny was flushed with anticipation. He recalled this feeling – the twined cables of fear and excitement. The anticipation grew in him for the sweet instant he would stand. During the war, all this had been forgotten, left behind, but now he was totally engaged.

Footy watched his mate become a dot on the blue. The Yank was out sixty yards.

Over deep water, Johnny turned to face the beach. He waited, hands gripping the edges of his board, ready to stand. He glanced over his shoulder for his ride. A swell threw him up a dozen feet and he let it pass. He studied the waves frothing toward him, looking for the right one.

And there the big boy came, churning from the open sea — a bearded giant roaring above the others. Johnny watched sunlight sparkle along its flanks, glowing turquoise within. Thirty yards from him, the top frothed in a mane that arced over and spilled down its face.

Johnny's heart beat fast as the breaker tossed him at the sky. He stood up on the wood, toes gripping, and at once he was moving. The surfboard shot landward while he struggled to find his balance. It had been years! But Johnny had been an expert rider, and now he stood to his full height. He adjusted his feet and raced with the wave.

The board responded like a live thing and Johnny laughed with delight. He bent his knees and balanced. He whipped through the wind, water frothing along the edges of his board. He held himself loosely, one foot forward, arms bent, hands out to either side.

He was twenty feet over the trough, all the power of the untamed Pacific beneath him. The pent-up stress of the last days burst out of him in a hoarse yell.

"Yeeeee-ha!"

Footy watched the great wave come with the tiny shape flying on it. As it churned towards the beach, the surfer grew in size. Footy had never admired Johnny more than he did right now.

The Yank's ability with a rifle was something, and the Aussie had been more impressed than he'd let on. But to see Johnny arrow through the ocean on a bit of wood put him in an entirely new league! In spite of Footy's personal crisis, his heart soared.

"Ace! Good on ya mate!"

For a few magical minutes, his own suffering was forgotten.

Johnny watched the land get closer and there was Footy. The breaker thundered over the shallows and the curl collapsed on itself.

Time to get off this train.

A stab of regret shot through him. It had been a great first run. He tipped the nose up, the wave left him behind, and he sank into the froth.

The water unrolled in a carpet along the sand. Another fell on it, and both boiled away. Footy saw the dark head bob on the waves. Johnny raised a hand and paddled out again.

An hour flew by as the Aussie watched his mate make run after run. Sure, he wiped out a few times, but he got in a lot of runs as well.

It was a treat to watch.

Johnny was absorbed in the dance with his board. The one thing he wished was that he could maneuver better, and turn! If only he could cut sideways along the flank of the roller, he could stay ahead of the crashing whitewater. But that wasn't the way it worked. Surfers just mounted their long boards and rode straight in. That was the way it had been done since time immemorial.

Still, the thrill was spectacular! The sense of time passing disappeared and the war washed out of him. Temporarily at least, the South Pacific gave him back his lost youth.

One of the things Johnny loved about surfing was the concentration. There was no daydreaming on the board! It took all his attention to stay in the bright world.

Let fear get the whip hand, and the dark power would take him down. The same strength that carried him could just as easily grate him on the coral.

To surf meant to balance on the knife-edge between ecstasy and terror – and that's what made the ride so sweet.

Johnny noticed the passage of the hours when all his muscles trembled. He was surprised to see another full-blown sunset painting the sky.

There was time for one more run. He picked a water bull, let it buck him to shore, and burst out on the sand. He tucked the board under his arm and trotted to camp.

"Struth mate!" Footy crowed. "Don't get a big head, but you're a ripper out there!"

Johnny laughed and went to rinse off.

153

Now Johnny had a new routine. He'd awake at dawn, brew coffee, fish for a couple of hours, then make breakfast and provision camp.

All he wore these days were his shredded shorts. When he fished, he added his sun-visor helmet against the glare. In the afternoon, Johnny grabbed his board and rushed into the surf. He'd be gone for hours.

In the evening, he'd check Footy's wound, and they'd sit by the fire and he'd describe the day's runs. There was an issue he and the pilot talked over ever more frequently. If only Johnny could find a way to steer his board! He'd remembered something a sailor had told him years ago. Hadn't the man said something about a keel?

"Bloody right mate. Without a keel, no sailboat can turn. You're just a tub in the waves. Same with aircraft, but upside down. The plane's tail keeps it stable and lets you turn. Without it, there's no control."

"Maybe I could mount a board sticking down?" Johnny said, "but still, how would I turn?"

"Well mate, when a boat heels, it automatically turns on the keel. Use your feet. Why not try that?"

"I've got to figure out how I'd attach it," Johnny said. "I don't have a lot to work with."

They got ready for bed. When they awoke in the morning, Johnny had a plan.

"I've got an idea," he said, and he talked it over with Footy.

"You've come to the right place, mate. I'm a born mechanic!" They put their heads together.

Johnny fetched another plank from the broken desk drawers, about a foot and a half long by a foot wide. Using his bayonet knife, he took the morning to carve this into a rounded-edge triangle.

"Like we said, looks like a shark fin," Footy said.

Johnny got his board and had Footy hold the keel upright on it. Johnny drew an outline with a stick of charcoal. Then he used a coconut to pound on the pommel of the knife, scoring the wood along the mark, then cutting deeper. Eventually, the blade cut through the other side and he kept working.

From time to time, he tried the fin in the hole. Footy held it in place while Johnny pounded it with a husk. At last it popped in – a good tight fit. Footy suggested he use the metal angle braces and screws from the desk to secure it on the bottom of the board. In short order, Johnny got that done.

"You might make a mechanic yet, mate," Footy told him.

His next time on the water, Johnny tried it out. It worked like a charm! Now when he torqued his legs, the point rotated, and the board shot in the direction he wanted to go. Then he used his weight to carve a turn and swooped back in the opposite direction. Soon he was riding in a new style, all over the face of the waves.

"It's a hundred times better," he enthused that night.

The following day, Johnny went surfing again. On his most recent run, he caught a magnificent comber whose top curled into a liquid tunnel. Johnny guided his feet so he was zipping along just in front of it.

A glance back showed him the tube, big enough to crouch in. He shifted weight onto his back foot, the board slowed, and he was inside. The light went green and water whooshed over his head. Bathed in mist, Johnny reached a hand and trailed fingers through the briny wall. When he shifted his weight forward, he shot into sunlight again.

From camp, Footy watched his mate ride with a cockiness which was dazzling. When Johnny came to the beach now, he spun the board with his feet, jumped in the water behind it, and paddled out to sea once more.

Alone in camp, the Australian forced himself to walk a little more each day. It was an arduous and painful process. He put on a brave front, but inwardly, he was seriously depressed. Johnny might be having some fun, but here he was with a truncated leg. He had to spend most of his time lying down, or at least propped against something. During the long hours, he tried to grapple with his future. What ate at him was the change from being an able-bodied fellow, to a one-legged cripple.

His one respite was watching Johnny surf. But when Yank-gazing got to be too much, he found himself searching the skies.

Where is our bloody rescue? Will it ever come?

And then what, mate?

I'll get meself to Aus, visit the relatives. Get fitted for a false leg. At least you've still got the knee. That will help. It was meager comfort.

You can still fly a plane, he encouraged himself, *don't let anyone tell you otherwise! You can still work the cargo business. Now you've got the perfect excuse to let others do the heavy lifting!*

He distracted himself by limping to the water and doing some fishing. Now he cooked more than Johnny did, but try as they might, neither came close to matching what Cat had been able to conjure up.

When it came to culinary creations, the prisoner had been some kind of artist.

154

Johnny was home – the bungalow covered in flowering bougainvillea. The scent of his mother's Saturday cooking filled his senses.

A sun-browned boy in shorts and Hawaiian shirt sat at the table. Mom was at the stove, making French toast. She brought a plate over and set a pitcher of warm maple syrup with it.

Dad came down the hallway. He was in his officer's uniform, cap on, hair neatly trimmed, rows of color bars on his chest. He was an executive who commanded thousands of men on a battleship and he looked like it.

"Smells like heaven!" he said, grinning at Mom.

His mother gave him her special smile. The man came and stood behind the boy. Johnny smelled his aftershave and felt strong hands on his shoulders.

"What's my Number One son up to today?"

"Your only son," Johnny responded – their old joke. "Going surfing on the north shore. Surf's up!"

Mom frowned.

"Oh, I wish you wouldn't!" she said. "I heard there's been another shark attack!"

"Mom!" The boy protested. "That was Maui!"

"Come here," Dad told her kindly. Mom brought a plate of toast for her husband and put it down. She placed a hand over his on their son's shoulder.

"I worry, is all," she said.

"Now, Honey," his father asked, "who do you see at our table?"

"My favorite boy," she said.

"You better look again," Dad smiled. "I see a man."

The dreamer watched his teenage self sit a little taller.

Dad put his arm around Mom's waist. She turned to him and their lips met. It was a quick kiss, but Johnny saw the love and his heart ached.

"I guess you're right," Mom said and looked at Johnny. "I guess I have to let you go."

"What are you waiting for?" Dad asked. "Vaya con Dios, son!"

Johnny opened his eyes and there was the magnificent ocean. The thundering waves invited him in.

155

A week since he'd started surfing again, Johnny was floating in deep water when a fist of fear squeezed his heart.

His sea legs were sure once more. He'd made six exhilarating runs and was waiting for his seventh. As usual, he was watching over his shoulder for the ideal ride when the scare came.

Fear, he knew well, was the surfer's dark companion. Sometimes the sense that a mouthful of giant teeth rushed up from below got the better of everyone. Johnny had felt it often enough in the past. It was nothing to be ashamed of, his Hawaiian buddies told him.

"Fear of the Landlord," they called it. Maybe today he'd come collect his rent. Sometimes the jitters got so bad, a guy had to call it quits and get onto dry land.

Why the shivers got him now, Johnny didn't know. He looked into the depths and saw his rippled legs against spears of light that met at a point below.

Catch the next wave! Sometimes when he stood up, the dread faded and he could keep going. Other times, it grew to near-panic and he had to get out.

Footy squinted into the light, trying to find the surfer in the raging peaks.

A swell broke over Johnny's head and the jitters got worse.

Okay, he told himself. *Take the next train to the station and get off!*

He was staring out at the rollers, and Footy was too far away to see.

A silver ball rose gleaming from the sea. It parted the water and threw drops like gemstones. A gleaming shaft rose out of the blue.

The blade sliced towards the surfer.

Johnny was facing away and did not see it.

Ten yards from the man, the shaft went down like a periscope. Now it was a sliver ball under the surface, trailing bubbles.

Over his shoulder, Johnny saw the monster he'd been waiting for.

156

He gripped his board as the breaker rushed up, shedding foam. He gauged the distance and tensed to rise. He was looking into the aquamarine wall when it was eclipsed by darkness. Something huge moved inside the wave and blocked the light.

The water rose like a wall and flung him up. He got on his feet, glanced back, and felt the stab of shock.

Rising out of the swell was the Samurai sword!

It rose in the liquid chaos, but Johnny was moving fast. He had to pay attention forward, or he'd be back in the sea.

He shifted his feet and sent his board shooting along the concave wall. The instant he could, he glanced back and saw the sword slicing after him.

Shock turned to terror when he took in the immense darkness behind it.

Again, Johnny had to look where he was going. Next time he could glance back, his heart raced.

Rising through the froth came the gleaming head of the Father. Cat's sword quivered in the empty eye socket, deep in the moon-scar.

The crocodile's one good eye stared at the surfer.

Johnny shifted his weight and fishtailed away. But the crocodile swept above him on the rising wall, water coursing through the scutes on its back.

The Father unsealed its nostrils and sniffed. Here was the One Prey! That knowledge even penetrated the anguish that speared its head.

The giant lunged at its prey and bit, but the animal dodged away. The clash of its own teeth rattled through the reptile's skull.

The Father whipped its tail and surged after him, the immense body sweeping as it drove forward. The crocodile was more at home in the ocean than the man could ever be, and it was immeasurably stronger.

And faster.

Long teeth slid along the surfboard's edge.

Footy sat grinning on shore. He'd seen the magnificent wave come and reckoned that this was the one his mate would take. Sure enough, Johnny rose on it and began the dance.

"Beauty!"

Footy lost sight of the Yank behind other waves – but there he came, going like a kangaroo at full hop.

A heartbeat later, all the joy died in Footy. He saw the dark monstrosity that chased his friend.

"The Father!" Footy shouted, his gut in free-fall. He jumped to his feet, forgetting there was only one of them.

He twisted and slammed down hard. Pain erupted and he rolled on his side and strained up. He got a glimpse of Johnny, the croc rushing right beside him. Footy grabbed his crutch and beat on the log.

"Come on, mate!" he shouted, "Faster! Much faster!"

Johnny fought valiantly to stay in front, but it was like a fly trying to outrun a bull.

"Come on Johnny," Footy fretted, climbing up on the crutch. "Come on!" Again he caught sight of the Yank, a nose ahead of his pursuer.

Footy had watched Johnny hone his new moves on his modified board for days, but he'd never seen anything like what the surfer did now! He was cutting the most inspired turns, using every bit of the wave.

Johnny knew the croc was too close. Desperately, he pointed his board straight down and dropped. Almost in the trough, he cut ninety degrees and rocketed along, working his legs to increase speed.

The Father caught up.

Johnny turned the nose up, crouched, and flew just in front of the snout. The wake washed over the reptile's head and instinctively, it closed its underwater eyelids. In the empty socket, the membrane sliced deeper on the razor edge. A dagger plunged into its brain and it lost sight of the One Prey.

Johnny flew up the breaker and ducked into the curl. The Father raised its head from the water, questing from side to side with its single eye.

Johnny's world was reduced to a green cone with a bright oval ahead. He barely caught his breath before he glanced down. Again, adrenaline spiked.

Darkness rose through the water below.

Johnny flashed into sunlight just as the Father's head came up behind. It snapped and this time, the teeth clashed against the butt of the board. The surfboard yawed and Johnny swung his arms, fighting for balance. He managed a turn as the croc bit again. It missed, but the sword almost sliced his leg on the way by.

Footy watched both Yank and croc burst out of the tumbling white water at the crest of the wave. The jaws opened as wide as Johnny was tall.

At the very last instant, the Yank seemed to jump right out of the mouth.

"Great hairy bollocks!" Footy screamed. "Get cracking!"

An intervening wave cut off his view and he squirmed with anxiety.

Johnny had used every trick he knew – even some new ones – and it wasn't enough. A flick of his eyes showed forty yards to the beach.

The boulder of the Father's head swept up with the sword quivering. The good eye glared and the croc swung its snout against the board. Johnny teetered, stood on one leg, and barely recovered.

The Father was too vast a foe. He could not outrun it, and for sure, he could not fight it.

Again, it slammed the surfboard with its head and Johnny dropped to his knees just to hang on. That slowed him, and the predator surged from behind and went underwater. Johnny stared down as the massive head moved under him. The sword was cutting the surface and grated against the wood. Now the Father's snout was in front of the surfboard and it began to rise. In a second, the man would be standing on its head.

Johnny did the only thing he could.

He stood and twisted, stepping on his back foot. His board spun a hundred and eighty degrees. The blade peeled off a shaving. Then Johnny was flying in the reverse direction, on the hunter's blind side.

The Father lunged through the surface, but the man had vanished. The reptile raised its half-blind head and swung it, staring for the One Prey.

The wave continued to bowl for the beach and Footy watched man and monster get close. His heart was in his mouth when the croc knocked his mate to his knees. He saw it go beneath the Yank. At the last instant, Johnny spun and his board skipped down the Father's flank.

"Sweet bloody yes!" Footy shouted.

Johnny's legs were shaking. This was the most challenging run he'd ever made – and it wasn't over. If he could reach the beach, and it was close, what then? His adversary was no fish – it would come out on its legs just like he did. He knew already, this croc could run. He'd seen it at Bumay's village.

But there was no time to think. He carved another turn to avoid the tail swerving at him.

Beyond, the waves petered out in foaming water. Johnny had to turn again and push for momentum.

Now he was just behind the crocodile's head again.

The Father had not spotted him yet. The nose of the board came parallel with the hulking shoulders. Again, Johnny shifted his weight to slow himself, but at any second, he'd be discovered.

His muscles cramped and his chest hurt. In dire straits, he formed a familiar plan.

Run!

"Where the hell are you?" Footy chewed a knuckle. The roller carrying the croc swept over the shallows and fell apart.

Johnny shot out of the surf onto the beach with the croc looming over him.

"Go mate, go!" Johnny heard that. The ocean spat him out and wood ground on sand. As Johnny leapt off, he kicked the board back between the monster's open jaws.

The Father chomped brutally. Splinters burst in its mouth, but there was no sweet bloom of blood. It grunted and shook its head, sending the ruined board flying.

Johnny knew Footy was helpless at camp and he ran another way. The Father raised up off its belly and chased at full run. Its clubfoot was clumsy, but it had healed. For short distances, it could run as fast as a racehorse.

Johnny heard the massive pounding and knew it was on his heels. The snout nudged his leg. Instantly, like the pass receiver he'd been in high school, he faked one way, and jumped the other.

His attacker followed the feint and its four thousand pounds drove it on. Johnny gained precious seconds. He dashed by the boulder where his fishing rod leaned. He had no weapon, but saw his helmet, snatched it up and jammed it on. The leaf visor fell off.

Now the Father both scented the One Prey and saw the Smooth-headed man. All its suffering made the urge to kill hit a crescendo.

Footy watched helplessly as Johnny and the croc blasted towards the point and into the trees. He could not see what was happening, and that was the worst!

Johnny ran blindly, branches tearing at him. The Father smashed through everything in its way. Johnny thought to climb a tree, but he'd have to pause and that would be it. He burst onto the river.

The Father was right behind and its massive weight made the bank collapse into brown water, almost taking the giant with it.

Again, Johnny gained precious seconds while the reptile scrambled, huge claws throwing clumps of clay.

Johnny was running as fast as he could, but the crocodile caught up and swung its immense head, clipping the man across the hips.

Johnny shouted as he flew sideways and smashed down.

From camp, Footy heard the faint cry and guessed the worst. Cussing madly, he scrambled to his feet and got his crutch under his arm.

Johnny was on his knees, winded, and bleeding from a dozen scrapes.

There was nothing left to do but stand and face the Father.

157

Ever since its foot had been blown off, the Father had suffered. But the penetration of its head caused unending torture. After it had killed its attacker, it had come to, floating far out to sea. It tried to swim, but the effort caused unbearable agony and again, it lost consciousness.

When next it was aware, it was beached against a coral head. It lay near death, awash in hurt, while light and darkness rolled over it in their turns.

The pain did not cease, but little by little, the reptile regained some energy.

The Father's instinct was to find its territory and hide. It began to swim, and after some time, it found itself in familiar waters in a place it knew well, and it continued toward the Big River.

But then, as the giant swam, it encountered the very creature that *was* its suffering. It tasted the ocean and knew the One Prey.

Then it saw the man himself, and wrath overwhelmed its wretchedness. By water and then by land, it chased him down and here he was at bay. The puny animal could not escape.

It bellowed triumph and bared its teeth for the kill.

But then the One Prey removed its head and struck him with it. Stars popped and the reptile was shaken along its length.

Johnny ripped off his helmet. He'd grabbed it for some protection, out of years of habit. It was all he had, and now it was his only weapon. He stepped to the crocodile and slammed the steel down – right on Cat's sword. The *katana* plunged deeper into the jawbone and it pierced a major nerve. Fresh blood surged into the eye crater and spilled down the great cheek.

Thunder clanged all through the Father's skull and its monovision jittered.

The man leapt away again, but the croc was after him.

Johnny began to count out loud:

"One – two – *three!*"

He jumped high into the air, as hard as he could, and threw forward his arms and legs.

The Father was five times as long as the man was tall: it surged up to take the prey in the air. It rose on its tail while its great hind legs drove it on, and its snout struck the man in the back.

Johnny shot forward and fell to earth, his hunter coming down behind him. His toes touched dirt and he lunged forward. He sprawled face down, winded and helpless, and glanced over his shoulder as the croc thundered down.

Johnny saw a blurred silhouette, forelegs spread wide.

The head slammed hard behind his feet.

And kept going down.

Beneath the beast, the forest floor flew open, displaying a deadly reception.

The massive body crashed into the spear-lined pit. It struck with such force, Johnny heard the pops as the razor points burst through the belly. Air rushed from the Father's lungs in a sound like a groan.

The Father found it had fallen into jaws far greater than its own. It felt the teeth bite in, all through its body.

Johnny rose to his feet on the far side of the pit and turned to watch the impaled creature. Thirty feet away, its tail thrashed impotently on the track, but the head and torso were nailed down.

The Father gazed at the One Prey through its Cyclops eye. In fact, it had no choice. Its head was fixed.

Johnny brushed himself off with shaky hands. He was truly banged up, but that was insignificant beside what he was looking at – the hunter that had tracked him all the way down the Raub River.

The Father was skewered. Hind claws ripped the mud and

the whipping tail knocked a palm out by the root, sending coconuts flying.

Johnny hunkered near the pierced head. The beast continued to jerk, but every move only drove it further down the hollow lances. Johnny heard the reptile's lifeblood gurgling out and pooling in the pit.

The Father stared at the One Prey as the points penetrated its inner sanctums. When they pierced a particularly sensitive organ, the beast hissed and shuddered so that the ground shook.

A voice spoke behind him.

"I thought the bleedin' Father got you, mate. Bloody happy I was wrong!"

Johnny turned and there was Footy dripping sweat, leaning on his crutch. He'd come through the plantation. Johnny managed a weak smile.

"You're in time for the end."

Footy limped closer and stared at the ruined carnivore. He sat on the edge of the pit with Johnny and they watched.

Peaks began to form under the scaled back and neck. The hide rose as if on tent poles, and then the angled razors cut through. They burst into sunlight, slick and red.

The Father's upper jaw jerked open. In the gory cavern, the men saw the glistening bamboo columns, Cat's sword shining at the back.

The single eye mesmerized Johnny. Strangely, it began to bulge. Then a point burst through, squirting liquid.

"Whoa!" Johnny breathed.

"Stone the crows!" Footy exclaimed.

The bellows breaths slowed and grew labored. At last the brute convulsed, causing spears to shudder and crack. The reptile quivered along its length. Blood gushed from its eye sockets and nostrils and pumped around the great teeth.

The Father's blind head slid down the spikes and it gurgled a great sigh. The dragon tail swung a final time. The body clenched like a mighty fist, relaxed, and went still.

The Samurai sword shivered in the scarred eye socket.

"Hell's – bloody – bells!" Footy breathed.

Johnny reached down and placed his hand on the iron head.

"This time for sure," he said, "the Father is dead."

158

A wide-body Empire-class flying boat soared along the New Guinea coast. The pilot manned the controls while the co-pilot handled navigation. Two crewmen sat in a lower passenger compartment and gazed through the windows.

Flying low, they approached the delta. From a long way off, the aviators had observed the muddy stain on the South Pacific that marked the egress of the Raub River.

During the war, the aircraft had done time with the Royal Australian Air Force. Recently it had been returned to its owner, the Queensland and Northern Territories Aviation Service – better known as "QANTAS." Operating a flying boat required significant training and skill, and the crew had remained with their craft.

With the end of war, the airline was frantically busy. But at last, management had responded to multiple requests for assistance from the Allied Army in New Guinea.

The crew had been given one day to fly to the Raub and re-trieve three survivors of something called "Operation Teeth."

"There's the Raub," the co-pilot called. "Righty-oh," the pilot said and banked the mighty four-engine plane so he could see down. "This is it, mate! This is where the Coast Watcher said the men would be."

"There!" the co-pilot called. A thick column of smoke had just ballooned over the trees.

The plane shot across the band of brown river water and a strip of green, and there was the beach. A glance showed a bon-fire burning, two jeeps, and an S-O-S on the sand.

The aircraft thundered over and came around for a closer look. From a hundred feet up, the aviators saw two men waving.

Again they were by. A line of jungle, and they turned over the Raub. They came back at treetop level and were treated to a startling sight. An enormous headless skeleton snaked among the trees! The pilot was reminded of dinosaur bones he'd seen in a museum.

Again, the plane fired through the smoke. A bare-chested man stood at the fire, waving his arms. Beside him was a smaller bloke waving a stick. Seemed he had only one leg.

At the sound of engines, Johnny had dropped his fishing pole and rushed to camp. Footy was there and he grabbed a branch from the fire and hopped down the beach. He shoved it into the long-prepared kindling and at once, flames leapt up.

The aircraft filled the sky and looked like the best thing they'd ever seen.

The flying boat roared over the ocean, turned, and came back.

The rollers were large, but in the last week, the storm had abated. Still, it was going to be a tricky landing. The amphibious craft skipped across them, and fell in.

There was a great splash and the blast of engines. A metal snout appeared in the surf, and then, wings. Props whipped the water as the craft powered for the beach.

Johnny and Footy went down to meet it.

The pilot slowed just offshore, waited for the next wave, and rode it onto the sand. Two crewmen dressed in crisp white shirts and shorts jumped barefoot out a lower door, grabbed hold of a pontoon and pushed.

Four engines died and the propellers stopped. A forward door opened in the fuselage, a set of metal stairs was hung, and one after the other, the pilots climbed down. Four airmen came to greet the castaways.

"You're a sight for sore eyes!" the tall one called in a wicked Yank accent.

"About time, mate!" the one-legged freckled fellow beamed. "What the hell took you so long?"

"G'day mate," the pilot grinned. "Fact is, we only just heard about you. Good to see you blokes. But we were told there were three of you?"

"Our prisoner didn't make it," the Yank said shortly. The pilot nodded and introduced himself and the crew. Everyone shook hands and the one-legged chap was most enthusiastic.

"Beaut to see you, mate! Tickled pink!"

There was a strange site near the surf – a massive white croc skull beside a roll of skin.

"Not to rush you," the pilot said, "and you do have a lovely spot – but we better shake a leg. If the waves get any bigger, we may all be here for days. Can we load anything for you?"

"I spotted a long set of bones on the river as we flew in," the co-pilot said. "I take it that's the brute's head down there? What's the story?"

"Yeah — about that," the one who introduced himself as Johnny said. "We do have some luggage, and we'll need your help to get it aboard."

"No bloody worries!" A muscular crewman clapped the Yank on the back. "How many bags can you blokes possibly have?"

Everyone got a chuckle.

159

The engines climbed in pitch as the aircraft lumbered over the Owen Stanley Range, on course for Port Moresby.

On the far side of the mountains at last, it tilted into the long descent. The pilot turned the controls over to his colleague and walked back from the flying deck. He passed the crewmen playing cribbage, came down the steps to the lower compartment, and stood studying his passengers.

The Yank and his one-legged mate were sprawled across the seats, asleep. Their hair was wild, they had stubble on their cheeks and chins, and they were about as sun-cooked as two blokes could get.

The Yank wore torn shorts made from Army pants and an unbuttoned shirt with the sleeves gone. The pilot glimpsed a scar going down his torso. Around his neck was a chain with metal tags, and a big croc tooth. Across his lap was a well-worn rifle. He had two knives in his belt, one a long cane cutter.

The Aussie wore a rag of a shirt and shorts. He had a brimmed hat over his eyes, and another big knife at his waist. The stump of his leg, capped in a sock, was propped on the cushions. The carved stick that was his crutch lay on the floor. Near it were two well-worn backpacks.

Bloody pirates! the aviator thought. *Blimey! I wouldn't want to run into them late at night on the Sydney wharf!*

His attention went to the rest of their "luggage." Coiled behind them was the roll of a massive scaled hide, tied with rope. He peered at the even more dreadful item beside it – a huge skull, all white bones and teeth.

The Father! He wrinkled his nose.

What a pong! Worse than low tide!

The pilot had balked when the men told him what they intended to bring aboard. His passengers were scheduled to disembark in Moresby, but he had to go on to Aus! The bigwigs would not like the stench, and he would get an earful.

But there was an impasse. The castaways refused to board without their treasure. They wore him down, and anxious to leave, he gave in. It was one of the stranger loads he'd ferried, but then, he'd grown up on a cattle ranch. Truth was, interesting cargo did not put him off. He'd help these men and take his lumps later.

While they wrestled the artifacts aboard, the castaways spun a fantastic tale of their long journey down the Raub river, Valley of the Cannibals along the way, and this bloody great brute chasing them. The croc had killed their Japanese prisoner and just about done Footy in as well. The pilot stared down at the lad sleeping and felt pity.

My word! Poor bastard is lucky to be alive!

The Yank had filled them in on the croc while they loaded.

580

Once the brute was dead, the men had managed to chop off its head. They'd rigged ropes and rolled it on palm logs into the ocean. The fish and crabs had done the rest.

Great bloody teeth! Same with the hide – skinned, soaked in saltwater and sunbaked.

It had all taken weeks, but then, as they said, what else did they have to do?

The pilot shook his head and returned to the cockpit.

160

Light played through the cabin and Footy drifted in and out of awareness. He'd been dreaming of the gorgeous girl in Moresby – the one he'd been after these two years.

Gwyn is a real ripper! What a beauty! In the last months, even though she hadn't fully spelled it out, he'd gathered she was planning to stay on permanently. From the get-go, the nurse had made it clear she would have nothing to do with a soldier, which Footy was when he met her. But once he'd left the army, he'd reckoned he had a real chance with Gwyn.

Just before this buggered mission, he'd proposed marriage, but she'd turned him down – *just for the moment,* he told himself. He hadn't mentioned her to Johnny for that very reason. *No bloke wants to look like a loser.*

But back there on the beach, he'd had plenty of time to sort through his options. Perhaps he still had a fighting chance with Gwyn!

She's a nurse, and I am a man in need of her skills. Instead of the worst thing that's ever happened to you, mate, this leg could be your saving grace!

He had truly enjoyed his bachelor years, hanging about with his mates. But eventually a lad had to grow up, do the right thing.

During his convalescence, Footy had renewed his determination to launch his cargo business. He would make Port Moresby home base, and spend his time hopping to Queensland and back.

With the war done, the place will come back to life. There'll be more people – more shops opening, more of the comforts a woman wants.

All of it meant more demand for factory goods from Aus, plantation produce to fly the other way, and passengers coming and going.

This was the right time to set up a house and take a wife. *I need someone who can get along in New Guinea, where it is obviously a bit raw. Who better than a woman who already knows what it's like – who's already here? Someone with her own interests and friends.*

Being a pilot, he'd be away from home a lot of the time. *Gwyn's the ideal choice – if only she'll have me!*

Talk to Doc Mac, the thought occurred. He was a mate Footy respected. And Doc was friends with Gwyn. *Don't be too proud to play the sympathy card,* he told himself. *Mate – do whatever it takes!*

The engines droned on. Johnny dozed and sometimes came to, having to remind himself they had really, finally, been rescued.

Operation Teeth was over – and more importantly, so was the war. His thoughts were on Gwyndolyn. He couldn't wait to see her, but now that he was actually on the way, he felt strangely shy. Truth was, he didn't know how things stood between them.

We were supposed to be gone three days. Instead, it's been what? Two months? More? She asked me to find my heart. What can I tell her?

I know this. My war is over. My enemy became my friend. What does peace mean? And a soldier like me – do I have any hope of a normal life?

When he was a boy, Johnny's future had looked straight ahead. He'd be a Navy career officer, like his forebearers. One day, just like his dad and granddad before him, he'd find a girl, fall in love, and they'd marry and have kids. He would go where his country commanded, and his family would go with him.

But now he knew, that path was closed off forever. In his very bones, he was done with war. He would be the first of the men of his family in generations to choose another course.

So the question was urgent. As a civilian, how would he make a living? A woman would need to know that!

As Johnny considered possible futures, he was shocked to discover that every one led him to Gwyn. All other roads appeared long and bleak.

And love. How gingerly he formed that word, even in his mind! Now, in the flying boat, for the first time since Pearl – or maybe it was really for the first time – he let the idea of deep love, true love, bloom as a possibility.

Could someone like him – a man who had seen the darkest, most brutal, aspects of human nature – could he find love?

Johnny felt the shift in the fuselage that told him the aircraft had crested the mountain range and turned into the long descent.

The Hard Case was heard from. *What's this trash about love? You're mooning like a schoolgirl!*

Johnny's mind went silent, and then some new part of him rose against the voice he'd depended on during his years of war. It was a calm, more mature presence in his mind.

Enough! Stand down now. For once, there was no biting answer. He probed the nascent feeling growing inside. He got a thrill like surfing, but this time, the sea was his very life.

Finally, he put it front and center. He did want love, he wanted it with Gwyn, and he wanted it more than anything. Johnny's eyes were closed, but he was wide awake.

How blind I've been! How did I not see this?

And then it came to him. It was the solemn promise his sixteen-year-old self had made. In the grim shadow of Pearl and the slaughter of his parents, he had vowed to avenge them, and his nation. That promise left no room for Gwyn.

But now he had fulfilled his vow. Incredibly, he had survived. This was a new day, rich with possibilities.

The aircraft soared through the changing winds over New Guinea. Johnny's ears popped as it tilted towards the Moresby airport.

And now Johnny made another promise, one formed as intensely as the first. *I am not sure who I am now. But I will find out what Gwyn wants, and if she'll have me, I will do my best to make her happy.*

A crewman stepped into the compartment to see if the passengers required anything.

He saw two wild men at rest, a hint of a smile on each face.

TEETH

Epilogue

*"We must go forward to preserve in peace
what we won in war."*

**– five-star General Douglas MacArthur,
accepting the surrender of Japan
aboard the USS Missouri
September 2nd, 1945**

"In this world there is room for everyone.
And the good earth is rich
and can provide for everyone...
but we have lost the way.
Greed has poisoned men's souls...
More than machinery we need humanity.
More than cleverness
we need kindness and gentleness.
Without these qualities,
life will be violent and all will be lost."

– Charlie Chaplin, The Great Dictator

"The world breaks everyone and afterward
many are strong at the broken places."

– Ernest Hemingway, A Farewell to Arms

161

5 Months Later

February 14th 1946

A Beach Near Port Moresby

It is a splendid day on the coast. A tropical breeze stirs the palms and the waves dance under the wide blue sky. There comes the rumble of big twin engines and an aircraft appears, flying low over the water. Although not nearly as grand as the Empire version, it is a stout flying boat.

The Grumman Goose has a fresh coat of white paint. On each side of the fuselage, a logo and letters are seen, bright red outlined in black. Inside a circle is a stylized crocodile head, jaws wide, displaying rows of teeth, and the words, "Croc Air."

The aircraft follows the coastal road lined with palms.

Fifteen miles from the capital, a village appears. Some fifty huts are revealed among the trees. It's an idyllic spot. A scrub-covered dune separates the dwellings from the beach. A clear river runs out of the hills, along one side of the homes, and into the ocean.

Sixty yards out, white foam outlines the coral reef surrounding a lagoon. Behind the village, vegetable gardens stretch back to the hills.

The Goose thunders over half a dozen black sedans driving along the road. These are slowing to turn into the native settlement.

Near shore stands a large round house with a shining corrugated metal roof. Beside it is a similar building, but with open walls. Nearby are two rectangular structures, also metal-roofed, with panel walls. Stacks of lumber and other building materials are arranged nearby.

The aircraft thunders overhead, wings waggling, and there is a glimpse of the pilot, hand raised. It sails out over the lagoon, banks, and comes back, angling lower. The aircraft make a picture-perfect landing, throwing up spray. The big Pratt and Whitney engines rev, and the craft comes on, plowing water. At the beach, wheels lower from the fuselage, and the winged boat drives onto the sand. The propellers tick over and stop.

The whole village is abuzz, hundreds of men, women and children busy on this magnificent day they've been preparing for weeks.

The cars proceed along the dirt road and park near the open-air round building. People of European heritage disembark. The women wear their best dresses and low-heeled shoes for the sand, while the men are all in white, wearing shirts and shorts, knee socks, and polished shoes.

Doc Mac's head of white curls emerges from one of the sedans. From another vehicle, dressed in his army uniform, Colonel Clint Waters steps out. Several months ago, he succeeded Henry Chambers as US commander. The officer is accompanied by his wife, Evelyn, who wears her pearls for the occasion. Other friends from the city get out and stretch their legs.

One of the newcomers stands out because he is taller and thinner than most. This is the Reverend Habakkuk Brown, a young man recently arrived from Australia. He is dressed like the other Aussie men, but has a long black cape around his shoulders, and carries a Bible.

A door opens in the side of the Goose fuselage and a man also dressed in white appears, looks toward the village, and waves. He hangs metal stairs and backs down, a little clumsily, onto the beach.

His shorts reveal a carved wooden leg, painted skin color, hinged foot attached. He wears matching shoes. His shirt has gold epaulets on the shoulders.

Footy turns grinning and beams at the crowd. And indeed, it is the Aussie pilot. His hair is freshly cut, and he has filled out since his ordeal on the Raub. He calls, and a score of native men run to form a human chain.

Footy instructs them, and they climb the ladder and begin to pass out the cargo – crates of food and drink, piled with ice chips.

The pilot walks toward the church.

"Footy! Over here mate!" Doc calls.

The man walks with barely a limp to greet his old friends. Doc introduces him to the Reverend Habakkuk Brown.

"Good to meet up again, Reverend," Footy says. Turns out, he was the one who ferried him from Aus a few days ago.

"As I told you, call me Hab, mate," the minister grins. There are handshakes all round, including with Colonel Waters, and some pecks on the cheek for the ladies.

The men clap the pilot on the back, with congratulations on this momentous day.

Footy looks around. Where is Gwyn?

He has not been here before, and he studies the buildings in detail. The large, round home is new, and construction is ongoing. There's a sign fixed over the double main doors. In neat, hand-painted letters, it reads, "The Good Shepherd Orphanage."

The main doors stand open, and a gaggle of children of various ages and shades of skin color, run excitedly in and out.

Others are lined up to shower at the stalls built along an exterior wall, ready with their towels.

On the far side of the edifice is a simple courtyard, a space between palm trees. There's a collection of school desks and chairs. And here is Gwyn herself, dressed in shorts and a blouse, sitting with a dozen children. These are already in their Sunday best – colorful sundresses for the girls, shorts and button-up shirts for the boys.

On her knee is a pretty little five-year-old, Sally, with sun-bleached hair, one of the nurse's long-term orphans. An older native teenage girl sits with them. This is Kiki, another orphan, and Sally's inseparable companion. They came to Gwyn together, years ago, referred by Doc Mac. Apparently, their people had all been killed during the war. Gwyn had never learned much more than their names, but now they are family.

A little mixed-race boy, Freddie, runs up and plops himself on Gwyn's other knee, pulls over a book, and begins to color. Gwyn runs fingers through his soft brown curls. He gives her a look of pure adoration.

A pretty young woman in a green frock walks through the interior of the home. She has a mass of red hair, brushed out and hanging down her back. Ruthie goes through the living room under a high, corrugated metal roof. The surrounding walls are inset with ten doors that give access to the bedrooms, each equipped with bunk beds.

She emerges in the courtyard. Children run and greet her happily. Clearly, they love their Auntie Ruthie, but today, she has her hands full.

"Gwyn!" she calls, "The guests are here. It's time, dear! You need to hurry up." Gwyn settles the little ones on their own seats, and enters the building.

Ruthie returns through the orphanage, goes out the main doors, and joins the townsfolk. Old friends get a kiss, and new introductions are made. She leads the group to a table near the church. Here, refreshments have been provided before the main event. She excuses herself and returns to the orphanage.

The church has a dirt floor with inset posts to support the roof. Woven-reed pony walls come half way up. The building is *al fresco*, the entrance open, and many footpaths lead to it. On the peak of the roof is a cross. Inside is a low wooden stage. On this stands a simple lectern. Rows of folding chairs are arranged on either side of the central aisle. Native women move about, placing glass jars of brilliant tropical flowers.

Outside, the entire village is abuzz. Preparations have been extensive, and the excitement has soared with the arrival of the aircraft and the cars from town.

To one side of the village, in a pretty place beside the river, groups of women tend several large *mumu* pits. Tendrils of steam drift through the coverings of earth, carrying a mouth-watering scent. Under the layer of dirt over each mound is a blanket of banana leaves, and below, a feast of leaf-wrapped vegetables packed around entire pig carcasses. The swine have been gutted and boiled, their skins scraped clean of bristles. To-day, six pigs will be served up – a major event in any village.

Groups of native women chat excitedly as they help one an-other dress. Some wear their finest grass-skirts, breasts bare, and they add tribal necklaces and, in their hair, insert bamboo combs, plumes and flowers. A few wear brightly patterned trade-store blouses and skirts.

Native warriors are also to be seen – strong, muscled men. Their skin shines with pig grease mixed with charcoal, and over this, they have painted bright lines and patterns on their torsos and faces. Some fluff the feather on their bark headdresses, while others tune the skin heads on their hourglass drums.

The men wear their finest pig tusks paired through their noses, turned down for this joyful celebration.

Ruthie knocks on a bedroom door and is told to come in. She enters to find her dearest friend, Gwyndolyn, putting on a final touch of lipstick. Gwyn's chestnut curls, grown to shoulder length now, are brushed back from her face, held in place by combs.

"Ready darlin'?" Ruthie asks. Gwyn puts a hand to her heart.

"I'm all aflutter. How do I look?"

The nurse wears a gorgeous white dress with three-quarter length sleeves, a beaded lace bodice, and a long, flared skirt. It is an heirloom lent to her by a friend, a plantation wife who wore it on her own wedding, many years ago. It has been altered to fit Gwyn's slender figure and looks like it was tailor-made for her. She will wear no veil, but a fashionable white cap waits on the dresser.

"You look absolutely smashing!" Ruthie beams. "By far, the most beautiful bride I have ever seen."

"I didn't think I'd be all sixes and sevens," Gwyn tells her and perches on the bed. Ruthie joins her.

"Darling, you're just nervous about what happens here tonight," Ruthie grins. "You remember everything I told you?"

"Is anyone ever really ready?" Gwyn asks.

Outside, hundreds of villagers come from all directions, making their way to the church.

Eventually Hab consults his watch and says the time has come. He leads the way into the building and a crowd follows him in.

The minister moves behind the lectern and opens his Bible. Footy walks in, smiling around at everyone, and takes his place at the head of the aisle. Doc Mac carries in a phonograph player with a large trumpet and fusses with it at a side table. The Caucasians file in and fill the front rows on one side, while Gwyn's children enter and take the seats on the other. Behind them, native women seat themselves in the rows. There's an excited hubbub all around the *"Haus Krise."*

From back in the village, drums begin to beat a rhythm. The pounding grows louder. Conversations taper off as the people crane over their shoulders.

From between the huts, a phalanx of warriors comes out dancing, broad smiles on each face. They are painted and feathered, but today, no one carries weapons. Instead, each man holds a drum which he slaps in rhythm with the others.

They approach the church and, still drumming, they enter. They peel off, left and right, and fill the back rows. Seated, the beat continues.

The one who walked behind them is revealed.

He is tall, broad-shouldered, dressed in the lightweight khaki uniform called chinos. He has sergeant stripes on the sleeves. On his shirt is an impressive display of colored bars and medals. Prominent among them are the Silver Star, two Bronze Stars, and four Purple Hearts.

You would hardly recognize Johnny from the man who survived Operation Teeth. His hazel eyes are clear, his tanned face is clean-shaven, and his glossy black hair is combed back. White teeth shine as he smiles at his friends. He has just turned twenty-one and he moves with the grace of a panther.

He weighs two hundred pounds now, and his body is thick with the muscle he has worked so hard to rebuild these last months.

Johnny strides down the aisle, nods at the preacher, and exchanges a grin and a warm handshake with Footy. They have not seen each other since the pilot left for Aus, although they have spoken several times by radio. The pilot steps to the left and Johnny takes his place at the center.

The drumming comes to a crescendo and stops. The congregation breaks into applause.

Doc Mac is at the phonograph, cranking the handle. Now he places the needle in the disc's groove, and the strains of the Wedding March emerge. He goes to the open door of the church and waits.

Ruthie approaches, carrying flowers. Before her walk two children, little Sally and Freddie, woven baskets in their hands. As they enter, the children throw handfuls of multicolored petals on the aisle. Ruthie, smiling ear-to-ear, follows them to the front. She takes her place opposite the two men.

The crowd turns expectantly to the entrance.

Gwyn emerges from the orphanage. She is a vision in white and carries a tropical bouquet. She, too, is beaming. She approaches Doc Mac who offers his arm, which she takes, and together, they begin to slow-walk up the aisle.

Footy taps Johnny's arm and whispers behind a hand.

"Mate, still time to make a run for it." Johnny chuckles, but his eyes never leave Gwyn.

Her own gaze is on him as Doc Mac brings her to the front. Gwyn gives her flowers to Ruthie. Doc places her hand in Johnny's, and he steps away. Johnny takes in her beauty and perfume and his breath catches.

Hand in hand, they face each other, the minister behind them.

The music ends. Doc lifts the needle and returns to his seat. There's some shuffling in the crowd. The minister clears his throat.

"Dearly Beloved," he begins. "We gather this day, in the sight of God and in the presence of this company, to join together Johnny Willman and Gwyndolyn Brooks in holy matrimony.

"Marriage is not to be entered into lightly, but reverently and in respect for God.

"Into this holy estate, Johnny and Gwyn," – he smiles at each of them – "have come to be joined.

"Today," Habakkuk continues, finding the passage with his finger, "I will read a selection from the Old Testament. For those who forget that it was God who created every pleasure, hear these words!"

He turns to Gwyn.

"Behold, you are beautiful, my love,
Behold, you are beautiful!
Your eyes are doves
Behind your veil.
Your lips are like a scarlet thread,
And your mouth is lovely.
Your cheeks are like halves of a pomegranate.
Your two breasts are like two fawns,
Twins of a gazelle,
That graze among the lilies.
You are altogether beautiful, my love;
there is no flaw in you.
Behold, you are beautiful, my beloved, truly delightful."

Johnny's eyes widen. Gwyn blushes, but the corners of her mouth twitch.

In the front row, Colonel Waters leans to his wife.

"What's this?"

"Shhh!"

The minister turns to Johnny.

"My beloved is radiant and ruddy,
distinguished among ten thousand.
His head is the finest gold;
his locks are wavy,
black as a raven.
His appearance is like Lebanon,
choice as the cedars.
His mouth is most sweet,
and he is altogether desirable."

"Struth!" Footy whispers. Even Doc Mac looks astonished.

Hab returns to Gwyn.

"You have captivated my heart, my sister, my bride."
His voice grows in confidence, Adam's apple bobbing.
"You have captivated my heart with one glance of your eyes.
How beautiful is your love, my sister, my bride!
How much better is your love than wine.
You are like a palm tree,
and your breasts are like its clusters.
I say I will climb the palm tree
And lay hold of its fruit!"

There are gasps from the first row. Johnny and Gwyn had not thought about what the sermon would be: Footy had made the arrangements, but had not asked about the service itself.

The couple looks at the minister – a little embarrassed, but electrified.

595

"What does the tall one say?" a warrior asks one of Gwyn's teenage boys in the back row. He whispers:

"Auntie Gwyn is a palm tree – and Uncle Johnny must climb and pick her coconuts!"

"Ahh!" The warrior smiles and nods approval.

"Oh! May your breasts be like clusters of the vine!" Hab continues:
"The scent of your breath like apples,
And your mouth like the best wine!"

Gwyn suddenly, desperately, feels a giggle rising and she pinches herself. Beside her, Ruthie stifles a snort. They dare not look at each other.

"As an apple tree among the trees of the forest,
so is my beloved among the young men.
With great delight I sat in his shadow,
And his fruit was sweet to my taste."

The minister takes a breath and considers both of them.

"My beloved speaks and says to me,
Arise, my love, my beautiful one,
And come away!
For behold, the winter is past,
The rain is over and gone.
The flowers appear on the earth,
the time of singing has come!"

Yes, thinks Johnny, *yes!* His cheeks hurt from smiling.

"Let my beloved come to his garden and eat its choicest fruits!" Hab thunders, slapping the lectern with a hand.

Dearie me! Ruthie thinks.

Strike me pink! That's Footy.

The minister looks to the congregation.

"Eat, friends, drink, and be drunk with love!"

There is stunned silence. Hab, smiling hugely, closes his Bible.

"Johnny and Gwyn," he says, "is it your intention to bring your lives together in sacred marriage under God? To share with one other your joys and sorrows and everything that comes – to bind yourselves to one another as husband and wife?

"Yes," they say together.

"Johnny, do you take Gwyn as your lawfully wedded wife? To have and to hold, to love, honor and keep her – for better or for worse, for richer or for poorer – in sickness and in health. And forsaking all others, keep only unto her, as long as you both shall live?"

"I do," Johnny says around the lump in his throat.

"And Gwyn," Hab goes on, "do you take Johnny as your lawfully wedded husband? To have and to hold, to love, honor and keep him – for better or for worse, for richer or for poorer – in sickness and in health. And forsaking all others, keep only unto him, as long as you both shall live?"

Gwyn stares into Johnny's eyes for long seconds before responding:

"I do!"

"Who has the rings?" the minister asks.

"Me," Footy said, patting his pockets – more and more frantically.

"Cor blimey! They're in me other shorts!"

597

Johnny frowns at him. Laughter bursts from the front rows while the villagers look mystified. But then, the Aussie pauses with a sly grin.

"Ahh no. Here they are!"

Footy tugs a drawstring bag from his pocket and hands it to Johnny. Johnny spills what's in it into his hand – three rings. He'd asked, and Footy purchased these in Aus. Along with the wedding bands, there's an engagement ring with a perfect-cut solitaire diamond. Johnny could find nothing like it in Moresby.

"The ring is a symbol of wedded love," the preacher goes on.

"Its perfect circle symbolizes unending love – the promise you make to each other."

Johnny slides the larger band into Gwyn's free hand, takes her left one and places the diamond on her finger. It sparkles like sunlight and Gwyn takes in a breath. Johnny adds the wedding band.

"With this ring I thee wed," he says.

"Now you, Gwyn," Hab says.

She slips the larger band onto his finger. "With this ring I thee wed," she says. Johnny and Gwyn gaze at each other on a rising tide of happiness.

"Those whom God has joined together, let no man put asunder!" Hab stares sternly at the attendees.

"Now, by the power vested in me by the Government of Australia, in this Territory of Papua... " he pauses dramatically:

"I pronounce you man and wife!"

A cheer rises from the front rows and is picked up by the crowd. There are tribal yells and a banging of drums.

Doc Mac steps to the phonograph and places another record on the turntable.

"You may kiss the bride!"

Johnny takes Gwyn in his arms. Their lips meet and they kiss.

At last, they turn to their friends, joy shining on their faces. Applause breaks out and people stand and cheer.

Doc Mac sets the needle and the music begins. He has no idea if this is appropriate, but his choice of records was slim.

The Andrews Sisters' "Boogie Woogie Bugle Boy," warbles out. Johnny and Gwyn, followed by Best Man Footy, and Maid of Honor, Ruthie, turn to exit. Gwyn's children are waiting. There are screams of delight and Johnny and Gwyn are showered with petals.

The congregation follows them out of the church.

162

Led by the newly married couple, the foreign guests, orphans and villagers make their way into the village. Now the women will begin to scrape the dirt off the *mumu* pits and the feast will soon be ready.

Gwyn tells her guests she wants to change her clothes. She asks Johnny to give her a few minutes, then come and meet her.

"I have something special to give you," she says to her husband as she leaves.

"I have something for you as well, Johnny," Colonel Waters says. He takes a letter from his jacket and hands it over. Johnny gets a flash of a very different letter given to him by another colonel. It seems like an eternity ago.

"These are your honorable discharge papers, Sergeant Will-man. They are signed by General MacArthur himself from his HQ in downtown Tokyo. We asked, and he said it was the least he could do. And he thanks you for your service. You'll see his own handwriting along the bottom: Duty – Honor – Country."

"Thank you, Sir."

"I've had a word with the admin as well," Doc adds. "You are all set to stay on. A fellow who can rid the villages of crocs is more than welcome. They're a plague on the people."

"Well, it's one of the few things I feel qualified to do," Johnny says. "I've had some success in the last couple of months, and truth is, I enjoy the work."

He excuses himself and goes to the orphanage. At Gwyn's bedroom, he knocks at the door and enters.

He finds she's removed the gown and slipped into a summer dress. She greets him with a smile.

"No need to knock anymore," she says. "You live here now." He's been bunking in his new office, one of the nearby buildings.

Again, they feel the mix of stomach butterflies and exhilaration.

Gwyn tells Johnny she has some gifts for him. She has secretly been working on her surprise for some time. She brings out several packages wrapped in brown paper, tied with string. He unwraps the first and shakes out a khaki shirt. It is army issue, he sees, but it has been modified. The sleeves have been cut off at the shoulders and neatly hemmed. Next, he finds a pair of dark brown shorts. A bag reveals a hat – it's an Australian "dig-ger" like Dingo's, but made from dark brown felt. Johnny ex-claims over the crocodile skin band someone has added.

"Just a teeny bit of the Father," Gwyn beams. "And you'll also need this."

She holds out a belt of stitched scales with a brass buckle. Johnny whistles.

"How on Earth...?"

"I have my sources, and my friends have sewing machines," Gwyn says. "There's more!" She goes to the closet and returns with a pair of brown boots. Yes, they may be used, but they gleam with polish and have new heels, a pair of balled socks in one leg.

"And finally!" From behind the dresser, Gwyn brings out Johnny's Springfield rifle in a croc skin case, complete with a shoulder strap. In her other hand, she offers his bayonet knife in a sheath of the same hide.

"Wow, Gwyn! This is really something! What's this all about?"

"Well, if you're going to be a crocodile hunter, you better look the part!"

"And you might want to look away," Johnny said. "I'm putting this on!"

Gwyn turns as Johnny strips down to his boxers. He lays the uniform on the bed and dons the new clothes. She can't help glancing and gets an eyeful of muscled chest and ribbed stomach as he steps into the shorts. The croc tooth necklace with dog tags is around his neck. He rarely takes it off.

I've seen him naked a hundred times. What's this I'm feeling! But there is a profound difference between that sick boy, and this vital man who seems to fill the room.

And later tonight...

She leaves the thought unfinished, while her cheeks burn.

"Okay," Johnny says. "How do I look?"

He wears the fedora flat-brimmed. His shirt is unbuttoned, showing chest and biceps — and of course, the scars. He runs the belt through the loops, and hangs the knife on it. He tugs on socks and then the boots.

He stands in front of her with a wide smile.

"Wow!" Gwyn says. It's all she hoped it would be.

"Thanks so much," Johnny says. "You really know how to make a guy feel special!"

They face each other, children's voices carrying from beyond the closed door. Johnny pulls Gwyn to him and kisses her full on the mouth. She feels his warmth and strength against her and melts into it. She kisses him, self-consciously at first, and then deeply. After long minutes, she pulls away.

"Good heavens!" she gasps.

"Right," Johnny says. "But we've still got a big day ahead!"

"Yes," Gwyn agrees. "There's the feast..."

Johnny picks up his encased rifle and puts the strap over a shoulder.

"Listen, wife of mine," he smiles into her eyes. "We'll save that for later. Right now I've got business."

"A meeting?"

"At my office. Gotta see a man about a croc."

He leaves Gwyn and walks away from the house.

163

Johnny exits the orphanage, greeting people as he goes. There's a grand party underway. He gets handshakes and congratulations, and lots of compliments on his outfit. He navigates the well-wishers, and walks beside the beach to one of the rectangular buildings. Over the main entrance he has mounted the bleached bones of The Father's massive head, facing out, the open jaws lined with teeth. A sign is screwed to the wall, black-outlined red letters on white board, "Croc Hunters." And below that, "Johnny Willman and Footy Carmichael."

Johnny steps through the door and there's the man himself. He and Footy stand before two wooden desks facing a couch and easy chairs. File cabinets line one wall.

"G'day again, mate!" Footy stares the Yank up and down.

"What are you got up as?"

"This is my new work uniform," Johnny shrugs. "Gwyn put it together." He stows the rifle in a corner.

"Of course, you look a sight," Footy says. "But Gwyn knows best so I won't say another word. It was a lovely wedding and a beautiful bride. Gwyn's too good for you, but there it is.

"Mate, I need to be serious a minute," he goes on. "You know I was sweet on Gwyn – we talked about that. But she chose you and that's the end of it – I'll never bring it up again. What Gwyn wants, Gwyn should have. But you ever hurt her..."

Johnny laughs and claps the pilot's shoulder.

"Same old Footy," he says. The pilot shows his trademark grin.

"You've done a brilliant job with our office! The Father's skull – that's the perfect spot for the toothy bastard. And we're already making money offa that skin.

"Like I said back there, I'm glad we did what we did with Cat's sword. I see it now."

"How's the leg?" Johnny asks.

Footy raps his knuckles on it. "I'm getting around pretty good.

"And we're officially partners. Got the paperwork done in Aus. Croc Air and Croc Hunters, Party Limited. Thanks for your investment, Johnny. I bought the Goose with the cash you sent. I'll be doing runs to Cairns and back, and all over the Territories."

"Well, I finally got my family inheritance," Johnny says, "I'm also helping Gwyn build this place."

"First we've got that other matter."

"Yes," Johnny says. "The rescue. Someone's got to get that poor missionary woman, Sarah, and bring her out."

"True," Footy says. "I was able to contact her people back home. They're waiting."

"And Mula," Johnny says.

"Right, mate. I've been on the radio with Rutherford. He sent a runner to the Uhuli village. Mula wants us to know, he's got croc skins to trade.

"From his long shopping list, I brought some things to get him started. Tea, coffee, sugar – a coupla outboard motors for his canoes, and petrol. He won't be getting firearms – against the law. But axes and knives, he can have. He says the Mambu nation is *gone-finish*. The river is much safter."

"Hey, we'll give him a ride in our Goose," Johnny enthuses. "That will be something to see! We'll take him along when we land downstream – remember the tribe?"

"Taifora, mate," Footy says. "Can't wait to see their faces when the Cargo Cult actually comes flying out of the sky!"

"We'll teach them about trade," Johnny says. "Real cargo has a price."

"We'll stop by Rutherford's plantation while we're in the neighborhood," Footy says. "Chas says he's ready to do business."

"Did you find buyers in Aus for crocodile skins?"

"Not much of a market right now," Footy replies. "But you know who wants skins? Or always did until the war came along? The Japs. They do wonders with them."

"We're going to sell to Japan?" Johnny asks. He hasn't considered this.

"The bloody war is over," Footy says. "The world has to get going again. I've got a plan. You and me, mate. We'll take the Goose hopping from island to island all the way to the Japanese islands. I've charted the route. It should be safe there – you Yanks are running things.

"But now, we better get back to your guests," Footy says.

"Right you are. Thanks again for the rings, Footy. You did great."

The friends return to the village.

At the refreshment table, they find Doc Mac with Colonel Waters and other men from Moresby. They freshen their drinks. The wives stand in another group, enjoying a lively conversation about all the new things showing up in the stores.

Doc Mac brings out a box of cigars, offers them around, and the men light up.

He raises his glass.

"Here's to Johnny and Gwyn, two of my favorite people. May you live long, Young Johnny, have many children, and always be faithful!"

"Hear, hear!" the Colonel says. "Bloody right!" Footy chimes in.

"Cheers!" The men clink glasses and drink.

"Your future is here now," Doc says to Johnny. "Perhaps one day, this will become a nation, and your children will become citizens. That will be well after my time."

Johnny nods thoughtfully. He has not thought that far ahead.

"This place a nation?" Colonel Waters is clearly dubious. Doc Mac places a hand on his arm.

"Mark my words, Colonel, these territories are merely entrusted to Australia. One day, the tribes will enjoy the benefits of laws and a parliamentary system founded centuries ago and an ocean away."

Ruthie approaches, waving at the cigar smoke.

"Men!" she says. "The wedding feast is ready!"

"Right you are," Doc says.

"I'm looking forward to it," the colonel says. "Evelyn and I have not had a chance to taste the island *mumu*."

Everyone moves in that direction. Footy takes the Irish nurse by the arm and leads her aside.

"Ruthie girl, half a mo', mate. I got a little something for you in Aus." He reaches into his pocket and produces a fancy glass bottle he gives to her.

"Ooooo. 'Indiscrete,'" she reads. "French!" She lifts the stopper and sniffs. "Lovely! Ta mate."

"I hope your boyfriend won't be offended," Footy says.

"He's flown the coop."

"Aww, not to worry," Footy says. "Maybe we can fix that, love!" Ruthie turns the full warmth of her smile on him. He offers his arm and she slips hers through. He feels her soft curves against him and flushes to the roots of his hair.

The outdoor dinner is delicious. Johnny and Gwyn eat together, chatting with friends. Gwyn is in her element, surrounded by her children, the villagers who have made her one of them, and all her dear friends from town.

164

A single candle gives light. Johnny lies under the sheet and waits for Gwyn. She is in the walk-in closet, with a mirror on the wall and a basin of water on a stand. A hurricane lantern hangs from a nail. She slips on her best silk nightdress, nothing under it. She uses cold cream to remove her makeup and dabs "Evening in Paris" behind her ears and on her throat. She blows out the lantern, returns to the room, and sits on the bed.

"My wife," Johnny says. He keeps his voice low, aware of all the sleeping children in this grand home.

"My husband," Gwyn breathes. "I love you."

She leans away, blows out the candle, and slides under the sheet. He puts an arm around her.

"You told me to find my heart," Johnny murmurs. "I've been waiting until tonight to tell you this. My heart is you, Gwyn."

He pulls her close. She wraps her arms around him. And now, at last, instead of nervousness, a delicious anticipation rises in her. They come together, and for Johnny, at least for a time, the war years fade away.

Gwyn feels his youth and yearning along her body, and she gives her own strength in return. For a time they became urgent until, at last, the darkness fills with spangled galaxies.

But this feels very different to Johnny than his experience on the beach. Now there's a real woman in his arms, and a soul beside him among the stars.

They must have slept because both stir when the first rooster crows. Inevitably, a new day has come. Soon the children will be up and the cycle will continue.

Their future is upon them.

"I never want to move," Johnny sighs. "You feel like home. I haven't felt home in a long time."

"You are home," Gwyn whispers against him.

"Welcome home, my love."

TEETH

Coda

A sweep of empty sand. Tattered canvas stretched between trees. Blankets half buried, sand sifting over charcoal.

On the far north shore of the island, there is a deserted stretch of beach. Conspicuous by their absence, two jeeps no longer sit here. At the point where the Raub River flows into the South Pacific towers a shade tree. In the dappled light below is a leaf-strewn mound. Beside it is the faded indent of a massive clawed foot, half full of water.

At the head of the mound, two sticks form a cross. Beside it, a rusted sword stands in the earth. From that dangles a helmet with torn netting. Inside, in a nest of twigs, two hatchlings squawk, beaks wide. The mother bird swoops up and lands. She carries an insect she feeds to her babies.

At the foot of the grave stands a curious marker. It is a homemade surfboard, its splintered tail buried in sand. On it is carved, letter by laborious letter:

Katsu
Soldier of Japan
Sept 2 1945

And beneath that, scrawled in charcoal so faded it is barely legible:

Since my country burned down
How clearly
I see the moon

TEETH

Afterword

I grew up in the South Pacific; New Guinea, the Philippines and Australia. I spent the better part of a decade on the great island itself, and developed a lifelong fascination for the place, the people, and its flamboyant history. As an adult and a documentary television producer, director and writer, I returned many times. I've also explored Asia, revisiting the haunts of my childhood and adding Japan, China, Hong Kong, Singapore and more. Today, the territories I knew as a boy are now the proud nation of Papua New Guinea, or PNG.

To see a little of my documentary footage, as more than 40-million viewers of You Tube have, and millions more on TV around the world, search the site for "Timothy James Dean." I'll meet you there, and you'll get up-close with the giant crocodiles and penis-gourd wearing warriors who populate this novel's pages.

This is the 2nd Edition of *TEETH*. When it was first published, I intended to write a sequel. However, I found I could not continue without the Father. He hatched in my imagination, based on the photograph you've seen in this book, simply as a gigantic predator – much like a great whale, shark or dinosaur.

But the Father would not remain a simple monster. He grew to be one of the principal characters in the story. Without him, I found I could not go on. I developed a serious case of "writer's croc," and turned to other projects.

I estimate that the maneater in the photo was about 20-feet long — a real predator that had attacked and eaten many natives before its reign of terror was ended.

But I wanted the Father in the book to be equal to the biggest ever recorded, a full 30 feet long, based on one killed in the region in the old days. That would be 10 feet longer and a couple of thousand pounds heavier than the crocodile in the picture!

I had a lot of other elements I wanted to include — an important one being both Johnny's and Katsu's complete stories. I also desired a satisfying climax to the love story — something I originally intended for the sequel.

Everything is now in this one epic adventure.

A word about historical accuracy: I have done my best to get the dates and events of WWII correct, and the history of Papua and New Guinea itself. The major real characters, especially General MacArthur, I tried to get right. The things he says are from the record and I hope I've done him justice. Other aspects, like the GIs' march across New Guinea, actually happened. This includes General Eichelberger and the things he spoke to the men bogged down at Buna.

On the other hand, General Yazawa is invented. He is modeled on several Japanese senior military men I researched, and it was the essence of these proud warriors I wanted to capture. However, this is not a textbook, it is an entertainment, and I hope you will forgive me for blurring the lines.

In addition, while I have explored some of the real rivers of the island, including the mighty Sepik, the Raub River is imaginary. The rivers of New Guinea are peopled with genuine tribes, and I do not pretend to speak for them. There is a real "Valley of the Cannibals," set in a different geographical location, so again, this is all part of the dreamtime of the novel.

Everyone else is fictional, but they live for me, and I hope you've come to see them as friends and acquaintances as well.

I want to thank a few people who assisted me along the way. First is Yasuyuki Kasai, the Samurai-descendant novelist. He enriched a number of aspects of Katsu's life, martial arts training and character, and he translated my haiku into Romanji (Japanese).

Another is Julie Price, who proofed the original MS – a huge job.

My most profound gratitude goes to Deborah, my wife, who read and reread the various versions of **TEETH**, over and over again. Without her encouragement, editorial observations and sharp eyes, this book would not be nearly what it is.

There are many others who provide knowledge and inspiration, and kept me going when the going got tough. I won't list you all – you know who you are, and I thank you from the depths of my heart.

This time, I can say with certainty, **TEETH** is finished. Dear Reader, I hope you found it edifying and enjoyed the adventure. Together, we traveled the same path – just at different times.

I wrote it for myself, and also, for you.

Timothy James Dean

TEETH

The Epic Novel Of War And Love

This is a work of fiction.

Except for certain historical figures and events depicted in a dramatized manner, the characters, names, places, and incidents are the product of the author's imagination. Any resemblance to actual persons, living or dead, is purely coincidental and unintentional.

The author acknowledges and respects the cultures, traditions, and histories of the Indigenous peoples of the South Pacific. While elements of local mythology, language, and custom may be referenced in this work, they are fictionalized and should not be taken as authoritative representations.

www.ingramcontent.com/pod-product-compliance
Lightning Source LLC
Chambersburg PA
CBHW030839030726
47495CB00005B/1294